Space Gamble

Volume 2: War

J. W. DELORIE

DENVER, COLORADO

Space Gamble
Volume 2: War

Outskirts Press, Inc.
http://www.outskirtspress.com

ISBN: 978-1-4787-0178-1

Outskirts Press and the "OP" logo are trademarks belonging to Outskirts Press, Inc.

PRINTED IN THE UNITED STATES OF AMERICA

Prologue

After a long and tedious trial, the Terran Tribune issues an arrest warrant for Acela Vega on the charges of murder and interference of an investigation. Marshal Scoop is determined to bring Acela Vega in front of the Solar Council on Earth; his only obstacle is Neptune One's administration. The Terran Tribune will not interfere with Neptune One; they need Dr. Niclas Gerlitz to complete his classified research before the Tribune's control on Earth vanishes completely. The conflicts between empires continue to grow, causing hostilities in the solar system and forming allegiances, as Neptune One struggles to stay neutral. The Eastern Empire is growing aggressive while gaining support from other organizations and establishments in the system. Tabitha Drake prepares for the Mech fight matches. Unable to defeat the top two Mech fighters in the system, this cycle she is determined to become solar champion. Tabitha's father, Captain Justin Drake, grows concerned as he watches more skirmishes increase throughout the inner system as new war ships arrive from both sides. Samuel Furgis can see hope as he witnesses the war ending between his mother and father.

Chapter One

Supervisor Stykes and Officer Armela stood close to the main vid com in glide tube station A, waiting for Marshal Scoop to arrive. Officer Armela looked around the busy station at the guests and staff waiting for their family and friends to arrive from the transport. His attention refocused when he saw the glide tube car entering the station. He felt a tap on his upper arm and watched Supervisor Stykes walk toward the "caution" painted area in front of the glide tube platform. "Ready to meet and greet, Juan?"

Officer Armela laughed slightly, almost a chuckle before answering, "Ready, sir."

Supervisor Stykes nodded in reply as the glide tube car slowly came to a stop. Its curved doors hissed open, allowing the crowded car to empty into the station. Marshal Scoop casually exited. Dressed in his law enforcement uniform, Marshal Charles Scoop stood tall. He had short, light brown hair and was in his early forties.

Marshal Scoop had spoken with Supervisor Stykes on the vid com but had not visited Neptune One in a very long time. Stykes approached Marshal Scoop with an extended hand. "Marshal, it's good to see you."

Marshal Scoop replied with a smile and a handshake. "It's

good to see you, Leaf. How's the station?"

Supervisor Stykes chuckled. "She's doing fine, no complaints, sir."

Officer Armela stepped in front of Marshal Scoop. "Sir, it's good to see you again. How was your trip?"

Marshal Scoop could not ignore the large man in front of him. Everyone knew if Officer Armela was given time away from his duties as an enforcer, he would always enjoy his quiet time in the exercise chambers, provided the special person in his life was busy. Huiling Li encouraged Officer Armela to visit the exercise chambers frequently; she was aware of the importance of quiet times.

Marshal Scoop did not enjoy long voyages, but his duties required extended periods on ships traveling in the inner system as well as the outer system. He frowned. "Very tedious trip, Officer. I wish they could shorten them."

Stykes laughed. "You know what that would do to the solar economy."

Scoop smiled. "Down to business, gentlemen, you know why I'm here."

Supervisor Stykes interrupted with determination. "Yes sir, however there is a problem with your warrant." Supervisor Stykes and Officer Armela grew serious. Marshal Scoop stood still, watching the guests and staff members leave the station. As the crowd thinned out, he looked Supervisor Stykes in the eyes with his own determination. "Leaf, we're not going to have a problem here, are we?"

"No sir, I'll let Director Furgis explain." Supervisor Stykes pointed to the hotel lobby.

Marshal Scoop was curious. "Director? Did he get demoted?"

Supervisor Stykes and Officer Armela chuckled heavily as Stykes answered, "No sir, it was a promotion."

The hotel lobby was crowded from the other ships' debarking passengers. Marshal Scoop followed the enforcers through the hotel lobby, watching the crowd and realizing Neptune One had become a well-desired spot for visitations for all kinds of patrons. Officer Armela was loud with excitement in his voice. "Sir, I see a VIP. May I join you in the Director's office later?"

Supervisor Stykes nodded. "Sure, Juan."

Marshal Scoop waited for Officer Armela to leave before asking, "That's not his little preacher girl he's talking about, is it?"

Stykes laughed loudly."If it was he would not even have asked."

They watched Officer Armela approach a small older woman and engulf her with a huge hug. He released the fragile woman and said, "Mrs. Alberts, I am happy to see you visiting us again."

Mrs. Alberts was excited. "Thank you, sir."

Officer Armela interrupted quickly. "Juan, ma'am."

Mrs. Alberts smiled widely. "Of course, Juan." She smacked him on the lower arm and looked around with curiosity before refocusing on the large man in front of her. "Where is that young man that helped me on my last visit? He was so nice."

Officer Armela laughed. "Do you mean Sam, Mrs. Alberts?" He looked down at Mrs. Alberts with a gentle smile.

The noise level in the crowded lobby grew, forcing Mrs.

Alberts to struggle. "I'm sorry, I didn't hear you."

Officer Armela leaned lower. "Are you looking for Sam Furgis, ma'am?"

Mrs. Alberts laughed. "Yes sir."

Officer Armela grinned as he reached for his ear com piece and instructed the communications device after hearing the familiar chime "Sam Furgis." Officer Armela nodded to Mrs. Alberts as he waited for a response. "How was your trip?"

Mrs. Alberts looked a little frustrated. "I made the mistake of taking the *Orion Princess*." She looked away with disgust in her expression before continuing. "I should have waited for the *Jupiter Queen*."

"Yes, ma'am, the *Jupiter Queen* is a fine ship." Officer Armela was interrupted by the chime of his ear com. "Sam Furgis." Officer Armela replied quickly, "Accept."

Samuel Furgis's voice grew deeper as he aged. A twenty-three-year-old tall black man, still learning the wagering business from his father Kennith Jackson Furgis, was pleased to speak with his friend Officer Armela. "Juan, what's up?"

Officer Armela smiled at Mrs. Alberts as he answered his ear com piece. "Sir, I have a dear friend of yours here. Mrs. Alberts would love to see you." He could hear the happiness in Sam's voice when he replied, "Absolutely, Juan, tell Mrs. Alberts I have her suite ready and I will see her as soon as I get this other business taken care of."

Officer Armela replied with professionalism in his voice, "Yes sir." The ear com chimed off and Officer Armela gently touched Mrs. Alberts' forearm. "Let's visit with Marco and take you to your suite. Sam will see you in a bit." Mrs. Alberts' smile grew wider as Officer Armela escorted the older lady to the front desk.

Sam Furgis sat at his desk looking over data pads from the solar pit. The vid com chimed, "Request entry," and Sam sat up straight, pulling on his old-styled Italian blazer Marco De Luca gave him. "Who?" The vid com responded instantly, "Supervisor Stykes." Sam was quick to answer, "Granted," and the doors to his office hissed open. Sam Furgis stood as he watched Supervisor Stykes approach his desk, followed by Marshal Scoop with a look of curiosity. Supervisor Stykes stood by the empty chairs in front of Sam's desk, waiting for Marshal Scoop to sit. "Director Furgis, you remember Marshal Scoop."

Sam leaned forward to shake Marshal Scoop's hand before sitting back in his desk chair. He leaned back with a grin and said, "What can I do for you, Marshal?" Stykes could see a slight look of surprise on Scoop's facial expression.

"Sam, you have a felon on this station who I need to take back to the Tribune."

Sam laughed. "I don't agree with the verdict, Charles." The room grew quiet, and the three individuals in Sam's office stared at each other for several moments. Scoop leaned forward. "Sam, the warrant is valid. Acela needs to appear in front of the Tribune."

Director Furgis held up his hand. "No sir, she does not; you know darn well once she leaves this station we will never see her again." Supervisor Stykes nodded at Sam and gestured to Marshal Scoop's uniform dress jacket.

Sam Furgis took a moment before realizing what Stykes was referring to. He leaned forward with a very serious look. "Charles, the vid com allowed you to carry your weapon off the transport because of your enforcement ID. I'll allow you to carry your weapon, but you keep it out of sight and cause no trouble." Marshal Scoop expected a problem with the Neptune One's administration. He was also aware of the diplomacy enforcers required at times. Supervisor Stykes interrupted quickly. "Do you have quarters, Marshal?" He stood up and moved back to allow the marshal room. Marshal Scoop and Sam Furgis stood from their chairs. "Marshal, if you need a room I'll inform the front desk," Sam said.

"No sir, I'm all set and thank you for the courtesy."

Sam nodded and watched the two enforcers leave his office. After hearing the hiss of the door closing, Sam sat back in his chair. "Vid com." The gentle female voice responded, "Ready," and Sam issued his commands: "Operator Furgis." The familiar chime was heard. The laser lights from the base of the vid com in the corner of Sam's office flickered before projecting the image of Kennith Furgis. "Sam, when's the astro tourney start?"

Sam chuckled before answering, "Next cycle, Pops, which reminds me, I need to talk with Mrs. Alberts."

Operator Furgis grinned with pride. "Very good, son, it's important to keep ladies like Mrs. Alberts happy."

Sam laughed. "I asked Marco to put her in a suite, Pops." Before Operator Furgis could respond, his son continued. "Marshal Scoop has arrived early." Sam Furgis lost his smile to a more serious look.

Operator Furgis was calm. "Yeah, I figured the transport would be early. Was he persistent?"

Sam nodded. "Not as much as I figured. I think he's up to something."

"Of course he is; if I was him I would try diplomacy first before asking help from operatives."

"How many do you think he has, Pops?"

Operator Furgis paused for a moment. "Not sure." Sam could see his father looking off to the side of his vid com. Operator Furgis turned his attention back to his son. "Sam, your mother wants to speak with you." The image of Raynor Furgis, a thirty-nine-year-old, full-figured black woman with origins from the old African continent on Earth appeared on the vid com.

Sam Furgis was happy his mother and father had reconciled again. His mother always talked with a pleasing voice to her son. "Sam, you're joining us for the Grav Ball match?"

Sam smiled widely. "Of course, Mother, I would not miss it."

His mother smiled with acceptance. Operator Furgis's image was once again projected on Sam's vid com. "Sam, keep an eye on Marshal Scoop. I don't need him interrupting the tournament."

Sam nodded. "Okay, Pops. Will you be at the Solar House later?"

Operator Furgis responded with a questioning tone. "Your credits?"

Sam laughed louder. "Of course. I'll meet you and Mom there."

Operator Furgis nodded with a smile, his attention on Raynor as the vid com in his office returned to the jazz recording. Both Kennith and Raynor enjoyed jazz music; Captain Justin Drake had introduced them to each other during a modern jazz concert on Mars. Operator Furgis leaned back in his desk chair. "Ray, do you mind if I switch to the solar news?" Raynor Furgis shook her head. Operator Furgis issued his commands to the vid com. "Solar news." The vid com flickered and projected a news commentator. "The Tribune steps in as tensions rise over the old Australian territories. The Western Empire remains in control as the Easterners accuse the Tribune and Westerners of collusion." The sidebar projected an image of Mars as the commentator continued. "Mars is not exempt from the hostilities as factions from both empires clash in violence."

Raynor Furgis interrupted quickly. "That reminds me, Ken, I need to place a vid later to Derek and find out what is really happening on Mars." She leaned forward. "Ken, put the sports back on." Operator Furgis sat up in his chair with his elbows on desk. "Vid com, sports." The vid com flickered before the lasers could project the sports news.

The sports commentator was describing the Grav ball match on Lunar One Colony. "The Lunar Landers played with determination; however, the Rovers take the victory back home to Mars." The vid com flickered and switched to the outside visual of the Earth Dome. "Preparations are under way for the upcoming Mech fight between Darkstar and Cronus. Tabitha Drake is a seasoned armor warrior and fought her way through the ranks, but everyone is placing their credits on Ben Swells; the veteran armor warrior is deadly, and with no rules in this open match, anything can happen." The vid com projected the last Mech fighter match. Cronus defeated his opponent with deadly precision, ending the match and his opponent's life. Raynor watched the Mech fighter explode and turned to Ken with concern.

Operator Furgis issued his command quickly—"Jazz"—and the vid com instantly projected the previous recording of jazz music "Ray, you don't need to worry about Taby. They underestimate her."

Raynor Furgis was now facing her ex-husband. "I hope so, Ken. When she's done with Swells, she has to take on Masoko at the champion fights." Operator

Furgis laughed. "I don't see any problem there. Is Mars City Central ready?"

Raynor looked at Operator Furgis out of the corner of her eye with a slight frown. "Of course. Will you be there?"

Operator Furgis grew serious. "I would like to." He paused. "Are you ready for the Grav ball match?"

Raynor was relaxed. "Almost. I was hoping to say hello to Justin before leaving."

Operator Furgis laughed. "You knew I wanted to speak with Just," he said, but Raynor interrupted while turning her chair towards the vid com. "Of course." Operator Furgis leaned back in his desk chair.

Captain Justin Drake's image appeared on the vid com projection. Captain Drake was smiling and his voice was slightly loud. "Ken, I see you lovebirds are making a good go of it this time."

Raynor Furgis laughed. "We're trying, Justin." Operator Furgis interrupted, leaning on his desk. "I hope you make it this time." He leaned back in his chair with a smile.

Captain Drake started laughing. "If I miss it I'll attend the next wedding. Is Sam the best man this time?"

"Of course. Ray wanted one of her Mars confederacy friends though."

Raynor grew angry. "Knock it off, Ken. That's past stuff unless you would like to discuss it now."

Operator Furgis looked apologetic. "All right, all right. Sorry, bad joke."

Captain Drake laughed, trying to maintain his composure while on the bridge of the SS *Hammerhead*. "I don't think I would miss this for anything." Operator Furgis leaned forward across his desk and grabbed Raynor's hand.

Captain Drake grew excited. "Ken, someone just came to my bridge, and she wants to say hello." Tabitha Drake leaned into the vid com with a smile. "Hey, guys."

Operator Furgis was glad to see Tabitha and thought of how she had grown into a very attractive young lady. She was twenty-eight years old and five foot ten, with muscles blending with her feminine side. Operator Furgis remembered when her brunette hair was short. "Taby, how's the trip with your father?"

Tabitha offered a slight chuckle before replying, "Dad's driving is fine; we should be arriving at Mother Earth soon, I hope."

Captain Drake interrupted with a smile. "We'll get there." He gently grabbed his daughter by the arm.

Raynor was quick to interrupt. "Taby, you give us a vid call before the match."

Tabitha Drake was always respectful to Raynor. "Yes, ma'am."

Operator Furgis laughed. "All right, Just, get back to driving the *Hammer* and stay away from the Earth conflict."

Captain Drake raised his eyebrows. "You got it, Ken," and the vid com in Operator Furgis's office switched back to the solar news.

Raynor was about to speak to her future husband when he grew excited and raised his hand to interrupt. "Wait." Raynor could see his attention was focused on the solar news. The news broadcaster was loud. "WH-12 was discovered nearly one solar cycle ago." The vid com projected a faint image of a clouded funnel; the edges looked wavy with a slight movement. Raynor laughed loudly. "Let me guess, Ken, you want to go through this wormhole and set up a casino on the other side."

Furgis looked amused. "Not a bad idea; let's find out if it's safe first. The last time they found something like this, their ships were crushed with all hands lost."

"Tell Justin, you guys can have another adventure together like the old days."

Furgis laughed. "And miss my wedding? Never. Vid com off."

Marshal Scoop walked around the solar pit slowly, observing the tables and the pit boss. Acela Vega easily spotted Scoop in his marshal uniform staring at her and decided to confront him. "Officer Scoop, how are you?" Scoop was impressed with the attractive Spanish woman. Acela was thirty-three years old, five foot nine, and was very beautiful with diamond jewelry to match her feminine beauty. Marshal Scoop matched Acela's smile. "Acela, how have you been?"

Acela replied calmly, "Very good, Marshal. Would you like to place a wager? I recommend the wheel."

Marshal Scoop nodded while smiling. "No ma'am, I'm here on business."

Acela turned to the podium, studying the data pad she

picked up. "Well, good luck with that."

Scoop laughed. "Not luck, Miss Vega, just time." He saw Officer Armela approaching and turned to face him.

Officer Armela stopped slightly past the marshal and looked at Acela. "Everything all right, Acela?"

"Of course, Juan."

Officer Armela quickly turned to Marshal Scoop. "You like to wager, sir?" He smiled mockingly.

Scoop laughed. "No sir, just looking around."

Officer Armela attempted to relax the conversation. "The Grav ball match is at the end of cycle—what side are you wagering on, Marshal?"

The marshal looked confused. "What are my choices again?"

Officer Armela laughed before answering. "Of course I'd wager on the Poseidons; however, the Marauders are very good." Marshal Scoop was nodding in thought. Armela continued, "You can check out their stats on the vid com or check with the sports depot."

Marshal Scoop was ready to answer, but he was interrupted by a gentle voice. "Juan." Both enforcers turned towards the voice to see Huiling Li smiling widely as she approached the solar pit.

Huiling Li was an attractive Asian lady in her early thirties, a petite woman who was hidden when close to Officer Armela. Huiling was excited and spoke quickly. "Good news, Juan."

Officer Armela laughed with delight as he put one hand on her back. "What's the good news, Huiling?" He respected Huiling as the pastor on Neptune One and knew the word gospel meant good news.

Huiling Li slowed her speech down. "My sister is arriving soon," she said, catching her breath.

Officer Armela looked surprised. "Good. When you said good news I thought you had a new idea for services." Huiling laughed. "I'm sure my sister will." She looked at Marshal Scoop. "Hello, sir, I did not realize you were visiting us again."

Officer Armela interrupted. "The marshal is here to arrest Acela."

Huiling looked at Marshal Scoop and gently laughed. "Good luck, sir" she said before walking away.

Officer Armela spoke quickly before Huiling was too far away. "I'll see you later." Huiling turned and smiled. Armela turned his attention back to Scoop. "Sir, do you have any news from Earth? I hear it's a mess back there." He was required to speak loudly over the crowd in the casino.

Marshal Scoop continued to watch the solar pit. "Only what they tell me, Officer."

"The solar news said the conflict is escalating and the aggression is growing."

Marshal Scoop looked agitated. "Like I said, I only know what they tell me."

Officer Armela laughed. "Okay, sir, would you like to join me in my rounds? First stop is the sports depot."

"Okay, Officer Armela, I'm a patient man. We can check those stats for the Grav ball match." Marshal Scoop pointed the way with an open hand. He followed Officer Armela through the crowd until the officer stopped in front of the dispensing lounge; Scoop could see another individual in a work uniform with the station's designation approaching. Officer Armela was excited and spoke loudly over the crowd. "Shaun, what's up?" Marshal Scoop stood next to Officer Armela as Engineer Trently walked around the station's guests. He approached with a smile. "I tell ya, Juan, this astro tourney is bringing in all types of wagers."

Marshal Scoop interrupted curiously. "I forgot to ask about that tourney."

Engineer Trently quickly looked at him. "Marshal, welcome aboard." Scoop accepted the engineer's hand greeting. Officer Armela laughed. "The marshal is here to arrest Acela." Engineer Trently started laughing, but Marshal Scoop did not look amused. "What's so funny, Engineer?"

Trently quieted down before answering, "I was just thinking of the odds the sports depot would give on you getting Acela off the station."

Marshal Scoop grew more agitated and slightly hostile. "I can give you the odds." He stared at Engineer Trently.

Officer Armela quickly defused the emerging confrontation. "Marshal, to answer your question, the astro tourney was designed to include all wagers. The idea is to have a marathon with the combination of all games of chance, not just one particular game."

Marshal Scoop calmed down. "That's new. Do you think it will work out?"

Engineer Trently laughed. "Of course. Acela Vega designed the tourney." He paused. "Juan, I need to get down to the engineering level. Dr. Gerlitz is installing something new on the bottom of the station." The twenty-eight-year-old engineer from old England walked away with a slight wave of his hand and a smile at the marshal. Before Armela and Scoop could continue on the security rounds, Officer Armela's ear com piece chimed. "Incoming transmission." Officer Armela stopped and, looking at the marshal, activated his ear com piece. "Source." The ear com piece chimed, "Supervisor Stykes." Officer Armela quickly accepted.

Supervisor Stykes' voice sounded confident. "Juan, we've got the miners' transport arriving. I'm caught up in something."

Officer Armela interrupted. "Understood, sir. I have the marshal with me; we'll both keep watch."

Stykes sounded reassured. "Thanks, Juan." Officer Armela's ear com piece shut off with a chime. Marshal Scoop could slightly hear the conversation. "I guess we're headed for the glide tube station."

Officer Armela chuckled. "Yes sir, if you don't mind." Marshal nodded. "Not at all, Officer Armela." They casually walked towards the lifts.

Engineer Trently activated the vid com outside Chief Tylor's office and instructed the vid com after hearing the chime "Request entry"; the vid com quickly and unknowingly scanned the individual asking for entry. Chief Tylor was interrupted by the vid com chime while talking with Dr. Gerlitz. "Entry requested." Chief Engineer Dan Tylor was calm and relaxed as usual.

A man in his late fifties with extreme experience in his trade, he answered the vid com with his heavy English accent. "Who's at my hatch?" The vid com immediately replied, "Engineer Trently." The chief could see Dr. Gerlitz smile with an approving nod. Chief Tylor nodded back at Dr. Gerlitz before replying, "Granted." Both heard the hiss of the door sliding open. Engineer Trently pulled out the vacant chair next to

Dr. Gerlitz and sat. "Dr. Gerlitz, how's your testing going?"

The chief was fast. "Shaun, that's what the good doctor is here for."

Dr. Gerlitz was grinning widely."Shaun, I need your assistance." Engineer Trently looked at his superior. Chief Tylor explained in his usual calm voice. "Shaun, Dr. Gerlitz has a device ready for testing, but he needs your assistance installing the device to the station."The chief leaned back in his chair.

Engineer Trently was quick to ask, "May I know what this device is?"

Dr. Gerlitz, a man from what was once called Germany, interrupted quickly and aggressively. "No, you may not see the device." He was in his late sixties, of average height and build, with an extensive list of work in the scientific field, including the HGE process now used throughout the system.

Engineer Trently was aware of the secretive and important work Dr. Niclas Gerlitz was involved in for the Terran Tribune and accepted his position. "Very well, Doc, I'll meet you on board *Research Two* after the safety checks."

Dr. Gerlitz was relieved the engineers did not persist in their inquiries. "Thank you, Shaun. I'll get my assistant and see you there." Dr. Gerlitz was quick to get up and leave the chief's office. Chief Tylor waited for his office door to close before saying, "Shaun, I think this new work of Dr. Gerlitz's has something to do with energy weapons."The chief could see that Engineer Trently was not surprised.

"I figured as much, Chief. I got a look at his device attached to *Research Two* and it has a very large chamber for Mortelis ore." Engineer Trently activated his data pad. "The power requirements are normal for a large stealth droid; it should not affect any systems."

Chief Tylor nodded. "You best get down there, Shaun, and try to keep Dr. Gerlitz out of trouble." Engineer Trently was not sure if the chief was joking.

Officer Armela and Marshal Scoop entered the glide tube station as the glide tube was arriving; the vid com announcement of the mining transport from Triton was already broadcasting. Both enforcers stood near the far wall, watching as the glide tube's curved doors hissed open, allowing new visitors to enter the station. The vid com announcement was recognized by the regular guests. "Welcome to Neptune One. If your stay here is for the astro tournament, please ID at the nearest vid com." Lines were already forming. Officer Armela smiled, shaking his head. Marshal Scoop was slightly confused. "What's the problem, Officer?" After a quick laugh Officer Armela answered while staring at the line of guests waiting to ID at the vid com, "No one except Operator Furgis thought this tourney would be accepted." He continued observing the patrons as the crowd grew with more glide tubes arriving.

Marshal Scoop realized this was not the usual number of guests to arrive at once. "I thought this was Furgis's idea."

Officer Armela interrupted quickly. "No sir, it was Acela's idea." He paused, watching another individual before continuing with a raised voice. "There he is." Officer Armela walked through the crowd. Marshal Scoop watched Officer Armela approach and shake hands with a muscular man in his mid-thirties; the man was over six feet tall and Spanish-looking. Marshal Scoop walked over to the two individuals as the crowd started to grow smaller. "Everything all right?" The marshal was calm. Officer Armela introduced his friend. "Marshal, this is Bruno Marvelous, the general foreman for the mining colony on Triton."

Bruno held his hand out in a greeting gesture. "Nice to meet you, sir."

Marshal Scoop smiled. "Any friend of Officer Armela's…" He grinned with a nod.

"What brings you to Neptune One, sir?"

Marshal Scoop grew serious. "Tribune business…and yourself?"

Bruno was relaxed and looked at Officer Armela. "Here to see my uncle." He chuckled. Officer Armela was ready to add more detail as to the marshal's reason for visiting but was interrupted by a very sweet voice. "Excuse me, Officer." All three turned to see a young lady in her early twenties with long, wavy blond hair. Officer Armela was quick to reply. "Yes, ma'am?" The young lady was shorter, and noticed Marshal Scoop and Bruno staring at her large chest. Officer Armela cleared his throat before she answered, "Sir, I'm looking for Sam Furgis." Officer

Armela wanted to laugh, noticing the look of surprise on Bruno's expression. He thought the young lady's accent was attractive. "Ma'am, I believe Director Furgis is in a conference at this time; however, if you like you can activate a vid com at any time and ask for him."

The attractive young lady smiled. "Thank you, sir, I'll check the vid after I find my room."

Before Officer Armela could respond, Bruno offered assistance. "Ma'am." Bruno Marvelous was grinning widely. "I'm heading to my room. If you would not mind joining me for the walk, I can show you to yours." Bruno politely pointed to the direction of the lifts with an open hand. The young lady laughed and winked at Officer Armela before walking in front of Bruno. Marshal Scoop watched the two walk away for a moment before turning to Officer Armela with wide eyes. "There goes trouble."

Officer Armela laughed loudly. "Which one are you referring to?" and Marshal Scoop joined in the laugh.

Officer Armela's laugh was quieter. "Marshal, that young lady can handle herself."

Marshal Scoop nodded. "Do you know her?"

Officer Armela smiled. "Sam told me about her."

"Where's her accent from?"

"I remember Sam saying something about old Texas before the Empires existed. Marshal, I need to continue my rounds."

Scoop followed the enforcer out of the glide tube station. They exited the lift on the casino level and were stopped immediately by Marco De Luca. "Juan, how's everything?" Officer Armela responded in his usual calm voice. "Good. Marco, you remember Marshal Scoop"

Marco De Luca held out his hand. Marshal Scoop accepted his hand shake with a smile. "How are you, sir?"

Marco was excited. "Good. I'm on my way to see Acela about the tourney—are you interested?"

Officer Armela started laughing. "The marshal's here on business, Marco."

Marco De Luca was aware of the marshal's visit. "That's too bad, sir. Acela set up a very impressive tourney." He nodded with raised eyebrows at the marshal before leaving.

As they walked through the casino watching the crowd wager at the various vid machines or tables, Armela said, "Marshal, you are aware that the staff of Neptune One is like family."

Marshal Scoop laughed under his breath. "Officer Armela, you are aware that I have a job to do for the Solar Council appointed by the Terran Tribune."

Armela nodded. "I guess it's a good thing Operator Furgis is declaring Neptune One neutral..." he held his hand out, stopping the marshal from interrupting before continuing, "...and will be an independent government."

Marshal Scoop started laughing. "And making Operator Furgis emperor."

Officer Armela did not laugh. "Operator Furgis has been holding conferences on establishing a council on the station." He stopped walking and looked at the marshal with a serious expression. "Rumor is Acela will be in charge of extradition."

Marshal Scoop laughed. "Very funny, Officer." He stared at Acela in the solar pit as they walked by.

Supervisor Stykes stood in the large arched entrance to the sports depot watching the numerous vid coms projecting different solar sports to wager on. His attention stopped on the vid com projecting the news but was interrupted as Marshal Scoop and Officer Armela approached. The marshal was a stubborn man, but he was pleasant-natured and always tried to show professional courtesy. "Leaf, what has your attention?"

Leaf Stykes grinned before answering, "The news on Mother Earth is getting worse."

Officer Armela interrupted with a serious tone. "What happened now, sir?"

Marshal Scoop looked around the sports depot, noticing most of the patrons watched the one vid com projecting the news. Supervisor Stykes motion to the vid com. "Hear for yourself." Officer Armela joined the others in the sports depot staring at the news broadcast. The newscaster was in the middle of his broadcast, but Officer Armela knew what the broadcast was about after the vid com's sidebar projected the scene of two small war ships sideswiping each other with Earth's moon in the background.

The broadcaster continued. "Eastern Empires' claim of the Terran Tribune colluding with the Western Empire now demands the Lunar colonies be turned over immediately to the Eastern Empires' control." The scene changed to the projection of the Southern American continent. "The Terran Tribune has announced the territorial Mech fighter match for South America will proceed." The vid com flickered, projecting two individuals in their armor warrior suits. The projection split, one side showing Ben Swells and the other Tabitha Drake as the voiceover continued. "Darkstar is determined to fight aggressively to the championship match; however, Cronus is the favored Mech fighter in this match." The vid com switched to the inside the Terran Tribune's counsel room.

Supervisor Stykes turned to Marshal Scoop. "Who's wagering on Charles?"

Marshal Scoop snickered. "The Eastern Empire."

Supervisor Stykes shook his head and frowned.

Officer Armela was quick to reply. "Not funny, Marshal, Supervisor Stykes was referring to the Mech fight."

Scoop sighed. "Just being honest, Officer. Something's brewing on Mother."

Supervisor Stykes quickly spoke with concern. "Unfortunately you're right, and it's not going to stop on Mother Earth either."

Officer Armela frowned. "You're right, hopefully they can come to their senses before this gets carried away and affects the whole system."

Marshal Scoop sighed again. "Not to seam glum, but look at the aggression the Easterners are displaying in every issue; they want it all." He lowered his head slightly with a negative shake.

Supervisor Stykes looked at the other vid coms in the sports depot before responding, "What do you think, Juan, the odds are for Swells?"

Officer Armela laughed loudly. "I think it's Taby's time. and Swells will be beat this time."

Marshal Scoop laughed. "You're probably right, Officer, but I know Ben, and he's not going to give up his number two position so easily; in fact he's determined to take on the Sword."

Stykes was ready to argue with his opinion of the Mech fight match on Earth but was interrupted by the chime of his ear com piece. "Incoming transmission." He grew quiet. "Source." The ear com piece replied quickly, "Engineer Trently." Supervisor Stykes looked at Officer Armela with a curious expression before answering, "Accept." A quick chime and Stykes could recognize Engineer Trently's voice. Trently sounded slightly excited. "Sir, we have a security breach on the hangar deck."

Supervisor Stykes' demeanor grew serious, and Officer Armela, hearing Supervisor Stykes' ear com only slightly, grew concerned. "Sir, what's Engineer Trently saying about a breach?"

Stykes held his hand up while he responded to Engineer Trently. "Shaun, we'll be down there immediately. Does the chief know?"

Engineer Trently replied, "Yes sir," and the ear coms shut off.

Supervisor Stykes looked around the area before talking to his fellow enforcers "Juan, Trently said there was a security breach on the hangar deck."

The marshal interrupted with great interest, "Leaf, that's where Dr. Gerlitz's shuttle is; you mind if I join you?"

"Not at all, Marshal, let's go."

The three enforcers walked calmly through the casino until they reached the lift, where their speed picked up after the lift entered the hangar bay level. A small hatch to the hangar bay opened, and Engineer Trently watched the three enforcers approach Dr. Gerlitz and himself as they focused on the engineering grav unit holding a small octagon sphere in suspension with the vid com on the grav unit displaying details of the device on its projection.

Supervisor Stykes was serious. "Trently, what's the breach?"

Engineer Trently looked away from the vid com projection to answer. "Sir, when Dr. Gerlitz started testing several power systems on his experimental device," Trently paused to look at Dr. Gerlitz with a disapproving expression before continuing, "this stealth droid deactivated near the shuttle."

Officer Armela interrupted. "What was it doing?"

Dr. Gerlitz spoke quickly with a shaky voice. "It was collecting data on my experiments." He was growing more agitated.

Marshal Scoop turned toward Supervisor Stykes after inspecting the droid. "This is Eastern, Leaf, I can tell by the configuration."

"We could not tell because the system was wiped clean after the droid was exposed," Engineer Trently said.

The marshal grinned and nodded. "They're programmed to self-eradicate; this droid is now scrap."

Supervisor Stykes did not look happy as he issued commands to Officer Armela. "I want a full report. I need to inform Director Furgis."

Marshal Scoop followed Stykes to the hangar bay hatch.

Chapter Two

Operator Furgis walked to the table where his son and Raynor sat in the Solar House. "You guys order yet?" He sat down, looking at the data pad to order. "I know what I want," he said. "I'm just waiting for a friend to join us."

Sam Furgis was smiling. Raynor knew what that look on her son was about. "Good for you, son. I can't wait to meet her."

Operator Furgis looked up at his son. "Her?" He started laughing. "Excellent, Sam. Will she be here soon?" Operator Furgis was smiling with pride.

Raynor Furgis reached to the center of the table and activated the table's vid com. "I'll order everyone one of those drinks you guys like so much."

Operator Furgis continued to look at the data pad and said, "Thanks, hon," and Raynor Furgis smiled widely.

Sam picked up his drink after the server was finished placing the order on the table. He was smiling with joy. "Here's to Mom and Pops. May you guys find happiness this time."

Raynor's eyes opened wide. "Thank you, Sam, you're so sweet." She grabbed her son's hand after the toast.

Sam looked at his father with surprise "Pops, you always get the steak with trimmings—what's up?" Kennith chuckled.

"I thought about trying something else, maybe the meatloaf, but it would not compare to your mother's."

Raynor interceded. "I told you to build me a proper kitchen, Ken"

His father started to reply, but Sam interrupted. "Here's to old times." He held up his glass.

Operator Furgis laughed. "I guess I'll have the steak." And he drank his Dou Zhe. After they placed their orders, he turned around to look over his shoulder, and his son stood quickly.

Sam was smiling. "Hey, baby, we've been waiting."

Raynor Furgis turned her head with a look of disgust. Operator Furgis stood and pulled the chair out that was in between Sam and his father. He watched as a blond, wavy-haired young lady with an attractive figure sat.

"Pops, I want you to meet Kelly Brown."

Operator Furgis shared his son's smile. "Nice to meet you, Kelly. How long are you staying with us?"

Kelly's accent was from the southern part of the old Americas. "Not sure yet, sir." She grabbed Sam's hand.

Sam looked at his mother, now staring at Kelly with a frown. "Mom, you remember Kelly."

Raynor quickly answered, "Oh yeah, I remember Kelly." She held her hand out. "How are you, young lady?" she said sarcastically.

Sam smiled, shaking his head. "Pops was getting hungry so I ordered your favorite, Kel."

Kelly grew excited. "They have squid?"

Operator Furgis coughed while Raynor laughed. Sam nodded. "Of course, Seth can get anything,"

Operator Furgis added, "At a price."

Kelly squeezed Sam's hand harder. "You're so sweet."

"It runs in the family," Operator Furgis said with a chuckle and gently smacked Sam's shoulder.

Kelly grew slightly more serious. "Who's Seth?"

Sam answered quickly, knowing his father would like to have explained. "Seth Adams is the owner of the restaurant, and he also owns Grav Zero." He squeezed her hand. "I'll be taking you there later."

Kelly smiled. "I can't wait."

Seth Adams approached the table. "Is everything satisfactory?"

"Excellent, Seth, thank you," said Sam.

Kelly looked up at Seth. "I'm Kelly, a good friend of Sam's."

Sam stood quickly. "My apologies. Seth, this is Kelly Brown, a close friend from Mars City Central."

Seth leaned forward and shook Kelly's hand. "It's a pleasure to meet you. Anything you need, just ask."

She nodded as Seth moved to the next table. Her curiosity continued to grow and finally she asked, "Sam, how is your arm?"

Sam smiled. "It's good, Kel, most of the time I forget it's a bio arm."

His father laughed. "He remembers after he shakes your hand." He turned to look behind him as Raynor waved; Huiling Li and Officer Armela approached the table. Huiling was cheerful as usual. "Raynor, hello." Raynor replied with the same excitement. "Hello, Huiling, Officer Armela." Officer Armela smiled standing behind Huiling.

Operator Furgis always enjoyed talking with Huiling. "And where are you guys off to?"

Officer Armela laughed. "Seth gave us our usual small table in the back." Huiling reached up and put her hand on the large enforcer's shoulder. "It's quiet back there."

Raynor interrupted. "It's more exciting here if you two would like to join us."

Officer Armela continued to smile. "Thank you, ma'am, but we looked forward to spending a little time together." Huiling's smile grew wider.

Sam stood and made introductions.

Huiling shook Kelly's hand. "Hello, Kelly, are you enjoying your visit?"

"Yes ma'am."

Huiling looked up at Officer Armela, continuing to smile. "This is Officer Armela."

Kelly's voice was gentle "I've already had the pleasure, ma'am."

Armela shook Kelly's hand. "It's good to see you again, ma'am."

Huiling grew a little more serious. "Will you be at services next cycle, Kelly?"

Sam answered Huiling's question quickly. "Yes, she will be there." Kelly looked at Sam with a surprised smile as they returned to their chairs.

Raynor laughed before looking at Kelly. "Since when do you attend services?"

Kelly Brown offered a sincere look. "I like services, ma'am."

Before Raynor could respond, Huiling said, "Ken, Senior Pastor Murray will be visiting the station soon." She paused for a moment to look at everyone at the table. "I would like to offer his services at your wedding." She held Officer

Armela's hand.

Ken looked surprised and was ready to answer, but Raynor was quick. "Thank you, Huiling, I was planning on asking you if you could do the honors."

"Hey, don't I have a say?" Ken said.

Raynor and Sam responded at the same time. "No." Raynor continued. "Ken, we're not using the solar net or 3-D world for our wedding." He attempted to answer but was quickly overruled. "That's final."

Sam laughed at his mother's authority and leaned forward to hit his father's shoulder. "Pops, you should know better than that."

His father nodded with a smile and replied with childlike sarcasm, "Senior Pastor Murray it is." Raynor cancelled her response as the servers placed the meals in front of the ladies first.

Huiling Li attempted to push Officer Armela toward their table, and the very large enforcer chuckled looking at Operator Furgis study his steak. "I guess that's my cue, sir—if you will excuse us." Furgis looked up at Armela and winked before they left for their table.

Sam looked at Kelly with a grin. "How's your squid?" Kelly was moving her food around and did not bother looking at Sam before answering with excitement, "Sam, this squid is real!" Raynor looked at Ken, trying not to laugh. She was amused at her future husband's look of concern at the cost of a favor from Seth Adams. Operator Furgis was enjoying his steak when the chime of his ear com piece was heard. "Incoming transmission." Operator Furgis accepted the transmission, which was from Chief Tylor.

Chief Tylor's voice was calm. "Sir, I hope I'm not disturbing you."

Furgis continued to eat. "Not at all, Chief, just enjoying a steak. What can I do for you?"

"Sir, I just wanted to inform you that Dr. Gerlitz is ready to launch."

"Thank you, Chief." Operator Furgis tapped his ear com piece to turn it off.

Sam inquired quickly, "What's up, Pops?"

"Dr. Gerlitz is taking a trip outside. I'll brief you in your office after we're done here."

Sam could sense that his father did not want to discuss Dr. Gerlitz openly. "Okay, Pops." Sam continued to eat.

The two couples walked casually from the solar house through retail level toward the lifts after enjoying their meal. Operator Furgis suddenly stopped and activated his ear com piece. Raynor looked surprised as she waited, trying to see the problem. Sam knew what the problem was as he gently grabbed Kelly's arm with a motion to stay silent and still. Operator Furgis instructed his ear com piece after hearing the chime, "Supervisor Stykes." After a brief moment Stykes answered, "Yeah, boss?"

Operator Furgis spoke with authority. "Leaf, Polly P is entering the lift with another guest again."

Supervisor Stykes had a slight chuckle in his voice as he answered, "All right, boss, I'll check it out."

Operator Furgis frowned. "Thanks, Leaf." The ear com chimed off.

Raynor finally realized what was bothering him. "Ken, you can't stop that."

Operator Furgis grew aggressive. "Oh yes I can!"

Sam stood silently next to Kelly, observing the conversation, as his mother said, "Good luck," laughing quietly. Operator Furgis lowered his voice as he watched guests walk through the level. "You think this is funny, Ray?"

"Of course not, I'm just saying good luck on stopping one of the oldest trades around." Raynor paused to calm her laugh before continuing. "Ken, I had the same problem on Mars, which reminds me…when we get to your office I need to call Fields and let him know when I'm returning to Mars." Raynor was looking off in the distance.

Operator Furgis grew frustrated and in a slightly louder voice said, "Well, we made a deal so we could have more control of the situation." He nodded, continuing to the lifts.

Dr. Gerlitz was sitting in the navigation chair as Engineer Trently entered *Research Two*, "Dr. Gerlitz, the safety checks are complete; ready when you are." Dr. Gerlitz nodded and looked over toward the pilot's chair. Dr. Gerlitz's assistant activated the touch screen controls and after clearance from flight control issued the commands to *Research Two* . The small vessel rose off the skid pads extending from the bottom of the shuttle. Engineer Trently checked the engineering console's data as the sound of the engines could faintly be heard. *Research Two* moved sideways away from the docking tube. Trently could see the docking tube retract into the wall of the station through the small window near the console. *Research Two* lowered its nose slightly as the engines pushed the small vessel forward toward the large hangar bay doors, leveling as the large opening grew closer.

Gases escaped through the thruster ports of *Research Two*

as the small vessel maneuvered around Neptune One. Dr. Gerlitz's assistant was working the touch screen controls with accuracy. Engineer Trently watched the data on his console with concentration before confirming with Dr. Gerlitz. "Doctor, I established an interface connection with the power port; ready for module docking, sir." He displayed the data on the navigations vid com for Dr. Gerlitz. *Research Two* emerged from the large opening as the hangar bay doors stopped in a full open position, and the small vessel continued straight, stopping in a 180-degree turn. The crew of *Research Two* could see the bottom of Neptune One. Trently worked the controls on his engineering station's chair to face the front of the shuttle.

Dr. Gerlitz pointed out the cockpit window before issuing orders. "There's the power port for the module. Engineer Trently, are you maintaining an interface with the docking port?"

Engineer Trently turned his chair to face the console. "Yes sir, ready for retractor cable with an eme." The electromagnetic emminator was already attached to the retractor cable. Dr. Gerlitz's assistant was ready to set a course for the shuttle when the vid com on the pilot's station chimed, "Incoming transmission." The pilot answered quickly, and the vid com flickered before projecting a young woman in her Neptune One uniform. "*Research Two*, please be advised, *Orion Princess* departing from docking spheres."

Dr. Gerlitz's assistant responded, "Confirmed, Neptune One."

Engineer Trently looked out the small round window near his engineer station. He watched the medium-size cruise liner push away from the docking spheres; gases dissipated quickly as the smooth-hulled vessel was released from Neptune One's control. The four large engines on the back of the ship grew bright briefly before becoming the typical small pointed blue flame thrusting the massive amount of tonnage through the vacuum of space. Engineer Trently adjusted his attention on the vid com display for the engineering console. "Dr. Gerlitz, we still have a firm interface with the docking port; eme ready, sir." Dr. Gerlitz did not look back from his navigation chair; he quickly nodded at the pilot, and his assistant worked the touch screen controls directing the small vessel to slowly move forward to the underside of Neptune One.

Research Two was a small but graceful vessel. The small shuttle maneuvered with dignity as it glided along the hull of the massive space station, turning at various points to adjust its course toward the very bottom. The research shuttle came to a complete stop in close proximity to the very bottom module power port, and the pilot and Dr. Gerlitz waited patiently for Engineer Trently. Dr. Gerlitz turned as quickly as his navigation chair would allow to face the engineering console. "Trently, report." The pilot remained patient. Engineer Trently ignored the pressure, continuing to work on his touch screen control console. Dr. Gerlitz was relieved to finally hear Trently respond. "Sir, the two interfaces are connected; they are networked and ready for deploying." Dr. Gerlitz smiled with a nod.

The pilot did not wait for Dr. Gerlitz to issue the commands, and the research shuttle slowly moved forward, the pilot watching the vid com display as the small vessel approached a position directly under the module power port at the lowest point on Neptune One. Engineer Trently activated the internal speaker system and focused on the engineering touch screen control console. "Sir, hold right there." Trently paused before continuing with more concentration. "Opening top bay doors." The shuttle jerked slightly as gases escaped. Engineer Trently continued to call out the progress over the speaker system as Dr. Gerlitz and his assistant watched the progress on the vid com display. The retractor cable with an eme attachment lowered from the docking port on Neptune One, and the small experimental module slowly floated from the top of *Research Two* into the magnetic control of the retractor cable.

Dr. Gerlitz was excited. "Report, Engineer."

Trently briefly studied the vid com display and rechecked with his engineering console before sending the vid com details to the other stations. He looked out the small window. "We have interface conformation, sir, just waiting for final docking sequence on the power port." A quick flash and a small jolt rocked the small shuttle. Engineer Trently was not wearing his safety harness and was knocked out of his chair. As the small vessel stabilized, Dr. Gerlitz removed his safety harness and entered the rear cabin of *Research Two* . Engineer Trently was trying to get up off the floor. Dr. Gerlitz kneeled beside him."Shaun, are you all right?"

Engineer Trently rubbed his eyes with both hands. "My eyes hurt." Dr. Gerlitz assisted Engineer Trently back in his engineering chair. "We'll get you to med lab." Dr. Gerlitz fastened the engineering chair's harness.

After instructing the pilot to return to the hangar bay, Dr. Gerlitz activated the navigation's vid com. "Neptune One." A brief moment later the hangar bay technician was projected. "*Research One*, you're clear for approach." Dr. Gerlitz was quick. "We have a med emergency."

The young woman in a Neptune One uniform did not look up. The vid com flickered with a new image of Dr. Avers, a tall, attractive, blue-eyed blonde in her late thirties "Dr. Gerlitz, what happened?"

"Dr. Avers, a power surge ignited a small amount of Mortelis, and Engineer Trently was flash burned."

Dr. Avers was working the touch screen controls on her med pad. "I have a med tube standing by, Doctor."

"Thank you, Dr. Avers," Dr. Gerlitz responded before shutting down the vid com. He picked up a data pad from the console's holster.

Research Two slowly climbed to the level of the hangar bay doors and turned to face the opening, which was growing larger as the doors slowly slid open. The landing skids of *Research Two* emerged from the bottom hull as the small vessel approached the massive entrance. *Research Two* was dwarfed by the large opening as the small vessel entered the massive hangar bay of Neptune One. On occasion a small amount of gas would release from the directional thrusters and dissipate quickly as *Research Two* slowly approached its berthing area. The massive hangar bay doors started closing, and the docking tube was ready to extend as the small vessel gently settled on the landing skids protruding from the bottom hull. A green light illuminated the cabin inside *Research Two*, and the gas seal of the docking tube could be heard. Dr. Gerlitz exited his navigation's chair and with the help of his assistant guided Engineer Trently out of his engineering chair.

Director Furgis's mother and father sat in the desk chair facing the vid com as Sam sat behind his desk, laughing at Kelly

Brown as she watched the motion recordings on Sam's office shelf. "Do you remember that, Kel?"

Kelly's face was red as she touched the small controls on the base to change the projected recording. She turned around with a slightly embarrassed laugh. "Yeah, I remember that stupid old toy. Everyone in the bar was laughing."

Operator Furgis looked away from the solar sportscaster on the vid com. "They called them Jack in the box."

Kelly shook her head as she pulled up a chair next to Sam. "Whatever they're called, they're stupid."

Raynor Furgis continued watching the solar broadcast but was shaking her head with a smile. Operator Furgis turned back to the vid com broadcast. "Nothing on Mother's Mech fight, Ray." Raynor opened her hand in a pointing gesture.

Sam leaned back in his desk chair and started to study his pocket pad; his father smiled, shaking his head at the small device. Before Sam could respond to his father's look, the vid com projected the words "incoming transmission" along with the familiar chime. Sam Furgis sat up in his chair and said, "Source." The vid com instantly projected Dr. Avers' name, and Sam could see his mother sigh. He accepted, and the vid com flickered quickly and projected Dr. Avers. Operator Furgis smiled. "Brook, what can we do for you?"

Dr. Avers smiled. "Ken, I wanted you to know that Engineer Trently is here in med lab."

Sam grew serious, replying before his father. "What happened, Brook?"

Dr. Avers was calm. "Sam, Shaun received a flash burn." Sam tried interrupting but Dr. Avers was quick as she held up her hand and continued. "He's fine; we have optical pads on his eyes and gave him a small dose of meda."

Operator Furgis interrupted. "We'll be down shortly, Brook."

Dr. Avers smiled. "Thanks, Ken," and the vid com returned to the solar sports broadcast.

Operator Furgis stood. "Ray, let's go to med lab and see how Engineer Trently is." Raynor was ready to stand but changed her mind when the sports broadcast for the station started.

"And the Grav ball match on Neptune One is bringing a lot of excitement from the outer system." Operator Furgis did not respond; he sat back in his chair. The occupants of Sam's office remained quiet as the broadcaster continued. "Lewis Rogers is a seasoned pro for the Mars Rovers, a twenty-four-year old black man weighing in at one hundred and eighty-seven with a height of six foot two." The vid com projected highlights of Lewis Rogers on the sidebar. The sidebar changed to Peter Robins's highlights as the commentator continued. "And in the number two spot for the Rovers is Peter Robins, a twenty-three-year-old white man weighing in at one hundred and sixty with a height of six foot"; Operator Furgis could see Raynor grinning widely.

The commentator continued as the vid com sidebar changed again, showing the highlights of Yasin Jabir. "The third and final Grav baller is Yasin Jabir from Mother's Old Persian area. Yasin is twenty-one years old and new to Grav ball." The sidebar switched to projections of droids racing around Mars. The commentator allowed the projections to continue briefly before adding more commentary. "Yasin is five foot eleven and weighs in at one hundred and sixty-five."

Operator Furgis spoke quickly. "Vid com pause." He took

a breath and turned his chair toward Raynor. "You actually believe your Rovers will beat my Poseidons?"

Raynor laughed. "Yasin may be new, but he's not inexperienced, and Lewis is the best Grav baller in the inner or outer system."

Operator Furgis smiled. "We'll see. Vid com continue," and the vid com unfroze the projection as Operator Furgis turned back to face the projections.

The commentator continued. "And here on Neptune One we have the Poseidons." The vid com switched the projection to highlights of the Poseidons. The commentator continued with enthusiasm. "Number one is Ali Fisher, a twenty-six-year-old white female weighing in at one hundred and forty-six with a height of five foot ten. Ali has been number one for the Poseidons for several solar cycles and has brought numerous victories." The sidebar switched images. "Assisting Ali is Nora Jackson, a black woman at twenty-two years. Nora has demonstrated agility in the arena. She is five foot eleven and weighs in at one hundred and fifty-one." The sidebar switched to the next Grav baller. "And finally for number three on the Poseidons' side is Ron Curtis, a twenty-three-year-old white male; his height is six foot one and he weighs one hundred and seventy. This match's favorite is the Rovers."

Operator Furgis quickly interrupted, "Vid com off," and turned to Raynor. "Favored or not, I think the Poseidons will take it."

Raynor laughed. "Would you like to wager on that?" She turned to her son and winked.

Before Operator Furgis could reply, Sam joined the conversation. "I'll take some of that action."

Kelly stood, putting her hand on Sam's shoulder. "I still don't see what the big deal is about Grav ball."

Operator Furgis grew excited, switching his thoughts from Raynor's challenge. "Let me explain…" He took a deep breath before explaining the rules of Grav ball. "Three players on each side fight to score by putting a Grav ball through a projected ring floating in the arena."

Kelly walked over to Sam's office shelf and picked up a crushed Grav ball. "This thing is metal." She turned to Sam, looking surprised.

Director Furgis stood and approached Kelly, taking the Grav ball from her with his bio arm. "This was the Grav ball Dr. Avers gave me." Sam turned to his father with a wide grin.

Operator Furgis held his hands up as his son tossed the heavy Grav ball to his father. Operator Furgis grunted softly before continuing. "The projection is about four foot in circumference and moves around in a fifty-foot radius. The Grav ballers, as they like to be called, have gravity suits on with small direction thrusters."

"It sounds like a child's game," Kelly said.

Sam laughed before continuing for his father. "I used to think so until Pops took me to my first match."

"I remember you calling me after the match, Sam," Raynor said. "The Rovers stomped on the Venus Vikings back home."

Operator Furgis interrupted. "Kelly, this Grav ball," he tossed it back to Sam, "floats with a motion sensor that moves the ball from any GB for five seconds; if the GB captures the Grav ball, he activates the ten-second delay for a quick pass to his offense partner while his defense partner moves with the ring." He activated the vid com.

Kelly stood behind Sam at his desk with her hands on his shoulders as the vid com replied to Operator Furgis's commands. Raynor laughed as it projected a cartoon motion vid recording of a Grav ball match. Operator Furgis shushed Raynor before explaining, "The match here on Neptune One will be at the Dome of Delphi."

"Don't ask about the name," Sam interrupted.

Operator Furgis squinted his eyes with a frown at his son. "The arena will be shortened to fifty meters and overseen by the game droid above."

Kelly moved closer to the vid com projection. "It still sounds too easy."

Operator Furgis laughed. "Have you ever seen old vids of people chasing little dogs? That's what it's like."

"They float around fighting over a Grav ball to put in a floating ring that moves," Kelly replied.

Sam was now standing behind Kelly and held her by the shoulder. "There is no intentional contact allowed, which makes it very hard to know the difference for the spectators. The game droid calls all fouls."

Operator Furgis chuckled. "It will look very chaotic, almost like a brawl at times, but the Grav ball was designed to move away from motion, remember?"

Kelly picked up the Grav ball from Sam's desk as she turned. "It's really heavy."

Sam laughed. "It has thrusters as well and will continue to move in the motion it was thrown in for ten seconds; if it travels out of bounds, it doesn't move too fast but is very agile and hard to follow."

Kelly started laughing. "And you guys make a lot of credits

on this!"

"We…" Sam paused.

Raynor took advantage of the pause. "Not if you bet against the Rovers."

Operator Furgis was grinning widely. He stood. "Now that we've got the Grav ball explanation done, I need to go to med lab and check on Engineer Trently."

Raynor slowly stood too. "I'll join you, Ken."

Sam picked up his data pad from his desktop. "Pops, what are you doing about Polly P?"

Operator Furgis looked at Raynor quickly before replying, "I'll let the director handle it."

Sam nodded with approval and activated the vid com as his mother and father left his office and contacted Supervisor Stykes. "Yes sir." Sam smiled, thinking of the days past when Security Supervisor Leaf Stykes would call him "kid."

"Leaf, I need you to set up a meeting with Polly P in your office."

Stykes sat up straight in his desk chair. "Right away. I'll have Juan detain her immediately."

Sam interrupted with a large grin and slight shake of his head. "Nothing like that, Leaf, I just want to talk business."

"Yes sir, I'll discreetly talk to her myself."

"Thanks, Leaf, let me know." The vid com shut off before Supervisor Stykes could reply.

Kelly stood in front of Sam's office shelves looking at the different vid cam motion projectors displaying Sam's captures. She held one base as she turned to face Sam. "Is your father going to approve of you making a deal with that woman?"

Sam stood from his desk chair with a grin. "He said the

director can handle it." Before Kelly could reply, Sam continued. "Besides, I've got Mom on my side." Kelly laughed, knowing what it felt like to have Raynor Furgis angry.

Sam walked over to Kelly, gently grabbing her arm. "No need to worry; let's meet them at med lab and see how Shaun is doing." Sam turned quickly to pick up his pocket pad from the desktop. "I need to stop by the solar pit and see Acela first." He gently guided Kelly out of his office.

Operator Furgis and Raynor walked into the lobby of the med lab. Raynor did not feel comfortable in med lab. She was aware of the attraction between Dr. Brook Avers and Ken. Dr. Avers exited Engineer Trently's exam room and walked into the med lab lobby to see Operator Furgis and Raynor waiting. "Ken."

Operator Furgis turned with a smile. "Brook, how's Engineer Trently?"

Dr. Avers smiled at Raynor. "Hello, Raynor."

Raynor grinned back. "How are you, Dr. Avers?" Dr. Avers turned her attention back to Operator Furgis. Raynor was slightly agitated watching Dr. Avers smile and grab Operator Furgis by the upper arm with a laugh. "Ken, Shaun is fine; we just removed the optical pads and his eyes are fine. Well, almost. He's still a little fuzzy, but he'll be all right in a short while."

Raynor stepped closer to her husband. "Do you mind if we see him?"

Dr. Avers could hear the aggression in Raynor's tone. "Of course, follow me." Operator Furgis allowed Raynor to walk ahead and saw the expression on her face as their eyes met.

Engineer Trently was sitting on the edge of the med tube

and looked up when Dr. Avers walked in to his exam room. "Engineer, you have some visitors." Trently smiled widely watching Ken and Raynor walk in. He staggered, trying to stand, and Dr. Avers moved forward quickly, grabbing him by the arm. "Thank you, Doc."

Operator Furgis stepped forward quickly but stopped as he watched Dr. Avers reach Engineer Trently first. "Trently, I came down to find out what this little vacation is about."

Raynor sneered, "This is no time for jokes, Ken. Shaun, how are you doing?"

Engineer Trently laughed. "Enjoying my vacation."

Operator Furgis put his hand on Trently's shoulder. "What happened, Shaun? I thought Dr. Gerlitz said this next step with his experiments was safe."

"It's my fault, sir. I scanned the entire module, but I did not catch a slight amount of Mortelis that escaped near the holding chamber." He lifted up his empty hands with a frown.

Raynor sighed. "Dr. Gerlitz and his Mortelis Canon." Operator Furgis and Engineer Trently stared at Raynor with surprise. She replied, "What?" Raynor's laugh lowered to a chuckle. "I'm the Regent of Mars; you don't think I know about these things?"

Operator Furgis grinned. "Engineer Trently is shocked because you know more than he does."

Trently laughed. "I'm not the only one."

Operator Furgis was ready to respond but was interrupted by his ear com piece chiming "Incoming transmission." He welcomed the diversion.

Supervisor Stykes sounded concerned. "Boss, we have a ship approaching from the other side of Neptune."

"We get ships here all the time, Leaf."

"This is the *Essex*, boss, an Easterner heavy cruiser," Stykes said. "Commander Kruger wants to speak with you."

Engineer Trently stood from the med tube. "I'll get back to Dr. Gerlitz, sir."

Operator Furgis nodded at Trently. "Leaf, tell Commander Kruger I'll be with him in a moment." He looked concerned as Raynor followed him out of the exam room, down the hall, and stopped in front of Dr. Avers' office. Raynor sighed quickly. "Ready, Ken." Operator Furgis activated the vid com entry.

Dr. Avers sat at her desk, gesturing with an open hand and a smile at the two chairs in front of her desk. Operator Furgis was quick. "Brook, do you mind if I borrow your office for a moment?"

Dr. Avers looked surprised. "Not at all, Ken." She picked up her med pad and smiled at Raynor. "I have to make my rounds." Raynor remained silent and sat in one of the vacant chairs while Operator Furgis sat in Dr. Avers' chair, turning towards the vid com and connected with Commander Kruger. "Commander, it's nice to meet you, I'm Operator Furgis."

Commander Kruger was six feet tall with short gray hair, a man in his late sixties and an accent from the old Eastern Empire. He was sitting in his command chair on the bridge holding a data pad. "Likewise, sir. I see that your station was once a military refit and repair station," he said smugly.

Operator Furgis was not intimidated. "Commander, Neptune One was once a military establishment; however, we are now an entertainment station."

"I see you still have functioning weapons."

"Yes, Commander. Neither empire can guarantee our

safety, and we have been attacked by pirate ships on more than one occasion." Operator Furgis looked quickly at Raynor.

Commander Kruger relaxed slightly. "Yes, I've heard of this." He set his data pad in the command chair's holster and leaned forward. "Sir, I need to refit the *Essex*; we just came through a skirmish with the Westerners."

Operator Furgis grinned. "I hope you and your crew are all right. We can provide medical assistance if needed."

Commander Kruger laughed. "No need, sir, but the *Essex* is low on ammo and I'm aware you help several Westerner ships on occasion." He sat back with his hands together, waiting for Operator Furgis to answer. He did not wait long.

Operator Furgis grew almost cheerful. "Any assistance our Eastern friend requires. I'll check my store if you could ask your guys to send a list of materials over."

Commander Kruger nodded. "If you have a data pad ready, I'll send it over the vid com as we speak."

After activating his data pad, Operator Furgis looked back up at the projection of Commander Kruger. "In the meantime, sir, we have a good Grav ball match we're preparing for if you would like to make a wager." Commander Kruger chuckled. "No thank you, but some of my crew will be over for a little R and R."

Operator Furgis did not have time to respond, as the vid com shut down. Raynor loudly sighed in a heavy exhale. "Nice guy, Ken."

Operator Furgis looked at his fiancée with annoyance. "I can tell this guy's up to something." He reactivated the vid com and instructed it to connect him to Supervisor Stykes. "Yeah, boss?"

Furgis sat back in Dr. Avers' chair. "Leaf, Commander Kruger is sending some personnel over for shore leave."

Supervisor Stykes was quick to reply. "Don't worry, boss, I'll keep an eye on the spies." Both nodded as the vid com turned off.

"Ken, does he always call you 'boss'?" Raynor asked.

Furgis laughed. "Don't ask, it's a long story." Raynor put her palms in the air. Operator Furgis was calm. "Do you have days like these on Mars?"

Raynor started laughing. "Of course," she said. "It's a little different; we already have both empires present on Mars, so these unannounced visits are less frequent." Raynor was shaking her head with a grin. Operator Furgis returned his chair to face the vid com and, after the chime and voice confirmation, asked for Chief Tylor. The vid com flickered briefly before projecting the chief sitting up straight at his office desk. "What can I do for you, sir?"

Operator Furgis held a great amount of respect for the chief and valued his opinion. "Chief, do you know anything about a Commander Kruger?"

The chief could hear the frustration in Operator Furgis's voice and looked surprised at the question. Operator Furgis waited for a moment, allowing Chief Tylor to think about his question before replying. "Sir, I never met the man, but I have been told he likes to play cat-and-mouse games. Does he still have that wannabe spy voice?"

Operator Furgis laughed. "Yeah, he still sounds ridiculous."

"Most of it is his real voice; I'm told he likes old spy books and vids."

Operator Furgis looked at Raynor, smiling. "It's not very

intimidating if that's what he's trying for."

The chief remained professional. "I asked Engineer Trently to check weapons and stores."

Operator Furgis interrupted. "He did ask for ammo; I'll send you the list."

"Sir, Engineer Trently also reports that Dr. Gerlitz is extremely nervous with the *Essex* here."

Operator Furgis finished his data pad transfer. "All right, Chief, I'll let Leaf know. Keep me informed." The vid com turned off.

Supervisor Stykes sat behind his desk listening to Polly P. As a twenty-three-year-old white female, at five foot nine, with dark hair, blue eyes, and a very voluptuous figure, Supervisor Stykes understood why others found this woman irresistible. He interrupted politely. "Ma'am, I'm not saying that you're not allowed company in your suite."

Polly P grew agitated. "Then what are you saying, sir?"

Supervisor Stykes remained calm, offering a slight laugh before replying, "How about working together?" He watched Polly lean back in her chair in deep thought. She remained silent for several moments.

"What do you mean by work together?" Polly asked.

"We will implement a set of guidelines for you to follow." Polly tried interrupting but Stykes held his open hand up and raised his voice. "In return you may discreetly allow a friend or two to work with you, provided you maintain control." He sat back in his desk chair.

Polly P continued to watch Supervisor Stykes. She was used to having her own way and the freedom of her own rules. She leaned forward and in a very low, feminine voice said,

"And if I say no?"

Supervisor Stykes laughed. "First of all, Director Furgis will meet with you in this office to approve of the arrangement personally." Polly tried interrupting but was denied once again by Supervisor Stykes' open hand and tone of voice. "Let me finish. If he agrees you will have complete discretion; however, you will be held accountable." Polly P stood and turned to walk toward the office door. Supervisor Stykes waited briefly before adding, "If you do not agree, Director Furgis has authorized me to use my discretion, and I have already spoken to Chief Tylor about the facilities you are using."

Polly P turned quickly to face Supervisor Stykes. "Tell Furgis I'll meet with him," and she turned and exited the office.

Director Furgis and Kelly Brown casually exited the lift on the casino level and watched the crowd in the wagering areas where the Grav ball match was drawing. Director Furgis smiled as he observed Marshal Scoop standing behind Mrs. Alberts as she wagered on a vid slot. Kelly tapped Sam on the arm. "What are we doing?"

"Patience, Kel," he said with a chuckle. "I'm looking for Acela." Sam watched Kelly trying to look through the crowd. He put his hand on Kelly's back as they started to walk toward the solar pit. Sam stopped when he heard the chime from his ear com piece followed by the gentle female voice, "Incoming transmission." Supervisor Stykes was transmitting. Sam accepted and Stykes could hear the crowd in the background as they spoke. "Sir, Polly is aware of your offer and will meet with you when ready."

Sam nodded at Kelly before answering, "Thanks, Leaf, I'll get back to you later." The ear com went silent.

Chapter Three

Sam and Kelly entered the solar pit and saw Acela speaking with Chayton. As they approached, two individuals entered the solar pit, one a tall, blond man with a slight limp and the other a shorter, medium-built black man. The blond man grabbed Acela's lower arm and roughly clamped her hand in a magnetic cuff. Chayton pushed the man back, and as the aggressive individual lunged forward again, Chayton turned sideways, catching him off-guard. The blond individual struggled as Chayton initiated a stranglehold around the his neck, but the struggle did not last long as Acela recovered quickly and used her left knee to impact the blond man in the groin. Chayton followed the him to the floor of the solar pit, landing with his knee on the chest of the attacker. Chayton and Acela could hear the grunt as he exhaled deeply.

The short black man was in between Kelly and Acela; he moved quickly, trying to push Kelly out of his way. The man was surprised to see Sam Furgis move quickly to block his attack after hearing Kelly scream. Sam reached for the man's throat, but the assailant leaned back quickly, and Kelly screamed once again as she witnessed the assailant drawing a transparent blade with extreme speed. Sam was aware of the approaching knife and leaned back, attempting to grab the assailant's hands; he felt a sharp sting on his check, and a burning sensation in his right eye as his hands met his opponent's hands.

The crowd sitting at the vid com wagering tables had already started a panic as they ran quickly from the immediate area; the main casino vid com already froze all tables and initiated an alarm for all enforcer personnel.

The struggle between Director Furgis and his aggressor ended just as quickly as it started, and extremely painfully for Director Furgis as the individuals in the solar pit heard a very loud pop. Sam fell backward, with his assailant landing on top of him. Sam could see through his left eye Marshal Scoop standing on the wagers side of a shut-down vid com table. He put his air pistol back inside his jacket as he entered the solar pit. Kelly Brown and Acela were already holding a ripped cloth to Sam's right eye. Marshal Scoop was hoping the injury was not as severe as the amount of blood suggested. As Marshal Scoop took control of the blond man, Chayton activated the vid com on the solar pit podium, informing Dr. Avers of the medical emergency and possible casualty.

Sam Furgis tried to stand but was forced back down by his three friends. Marshal Scoop watched him, impressed with the young man's courage. He activated his ear com and contacted Supervisor Stykes, who was already entering the lift from the administration level. Officer Armela and Huiling stepped aside, allowing Stykes room in the lift. Officer Armela was first to speak. "Weapons discharge in the solar pit."

Supervisor Stykes interrupted him. "Acela."

Huiling let go of Officer Armela's arm as the doors to the lift hissed open. Stykes exited the lift on the casino level, followed by Armela and Huiling. He could already see Kennith

and Raynor Furgis standing in the solar pit as Dr. Avers oversaw the med tech carefully lift Director Furgis onto the med
tube. Operator Furgis turned to Marshal Scoop with anger.
"What the heck are you doing?" Before Marshal Scoop could
reply, Operator Furgis continued loudly. "Every time you're
on my station, someone gets hurt."

Raynor grabbed Ken's arm and shoulder. "Not here, Ken."

Marshal Scoop walked over to Supervisor Stykes, who said
angrily, "Marshal, you need to get your guys under control."

Scoop sighed heavily in response. "They're not my guys."

Supervisor Stykes was sarcastic. "No, they're not." Officer
Armela was holding the blond individual. "They're ours now."

Huiling was kneeling next to the short black man. Operator
Furgis and Raynor followed Dr. Acela and the med tube containing their son to med lab. Dr. Avers was watching the data
on the med tube's med pad while following the med techs to
med lab "Ken, Sam will be fine."

Before Operator Furgis could reply, Raynor snapped,
"Fine? He was stabbed in the eye and you say fine?"

Operator Furgis remained quiet as he walked next to
Raynor, pulling her closer with his arm.

Huiling Li followed the next med tube with the black man
inside to the med lab, knowing there was no rush; the hardened
plastic projectile from Marshal Scoop's air pistol was accurate
and deadly. Governor Bob Davis joined Marshal Scoop as he
followed his fellow enforcers to the security headquarters.
"Marshal Scoop, I need a full report for the Solar Council."

Marshal Scoop chuckled. "Yes sir." The marshal had known
Governor Davis for a long time and always found his old Irish
accent, tweed cap, and his short, round body extremely hard

to take seriously.

Acela Vega filled out a security report on the solar pit's vid com after authorizing the casino's main vid com to reactivate the vid tables and allow the wagers to continue their individual wagering. Acela Vega was cautious, almost paranoid, as she watched people around the casino level, noticing the extra enforcers Supervisor Stykes had assigned to patrol. Chayton was concerned for Acela and did not want to leave the solar pit; he watched the extra patrols as well and smiled when he noticed Marco De Luca approaching.

Marco De Luca was in his early forties, a very well-dressed man from old Italy and promoted to front desk manager. Marco was usually comical but he appeared serious as he slowly approached Acela, grabbing her arm gently. "Acela, I saw the vid com recording. Are you all right? How's Sam?"

Acela smiled at Marco. She thought of him as a close friend, especially when he helped her during her trial period on Neptune One. Ken Furgis accepted Marco De Luca's recommendation for Acela's position as senior pit boss. He enjoyed Marco's sense of humor and respected his insight into other's characters.

Acela Vega grew more cheerful. "I'm fine, Marco, thank you, and as soon as I get the pit fully operational, you can join me and Chayton when we see how Sam is." She nodded at Chayton.

Marco looked Chayton up and down, inspecting his suit. Chayton also wore nice suits, and both men enjoyed razzing each other. Marco started first. "Sure I'll join you. Should we stop by Chayton's quarters?"

Acela looked confused and asked, even though she felt she

should not, "For what?"

Marco grinned. "So he can change."

Acela laughed. "Enough. I'm ready; let's go." Chayton smiled, shaking his head at Marco.

Supervisor Stykes and Officer Armela entered the med lab lobby and approached Operator Furgis. Raynor looked very concerned about her son as she turned quickly to Supervisor Stykes. "Leaf, do you have that bast—"

Operator Furgis interrupted. "Who's watching him, Leaf?" He gently rested his hand on Raynor's shoulder.

Supervisor Stykes answered with a gentle tone as Raynor stared, "Marshal Scoop is in the holding chambers."

Raynor shrugged Operator Furgis's hold off and stepped toward Stykes. "Do you think that's wise?"

Supervisor Stykes looked at Operator Furgis. "Boss, whatever the feelings about the marshal, he's still a marshal, and I trust him as such." Operator Furgis regained his comforting hold on Raynor.

Officer Armela spoke loudly but compassionately as he interrupted the conversation. "Ma'am, how's Sam?"

Raynor was having trouble holding the tears back. Operator Furgis pulled her closer and answered for her. "Dr. Avers said he will be fine, Juan, we just have to wait." He was interrupted by the hissing sound of the med lab lobby door opening. Raynor forced herself away from Operator Furgis as she watched Huiling quickly enter and walk directly to her. Huiling and Raynor hugged tightly for several moments. After hearing Officer Armela cough, Huiling let go with watery eyes, staring briefly at Raynor before inquiring, "Is Sam okay?"

Raynor never thought she would like Huiling Li because of

her convictions, but she found the young Chinese woman very easy and pleasing to speak with. Raynor Furgis was always busy as the Regent of Mars and had her beliefs, but it was not until she met Pastor Huiling Li that she started to explore those beliefs more deeply. The full-figured black woman smiled as she wiped her eyes. "Brook said he will be fine; we're just worried about his sight." Operator Furgis had a look of confusion after hearing Raynor say "Brook." He knew Raynor did not hate Dr. Avers, but he was aware of her uneasiness and was pleased that she trusted Dr. Avers in her field. Operator Furgis held his hand out for Huiling and was ready to speak with her when they heard the hissing sound of the door again, and Acela Vega walked into the med lab lobby followed by her companions.

Acela went directly to Operator Furgis. "Ken, how's Sam?"

Raynor answered quickly, "He's fine, Acela. We're just waiting for Brook to let us know about his eye."

Acela could see the worry in Raynor's watery eyes. "God bless Sam. In my book Sam is a hero." She paused to quickly look around the lobby at the individuals waiting for news. "If there is anything I can do…" Acela was holding Raynor's hand tightly. Raynor knew Acela and Operator Furgis had grown close, but this did not bother her. She also knew of Acela's preference.

Acela was slightly older now than the day Kennith Furgis appointed her senior pit boss. She was still a very attractive Spanish woman with curves that captured the attention of both genders.

Kennith Furgis was once again interrupted as Dr. Avers appeared in the entryway. Operator Furgis gently pushed his way through the group with Raynor following. "Brook, talk to me."

Dr. Avers smiled at both before responding. "Sam is all right."

Raynor interrupted abruptly. "What about his vision?" Operator Furgis held Raynor gently by both shoulders.

Dr. Avers looked at the small group. "Ken, Sam is awake and fidgety as usual, but he needs to stay still. I have an optical pad on his right eye." Dr. Avers held both hands together behind her.

Raynor did not welcome this news and was slightly loud. "Does that mean his eye will be okay?"

Dr. Avers moved her hands to the front. "I did not say that."

"Tell us what's happening, Brook," Ken said.

Dr. Avers took a deep breath before exhaling. "Ken, Sam's eye has major trauma; if the optical pads do not heal the injury, then I will have to replace the eye."

Operator Furgis touched Dr. Avers on the arm with a smile. Raynor was not so accepting and used some foul language before turning to Huiling. "I'm sorry, Huiling." Raynor smiled with a small bow of her head.

Huiling smiled back. "It's okay, Raynor." She turned her attention to Dr. Avers. "Brook, can we see him?"

Dr. Avers looked cheerful. "Ken and Raynor first." She stepped to the side, allowing both parents to exit.

Director Furgis sat up on the exam table holding his right eye as his parents walked into his exam room. "Pops, Mom." Dr. Avers walked quickly to Sam before either parent could react. "Sam, you need to lie down and rest, let the optical pad work." Sam frowned as he lay back on the exam table.

Raynor stood near Sam, holding his hand. "Sam, are you all right? What did they do to you?"

Sam sighed briefly. "Mom, I'm fine. Dr. Avers has taken care of me before. I'll survive." Dr. Avers looked up briefly from her med pad to smile at Sam.

Operator Furgis was on Sam's other side, squeezing his shoulder gently. "I tell you, son, you just can't stay out of the thick, can you?"

Sam started laughing. "At least the meda is good."

Dr. Avers grew serious as she holstered the med pad. "We need to keep an eye on that dosage. Meda is highly addictive." She smiled at Sam. "I'll let the others know you're ready to see them." She winked before walking toward the sliding door.

Huiling entered Sam's exam room, followed by Acela and Officer Armela. Sam looked at his three friends and wondered where Supervisor Stykes was. "Juan, where's Leaf?"

Officer Armela stepped forward quickly. "Supervisor Stykes received a call from Dr. Gerlitz in *Research Two* . How are you doing, sir?"

Sam chuckled. "Leaf's always busy."

Acela moved closer and held Sam's hand. "I'm so sorry, Sam."

Sam interrupted, trying not to turn his head too far as he looked at her. "No need to apologize, Acela, I'll be fine."

Acela wiped her watery eyes quickly. "In any case, Sam, I thank you from the bottom of my heart." She smiled widely.

Huiling smacked Sam's knee. "Hey, young man, you all right?"

Sam laughed. "GF, Huiling."

Huiling was excited. "God First." She looked at Raynor, smiling. Kelly Brown laughed, holding Sam's arm, but she remained quiet while next to Raynor.

Supervisor Stykes entered the docking tube for *Research Two* and saw Dr. Gerlitz standing in the entry hatch to the small vessel. As Stykes approached, he could see the angry look on Dr. Gerlitz, who said aggressively, "Supervisor Stykes." He took a deep breath, allowing Supervisor Stykes to respond.

"Sir, what seems to be the trouble?"

"Security is the trouble," said Dr. Gerlitz as he stepped aside, allowing Supervisor Stykes to enter the shuttlecraft.

Stykes saw Dr. Gerlitz's assistant kneeling with one knee on the back of an individual who was face down. His eyes grew wide with surprise. "May I ask what is happening here?" Dr. Gerlitz stepped around Supervisor Stykes as he entered the shuttlecraft.

Dr. Gerlitz's assistant looked up at Supervisor Stykes; his hands were shaking as he picked up his data pad from the floor of *Research Two* . "We needed some data from the engineering console, and when we entered we found this man sitting at the console." Supervisor Stykes sighed and shook his head.

Dr. Gerlitz stepped in front of the man, attempting to look up from his prone position. "I want to know who he is."

Supervisor Stykes grabbed Dr. Gerlitz from the back of the shoulder hard after hearing his tone. "I'll handle this; let him up." Stykes pulled out his air pistol. Dr. Gerlitz's assistant stood back, allowing the intruder to rise to his feet. Stykes stepped back in the cramped aft compartment of *Research Two* . "Turn around, hands behind your back. Any sudden moves and they'll be your last." The intruder complied slowly as Dr. Gerlitz and his assistant stood aside and watched Supervisor Stykes put his mag cuffs on the man.

Supervisor Stykes escorted the individual through the

entry hatch to *Research Two* into the docking tube, and then used his ear com piece to contact Operator Furgis.

Operator Furgis was smiling at Raynor, knowing his son was injured but in no life-threatening danger. "Ray, I think you need to help Sam with his duties as director."

Raynor looked surprised as she turned to her son with a smile. "And what duties are those?"

Sam laughed. "I was supposed to meet with Polly P shortly." Raynor looked back at Ken and was ready to speak when she was interrupted by his ear com piece chiming. It was Supervisor Stykes. Operator Furgis turned and walked toward the door, leaving Raynor and her son wondering.

"Boss, we got a situation here."

Operator Furgis turned back to face his family and watch the others. He remained calm. "Explain, Leaf."

Supervisor Stykes was also calm. "I have an individual in mag cuffs and we're headed for security headquarters."

"For what reason?" His ear com piece was silent. Operator Furgis watched his family and friends waiting to hear the news.

Supervisor Stykes finally replied, sounding out of breath. "Sorry, boss, this guy refused to move for a while."

Operator Furgis watched Officer Armela exit the exam room quickly. "What's the problem, Leaf?" His tone was growing louder.

"Dr. Gerlitz found this guy looking through the engineering console on *Research Two*," Stykes explained. "It gets better, boss. I believe this guy is from the *Essex*."

Operator Furgis took a deep breath. "I'll meet you in security headquarters, Leaf. I believe Officer Armela is already on his way."

"See you there, boss." Both ear com pieces chimed off.

Dr. Avers exhaled quickly as she approached Operator Furgis. "Ken, Sam needs rest now."

Operator Furgis grabbed his son's shoulder. "We'll see you soon. Anything needed let us know." Raynor leaned forward, kissing her son on the forehead before Sam could answer. Kelly looked over at Dr. Avers as Sam's visitors exited. "I want to stay.' Dr. Avers nodded. Sam laughed when he heard his father telling his mother to speak with Polly P as they exited the exam room.

Raynor turned to Operator Furgis as soon as the exam room door was heard closing. "Okay, Ken, I'll take care of Polly while you're having fun with Leaf." Operator Furgis laughed loudly. They entered the med lab lobby and activated the vid com so that Raynor could contact Polly P.

Raynor could see the attraction men had for the young, beautiful white woman. Polly P answered with an exotic voice. "May I help you?"

Raynor chuckled. "We have some business to discuss."

Polly's voice grew erotic. "I can find some time, honey."

"Sweetie, if you want to stay in business, you'll find time to meet me in Director Furgis's office immediately."

Polly was leaning back in a pink body chair but sat up and leaned forward before answering, "All right, I'll be there soon." The vid com shut down.

Operator Furgis's laugh grew deeper as he exited the med lab. His ear com piece offered the familiar chime and gentle voice; he reached up and activated the communications device. "Chief Tylor." After a brief pause he could hear the chief's voice. "Yes sir." Operator Furgis stopped in the middle of the casino, watching Raynor casually walking toward the lifts with a large grin. He observed Acela and Chayton in the solar pit from across the casino area. "Dan, I need to know how the intruder got through the vid coms on the docking tube and entered *Research Two*."

"I have Engineer Trently checking that out at this time; he'll send a report to security headquarters ASAP, sir."

Operator Furgis grinned. "Thanks, Chief," and he walked toward the security headquarters.

Supervisor Stykes turned toward the entry door to the holding chambers, heard the hiss from the door opening, and saw Operator Furgis approaching. Stykes moved closer to the entry door, noticing the familiar angry look on Furgis. "Boss, Officer Armela is questioning the perp now." He handed Operator Furgis a data pad and continued to explain the contents. "Lt Jeff Mead, Operations Officer for the SS *Essex*." Operator Furgis walked to the transparent wall of the holding chamber.

Supervisor Stykes continued. "Five-foot-eleven white male with short brown hair and brown eyes"

Operator Furgis grinned. "I can see that, Leaf."

Stykes remained calm. "Boss, take a look at his left hand."

Operator Furgis looked carefully and then looked back at his data pad, inputting commands for a 3-D projection of the ring on Lt. Mead's finger. The data pad projected a small image of a rotating ring. Operator Furgis shook his head before ending the data pad's projection. "It's an Easterners' ring of Elites."

"Why is an Elite looking around Dr. Gerlitz's shuttlecraft?"

Operator Furgis handed the data pad back to Stykes. "It's time I ask Commander Kruger."

Operator Furgis left the holding chamber, entered his office, and activated the main vid com before sitting in his desk chair. Before he could issue a command to his vid com, it interrupted with a communication from Acela Vega. Operator Furgis accepted with enthusiasm and the vid com projected the beautiful senior pit boss.

"Ken, I have a gentleman here who wants to enter the astro tourney." Acela was calm and relaxed as always.

Operator Furgis could see the action in the pit behind the gorgeous and curvy Spanish woman; he was always impressed with Acela as a pit boss and a lady. Operator Furgis finally answered with a respectful tone, "Acela, I thought the tourney already started."

She nodded. "He says he's a friend of yours and does not mind starting late."

"Who is he?"

Acela instructed the vid com to focus on the new arrival. Operator Furgis grew excited as the vid com projected a white man, five foot nine, with brown eyes and blond hair, weighing around one hundred and sixty pounds with a suit that would rival Marco De Luca's.

The man greeted him happily. "Kenny, you old hound dog."

Operator Furgis started laughing. "Dunc, what in the system are you doing here?" He let out a sigh and continued before his friend could interrupt. "Acela Vega, meet Duncan Jennings." Operator Furgis watched the vid com in his office project Duncan and Acela shaking hands. "Acela, Duncan is a really good friend of the family; if you have no objection, I say let him sign up." Acela nodded with a smile. Operator Furgis was not finished. "On one condition."

Duncan Jennings looked at Operator Furgis with a grin. "What?"

Operator Furgis laughed. "As soon as I get done with a transmission, you meet me at the solar house." He watched Duncan nod with a smile as the vid com switched to ready mode.

He sat back in his chair, shaking his smile off and activated his vid com. Operator Furgis's voice was slightly deeper now. "SS *Essex*." He waited patiently until the communications officer answered.

"This is the SS *Essex*."

Operator Furgis leaned forward. "No BS, ma'am, put Commander Kruger on the vid now," and the vid com projection flickered before a projection of Commander Kruger appeared sitting in the SS *Essex's* command chair.

Commander Kruger was arrogant, almost disrespectful. "A little busy here, Furgis. A warship is a lot different to operate than a vid machine." He was chuckling with a wide grin.

Operator Furgis waited for a moment to steady his diplomatic nerves before answering, "Commander Kruger, can you please explain why Lt Mead was caught infiltrating one of our secure research shuttles?"

Commander Kruger leaned forward. "Did you ask Lt Mead?"

"Yes, right after we put him in the holding chamber." Operator Furgis's voice grew slightly louder. "He stated he needed a secure transmission." Commander Kruger was no longer laughing; he sat back in his command chair quietly. Operator Furgis waited for several moments before continuing. "Well, Commander?"

"Furgis, I do not appreciate one of my command officers sitting in your holding chambers."

Operator Furgis quickly interrupted with a grin. "No need to worry, sir, my enforcers are with him."

"I want him out now."

"As soon as we find out what he was looking for."

Commander Kruger laughed and sat back in his command chair. "He already told you; he wanted a secure transmission. Furgis, he is my operations officer and has a right to a secure transmission."

Both vid coms remained silent for an extended period while each individual waited for the other. Operator Furgis was first. "Very well, Commander, we'll release him after we check all the systems on the shuttle."

Commander Kruger grew aggressive once again in his response. "You'll release him now or my enforcer will be there to release him."

Operator Furgis was pleased at this statement and grinned widely. "Very well, Commander, I'll release him and have him escorted back to his shuttle along with all other personnel from the *Essex*." He leaned back in his desk chair, watching the projection of Commander Kruger with a very large smile.

"So now you're telling me personnel from the Eastern Empire are not allowed on Neptune One."

Operator Furgis was starting to enjoy the conversation. "No sir, I'm saying personnel from the *Essex* are not allowed on Neptune One due to station security policies being violated." He could see the irritation from Commander Kruger. "All personnel will be escorted off the station immediately."

Commander Kruger was angry. "This is not over, Furgis."

"Feel free to file a complaint with the Solar Council on Earth; in fact Governor Davis is in his office if you would like me to link your transmission."

Commander Kruger relaxed. "Very well, Furgis, I also need to warn you of the pirate ships in the area—be careful." The vid com returned to the solar news about the wormhole designated WH-12.

Operator Furgis leaned back in his chair and continued to watch the vid com projection of the news; he was interested in the commentary about the upcoming Mech fight between Ben Swells and Tabitha Drake. Watching the news about the wormhole was interesting, but when the vid com projected the 3-D image of Earth dome with the Armor Warriors on the sidebar, Operator Furgis grew excited. His excitement ended when the vid com chimed in and Raynor was projected flowing across the projection area in midair. Operator Furgis leaned forward and adjusted his suit jacket. The vid com flickered quickly as the lasers replaced the solar news image with the 3-D image of Raynor sitting at his son's desk. He could see the beauty in her, but he could also see the professionalism as she said, "Ken, I have Polly P waiting outside. Would you like to sit in?"

Operator Furgis raised an open hand, his left hand in response. "It's all yours, Ray."

Raynor Furgis laughed, and Ken was confused. "What's so funny about Polly P? She brings trouble to the station."

"Maybe so, Ken. It's the oldest profession around; it even goes back to the Bible—you know, that book you like to avoid at all costs."

"Ray, if I need a history lesson about the book I like to

avoid, I'll ask Huiling." Raynor started laughing, but Operator Furgis was still tense about the subject. "Ray, can you just handle the matter? If I take care of it, Polly will be on Kruger's ship." Raynor continued to laugh. Operator Furgis was growing a little annoyed at the conversation but took care in his tone with his fiancée. "What's so funny, Ray? This is serious."

Raynor toned down her laugh, knowing it was bothering him. "Sorry, Ken, when you said that I pictured Polly sitting next to Kruger on the *Essex*." Operator Furgis decided to share the laugh with his future wife. Raynor Furgis calmed and grew serious. "Ken, I got some intel from Derek; he said Kruger has at least two more ships in the area."

Operator Furgis was silent for a moment before saying, "Tell Mr. Fields I appreciate the heads-up. Any idea which ships?"

Raynor picked up a data pad from her son's desk and took a few moments to look over the data before looking back up at her fiancé. "He mentioned only one." She paused to scroll through the touch screen of her data pad. After several minutes she said, "The SS *Staton* commanded by…" Raynor scrolled through the touch screen of her data pad quickly. "…Jonathan Edwards. You ever hear of him?"

Operator Furgis was quiet for a moment. "No, I never heard of Edwards, but the *Staton* is a small destroyer usually patrolling around its home base on Deimos."

"Yeah, I know the base; in fact as Regent I filed a complaint with the Solar Council against having a military base on one of Mar's moons." Operator Furgis could see her anger. "I was told the Eastern Empire established this base to protect their interest on Mars."

Operator Furgis sighed quickly. "It seems they have an interest in a lot of things."

Raynor shook her head. "Ken, I just wanted to give you heads-up."

Operator Furgis smiled. "Thanks, Ray, and have fun with Polly."

Raynor laughed and the reception vid com in Director Furgis's office lobby chimed, followed by a gentle female voice. "Polly P, please enter." Polly P stood slowly and walked in. Raynor looked up after hearing the hiss of the entry door. "Sorry for keeping you waiting, Polly." Raynor stood and walked to the front of the desk, pulling out a chair. "I had some important business that suddenly popped up."

Polly P sat in the chair Raynor offered and replied with her usual calm feminine voice, "No trouble at all, ma'am."

Raynor sat back in the desk chair. "I'm not sure if you're aware of my son's accident."

Polly leaned forward and said in a sympathetic voice, "I heard something happened. Is Sam all right?"

Raynor nodded. "He'll be fine, Polly. However, while he is recovering he asked me if I could speak to you about our situation."

"What situation is that?"

"Let's knock off the BS. Everyone knows you sell booty." Polly started laughing. Raynor chuckled before continuing seriously. "You may continue, with some provisions."

Polly P was curious. "What provisions are we talking about? You want a percentage?"

Raynor was taken by surprise. "Absolutely not!" She stared at Polly and continued. "We will not accept this station turning into a brothel; however, we also realize this type of establishment attracts individuals who want and individuals who offer."

"And the problem is the offering part..."

"Very good."

Polly P did not appreciate the sarcasm and grew more serious. "What is your suggestion, ma'am?" She stood. Raynor stood as well and walked around the desk. "The policies are here on this data pad; we know as you become more successful in acquiring more clients, others will want..."

Polly P interrupted quickly. "...work. I understand. You want us working for you."

Raynor laughed. "I want them working for you and I hold you accountable—take it or leave it."

Polly P thought for a moment and then held her hand out. Raynor watched Polly P exit Sam's office with the data pad as she wiped her hand with tissue from her son's desk. Raynor activated the vid com and contacted her future husband.

"How did it go, Ray?"

"Ken, you have a new employee."

"That's not even funny."

Raynor started laughing. "All right, Ken, I'm sorry but your problem has been dealt with." Raynor paused. "Any word from Dr. Avers?"

Operator Furgis shook his head softly. "Brook said the optical pad healed the wound."

Raynor was confused. "Then why are you concerned, Ken?"

"Sam has only regained half his vision and decided to have a bio eye replacement."

Raynor leaned forward. "It's his decision. Brook said he will regain full sight with no problems, correct?"

Operator Furgis sighed. "She said it is a common procedure and Sam should be back in no time." He looked very depressed.

"I'm worried for our boy too, Ken, but we have to have faith. Dr. Avers is very good at what she does, and besides, Huiling is putting in a good word."

Operator Furgis started laughing. "Huiling put a good word in, so everything will be fine. Sam has been through some bad times in the last five solar years."

"Kenny, it's not your fault. Meet me at the Solar House— my treat."

Operator Furgis shook the depressive feelings off and regained his composure quickly. "All right, Ray, Seth owes me one." The vid com shut down.

Operator Furgis stood from his desk chair and was ready to leave his office when he heard the familiar chime of the vid com. After taking a deep, relaxing breath, he answered the call from Supervisor Stykes. "Leaf, what can I do for you?"

Supervisor Stykes was sitting at his desk holding a data pad. "Boss, we got a transmission from the SS *King David*. The ship should be arriving earlier than expected." Furgis picked up the data pad resting on top of his desk. Stykes activated his data pad, using the touch screen controls with accuracy. "You ready for download, boss?" Operator Furgis nodded as he watched the data download. "Boss, check out the ship; it's massive. It could rival any carrier in either fleet."

Operator Furgis was quick to activate the vid com and contact the *King David*. The vid com projected an image of the ship, and he thought he could reach out and touch the impressive ship. Supervisor Stykes was excited. "I'm glad this ship belongs to the Solar Council, boss. If either empire puts armament on this, it would be a juggernaut."

Operator Furgis laughed. "They already have." He stopped to look closer at his data pad.

Supervisor Stykes watched the 3-D projection of Operator Furgis in the sidebar of the vid com, "What did you find, boss?"

Furgis looked back toward the vid com. "Enhance section four, grid three."

They leaned back in their chairs as the 3-D projection of the SS *King David* increased in size rapidly. Supervisor Stykes laughed loudly. "Wow, that's a big ship. If it wasn't a projection I could sell rides at the Armstrong Festival."

"Leaf, do you notice the docking sphere ports in this section?"

Supervisor Stykes was confused. "I see several docking spheres along this section." He stood back from his desk for a better view of the 3-D image.

Operator Furgis waited for Supervisor Stykes to arrive at his own conclusion. "There are several docking spheres in one section on a ship of this size."

Operator Furgis was quick to add to Stykes' observations. "Leaf, what do you notice about the docking sphere hatches?"

Supervisor Stykes studied the 3-D image for a brief moment before growing excited and slightly louder. "They're single hatches, no air locking chambers as well."

Furgis watched Stykes return to his chair with a large grin. The SS *King David* was a very large vessel operated by the Solar Council for exploration missions and manned by troops loyal to the council. The Solar Council contracted the operations of this ship with personnel who were devoted in their spiritual convictions. The ship itself was not very sleek or graceful in looks; the sides were designed with squares and spheres of all sizes, and antenna of different lengths came from all areas of the ship. The conning tower was almost the whole length of the top of the vessel followed by four extremely large engines.

Supervisor Stykes was quick to make another observation. "Boss, how many troposcopes does this ship require? The bow of the ship has several large arrays and more than a handful of smaller arrays."

"Good observation, Leaf. The ship is designed for exploration and is required to have numerous trops; however, I believe some of those are weapons arrays."

The vid com chimed with no voice-over, and Operator Furgis watched the name "Raynor Furgis" float across the image of the SS *King David*. "Leaf, the boss is calling. I'll get back to you."

Stykes laughed. "You got it, boss."

Operator Furgis accepted the transmission from Raynor. "Ray, what's up?"

Raynor looked slightly disappointed. "You know what's up. You joining me or should I sit with Officer Armela and Huiling?"

Operator Furgis grinned, shaking his head. "Sorry, babe, I got a trans from Leaf about the…"

Raynor interrupted quickly. "*King David*, I know."

"I can never get used to you knowing everything before I tell you."

Raynor laughed. "Huiling just told me, which brings me to the next subject." Operator Furgis knew he was required to proceed with caution after Raynor went from joking to instant seriousness with a new subject. "We have changes in our wedding plans." Before Operator Furgis could interrupt, Raynor continued. "Now's not the time to discuss the arrangements—just giving you a heads-up so you're not taken by surprise."

Operator Furgis chuckled. "You never take me by surprise, Ray."

Raynor laughed. "Are you coming down or will I be joining Huiling?"

"I'll be there as soon as I'm done talking with the *King David*." The vid com interrupted with the familiar chime and no vocal. Operator Furgis ignored the first chime, trying to end the transmission with Raynor quickly. "Ray, have you heard from Sam?"

Raynor shook her head. "It's about time you ask. Sam is fine with his bio eye; he's on a light dose of meda and Dr. Avers released him with an eye patch full of optical gel."

Operator Furgis smiled with pride he felt for his son. "Thanks, Ray, I'll stop by his office and see how he's doing. Go ahead and join Huiling, I'll see you in a bit."

The vid com switched to the transmission from the SS *King David*. Operator Furgis leaned back in his chair again with his best diplomatic smile. "Accept SS *King David*."; the vid com flickered briefly before displaying a tall, older black man in a very nice suit. Captain Murray was a fit man at sixty-nine years old.

Furgis was unaccustomed to seeing a solar ship captain in a suit, but he adjusted his train of thought and answered with respect in his voice. "Captain, how are you, sir?"

Captain Murray was quick to reply with a smile and friendly demeanor. "I'm doing very well, Mr. Furgis. Pastor Huiling has spoken very highly of you."

"Thank you, sir, we all respect Pastor Huiling here."

Operator Furgis adjusted his suit jacket.

"We should be arriving soon, Mr. Furgis. I hope you don't mind a brief visit. I'm looking forward to watching the Rovers in action again."

Operator Furgis lost some of his smile; he took the Grav ball matches seriously and was fond of Neptune One's team.

Captain Murray grew slightly concerned as he watched the 3-D image of Operator Furgis projected on his bridge. "Mr. Furgis, I hope I didn't offend you."

Operator Furgis's smile reappeared quickly. "No sir, I just have a lot on my mind, and to be honest I'm looking forward to watching the Poseidons teach the Rovers how to play Grav ball."

Captain Murray started laughing, knowing Operator Furgis was slightly more relaxed. "I understand Huiling offers grief share at her church."

"Thank you, sir, for your kindness and I mean no offense, but I haven't been called Mr. Furgis since my days on the Hammer. They call me Operator Furgis these days."

"I'm sorry, sir. Operator Furgis it is. I am looking forward to some of your well-known hospitality." Captain Murray was genuinely smiling with the utmost respect.

Operator Furgis felt a little uncomfortable correcting Captain Murray. "Captain Murray, you can call me Ken, and I look forward to seeing you too. The first meal at the Solar House is on Neptune One, sir." He waited quietly for Captain Murray to respond, knowing he was quickly becoming a new friend.

Captain Murray looked away from the vid com briefly before responding. "Sorry, Ken, the dust from Neptune's rings sometimes fools the trops. We should be arriving soon, and I look forward to sharing a meal with you."

"My pleasure, Captain Murray."

"Ken, when I'm off the ship you can call me Pastor Murray or, if you like, Don."

Operator Furgis was slightly surprised. "Very well, sir, we'll see you soon." The vid com shut down.

Chapter Four

Huiling Li and Officer Armela waited close to the glide tube station, anticipating the arrival of the passengers from the SS *King David*. The glide tube station was crowded due to the traffic from numerous ships departing and arriving for the astro tournament and grav ball match. Huiling's height was causing her difficulty in watching for her sister through the crowd; however, Officer Armela could look farther through the traffic of patrons. Whenever Officer Armela was with Huiling he would show his affection; this sometimes caused Officer Armela to tease with compassion. He moved behind Huiling and grabbed her by the waist, lifting her above the crowd with ease as Huiling shouted, "Juan, good gracious!" Huiling stopped yelling as she saw Pastor Murray walking through the lobby greeting everyone with a smile.

Huiling was demanding in her gentle feminine way. "I see him, put me down." Officer Armela gently set Huiling on her feet as Pastor Murray approached, followed by a short, petite Chinese woman. Huiling hugged Pastor Murray with one arm. "Senior Pastor Murray, welcome to Neptune One."

Pastor Murray was laughing as the hug ended. "I see you're still playful."

Huiling's face turned slightly red as she turned to Officer

Armela. "Pastor, this is Officer Juan Armela, a very good friend of mine and a true follower." As Pastor Murray shook hands with Officer Armela, Huiling turned to her sister, who was waiting in anticipation. No words were exchanged at first, just two petite Chinese women hugging each other so tight other travelers would look twice as they passed.

Huiling slowly exited the embrace and looked at her sister in eyes that started to turn watery. "Sis, how was the trip?"

Huiling's sister looked at Pastor Don Murray. "Beautiful. The good Lord has blessed Captain Murray with a gift."

"And Mom and Dad?"

"They're doing great, sis. I thought you spoke with them in 3-D world?"

Huiling laughed. "Of course. I wanted to hear it from my own sister. I have someone you need to meet." Huiling turned to Officer Armela and Pastor Murray.

Before Huiling could speak, Pastor Murray gave a belly laugh that stopped several patrons. "They will never win." He looked at Huiling, his laugh growing softer. "Huiling, my good friend Officer Armela here says the Poseidons will prevail over the Rovers."

Huiling laughed. "Sorry, Pastor Murray, I'm with Juan." She turned to her sister, gently grabbing her arm and directing her in the center of the group right in front of Officer Armela. "Juan, I would like you to meet my sister, Hui Yan Li."

Armela shook Hui Yan's hand. "Pleased to meet you."

Hui Yan smiled widely. "My pleasure, Juan. My sis has talked a lot about you." Everyone could see the excitement on Huiling's expression.

Pastor Murray interrupted. "Huiling, could you show us to

our quarters please?"

"Of course, and later Raynor Furgis would like to meet you." Huiling stepped aside, allowing her visitors to follow Officer Armela.

Operator Furgis entered Chief Tylor's office and approached an empty chair in front of the chief's desk. Furgis could see a 3-D schematic projected from the vid com in front of Dr. Gerlitz, Engineer Trently, and Marshal Scoop. Operator Furgis sat in the empty chair next to Governor Davis. "All right, Chief what did we find?"

Chief Tylor was quick, knowing Governor Davis was interested in having the situation explained. "Sir, in light of the recent espionage, Governor Davis has authorized Dr. Gerlitz to debrief us on his new experimental cannon." Operator Furgis watched the smile on Governor Davis's face grow wider. Dr. Gerlitz turned toward the desk, leaving Marshal Scoop and Engineer Trently studying the vid com's projection of the new weapon. Dr. Gerlitz spoke with pride. "Operator Furgis, as you know the HGE experiment was a huge success." He paused in thought for a brief moment before continuing. "I have managed to develop a means of controlling the implosion of Mortelis ore at the molecular level; without getting into any descriptions you would not understand, I can simply say this new energy cannon will change weaponry forever." Dr. Gerlitz was smiling with pride.

Engineer Trently turned around and joined the conversation. "Chief, this cannon is amazing; it uses RC current generated from the Mortelis, creating energy that would exceed…" He looked up at the ceiling in thought. "…I would guess around six million large calories."

Dr. Gerlitz interrupted. "Close, but I would say more. The trick was designing a structure to collect this amount of electrical heat and deliver it to its target." He stood, holding his data pad, and walked over to the vid com next to Marshal Scoop.

Marshal Scoop looked at Dr. Gerlitz quickly before walking over to Operator Furgis. "Mead was either looking to copy the schematics or trying to find a flaw to exploit." Operator Furgis nodded.

Engineer Trently was excited. "Dr. Gerlitz, how did you create RC power? I thought rotating between AC and DC at the required speed was impossible, and that much amperage generated…"

Chief Tylor interrupted. "Trently, you can discuss physics with the doctor later; right now we need to check every vid com command protocol for that cannon."

Dr. Gerlitz was proud. "The MC is secure. I just worry about unauthorized copies. That can become extremely dangerous."

Operator Furgis held up his hand as the individuals in the room started speaking at once. "Enough." He gained the attention of everyone with his loud voice. "What do you mean exactly, Dr. Gerlitz?" Dr. Gerlitz looked at the schematic almost in a trance. Operator Furgis grew impatient. "Dr. Gerlitz?" Furgis stood and walked over to the vid com Dr. Gerlitz was studying.

Dr. Gerlitz looked at Operator Furgis, shaking his head. "Ken, the smaller designs are easy to control, but the larger cannon we are testing now is still a prototype, and on occasion the targeting emitter fails or the charge does not travel."

Furgis shook his head in confusion. "You're saying this cannon could explode with the energy of a Mortelis ore implosion?"

Dr. Gerlitz refocused. "Not the one on the station. My concern is if someone tried to copy the design without knowing these issues."

Marshal Scoop interrupted with a sarcastic laugh. "That's a pretty good deterrent."

"Not now, Scoop," Furgis said. Marshal Scoop smiled, shaking his head.

Operator Furgis held his hand up, quieting everyone in Chief Tylor's office. "Dr. Gerlitz, I need as many of these smaller cannons ready to go and a complete safety check on the larger one you installed on my station."

Governor Davis looked surprised as he stood. "May I remind you that Dr. Gerlitz and his experiments are solely for the Terran Tribune?"

Operator Furgis turned to Governor Davis quickly. "Sir, may I remind you that we have declared independence from the Terran Tribune and that these experiments are at Neptune One's expense?" He turned to Chief Tylor. "Dan, check the design for the Hammer and our own shuttles. I need to know if these cannons will work on our ships."

Chief Tylor nodded at Engineer Trently, who immediately exited the office, with Dr. Gerlitz close behind. Operator Furgis waited until the door closed before continuing. "Gentlemen, let's not act stupid; we all know the Eastern Empire will eventually make a move for control of the inner system." Furgis stood close to Chief Tylor's desk, and Marshal Scoop sat in the chair next to Governor Davis. Governor Davis looked annoyed. "How do you know that? The Eastern Empire and Western Empire have been working directly with the Solar

Council on Earth."

Operator Furgis laughed lightly in response. "Call it a gut feeling, Governor. That's one reason Neptune One has declared independence from any government; we will remain a neutral entity for now."

Chief Tylor and Marshal Scoop nodded in acceptance.

Marshal Scoop stood. "Sir, I'll check with my contacts to see if they have any intel on the Easterners' plans, if any plans do exist."

Operator Furgis stopped Scoop before he could exit. "Marshal, I trust this thing with Acela will wait until we find out what the Easterners are up to."

Marshal Scoop smiled with an accepting nod and exited the chief's office. Governor Davis stood as well, starting to walk toward the exit. "I hope your gut feeling is wrong, Ken." He slowly exited the office as well.

Chief Tylor leaned back in his desk chair. "Sir, you think the Easterners are building up their forces to attack the Westerners?"

"Chief, I believe they are. The Hammer should be at Earth for the Mech fight match by now. I'll give Justin a transmit; I know he'll be poking around for the Westerners."

"Tell Captain Drake we got some new weapons for the Hammer or any of his other friends."

Operator Furgis nodded with a grin. "I'm sure he'll be happy about the good news; in the meantime I need to get to the other battle." He stood at the same time Chief Tylor stood.

The chief was confused. "What other battle?"

"The wedding, Chief!"

Sam Furgis was sitting at his desk chair talking with his

mother and Kelly when the vid com alerted him to a visitor. His office door slid open with a hissing sound, and Huiling Li walked in and stopped directly in front of Raynor Furgis. Raynor shared her son's smile as she touched Huiling on the upper arm. "Huiling, it's good to see you." She looked at the others who were that followed Huiling into Sam's office.

Huiling Li stood aside and introduced Pastor Murray to everyone. Sam extended his hand. "Sir, it's a pleasure to meet you. Welcome to Neptune One. May I introduce you to a good friend of mine, Kelly Brown?"

"Pastor, Huiling has spoken very fondly of you," Kelly said.

Raynor let out a little scream of excitement and turned to her son, quickly guiding Hui Yan Li. "Sam, look who's here!"

Sam smiled widely, offering his right hand in greeting. As Hui Yan stepped closer and hugged Sam with one arm, Sam could not stop thinking how identical Hui Yan was to Huiling. Hui Yan was a petite woman also with green eyes; Sam noticed Hui Yan liked to wear purple also, and he guessed she was in her early thirties.

"Hui Yan, I'm Kelly, Sam's close friend."

Hui Yan let go of Sam and grabbed Kelly's extended right hand with both hands. "Nice to meet you, Kelly; my sis has told me about you."

Kelly laughed. "I'm not that bad."

Hui Yan laughed louder. "What a sweetheart."

Huiling grew more cheerful as she turned back to Sam's mother. "Ray, I've got a surprise."

Raynor Furgis could not stop smiling. "I know. Ken said it was all right for Pastor Murray to perform the wedding." Sam started laughing as he put his arm around Kelly's waist and spoke softly into her ear. "He really had no choice." Kelly laughed too.

Huiling's excitement quieted. "No, Ray, I'm speaking about Acela and Marco."

Raynor was surprised. "No, I thought Acela liked…"

Huiling interrupted quickly. "They booked Arina Petrov for the wedding."

Raynor screamed with a high pitch, and Pastor Murray narrowed his eyes with a smile.

Kelly made a mistake in answering the question she had seen in Sam's eyes. "I'm sure she's there for the Grav ball match as well."

Raynor turned toward the blond girl wearing a tight blouse and pants. "Honey, it's my wedding and I say Arina is here for me."

After looking at Raynor's eyes, Kelly Brown decided to remain quiet. Sam laughed. "Mom, the whole deal is one package, especially with Pastor Murray giving the service."

Pastor Donald Murray interrupted. "Arina will be the main attraction. I'm hoping she performs 'Amazing Grace.' I saw a vid recording that was awesome!"

"Of course she will!" Huiling said enthusiastically. She stood close to her sister and Sam watched in amazement—if their purple shirts were different, he could not tell them apart.

Pastor Murray grew serious. "Are all the arrangements made? We don't have much time."

Huiling answered first. "Yes sir, the entire senior staff has been given their assignments and briefed."

Hui Yan interrupted. "We're on a schedule; shortly after the match we need to leave," and Don Murray gently placed his hand on the bottom of Hui Yan's neck.

Sam realized what Hui Yan was saying. "Are they sure the wormhole is stable?"

"That's what they say. In any case we're going to find out."

Pastor Murray laughed. "No need to fear when you have the shepherd on your side."

Sam Furgis chuckled, pointing up. "GF."

Pastor Murray was slightly surprised. "Absolutely, son."

Everyone turned to the vid com after hearing the chime. "I know who that is," said Sam. "Granted." The office doors opened with a hiss.

Operator Furgis entered his son's office followed by Chief Tylor and Supervisor Stykes. Sam's father greeted Don Murray first and introduced his staff.

"How long will you be with us, Don?" Chief Tylor asked.

Pastor Murray laughed before answering, "Until we get a little bit of business done." He smacked Operator Furgis on the arm. Sam felt compelled to add to the conversation. "And watch the Poseidons give out some lessons."

Operator Furgis laughed as he grabbed his son by the head, lowering his forehead for a fatherly kiss. Sam was not amused. "Pops, knock it off."

Raynor Furgis laughed at the affectionate display before interrupting. "Besides, they haven't won yet, right, Don?"

"I already told them about grief share."

Huiling and her sister started laughing.

Operator Furgis became more serious as he watched his son move to his chair next to Kelly. "Sam, we need to transmit to the Hammer."

Huiling could see that Operator Furgis had business on

his mind. "Pastor Murray, would you care to join Hui Yan and myself at the dome? We have some preparations to go over."

Pastor Murray approached Raynor, grabbing her hands while smiling with great joy. "We'll see you guys before the match." He nodded at Operator Furgis, "Blessings to all," and followed the twin sisters out of Sam's office.

Raynor looked at Kelly sitting in her son's desk chair. "That means you too, sweetie."

Before Kelly could respond, Sam interrupted. "Kel, can you help Acela and Marco?" Kelly did not reply; she stood and slowly walked to the entry door. Before she left, she heard Operator Furgis say, "Ray, take it easy."

Raynor started to respond, "That little miss prissy is a sl—"

Sam interrupted quickly. "Mother, we don't need another fight."

Operator Furgis was in boss mode. "Everyone grab a seat. Sam, get Just on this thing." He pointed to the vid com and sat next to Raynor. Sam adjusted his eye patch and sat down.

His mother grew concerned. "How is it, son?"

Everyone in his office turned from the vid com and stared at Sam, who stopped in the middle of adjusting the eye patched and laughed, lowering his hands and picking up a data pad from his desk. "It's fine—maybe a little annoying, but Brook said it will be off soon."

Supervisor Stykes turned back to face the vid com. "Aaarrgh, me maties, no Davies here." Operator Furgis watched a grin grow on Chief Tylor as the vid com activated.

Sam instructed the main vid com to contact the SS *Hammerhead*. The system was slow due to the skirmishes from the two empires in the system. Several solar network relay modules in sensitive areas throughout the inner system had been targeted for destruction, while others were seized for military use. Chief Tylor watched the vid com flicker as he relaxed in his chair. "The net will fail altogether if they don't leave those modules alone."

Operator Furgis replied sharply, "That's the idea, if we have no communications."

"They think Neptune One will be easy prey if it's dark," said Ray.

Operator Furgis sighed. "That reminds me...how's the *Carmela* doing?" Supervisor Stykes looked at Furgis with curiosity. Operator Furgis grinned. "The SS *Carmela* is bringing us some much needed supplies from Mars."

Raynor laughed. "You didn't get the memo?"

Stykes frowned. "Guess not."

The vid com flickered with a blurry 3-D image, and Stykes turned to face the image of Captain Justin Drake, who sat in his command chair on the bridge of the SS *Hammerhead*. The individuals in Director Furgis's office watched Captain Drake yell at his subordinates with commands. "Clear it up, enhance the vid!" After a quick pause Captain Drake continued, staring directly into the vid com. "Kenny, is that you?"

Suddenly the vid com projected a perfect 3-D image of Captain Drake. Operator Furgis laughed. "Just, are you fiddling with those knobs again?"

"Don't get personal," Captain Drake said with a grin and looked around Sam's office.

"Just, how's Earth?" Ray asked.

Captain Drake smiled. "Just when you think you don't miss her, you see the big blue ball again and the beauty grabs you."

Supervisor Stykes interrupted. "How's Taby, sir?" and Captain Drake could not hide his pride. A very large smile grew. "Almost ready to take out Ben Swells, aka Cronus."

Sam picked up on his smirk. "Why do these guys pick false gods' names for call signs?"

His father laughed. "I understand where you're coming from, Sam, but think what the crowd would do if you introduced Fee-Fee the killer robot!"

Raynor joined Supervisor Stykes in a large laugh. Sam looked annoyed at his father's comment. "Fee Fee or Thor, it does not matter. Darkstar will put him down." No one argued with Sam Furgis.

Operator Furgis could not hold his curiosity back any longer. "How is the Mech fight, Just?"

Captain Drake leaned back in his chair before answering. "Taby's planet-side at the Earth dome with Hobbs, prepping for the warrior match; the match is scheduled for next cycle."

"We'll probably have to see it on vid recording. I don't see the solar net clearing up anytime soon," said Chief Tylor.

"That brings me to the next question, Just." Operator Furgis turned around in his chair and nodded at his son. Sam picked up the data pad from the top of his desk and activated the touch screen controls. After several moments he nodded back at his father. "Secure transmission locked in, Pops."

Captain Drake spoke quickly. "Sam, before we continue…" He leaned forward in his chair. "…what is that patch on your eye for?"

After adjusting the eye patch, Sam said, "Some fool attacked Acela, and I got in the way."

Captain Drake nodded and looked at Raynor and Ken. "So

what's up, number one?"

Raynor chuckled. "Don't let Mela hear you. She'll think you're replacing her."

Captain Drake laughed. "She'll probably replace *me*."

Operator Furgis leaned forward. "Just, do you have any intel? I feel something in the air."

"Ken, there have been a lot of reports about fighting in the belt, but there is also talk about several major buildups around Venus and Mars."

"Anything heading our way?"

Captain Drake picked up his data pad. After several moments he called down to his operations station. "I need updated intel."

Commander Mela Finch stepped into the video range of Captain Drake's vid com. She was a pleasant young woman, but stern in her command. "Ken, how are you?"

Operator Furgis was always impressed with his replacement as Captain Drake's first officer. "Doing good, Mela. Are you keeping Just in line?"

"No need, Ken. Captain Drake is one of the finest captains in any fleet." Mela stood at attention next to Captain Drake's command chair.

Raynor laughed. "I agree."

Mela was excited to see Raynor sitting next to Ken. "Ray, are you still with that old warrior?"

Captain Drake continued to study his data pad as his smile grew. Before Raynor could answer, Captain Drake looked up and answered Operator Furgis after nodding at Mela. "I know you're aware of the *Essex* and *Staton* in your area." Operator Furgis nodded as he watched Mela Finch leave the vid com's range. "There is a report of an Eastern fleet around the belt on Jupiter's side; this fleet is a carrier fleet, including the *Courageous*."

Operator Furgis could see a slight grin on Chief Tylor's face. "Anything else in this area, Just?" he asked.

"Two Eastern destroyers. There are reports of these engaging pirate ships in your section, so be careful, Ken. I've got a bad feeling about this. The Terran Tribune thinks they have everything under control, and you know how that works."

"Yeah, we both know, but I have a surprise for the Easterners." Operator Furgis grinned widely, nodding at the chief.

Captain Drake was calm. "Yeah, I know, Gerlitz is almost done with his Mortelis cannon."

Raynor noticed the shock on Ken's face and started laughing. "Baby, you need to work on your intelligence department; that little pudgy man developed a secret weapon on your station that everyone knows about."

Captain Drake joined the laughter. "That pudgy man developed the next super weapon, and it's at your disposal." Operator Furgis frowned heavily.

Supervisor Stykes interrupted. "Sir, we already stopped an attempt at espionage, and the prototype is almost ready."

Furgis held his hand up quickly. "Just the prototype is a large cannon; however, we already have several smaller cannons ready for refitting."

"As soon as we leave Earth and make a stop at Mars for Taby's champion fight, we'll be there for a refit," said Captain Drake.

Raynor leaned forward. "Feel free to bring some friends." Captain Drake responded with a grin and a nod.

Furgis looked at Chief Tylor. "Dan, can you give Just the

specs so we can speed up the refit time?"

Chief Tylor pulled out his data pad. "Interfacing with your vid com now, sir."

Captain Drake looked down at his operations station; Furgis could hear Mela acknowledging. Drake nodded at Furgis. "We'll start preparations, Ken. Your job is to keep the Easterners away from Gerlitz; if they can't get the specs they'll try grabbing Mr. Pudgy."

"Will do, Just; see you on the return side." The vid com shut down. Furgis turned to Chief Tylor. "Dan, it's important the refit goes without any hitches." He turned to Supervisor Stykes next. "I want to see Dr. Gerlitz in my office immediately, and from now on he is to be accompanied by two enforcers at all times."

Tylor and Stykes quickly stood and exited the office. Furgis was now standing and frowning at Raynor. "Mr. Pudgy? Come on, Ray, you're not helping."

Sam started laughing. "It does fit, Pops, but you're right, it's not appropriate. I'm gonna have Marshal Scoop meet you in your office along with Davis and Gerlitz."

Ken and Raynor exited their son's office. Furgis watched his future wife enter the lift on her way to the Delphi dome for the wedding preparations, and he entered his office in anticipation for his three guests to arrive. He was ready to pick up his Voodoo Stratocaster, thinking there was enough time to relax and play the famous guitar, but he realized he was mistaken as his vid com announced three visitors: Governor Davis, Dr. Gerlitz, and Marshal Scoop.

Operator Furgis stood by his desk, gesturing to his guests to sit. Marshal Scoop waited for Governor Davis and Dr.

Gerlitz to sit directly in front of Operator Furgis's desk before pulling another chair over to join them. Furgis noticed Governor Davis was nervous.

"Ken, we have a situation."

Operator Furgis interrupted. "We all know what the situation is. I have two enforcers outside who will escort Dr. Gerlitz wherever he goes."

"I have asked the marshal to escort the doctor," Governor Davis said.

Operator Furgis exhaled deeply. "No sir, Neptune One is still an entertainment resort and will act as such. Acela is still hosting the astro tourney as well as the Mech fights and droid races. I need the marshal to assist Supervisor Stykes and Acela Vega with the safety of the station's patrons."

Governor Davis thought for a brief moment. "As long as you can guarantee Dr. Gerlitz' safety."

Marshal Scoop smiled and Furgis laughed. "Bob, no one can guarantee anyone's safety." Scoop was quick to add, "I've worked with Operator Furgis's enforcers; they'll do the job, and besides, Operator Furgis is correct when he said my first priority should be the general public of the station."

Operator Furgis was surprised the marshal agreed. "Do you have any intel, Marshal?"

Marshal Scoop smiled with a sideways nod. "Nothing you don't already know. But there is one thing. You know the old man for the Eastern Empire is gravely ill." Operator Furgis nodded and held up an open hand. "Rumor is that his son has taken over."

Operator Furgis exhaled deeply and sat back in his chair, folding his hands and looking out the observation window in his office.

Dr. Gerlitz was irritated at the lack of knowledge in politics of the Empires. "What does all this mean?" he said loudly.

Governor Davis frowned. "Niclas, the son is irresponsible and is only after more power and control."

"Bob, they all are," Dr. Gerlitz replied.

"Not like this guy. He doesn't care."

Dr. Gerlitz laughed. "His father will probably survive."

Marshal Scoop looked at Operator Furgis with skepticism. "Not likely." Operator Furgis nodded in agreement, and Dr. Gerlitz continued in a more serious tone. "Well then, maybe someone will take him out."

Operator Furgis looked at Marshal Scoop. "Not likely." Scoop returned the nod of agreement. Furgis stood. "Dr. Gerlitz, I believe your escort is outside."

Dr. Gerlitz joined his companions as they all stood and was ready to make a comment when something caught his attention on the shelf in Furgis's office. He walked over to the vid rec display and picked it up off the wall shelf. Turning to Operator Furgis with excitement, he said, "Sir, I did not realize you followed my work closely."

Operator Furgis smiled and gently removed the vid rec base from Dr. Gerlitz's hands. "These are from Sam." He instructed the vid rec base "Random," and it chimed and started switching between short recordings stored in its memory. One of the recordings showed Operator Furgis and Chief Tylor watching Sam, Dr. Gerlitz, and his assistant walk through the docking tube from the research shuttle, and several of the other recordings showed the impressive station through the small window of the shuttle. Operator Furgis set the vid rec back on the shelf. "The good old days when my boy was interested in vid recordings. I think he's going to blow the dust off and use it at the wedding." He stared at the other recordings, but his thoughts were interrupted by Marshal Scoop.

"Sir, we need to get." Furgis shook the nostalgia away and turned toward his door, watching his guests leave. Before Governor Davis could exit, Furgis loudly said, "Governor, could you stay for a moment please?"

Davis turned and slowly returned to his chair in front of Operator Furgis's desk. He waited for Furgis to sit before asking, "What else can I help you with, Ken?"

"Bob, I spoke with a friend on the Terran Tribune political board."

Governor Davis laughed. "Every board on the Tribune is political."

Operator Furgis shared in the governor's laugh before continuing. "He has recommended you for Neptune One's unofficial ambassador."

Davis was not surprised. "So they recognize Neptune One's independence."

Operator Furgis grinned. "They have no choice, and until it is official with them, we need an unofficial ambassador. The job's yours if you're interested."

"It would probably be safer here than at the Tribune," said the governor. "I think we both know the Tribune's in trouble with this new kid at the Easterners' helm."

Operator Furgis smiled and stood, holding his hand out over his desktop. "I'll throw in a bigger office and a new vid com receptionist."

Governor Davis accepted Furgis's hand with a nod and a

smile before exiting the office.

Operator Furgis sat back in his desk chair, picked up his data pad, and contacted his wife-to-be. "What took you so long?"

The vid com projection of Raynor Furgis offered such life-like detail, Operator Furgis could tell from her eyes that she was not ready for any teasing. "No time for games, Ken. Are you coming up to help with the wedding?"

Furgis knew his fiancée would not like his answer. "I'll try. Is Sam with you?"

Raynor looked around briefly before answering. "I don't see him; he's probably with Dr. Avers."

"Okay, Ray, I'll see you in a bit." Operator Furgis heard "Love ya" before the vid com shut down, followed by an incoming transmission. Operator Furgis accepted with a sigh.

"Hey, boss, you busy?"

Furgis exhaled. "Not at all, Leaf. What do you have?" Supervisor Stykes was interrupted by the vid com before he could reply.

Operator Furgis spoke quickly. "Stand by, Leaf. Vid com, who's at my hatch?"

"Director Furgis."

Sam casually walked into his father's office, accompanied by Kelly. "Pops, you ready for the big moment?" Kelly Brown was smiling with excitement as they both sat in front of his desk. Operator Furgis grew excited also when he noticed his son was not wearing his optical pad. He quickly got up and walked to the front of his desk, grabbing his son by the sides of his head and looking him straight in the eyes with a wide smile. Sam smiled and shook the hold off. "Pops, what's up with you?" Kelly was laughing with compassion as Sam stood. He no time to gain his composure, as his father grabbed him by the shoulders, pulling him in for a bear hug. Sam laughed and wrestled from his father's grip.

Operator Furgis stepped back, looking directly into his son's eyes. "It looks exactly the same."

Sam grinned. "Of course it does, and it works the same, so no more grabbing." Operator Furgis could hear Supervisor Stykes laughing. He returned to his chair. "Sorry, Leaf, I forgot you were there for a moment."

"No problem, boss, I'm kinda used to it," he said. "And Director Furgis, now that you can see again, I expect you will want to continue your boxing lessons." Both Operator Furgis and Kelly gave Sam a look of surprise.

Operator Furgis interrupted. "We'll talk about that later. Leaf, what was so urgent?"

"Sorry, boss, the SS *Staton* has come into range of the troposcope, and the *Essex* has disappeared behind Neptune."

"Switching one ship for another," said Sam.

"Stand by, Leaf," Operator Furgis said and then instructed the vid com to overlay Chief Tylor. Furgis looked at Kelly with a smile. "Kelly, I don't want to be rude, but this is business."

Kelly quickly stood up. "Not at all, sir, I understand." She leaned over Sam, stopping him from getting up from his chair as his father already had. "I'll join your mother. She's almost ready."

Operator Furgis sighed. "Good luck with that."

Kelly left the office as Chief Tylor appeared on the vid com. Operator Furgis sat back in his desk chair, looking at the split screen of the vid com; both individuals were displayed in a 3-D projection at their desks. Sam looked at his father. "Pops,

I got this." Operator Furgis leaned back with a smile, listening closely. "Leaf, how's the security measures for Dr. Gerlitz and his lab?" Sam asked.

Supervisor Stykes adjusted his enforcer uniform quickly and he sat straight. "Lil boss…"

Director Furgis interrupted. "'Sam' will be fine." Operator Furgis laughed, knowing his son was not aware of the carrier costumes of names.

Supervisor Stykes felt slightly uncomfortable as he continued. "I have two enforcers escorting Dr. Gerlitz and two enforcers outside his lab with another inside. I also have stealth droids in sensitive areas around the station." He picked up his data pad.

Chief Tylor interrupted calmly as the opportunity permitted. "Director, we also have a maintenance shuttle operating close to the MC, and Engineer Trently has initiated security blocks on all command codes for the main vid com."

"Where is Trently?" asked Operator Furgis. Chief Tylor activated his ear com piece for audible transmission only, but Furgis interrupted loudly. "No need, Chief, I just wanted to know where Trently and Armela are."

"Mrs. Furgis asked for Engineer Trently's assistance at the dome, sir."

Operator Furgis was always impressed by the chief's professionalism. Supervisor Stykes answered for his crew. "Boss, Officer Armela is also with Mrs. Furgis." Sam started laughing.

Operator Furgis smiled. "I thought Armela would be watching Acela, and Trently would be assisting Gerlitz."

Supervisor Stykes remained calm. "I believe he is."

Sam could not resist pointing out his father's mistake.

"Pops, you forgot to put Mom in the equation."

Operator Furgis frowned as he looked at his son. "We have a very strong tourney going on and a station full of Grav ball fanatics wagering throughout the…"

Sam interrupted. "Mom and company have hyped up your wedding so much, most of our patrons are placing wagers on everything about it." Operator Furgis lowered his head and sighed.

Chief Tylor knew not to remark on the situation, but Supervisor Stykes could not resist. "I wager Raynor will turn Neptune One into lil Mars within a few cycles."

Sam leaned back in his chair with a blank expression as he watched his father look up at the vid com. "I wager that if my enforcers are not more responsible in the future, I'll have a new security supervisor."

Chief Tylor interrupted the uncomfortable conversation. "Sir, I'll replace First Class Engineer Trently with a crew of third-class engineers and reassign Trently to the MC."

Supervisor Stykes was next. "Boss, I apologize for the humor. I'll let Officer Armela know he's required to escort Acela back to the pit." He sat up straight, imitating the chief.

Operator Furgis leaned forward on his desktop, shaking his head. "It's all right, Leaf, it's I who needs to apologize. I've got a lot going on. I'll talk to Ray and let her know she needs to start clearing these assignments through my senior staff."

"Pops, the wedding is almost here, and most of our guests will be heading toward the dome anyway," said Sam with a smile.

Stykes interrupted, trying not to be humorous. "Then you can relax on your honeymoon." Chief Tylor looked away with a frown.

Sam was quick to answer before his father could respond. "The honeymoon was postponed. Mom needs to get back to Mars immediately."

"All right, guys, I know you all care, but keep in mind that you're my senior staff as well." Operator Furgis paused for a moment to calm himself. "Besides, I'm hoping to join Ray on Mars for the championship Mech fight." Sam smiled. "I have good news for the station." Operator Furgis stopped and waited until he was sure he had everyone's attention.

Sam leaned forward in anticipation. "Well, what's the good news?"

"Marshal Scoop is staying on the station to assist in the security for the Mortelis cannon and Dr. Gerlitz. Leaf, he will be reporting directly to you, and to answer your next question, he has given his word he will not cause any trouble for Acela." Operator Furgis watched Supervisor Stykes nod in approval.

Sam Furgis grinned and started to rise out of his chair, but his father interrupted quickly. "I'm not done." Sam sat back in his chair. "Governor Bob Davis accepted a position as our new ambassador." Everyone started moaning. Operator Furgis laughed. "I knew everyone would be full of joy." Furgis grew serious. "I know Davis, now Ambassador Davis, can be irritating, but he is the best man for this position." Operator Furgis adjusted his formal jacket he was wearing with pride and allowed the three individuals to continue discussing the matter. He watched them quiet down, and the chief loudly questioned the decision.

"As an independent government, do we need an ambassador?"

Sam set aside his personal feelings and spoke as Director Furgis. "If we don't have any type of representation with others as an independent, they could say our authority is a violation of solar law."

Operator Furgis was proud of his son.

Supervisor Stykes was quick to add, "Or they could accuse us of siding with the Western Empire and force us to concede to joining them."

Chief Tylor was calm as usual and tried to speak through the chatter of Sam and Stykes debating the choice of Bob Davis as ambassador. Operator Furgis held up his hand. "Chief Tylor, it's your floor." The others quieted.

"The Eastern Empire will be more concerned with Neptune One joining forces with the Western Empire, if that is your intention, sir." Operator Furgis again held up his hand as he noticed both his son and Supervisor Stykes wanting to interrupt. Chief Tylor continued. "I do not mean to be disrespectful; however, I need to know so I can prepare my department and the station. We also need to stay neutral as long as possible. This station is in a very strategic spot for intel and commerce." He leaned forward, elbows on his desk.

Operator Furgis leaned forward as well, and issued commands to the vid com. "Reconfirm security protocol. Is this vid com transmission secure?" All individuals waited after hearing the chime. After a quick moment the vid com chimed once again, followed by the gentle female voice. "Transmission is secure." Operator Furgis sat back. "Chief, it is my intention that we join with the Western Empire only if the Eastern Empire starts trouble." Operator Furgis was quiet, waiting for a response. After no response was heard, he continued. "I don't personally know this young kid taking over the Eastern Empire, but I can read between the lines on the intel reports."

Chief Tylor was quick to offer support. "Either way, sir, you have the support of the engineering staff."

Operator Furgis grinned with a nod. "Chief, I always respected your candor. Thank you for once again offering your trust and loyalty."

Supervisor Stykes said, "Boss, you also have the security department behind you, although I hope we can remain neutral."

Chief Tylor said, "Probably not, Leaf. We need to get this station ready to join the Western Empire in defense of this sector at a moment's notice." He was serious.

Operator Furgis smiled. "Dan, if you could get with Leaf as soon as possible, I would appreciate it."

"Chief, I'll meet you in your office," said Stykes, and both nodded as the transmission ended.

Sam turned his chair to fully face his father. "Pops, do you trust the chief?"

His father was not surprised at his son's question. "Of course I do. The chief was aboard this station before I took over."

"The chief was an Easterner?"

Operator Furgis laughed. "It's good you have concerns, Sam. The chief and I have been through a lot, and my gut tells me he is loyal and dependable."

"I didn't mean any disrespect."

Sam's father stood. "None taken, son." He walked over to his son, grabbing him by the back of the neck. "I was very impressed by the way you acted in this meeting, Sam. You're ready to take over if needed."

Sam laughed. "Does that mean you're going on the honeymoon?"

It was his father's turn to laugh. "Not at all, son, but it's almost that time, and we need to get to the dome." He gently pushed his son toward the office door.

Chapter Five

Raynor stood next to the middle lift the fight droid used to enter the Dome of Delphi, waiting for Huiling Li and Senior Pastor Murray to arrive. Hui Yan Li approached. "Hello, Ray."

Raynor looked around the large fight droid maintenance bay. "Where are your sister and Pastor Murray?"

Hui Yan's smile slowly grew with compassion. "No need to worry, Ray, they'll be here. Right now we need to move to the upper level before the ceremonies start; the guests for the Grav ball match are already arriving." Hui Yan stopped and stared at Raynor. Mechanical equipment started coming alive in the large bay.

Raynor looked at Hui Yan with concern. "Are they here for the Grav ball match or my wedding?"

Hui Yan held Raynor's arm. "We have to go." Raynor walked slowly beside Hui Yan toward the personnel lifts.

Hui Yan was compassionate. "Huiling told me about the time constraints and that if you wanted a large wedding, you would have to share with other station activities. Besides, I think everyone is looking forward to hearing Arina Petrov sing for you."

Raynor chuckled. "I think she's here for the Grav ball

match." Raynor and Hui Yan approached the lift, trying to speak louder than the mechanical equipment that had begun to activate.

Hui Yan continued. "Ray, you look beautiful in that dress. Where did you find such a lovely yellow?"

Raynor smiled. "It was a gift from my brother and his wife," and Hui Yan laughed. "Very nice, just like the gift Dr. Avers and Acela gave you."

Raynor stopped at the lifts doors as the hiss was heard over the equipment noise. "What gifts, Hui Yan?" She looked down into the petite woman's green eyes.

"Dr. Avers and Acela arranged for Arina Petrov to sing for you." Both ladies stepped inside the lift.

Operator Furgis and his son walked through the fight droids hangar toward Huiling and Pastor Murray. Operator Furgis could see Acela and his good friend Duncan Jennings waiting patiently with the others. No words were exchanged as Ken approached Duncan, and both wrestled in a friendly bear hug. As the two separated, Operator Furgis's excitement showed. "Dunc, you decided to attend!"

Duncan laughed. "Of course," he said, speaking slightly louder as the mechanical equipment slowed in the noise they generated as each piece was ready for its individual function. Operator Furgis turned toward Pastor Murray. "Even though I wanted a small, discreet wedding, I very much appreciate this honor, sir."

Huiling interrupted. "All right, guys, let's take our positions on the lifts before the fight droid starts introducing players for Grav ball."

Sam laughed as he shook hands with Duncan. "What's the

difference?" he said in a low voice. Duncan laughed as they walked onto the secondary lift.

The fight droid had already ascended to the Delphi dome and hovered high above to project highlights in 3-D of previous Grav ball matches onto the arena floor. After several minutes of the crowd cheering and booing in the seats around the arena, the fight droid shut down all lighting from the center of the arena. Supervisor Stykes and Officer Armela sat at their consoles in the security booth with an open vid com transmission to the engineering booth on the opposite end of the arena. Supervisor Stykes was in full communication with Chief Engineer Tylor and First Class Engineer Trently as the fight droid started the proceedings.

Chayton and Marco De Luca occupied the same sky box Seth Adams controlled, both individuals still engaged in their friendly fashion wars. Each wore one of their finest business suits and harassed each other over their attire. Seth Adams listened to the teasing for a moment before laughing loudly as he stood, gaining the attention of both individuals. As they turned to watch him, Seth stood straight, almost like he was modeling his newly acquired suit. Marco and Chayton became quiet after noticing the Bronee Vanquish IX suit Seth proudly displayed. Seth smiled widely. "Gentlemen, if you watch closely you will see my new station ad for the Solar House and Grav Zero." He sat quickly to work the controls in the sky box, causing the whole box to move slightly forward and lean toward the arena floor. He waited patiently through the advertisements from other sources, including the Andromeda cruise lines. The fight droid went dark for a quick moment before scenes of dancing in the Grav Zero club and guests eating real beef and fruits in the Solar House appeared. The ad continued with an overlay projection of Seth Adams announcing the offerings of the solar rock music to dance to and the smooth, cosmic symphonies to dine to. Chayton and Marco were impressed and turned at the same time, smiling at the owner of the finest club and restaurant on this side of the belt. Seth leaned forward and handed his two friends small chips to link with their data pads. Marco could not resist asking, "What's this, Seth?" Chayton looked at Seth with curiosity as well.

Seth grinned and nodded. "They're comps to the Solar House, my friends. Link them to your data pads and use them anytime." Both gentlemen nodded in thanks.

Dr. Avers, Dr. Cole from Triton's mining colony, and Kelly Brown watched the advertisements from their sky box. Dr. Avers was laughing loudly. Kelly watched Dr. Cole with a smile before asking, "What's going on?"

Dr. Avers shook her head. "That Seth is an amazing businessman; he finds opportunity everywhere."

Dr. Cole shook his head with a grin as he added, "You can't blame the guy—as the station grew in popularity to become one of the finest destinations, so did Seth's establishments." Dr. Avers nodded in agreement. Dr. Cole looked at her. "I heard rumors that Seth is opening a 3-D café station so guests can plug in after the Solar House or coming out of Grav Zero."

Kelly interrupted. "No need to worry, Sam won't allow it."

The arena grew dark once again.

Supervisor Stykes worked the touch screen console with ease, and the carbon electric glass dome started opening to reveal the awesome openness of the stars and the giant blue planet of Neptune. The patrons of the Delphi dome were mesmerized as the sight was revealed, forgetting the unforgiving and destructive atmosphere the gentle-looking giant hid. The gaseous rings of Neptune could be seen through the transparent dome along with ships of various types arriving and departing. Operator Furgis's senior staff was caught quickly by the beauty the universe offered but soon returned to their tasks. Supervisor Stykes and Chief Tylor took an extra look for Easterner ships. On occasion a small streaking flash could be seen flowing across Neptune as the white clouds slowly moved across the horizon, and the very top of Neptune's moon, Triton, was visible as well.

In a quick moment the bright spot light from the fight droid appeared, focusing on one spot of the arena floor. The light dimmed, revealing a tall black man in his late sixties standing alone in the middle of the arena floor. Pastor Murray straightened his suit and started to address the crowd in the stadium of the Delphi dome. "Ladies and gentlemen, brothers and sisters." He paused as the patrons switched their attention from the stars to the pastor. The Delphi dome became quiet and serene, and Pastor Murray continued. "I have authority from the Solar Council to make the following announcement. More importantly, I have permission from the bride and groom." Laughter came from the stadium.

As the laughter quieted down, Pastor Murray continued with his announcement. "I'm sure everyone has seen the solar news broadcasts of the wormhole designated WH-12." Pastor Murray held his hands high with open palms. "What has not been revealed to the citizens of this great system is that a reconnaissance droid from the Solar Counsel has transmitted a broken signal from the other side of this magnificent creation."

He again waited for a moment as he heard slight murmur from the crowd. He pulled out his pocket pad and worked the touch screen controls.

The crowd in the Delphi stadium let out "Ah's" and quiet chatter as the fight droid projected the wormhole in 3-D floating in midair above the floor of the stadium. Pastor Murray continued. "Brothers and sisters, as you can see the beauty and power of this wormhole, which is not too far from here." He again worked the controls of his pocket pad, causing the 3-D image of WH-12 to shrink into a map of the outer system. Pastor Murray stepped forward and turned, straining to look up at the projection as he continued to operate his pocket pad. The fight droid highlighted several sections and astro bodies. "Neptune One is here orbiting Neptune on the outer edge of the habitable system. The dwarf planet Pluto is here inside the Kuiper belt, along with its other sister astro bodies." The fight droid highlighted several larger bodies in the Kuiper belt.

Operator Furgis stood unseen in the dark behind and far below the 3-D projection. Huiling, Acela, and Sam watched on in amazement. Furgis looked at Acela. "I need to get one of those pocket pads." Acela hushed Operator Furgis as Pastor Murray continued.

"WH-12 is here." The fight droid magnified the projected area of the wormhole. Pastor Murray laughed. "WH-12 was discovered awhile ago by the closest mining station in the Kuiper belt."

Pastor Murray allowed the fight droid to change 3-D images of several different mining stations in the Kuiper belt before stopping at the particular one he referred to. The crowd in the stadium grew quiet as they studied the image; the miners from Triton were respectful and proud, as most of them had family working in these various mining stations throughout the K belt.

Pastor Murray continued. "The hole was discovered by a Solar Counsel safety inspection team. The area has always been void of any activity or bodies; therefore, no one ever realized what opportunity was given to us until these inspectors crossed that particular expanse by accident." The fight droid showed the wormhole and the two mining stations on the extreme opposite sides.

Pastor Murray instructed the fight droid to slowly move a highlighted line designating the flight path of the inspectors' shuttlecraft. As the line moved across the projected display, Pastor Murray said, "Eventually new technology was developed to allow a reconnaissance droid to enter WH-12." He paused to allow the excitement from the crowd to calm. The fight droid changed the image of the outer system containing the WH-12 to an image of the reconnaissance droid.

Engineer Trently was heard talking to Chief Tylor from the main vid com in the security booth. "I would love to inspect that droid."

Supervisor Stykes said, "So would the Easterners; in fact I'm starting to understand why Neptune One is important to them."

Both vid coms in each booth chimed quickly with an override from Operator Furgis. "Enough, guys, we'll discuss this later. Right now let Pastor Murray finish."

Pastor Murray remained quiet, and the stadium slowly joined him; eventually the entire stadium was silent, with the 3-D projection of WH-12 floating in the middle of the coliseum. Pastor Murray spoke softly as the quiet of the stadium allowed. "What I am now going to share with you has just begun to be released on the solar network." He increased the volume of his voice slightly as the murmurs of the crowd started once again. Operator Furgis and his senior staff realized the importance of the secrecy that was given to this information.

"We believe life may exist on the other side of this wormhole," said the pastor. The crowd in the Delphi dome went into ranting and raving, and the commotion was loud.

Supervisor Stykes acted quickly, initiating the controls on the security booth and initiating panic mode. The seats in the general admission area grew stronger with gravity, causing the individuals to sit immediately back into their seats; the people in the rows struggled to return to their section or find rare empty seats temporarily. The fight droid sent flashes of yellow streaming light in every direction at random followed by a loud, intermittent, irritating whistle. As the crowd calmed to a manageable level of control, Supervisor Stykes slowly brought the stadium back to normal and started instructing his enforcer team to various sections of the Delphi dome. Officer Armela joined the enforcers to patrol the dome.

Pastor Murray stepped forward into the projected light from the fight droid. "Brothers and sisters," he was holding his hands high with open palms again, "please calm yourselves." As he lowered his hands he loudly quoted a favorite of Sam Furgis's: "Be still, ladies and gentleman." The crowd responded and became silent once again. The fight droid started projecting the wormhole as Pastor Murray worked his pocket pad, and the lights flickered, allowing the projection to rotate at random. Pastor Murray looked over the crowd with a smile.

"Brothers and sisters, please allow me to continue. I understand the news is very exciting, but please have patience as I show you the actual transmissions from the droid."

The fight droid projected the 3-D image the reconnaissance droid had transmitted back through WH-12, and Pastor Murray narrated. "As you can see, the transmission is very garbled and full of static." He allowed the transmission time to clear up to show enough detail for explanation. "We believe this sun to be Furoy in the Aldresia constellation." The fight droid magnified out to a generated 3-D image of the newly discovered star. Pastor Murray continued following the fight droid's projection. "Furoy has one planet in the habitable zone." He quieted, allowing the patrons of the Delphi dome to murmur. As the crowd grew quiet again, Pastor Murray instructed his pocket pad to continue. "The planet is designated as Eos. I'm not sure why we need to name planets after false gods. This is the second planet from Eos." The fight droid generated a projection of the inner Furoy system. "Eos is estimated to be two point six times the size of Mother Earth and has a year of two hundred and eighty days. Eos is estimated to have an average temperature of seventy-four degrees, and its orbit is closer to its smaller sun than Earth is. We also believe Eos has an atmosphere much like Earth's. A rough guess would be…" Pastor Murray worked the controls on his pocket pad before continuing, "…seventy-nine percent nitrogen and nineteen percent oxygen."

The 3-D projection zoomed into Eos, and the crowd gasped as the view flew through the clouds and slowly passed mountains and oceans. Pastor Murray smiled. "Please remember that this is a generated guess of the planet Eos; however, we do know that this planet offers water in all three stages and has two satellites." The fight droid's projection of Eos zoomed out until the two moons were shown in orbit of the larger Earth-like planet. "The gravity is slightly heavier on Eos, and the heavier density of the habitable satellite gives it the equivalent gravity strength of Earth." Pastor Murray grew quiet to allow the stadium spectators to chatter amongst themselves until a bright flash from the fight droid quickly caused silence.

Operator Furgis looked at Huiling and winked. He spoke softly in consideration of the acoustics of the dome. "I like his style. He knows how to get your attention."

Huiling leaned forward and whispered, "You should have seen him in seminary school." She returned the wink. Operator Furgis grinned, turning back his attention to Pastor Murray as the narration continued.

"These are actual images from the recon droid." The projections were filled with static and distortion. Pastor Murray worked the touch screen controls on his pocket pad before looking at the crowd through the stadium again. "I apologize for the quality, but this is the best the recon droid could give us. As you see the planet Eos in the distance, you can read the sidebar." Pastor Murray issued commands to the fight droid, causing the sidebar with the detailed information to zoom in front of the 3-D planet. He looked up at the projection and instructed the fight droid to highlight certain data. "The Solar Council estimates here that Eos is seven hundred and fifty-eight light years from us." He paused as the roar of the chatter from the crowd in the stadium once again took over.

As Pastor Murray worked his pocket pad, the fight droid projected a 3-D image of the SS *King David,* which was presently in orbit around Neptune One. One of the ships that could be seen through the transparent carbon electric glass dome was the SS *King David*. The image of the very large vessel shrunk, allowing the fight droid to project the entire sector containing Neptune One and the Kuiper belt. The droid was now projecting the image of the course from Neptune One and the wormhole; the highlighted line flowed from Neptune One through the belt until reaching the voided space close to the outer edge of the Kuiper belt.

The spectators in the stadium grew excited, some with cheers and others with shock, as Pastor Murray held up his open-palmed hands and made his next announcement. "Brothers and sisters." The 3-D image of the SS *King David* was at the start of the highlighted line near Neptune One. "The Solar Counsel has authorized the *King David* to explore this wormhole and Eos. I believe it is God calling for us to seek out our brothers from this world, and with the will of God may we find new friendship in this harsh universe." The crowd was cheering so loud the minor booing was overcome.

Pastor Murray was smiling widely with excitement as he walked around the front of the stadium, shaking his fist up high. As the crowded stadium quieted down to chatter, Pastor Murray continued. "The *King David* is manned by my command staff, accompanied by the military personnel from the Solar Counsel."

The fight droid projected the SS *King David* traveling through the Kuiper belt and passing several mining stations. "As we pass through the Kuiper belt, we will be making frequent stops at the different mining stations for cargo and personnel, including scientists and researchers—including a good friend of mine, Terry Pines, a geologist who is ready to explore new worlds." The crowd started cheering.

After several minutes the Delphi dome grew quieter. Pastor Murray relaxed and stood still as he looked around the stadium. "Brothers and sisters, if you wish, the *King David* can deliver any personal belongings or messages for the families and friends serving in the Kuiper belt; there is more than enough room. If you do not have a data pad or a pocket pad available, please use the nearest vid com, and my first officer Hui Yan Li will see that your request is answered." Pastor Murray could see the nodding approval of the crowd, as most pulled out data pads and pockets pads.

The focused light from the fight droid widened around Pastor Murray as he stood in the front of the stadium. He stepped to the side of the area illuminated by the fight droid and opened his hands. "Brothers and sisters, we all have the privilege of honoring the commander of this great station…" Pastor Murray paused as Operator Furgis walked into the light, with a wide smile and dressed in a well-fitted tuxedo. "Kennith Jackson Furgis, operator of Neptune One and soon-to-be husband." The crowd stood, applauding and cheering. "His son, Samuel Lafayette Furgis, Director of Neptune One." Sam walked into the illuminated area smiling; he had never liked the name Lafayette.

Sam whispered in his father's ear, "Wish you were eating strawberries in your office, Pop?" His father's grin grew, and Pastor Murray continued. "Acela Vega, the station's senior pit boss."

Ken Furgis nodded at Acela as she walked into the illuminated area. He was proud of his friend, knowing she was more than a senior pit boss. He relied on Acela for all wagering games, sports wagering, and tournaments like the astro tourney, which had temporarily stopped for the Grav ball match. Acela stood slightly behind Operator Furgis, wearing a short pink dress and diamonds gleaming in the light. Even Pastor Murray looked twice at the dazzling woman before announcing one of his favorite students. "And Pastor Huiling Li." The crowd continued to stand, applauding again as Huiling entered the illuminated area.

Officer Armela was now in the engineering booth with Chief Tylor and Engineer Trently. He was excited as he watched the young Chinese woman walk into the illuminated area and stand by Acela. His thoughts were of Huiling's beauty as she stood in her purple full-length dress with her diamond broach that held the capital letters GF captive in a circle. Officer Armela exhaled quickly. "She's lovely."

Engineer Trently agreed. "Yeah, if I didn't know Acela's preference, I would date her." He lunged forward in his engineering console's chair as Officer Armela laughed and smacked him on the back. "Sure you would." Trently's response was interrupted by Armela's ear com piece chime, followed by his superior's voice. "Juan, is everything all right over there?"

"Yes sir, I was checking the droid systems with Shaun."

Chief Tylor smiled as he rested his hand on the large man's shoulder. He activated the vid com in the engineering booth and, after hearing the chime, watched the 3-D projection of Supervisor Stykes appear. The chief was excited for his good friend Operator Furgis. "Leaf, we're all set here."

Supervisor Stykes relaxed. "Excellent, Chief. Tell Juan to check out the droid hangars and get with the other enforcers escorting Arina."

Officer Armela stepped into view of the vid com. "Got it, sir, I'm on my way."

Supervisor Stykes worked his touch screen console in the security booth, checking with his enforcers on assignment throughout the Delphi dome. When the main vid com chimed "Incoming transmission," he swiveled his console chair to face the main vid com in the security booth. It was Marshal Scoop, looking calm and relaxed.

"Leaf, you will be getting notice soon of a shuttle docking from the SS Staton."

Stykes snapped, "Where is the Staton?"

Marshal Scoop raised his eyebrows. "Not sure, but I can ask when they arrive in the grav tube station."

"That's all right, marshal, you need to babysit." Supervisor Stykes paused briefly before adding, "It's too bad—you're missing a good time."

Marshal Scoop smiled. "I'm watching on the vid com while Dr. Gerlitz and his assistant are doing some type of calculations for his MC. Just thought I'd give you a heads-up."

"Thanks, Marshal." Both vid coms shut down. Leaf turned his attention back to the arena floor, where the wedding of his boss was taking place. He admired the faith and strong convictions Pastor Murray held, knowing that someday he may acquire something as strong.

Pastor Murray was already calling the bride down. He activated his pocket pad to start the vid com-generated wedding music, and the fight droid focused a tight beam of light shining at the top end of the stairs where Raynor Furgis, Pastor Hui Yan Li, and Duncan Jennings stood waiting. The spectators in the stadium remained standing and quiet as the music continued, and the three individuals in the bride's party started descending the stairs slowly. Raynor was holding hybrid roses grown on Mars. The roses were red, but a pink stripe shot up each petal, and the tips, crowned with light purple, were impressive to the spectators as she slowly passed.

Hui Yan Li and Duncan followed Raynor down the aisle slowly; both would on occasion touch people on the shoulder with a smile as they passed. The wedding music continued as they stepped onto the arena floor and continued their slow march toward Pastor Murray and Operator Furgis. As Raynor approached, the fight droid merged the two lights together and widened the area that was illuminated; it was careful not to shine too bright, concealing the view of the stars and the SS *King David* slowly gliding past the blue color of the planet Neptune. Raynor approached Pastor Murray, and Kennith stepped slightly forward and turned to join his future wife; he grabbed her hand gently with a smile and nodded at Pastor Murray.

Chayton looked over at Marco De Luca with a wide smile. "I'm impressed with Raynor, very stunning."

Marco nodded in agreement and answered without looking at Chayton, "I love those flowers. We need to set those around the front desk."

Seth Adams leaned forward in his seat and said, "Marco, talk to me later; we can make an arrangement."

Chayton interrupted with a laugh. "Don't tell me you got the flowers."

Marco added, "And probably the rings as well." They both turned their heads, looking back to face Seth. They saw a very well-dressed businessman grinning back at them.

Seth answered with pride, "Of course, and wait till you see what Operator Furgis chose."

Before either could respond, the vid com chimed, requesting permission for Dr. Avers to join them.

Dr. Avers slowly walked down the skinny steps and sat in the empty seat Seth was reserving. "Sorry I'm late, Seth. I stopped in to speak with Kelly and Dr. Cole."

Chayton turned quickly in his seat. "Everything all right, Brook?"

Dr. Avers smiled. "No need to worry, guys, doctor stuff." She leaned sideways into Seth and spoke softly. "What did I miss?"

"You didn't miss any of the good stuff," Seth replied. "They're getting ready to start their vows I think."

"I'm glad I didn't miss any good stuff." Dr. Avers focused on the arena floor, hoping someday…

Pastor Murray held his open hands up in the air and was loud as the fight droid projected the 3-D image of him around the edges of the stadium. "Brothers and sisters." Pastor Murray paused to turn in several directions to observe the quiet spectators in the stadium. "We are gathered here today to witness the joining of Kennith Furgis and Raynor Furgis in holy matrimony." The crowd applauded as Pastor Murray lowered his hands. "Raynor and Kennith have both asked for readings, and at this time I would like Raynor to start." He stepped alongside Raynor as she spoke.

"I have asked the lovely Hui Yan Li to read for me" she said, and Hui Yan Li stepped in front.

The Delphi dome remained completely quiet as Pastor Hui

Yan Li read from her pocket pad. "Put on then as God's chosen ones, holy and beloved, compassionate hearts, kindness, humility, meekness, and patience, bearing with one another and, if one has a complaint against another, forgive each other, as the Lord has forgiven you, so you also must forgive. And above all these put on love, which binds everything together in perfect harmony. And let the peace of Christ rule your hearts, to which indeed you were called in one body. And be thankful. Let the word of Christ dwell in you richly, teaching and admonishing one another in all wisdom, singing psalms and hymns and spiritual songs, with thankfulness in your hearts to God. And whatever you do, in your word or deed, do everything in the name of the Lord Jesus, giving thanks to God the Father through him." Pastor Li smiled deeply at both Ray and Ken as she heard a light applause.

Pastor Murray stepped forward and Pastor Hui Yan Li moved next to Raynor. He looked at Ken. "Kennith Furgis, would you like to read?"

Operator Furgis said, "I have asked my son, Samuel Furgis, to read." Pastor Murray stepped aside, allowing Sam to move up front and face his mother and father. He pulled out his pocket pad and looked around the stadium before reading. "If I speak in tongues of men and of angels, but have not love, I am a noisy gong or a clanging cymbal. And if I have prophetic powers, and understand all mysteries and all knowledge, and if I have all faith, so as to remove mountains, but have not love, I am nothing. If I give away all I have, and if I deliver up my body to be burned, but have not love, I gain nothing. Love is patient and kind; love does not envy or boast; it is not arrogant or rude. It does not insist on its own way; it is not irritable or resentful; it does not rejoice at wrongdoing, but rejoices with the truth. Love bears all things, believes all things, hopes all things, and endures all things." He lowered his pocket pad, not sure if this was acceptable.

Pastor Murray stepped forward and shook Sam's hand and then looked at the spectators in the stadium. "Can you feel the love?" The spectators cheered. "Can you feel the love?!" This time everyone in the stadium was standing and shouting, "Feel the love." Pastor Murray whispered softly in Sam's ear. "You did good, my son." The spectators sat back in their seats and his father rubbed the back of Sam's head with proud and watery eyes. Raynor leaned around Ken and grabbed Sam by the upper arm. Sam could see her lips moving with no sound: "Thank you." He was happy that his mother and father were pleased.

Pastor Murray allowed the spectators to regain their seats and quiet down before continuing. "I have asked Pastor Li… the *other* Pastor Li…Huiling Li to read as well." He stepped aside, allowing Huiling to walk in front of Ken and Raynor.

Officer Armela patrolled the armor rooms used for the Mech fighters, Grav ballers, and other events held in the Delphi dome. He stopped at a main vid com after hearing Huiling's name on his ear com piece and activated the device. The 3-D projection of the wedding proceedings were projected, and Officer Armela smiled widely with compassion as he watched Huiling start to give her reading.

Huiling activated her pocket pad, looking from the wedding couple to the stadium and back to her pocket pad. "So we have come to know and to believe the love that God has for us. God is love, and whoever abides in him. By this is love perfected with us, so that we may have confidence for the day of judgment, because as he is so also are we in this world." Huiling paused, looking at the couple in front of her with a smile. "There is no fear in love, but perfect love casts out fear. For fear has to do with punishment, and whoever fears has not been perfected in love." She looked up at the stadium, and her voice grew louder. "We love because he first loved us. If anyone says I love God, and hates his brother, he is a liar; for he who does not love his brother whom he has seen cannot love God whom he has not seen. And this commandment we have from him: whoever loves God must also love his brother." Huiling winked at her sister as she watched with a smile.

Pastor Murray knew Huiling and was expecting more; his suspicions were confirmed as Huiling glanced at her pocket pad once again before continuing with great authority in her voice. "And he said to him, you shall love the Lord your God with all your heart and with all your soul and with all your mind. This is the great and first commandment. And second is like it: you shall love your neighbor as yourself." Huiling paused, looking up and around at the stadium before ending her speech with a simple gesture. She pointed up and yelled, "GF!"

The spectators answered with their own shouting, "God First, God First!"

Pastor Murray noticed that not all spectators were joining in on the chant. He stepped forward and hugged Huiling very tightly; she was like a daughter to him, and he felt a lot of pride when he watched her preach about the word. Huiling returned to stand next to Acela as Pastor Murray took back control of the crowd's attention. Acela and Raynor hugged Huiling, and Pastor Murray held his hands up and walked around the front of the wedding party. "Brothers and sisters," he waited for the spectators to calm, "we are gathered here to unit these two." Pastor Murray motioned for Ken and Raynor to move forward and closer, and the stadium quieted again. "Three things are too wonderful for me; four I do not understand: the way of the eagle in the sky, the way of a serpent on a rock, the way of a ship on the high seas, and the way of a man with a young woman." Pastor Murray allowed Raynor and Ken Furgis to stare closely into each other's eyes. As the bride and groom continued to smile, they turned to Pastor Murray, and he watched for their approval to continue. "Raynor Furgis, would you like to state your vows?"

Raynor Furgis turned back to Ken Furgis and grabbed his hands. "Kennith Furgis, do not urge me to leave you or to return from following you. For where you go I will go, and where you lodge I will lodge. Your people shall be my people and your God my God. Where you die I shall die and there I shall be buried. May the Lord do so to me and more also if anything but death parts me from you."

Hui Yan Li stepped closer, holding a tiny silver pillow. Raynor took the polished tungsten wedding band, which was pressed with inert Mortelis in the center of the band, and placed it on Kennith's finger. The spectators in the stadium offered a slight laugh as the fight droid picked up and broadcasted the whisper Raynor said to her husband: "You're mine now." Ken and the rest of the wedding party joined in the fun.

Pastor Murray smiled at Ken with a nod of approval. Ken held his wife's hands as he started his vows in a low and gentle voice. "I am yours now." Pastor Murray laughed, allowing the crowded stadium to join in on the compassionate fun as well.

After a brief moment smiling at his wife, Ken continued. "Two are better than one, because they have a good reward for their toil. For if they fall, one will lift up the other. But woe to him who is alone when he falls and has not another to lift him up! Again, if two lie together, they keep warm, but how can one keep warm alone? And though a man might prevail against one who is alone, two will withstand him. A three-fold cord is not quickly broken."

Samuel Furgis stepped closer, allowing his father to take the wedding ring from him. Kennith slid the three-point carat weight Martian diamond in a platinum ring onto Raynor's finger. "I love you, Ray." Raynor grabbed Ken by the sides of the head and kissed him with great compassion.

Pastor Murray stepped forward with a smile and excitement in his voice. "I was asked to add something." He pulled out his pocket pad and studied the device for a moment before saying, "Then the Lord God said it is not good that man should be alone; I will make a helper fit for him. Have you not read that he who created them from the beginning made them male and female, and said therefore a man shall leave his father and his mother and hold fast to his wife, and the two shall become one flesh." Pastor Murray looked at the bride and groom. "So they are no longer two but one flesh. What therefore God has joined together, let not man separate." Pastor Murray smiled and spoke directly to Kennith and Raynor Furgis. "Under God's law and authority from the Solar Council I now pronounce you man and wife. You may kiss the bride again." He gave Raynor a friendly wink, and the couple engaged in a long kiss. The fight droid started a laser light show as beams of different-colored light hit the individuals on the arena floor as well as in the stadium.

The wedding party casually lined up behind the bride and groom as they walked to one of the Mech fighter lifts, the laser lights from the fight droid continued as the lift started its slow descent. The party could not ignore the fireworks that started from the *SS King David* in orbit outside the Delphi dome, these fireworks where as bright and distinctive in color and size as the laser light show from the fight droid. The crowd watched the fireworks and light show as well as the wedding party lowering into the under bays of the Delphi dome. The fight droid closed the lift door as the individuals disappeared and the celebration slowly ended allowing the stadium to become quit with murmur once again.

"Wow, that was beautiful." Dr. Avers was excited and very loud.

Seth Adams chuckled as he looked over at her. "Yeah, put my wedding to shame."

"Where was your wedding?"

Chayton and Marco De Luca turned to listen as Seth opened up about his personal life. "I was married on Lunar One. It was a not religious ceremony." Seth was careful, knowing that Dr. Avers' husband was killed in an accident on Lunar One.

Marco was quick to interrupt. "That's a shame. I think Pastor Murray was very good, and Huiling was outstanding."

Dr. Avers was surprised. "I didn't know you believed, Marco."

Before Marco could respond, Chayton casually said, "I think they should have gone with the Great Spirit on a vision quest." He straightened his jacket.

Seth laughed. "I'm glad we managed to get away from those arguments about religion and learned to have tolerance of each other's beliefs." He leaned back in his chair.

Chayton smiled with a nod of acceptance. "You're absolutely right, Seth. I remember reading an article on the solar net about secular humanism."

Marco looked puzzled. "I heard someone mention that before."

"I was at the same place, Chayton," said Dr. Avers. "It was a form of government-imposed religion." She grew quiet as she lost her train of thought.

"Secular humanism was tried by several governments in the far past," Chayton explained. "It states that God—or in my case, the Great Spirit, whose name I choose not to say out of respect—does not exist."

"Then what did they believe?" asked Marco.

Dr. Avers took over. "Marco, secular humanism states that we are our own gods, and we rely on our own morals for proper judgment."

"I'm not a super believer in anything particular," said Seth. "In fact I'm thinking about exploring Huiling's service. But I do know that this universe was not created by some gases accidently mingling together."

"Seth, how in the universe do you know that?" asked Marco.

"If this universe was an accident caused by gases accidently colliding, then you and I are accidents." Seth used an open hand to gesture at everything in sight of his group. "Everything was an accident, and we have no purpose, causing more of a struggle for humankind to survive in an accidental universe."

Dr. Avers was a little insulted. "I was created in the image of God."

Chayton nodded in agreement. "What's good about love and tolerance is that everyone can choose."

Marco laughed. The other three grew quiet, shocked. Seth was first to ask, "What's so funny?"

"I was just thinking of Operator Furgis. What freedom of choice did Ray give him?" The other three were quiet in thought before they shared Marco's humor.

"Marco, if you're serious about services, join us in Recovery Celebration," said Dr. Avers. "It completely gave me a new way of looking at things. Pastor Huiling holds these meetings in her church, and we're all brothers and sister no matter what you believe."

Marco looked like he was in deep thought. Chayton answered for him. "Brook, tell Huiling we'll be there."

Seth started laughing as Marco looked at Chayton in disbelief. "Speak for yourself, thank you." Chayton responded with a laugh and Marco said, "All right, Brook, I'll give it a try."

"Marco, we'll make a new man of you yet!"

Dr. Avers chuckled. "Seth, stop." She caught her breath before continuing. "Marco, don't listen to these guys; you'll really enjoy the meeting." Marco nodded with a smile and hit Chayton on the shoulder.

Dr. Avers sat back in her sky box seat once again and activated her ear com piece. Acela Vega answered with her usual sensual voice. "Hi, Brook." Dr. Avers smiled as her companions in Seth Adams' sky box struggled in silence to listen to the ear com piece. "Acela, what's happening? I can see the stadium is getting restless waiting."

"Ken and Ray are almost changed and will be in their sky

box soon."

Dr. Avers smiled with a nod to her companions. "Is Arina Petrov ready"

Acela could hear the excitement in Dr. Avers voice. "Yeah, I just came from her dome quarters and she's ready to go. Tell Leaf we're just about ready." Both ear coms shut down with a chime.

Seth Adams asked, "Are they ready or what?"

"Stop getting hyper," Dr. Avers responded. "Yes, they're ready." Marco and Chayton started laughing. Dr. Avers activated the main vid com in Seth's sky box and issued commands. The vid com flickered for a moment before a 3-D image of Supervisor Stykes appeared. "Leaf, Acela said they're on their way to the sky box now. We're ready to go!"

Supervisor Stykes laughed. "Okay, Brook, I'll inform the chief and we'll get started with the announcements."

"And, Leaf, just to let you know, Arina will play her new instrument." The vid com chimed off. Supervisor Stykes was smiling.

Marco turned to Dr. Avers with a curious look. "What is this new instrument, Brook?"

Dr. Avers was ready to answer, but Seth pulled out his pocket pad and linked to the sky box's main vid com, projecting an instrument in 3-D floating above the base of the vid com. "It's called an ESIC. It's like an ancient guitar that musicians still use a modern version of today, but the ESIC was designed for empaths. The long neck has semicircular bubbles for the musician to glide their hands over, and at the larger base is a semicircle bubble the musician holds their hand slightly above. The clouded colors of the domes Arina's hands will glide over will change colors as the instrument picks up her musical empathy."

"Seth, I had no idea Arina Petrov was an empath," said Chayton.

Dr. Avers was quick to respond. "She's not an empath as you and I think of an empath. Arina is a musical empath; her abilities are focused only on music."

Seth added, "That's what makes her one of the most beautiful singers anyone has ever heard. Watch and you'll see something wonderful." He shut down the sky box vid com.

Chapter Six

Supervisor Stykes activated the security booth's main vid com and waited for the chime before issuing his commands. Chief Dan Tylor was projected in 3-D in front of him

"Chief, we're ready on this side."

Chief Tylor turned and watched Engineer Trently nod with approval before answering in his usual calm manner, "Let's get it started, Leaf."

Supervisor Stykes smiled as the vid com chimed off. Before he could activate any control on his touch screen console, the vid com chimed. It was Officer Armela. Stykes responded immediately. "Juan, we're ready to get started."

"Yes sir, I'm just letting you know a handful of Easterners from the *Staton* are on their way to the dome. I'll be there in a minute, sir."

Stykes was grateful to have a proficient and well-respected man on his enforcer squad. "Thanks, Juan. Operator Furgis and his guests are not in their sky box yet, so I think I can stall the starting announcement for a little longer."

The entry door to the VIP sky box hissed open, startling Dr. Cole and Kelly Brown; both stood and turned quickly to see Raynor in her dress uniform from the Mars Independent Army. Every once in a while she would still hear the joke "If you go Mars army, you go MIA." Raynor was too proud to laugh at such humor. Following Raynor was her son, Samuel, wearing his relaxed dispenser-generated slacks and wraparound shirt the younger generation appreciated. Sam immediately sat next to Kelly after a long, sensual kiss was given to the young lady standing in respect. Raynor looked at Kelly with a neutral look as she let go of Sam; this was very uncomfortable for Kelly, and Sam realized this was the reason she was quieter on Neptune One than on Mars.

Operator Furgis allowed his good friend Duncan Jennings to enter next and sit on the other side of his son. Acela Vega decided to join Huiling and her guests at their sky box. Operator Furgis sat next to his wife, wearing a formal suit that could rival Seth Adams' Bronee Vanquish IX, and it should as it was the wedding gift from Seth himself.

Kelly turned to Raynor, holding her hand out and speaking softly. "Congratulations, ma'am." Raynor stood quickly, causing the others in the sky box to pause their conversations in surprise. Raynor fought her urge to express her disapproval and offered two open arms.

Kelly accepted the hug from Sam's mother, and Raynor whispered in her ear, "We'll talk later." Kelly let go, displaying a quick smile before returning to the worried look she usually offered around Raynor Furgis.

Sam held Kelly's hand when she returned to her seat. "You okay, Kel?"

"Yeah, I guess—just wasn't expecting that!"

Sam laughed. "It's a start, Kel. Let Mom set you straight and she'll like you better. Let her think that. We're the younger generation and we do it our way anyway."

Kelly started laughing.

Operator Furgis leaned forward, grabbing his son by the shoulder. "Are you guys ready?"

Sam turned, looking into his father's eyes with pride. "You got it, Pops."

Before his father could respond, Kelly handed him something. "Sir, this was left for you."

Operator Furgis laughed. "I told you before you can call me Ken." He took the cryobox from Kelly, and Raynor leaned over, allowing her shoulder to rest on her husband's shoulder. "What is it?" Operator Furgis activated the cryobox, causing a small 3-D image of Seth Adams to appear above it. "Congrats, guys. I know how much you enjoy these, Ken, so I'm offering one more gift for the newlyweds." The image disappeared.

Raynor looked at her husband with squinted eyes. "I know there are strawberries, Ken. What else would he give you in a cryobox? Ken opened the cryobox and offered his son and Kelly a strawberry with a wink. He already knew Ray, Duncan, and Dr. Cole were not interested and did not offer.

Operator Furgis activated the skybox's main vid com to contact Huiling. He smiled as he realized he was not looking at the image of two Huilings, but her sister was also in the skybox. "Huiling, is everyone ready in there?"

The lovely Chinese woman he was looking at responded with excitement, "We're all set here, Ken."

Pastor Murray leaned closer to the vid com. "Remember grief share, Ken," and Raynor started laughing.

Operator Furgis chuckled. "We'll see, Pastor, we'll see." He instructed the vid com to switch transmission to the security booth, and Supervisor Stykes swiveled in his console's chair. "Hey, boss."

Operator Furgis smiled in response. "Leaf, are we ready?"

"Just waiting for you, boss."

Operator Furgis could hear the teasing in his voice, and his smile grew wider. "I'm sure the crowd can wait for the owner to arrive."

"The Solar Counsel is coming?"

Operator Furgis laughed with a touch of irritation. "No, but the guy who can replace you is here and waiting."

Raynor laughed also. "Leaf, I suggest we get started."

Supervisor Stykes was respectful. "Yes ma'am."

Operator Furgis looked at Raynor with a grin. "If I didn't like that guy..." Raynor patted his hand as his other guests tried not to laugh.

The Delphi dome went completely dark with only slight illumination emanating from the vid coms in the skyboxes. A bright light from the fight droid hovering far above the arena floor blinded the Delphi dome briefly before the flash turned into a 3-D projection of the star Sol. As the brightness of the star's projection dimmed, the image quickly grew outward, and the different astro bodies of the solar system appeared, accompanied by a faint modern organ sound effect. The different colonies and human establishments appeared as the image grew; the spectators were awed by a small image of Neptune One that appeared around the giant bluish planet and continued further, excluding the WH-12 wormhole.

The 3-D image slowly passed Neptune One, and Operator Furgis could make out its defining features, with a long cigar-shaped tube extending out from the side allowing larger vessels to dock with one of the five docking spheres toward the end of the docking tube. The smooth, squared side allowed for the numerous windows to shine light through, and the Delphi dome at the top was like a flashlight for the universe. Operator Furgis started reminiscing about the early days when he required permission from the Solar Counsel to modify the old military station for entertainment use. He also recalled some of the terms he was required to agree to. Raynor leaned into her husband with a slight smile. "You okay, Ken?"

Operator Furgis awoke from his daydream. "I was just thinking of how far we came from being a puppet for the Solar Counsel to declaring independence," and Raynor chuckled. He looked at Raynor with surprise. "What's so amusing?"

Raynor grew serious. "Ken, now you understand, or at least I hope you understand, why I did not fight the charges and left the Hammer to fight for the independence of Mars."

Operator Furgis nodded. "I understand, but taking my son away was very painful and then not keeping in touch was even more painful." He was looking directly into his wife's eyes.

Sam continued to concentrate on the news, knowing the battle was growing behind him; each word from his mother or father caused a slight disapproving nod of his head. Kelly held his hand tightly.

"What did you want me to do, take a vacation from the fight for independence?" Raynor asked her husband.

"You put Sam in danger."

Before Raynor could respond, Sam turned and loudly interrupted. "Would you guys like to go back down to the arena floor and start your first fight, or can you get over it and let the rest of us enjoy the solar news?"

Operator Furgis nodded with a smile and looked at his

wife. "I'm sorry, baby, you're right. I need more acceptance."

Raynor calmed. "It's all right, we'll talk later."

The smile on her son's face grew as he continued to watch the solar news projected in 3-D above the arena floor. The broadcaster for the solar news could be heard clearly as the skybox grew quieter.

"The clash between the Eastern Empire and the Western Empire has left two stations destroyed and one research station severely damaged. The Solar Counsel has received no response from either side as to the reason for the skirmish in the Venus sector; however, the Counsel did mention accusations of weapons technology was the cause of two small frigates challenging each other outside the Lunar One's docking sphere orbiting above. No shots were fired, and only one injury reported from the Western Space Fleet."

Operator Furgis leaned forward and tapped his son on the shoulder. "Don't you have a friend on Moon Colony One?"

"Yeah, Pops, John Moss, but I haven't talked to him since I quit Three D world."

Raynor smacked her husband's upper arm. "Ken, leave Sam alone and pay attention to the news."

Sam and Kelly chuckled, but Duncan Jennings and Dr. Cole laughed loudly as they turned their attention back to the solar news broadcast. The fight droid projecting the newscast followed the cues of the broadcaster and zoomed the 3-D projection from the Lunar orbiting docking sphere through space and into Earth's orbit. As the view quickly flew through the clouds and emerged above Earth dome, the broadcaster continued. "The Mech fighters are preparing for their match here on Mother Earth." The view quickly came down on top of the stadium and through the concealed top. It hovered above the projection of the empty stadium as the images of the armor Warriors appeared in the sidebars accompanied by their individual statistics. The broadcaster started with Tabitha Drake, the visiting challenger from Neptune One.

Operator Furgis noticed most of the spectators, including a lot of miners from Triton, cheering as the broadcaster continued. "Tabitha Drake"—the broadcaster paused to allow the 3-D image of Tabitha highlighted above flashes of her previous Mech fights unfolding. The image quickly flickered and changed to a new projection; Tabitha was standing on the bridge of the SS *Hammerhead* looking out over Earth.

The news broadcaster asked, "Ms. Drake, how do you feel arriving at Earth to challenge one of the best armor warriors in the system?"

The image of Tabitha turned from the SS *Hammerhead's* command bridge observation window and spoke with authority. "Ben Swells is a good Mech fighter, but to say he's the best…" she paused to chuckle, "…we'll see." Her grin was wide.

"You think you will beat Cronus?"

"Of course," she said. "It's just a matter of how much of a fight he wants to give me."

The broadcaster laughed. "How's it feel to fight your way from Neptune One all the way to Earth, last stop to the solar championship match?"

Tabitha paused to shake her head with a smile.

After a moment the news broadcaster grew impatient. "Your followers are waiting."

Tabitha remained respectful. "Neptune One is awesome."

There were cheers in the Delphi dome. She stepped aside to allow the recording droid to display the image of Earth. "And it is a great pleasure to be back at Earth, but my business here is to show that I will be the next solar champion. The support from my family on Neptune One will make that possible."

Operator Furgis smiled with pride, feeling Earth could hear the cheering from the Delphi dome on Neptune One.

The broadcaster quickly added, "Of course, I met Ken Furgis once on business to Neptune One. Good luck, Tabitha."

The stadium grew quiet and the individuals in Operator Furgis's sky box turned to look at Ken putting his open hands up in the air and shaking his head in disbelief.

Just as the broadcaster wished Tabitha good luck, the fight droid switched the 3-D image to Ben Swells, with recorded images of previous fights. Ben Swells was a six-foot white man with blue eyes and short blonde hair; his call sign was Cronus after the Greek god who overthrew Zeus. The broadcaster was more enthusiastic in announcing Ben Swells.

"Cronus—most fanatics say he will be the next solar champion, taking down Noyami Masoko from Venus Four. Fortunately, Venus Four was not one of the stations destroyed or damaged." The fight droid projected the image of Venus Four quickly before returning to the recordings of Ben Swells' Mech fight matches.

After several moments of displaying his statistics above the vid com recordings from the fight droids, the 3-D image flickered and changed to the projection of Ben standing outside on the rolling hillsides with a saucer-shaped house held suspended in the air by a large column underneath. The news broadcaster calmly started his interview, looking at the spectators first.

"Ben Swells, one of the best Mech fighters in the system."
The broadcaster turned to face Ben, and both glanced at a vid
com recording droid that accidently lowered into view behind them. The news broadcaster recovered quickly with a
slight chuckle. "Not all your fans are human." Ben laughed.
The broadcaster continued. "How does it feel to be so close to
the championship match?" The broadcaster stood next to Ben
Swells with his hands behind his back listening to instructions
on what to ask from his ear com piece.

Ben was a gentleman. "Beating Masoko will be a great
challenge. However, I have to beat Darkstar first."

"That should be no problem for you."

"I am one of the best armor warriors," Ben said. "I trained
and earned the right to say that throughout my career as a
Mech fighter." He looked back up at the area where the droid
was hovering. "I met Tabitha Drake and I do not take her challenge lightly."

The spectators in the Delphi dome stood and cheered,
causing the fight droid to pause the solar news broadcast.

Everyone in Operator Furgis's sky box was nodding with
approval as they looked at each other. Furgis activated his ear
com piece and asked for Chief Tylor. The very heavy English
accent the chief spoke with could be faintly heard from everyone in the skybox.

"Sir, what can I do for you?"

Operator Furgis took the pausing of the fight droid as
an opportunity to speak with the chief quickly. "Dan, you're
right, Swells is an okay guy."

"Yes sir, I met him long ago in one of his earlier matches."

Operator Furgis was smiling. "I'll get with you later, Chief."

The fight droid interrupted as it started broadcasting once again.

"Ben Swells, a twenty-nine-year-old seasoned armor warrior will be testing his abilities against Tabitha Drake, a twenty-eight-year-old young lady from the outer system."

Operator Furgis did not respect the tone the broadcaster used while saying "outer system." The fight droid flickered again, and then projected a red planet in distant space and started to accelerate the view until the skies of Mars were visible. The solar news broadcaster's tone grew serious.

"On Mars there was a slight issue with military forces as the Eastern Empire insisted on a training base on Deimos, and now I'm told…" he held his hand to his ear com piece, "…they also want to place forces in Mars Central City."

Operator Furgis looked over at his wife. He could see the anger on her face. His son turned around. "What's that about, Mom?"

Raynor Furgis took a deep breath and said, "Derek will allow Easterners in Mars city and then the Westerners will want to put their forces there in retaliation." She looked at her husband with concern. "Derek Fields is a good guy, but he's not good with politics."

"Ray, you can be on the next transport." Sam and Kelly both turned back around in their seats again as Ray calmed.

"Thank you, babe, but I'll catch the transport back to Mars city after Seth's gathering at Grav Zero."

The news broadcaster continued his 3-D narration. The image created from the lasers of the fight droid showed the atmosphere of Mars slowly disappear and turn into stars with a small moon slowly growing larger in the distance. "Deimos, sister to Phobos, is almost terra formed with the larger Phobos gaining ground." The fight droid directed the generated 3-D image of flight to enter Deimos. It showed very light clouds passing the view, and the image focused on the ground approaching slowly where several domes appeared. These domes were scattered around the surface of the moon with large amounts of foliage around each dome that would thin out as the distances between terra domes grew.

The news broadcaster continued in a louder voice. "The Eastern Empire accusing the Westerners of sabotage and espionage has increased its forces to protect its assets on Deimos." The 3-D image quickly traveled through the generated atmosphere of Deimos and through space until descending into the lighter atmosphere of Phobos. The news broadcaster grew quieter. "On Phobos the Western Empire has stated to the Solar Counsel and the solar news that they are assisting the Martians with their Phobos project and that no military will remain on Phobos when completed."

Duncan was first to ask Raynor why she was scoffing so loudly. Raynor shook her head briefly while looking down with a grin. "The contract was that the Western Empire would not have military forces on Phobos at all." She looked at her husband with disgust.

Operator Furgis responded, "Then why did you allow them to station forces there?"

"They put Tobine repeater rifles on everyone they called scientists or technicians and said it was for the protection of the project and its personnel. They're almost as bad as the Easterners."

Sam turned toward his mother with sarcasm of his own.

"Don't let the chief hear you."

His father grew angry. "Enough about the chief; he's no longer an Easterner and he's been on this station longer than anyone."

Sam looked at Kelly and rolled his eyes. His mother said, "He's definitely not the problem, Sam." Dr. Cole was nodding as he watched Operator Furgis start to calm.

The fight droid was projecting the traveled course of the generations again; the view exited Phobos and travelled until entering the asteroid belt. The news broadcaster's voice grew louder. "Minor skirmishes reported in the inner belt; however, no major conflicts at this time." The view slowly passed numerous asteroids before he continued in softer speech. "In fact it has been reported that several new private operations have been started, with the Solar Counsel's blessings of course." The broadcaster offered a slight chuckle. A large rock that was extremely hard to distinguish from a typical rock appeared above the 3-D asteroid belt projection. "Mortelis ore was found deeper inside several of the smaller asteroids. We all wish them luck; more Mortelis ore is needed."

There was silence as the projection continued on its path through the system. As the path the fight droid projected above the Delphi dome's arena floor emerged from the inner systems' asteroid belt, it closed in on the giant planet Jupiter. The projection quickly changed course and entered the inner moon of Io, and the view was magnificent. Io was one of the first successful terra-forming projects in the solar system, and it had a very large population compared to other terra-formed astro bodies. Io not only offered mining for precious resources, it was also an established entertainment destination larger than Neptune One and offering more Earth-like amenities. The spectators of the Delphi dome sighed as the 3-D image flew over the beautiful manmade terrain of Io, slowly zooming in and out with different features of the living moon.

Senior Pastor Murray leaned forward and gently rested his hand on Huiling's shoulder, causing her to turn with a grin. Acela turned to look at the senior pastor. Pastor Murray was loud enough for everyone to hear. "Amazing what we can do with the Father's help." Huiling returned the smile. "GF, Pastor." Pastor Murray smiled at her and quietly responded. "God First." He pointed up.

"Pastor Murray, have you ever been to Io?" Acela asked.

Pastor Murray laughed. "No, Acela, it is one of the few places I have not yet visited."

Huiling interrupted softly, looking over at Acela. "Senior Pastor Murray's district does not include Io."

Acela smiled at Huiling before looking back at Pastor Murray. "I have friends on Io, Pastor, if you ever want to vacation there." She offered an innocent wink at both Pastor Murray and Huiling.

Pastor Murray was quick to respond. "Maybe we can all visit after the *King David* returns."

Acela laughed. "I'm sorry, Pastor. I probably won't be leaving Neptune One for a while."

The solar news broadcaster's voice grew slightly louder, gaining everyone's attention, as the 3-D projection entered Jupiter's moon, Europa. "On this lovely little moon of Europa, the atmosphere is becoming more breathable." The fight droid projected the 3-D view of Europa, the dense foliage and growing trees along with a bluish mist barely recognizable in the air. "The air is almost filtered from the Mortelis gas that was generated from the terra-forming generator on the northern hemisphere many years ago."

The fight droid pulled back from the large moon. It passed Jupiter's largest moon of Ganymede. "The construction of more terra domes is almost complete, with the hope of adding more colonies in the outer system." The droid's projection increased in speed as its course took it toward Saturn. The gas giant grew in size, displaying a yellow hue about the atmosphere with electrical discharges known as partial discharge that were caused by the metal hydrogen particles traveling through the windy atmosphere; the discharges could be seen shooting through the upper layer of Saturn. As the fight droid approached the rings, it veered off and entered the atmosphere of Titan. The news broadcaster continued as the fight droid glided gracefully through Titan's atmosphere, showing the vegetation and once-domed cities. "Saturn Five, combined with Saturn Six on its sister moon of Rhea, has one of the most lucrative mines in the outer system." The fight droid started the ascending view.

Pastor Murray rested his hand on Huiling's shoulder, and as she turned Acela could hear the compassion Pastor Murray offered in his talks. "Look at the beauty of these places the Father allows us to inhabit."

Huiling smiled and responded softly, "The Father provides, sir." She turned to Acela after winking at her sister. "God First."

Acela smiled. "GF, Huiling."

The fight droid's 3-D projection exited the atmosphere of Titan and moved slowly past Rhea before accelerating toward the next stop. In the far distance another giant planet was growing larger, and the spectators in the Delphi dome's stadium knew it was Uranus from the brighter light blue atmosphere with slightly larger rings than the planet they had come to know as home, Neptune.

As the projection of Uranus grew in size above the arena floor, the fight droid changed course and entered the giant's satellite. The news broadcaster began his narration. "Uranus Two on Titania is also flourishing in its production and research, but the Eastern Empire has reported destroying and chasing several pirate ships in that sector. We thank God for the Eastern Empire and its protection of the outer system." The fight droid projected several solar warships in the distance of Titania exchanging missiles and small ordinance fire.

Operator Furgis looked over at Duncan Jennings and Dr. Arthur Cole, offering his best sarcasm. "Thank God for the Eastern Empire." Both recipients chuckled and shook their heads, and Sam turned to his father. Ken Furgis was already holding his hand up. "I don't want to hear it." He noticed his wife looking at him with amusement as she asked, "Hear what?" Ken shook his head with a smile and whispered, "It's probably about the chief." Sam continued to watch the 3-D news projection as he held Kelly's hand. Operator Furgis grew slightly excited. "We should be next," anticipating the news broadcaster was working his narration outward from the inner system.

The spectators in the stadium of the Delphi dome stood quickly and cheered as the fight droid's projection entered the Neptune sector. In the distance a large blue planet grew larger, displaying more detail of the rings around the giant gas planet known as Saturn's sister. The view went directly through the three sets of rings, showing the chunks of ice and rock pass by. Some were small and others larger, and they all had cosmic dust suspended in their immediate area of orbit. The view penetrated the outer edges of Neptune's atmosphere, showing the turbulence under the deceiving projection of the planet with only partial lightning discharges flowing across the outer atmosphere on more than one occasion.

Triton's miners cheered as they watched the projection of Triton, one of Neptune's satellites and home to most of the miners in the stadium. This moon was dark and very harsh, and there was no terra forming on Triton due to the geological activity of the astro body. The mining conditions were extremely dangerous. As the view slowly moved across the battered surface, the miners sat back down in their seats, murmuring. Dr. Cole was speaking softly to Duncan Jennings about the conditions on Triton. Operator Furgis interrupted. "It's good to have a small vacation, wouldn't you say?"

Dr. Cole laughed. "Absolutely, sir, and thank you." Operator Furgis nodded.

In the high orbit of Neptune was the famous station Neptune One, and the spectators cheered with enthusiasm as the fight droid took the 3-D view slowly from Triton to the station. Neptune One was very impressive, with five docking spheres at the end of the docking tube that stretched out like a long pipe, and entered at the front desk level in the middle of the massive station. The sides of the space station were square with smooth sides and rounded corners, and the massive hangar bay doors were visible on both sides. These doors allowed larger war ships to refit and repair without delay and would occasionally be used by both empires.

Smaller lights emitted through the numerous windows throughout the large space station, but this was not as impressive as the light shining like a beacon from the Delphi dome on top of Neptune One.

Seth Adams leaned over the shoulder of Marco De Luca with a grin. "This would have been a good spot for my Grav Zero solar ad."

Marco turned, laughing. "The whole station is your advertisement."

"Marco, do you blame him?" added Dr. Avers.

Chayton followed with a laugh. "He is a businessman; look at his suit." Marco returned the laugh as he watched Chayton look him up and down.

The view from the fight droid's 3-D projection flew through the docking sphere past a glide car and down the glide tube. It entered the glide tube station and the announcer said, "The former military station has been upgraded to offer any visitor full amenities—whether you're staying in basic quarters or a large suite." The fight droid's path quickly passed the Solar House and Grav Zero. "Neptune One has numerous places to grab a good meal and then, if you're interested, work it off to the new solar wave music in one of the clubs." The 3-D projection passed the Grav Zero club and flew quickly into a lift. The narrator continued as the lift doors opened, showing the casino level. "Or if you desire a challenge, you could always try to break the vid on one of the many wagering games offered." The fight droid paused at several touch screen vid tables, allowing the viewers to watch the table and very tightly dressed male and female dealers.

The news broadcaster's tone picked up slightly. "We

commend Kennith Furgis for the great job he has done with the old run-down military station."

The fight droid projected the 3-D image of Operator Furgis as he was in his not far past younger years. Raynor was impressed with her husband as she turned to him with a look of appreciation. "Not too bad, honey." Sam and Kelly laughed and looked back to watch Ken straighten his dress jacket. The fun ended when a 3-D image of Acela Vega appeared next to Operator Furgis; the spectators cheered for the very attractive Spanish woman, and several of the miners quickly offered cat calls, but the stadium became silent as the fight droid projected the word above Acela: WANTED.

Operator Furgis activated the main vid com in his sky box and quickly contacted Acela. The vid com flickered quickly and projected the 3-D image of Acela from her sky box into Operator Furgis's. She was smiling.

"Acela, you didn't tell me you were wanted."

Acela laughed. "Ken, you know everyone wants me."

Operator Furgis laughed, and Raynor reached over and activated the controls on the arm of her husband's chair. "It's all yours, Acela." The solar news broadcast paused as the 3-D image of Acela Vega took command of the stadium. She smiled as she spread her arms out with her palms open in a friendly gesture. "Everyone wants me." The crowd in the stadium were excited, with cheers along with her name heard throughout the Delphi dome.

The crowd quieted to a whisper as the well-dressed and very beautiful Spanish woman wearing a large diamond necklace covering the sight of her very low-cut top and accompanied by smaller diamond jewelry started to speak in a sensual voice. "Do not worry, my friends, the astro Tourney will continue next cycle after the Grav ball match." The crowd stood and grew extremely loud again, and the cheering was confusing with numerous chants being raved and echoed through the Delphi dome.

Operator Furgis smiled until he saw his wife staring at him with a curious look; he changed his smile to a grin and activated his ear com piece to contact Acela.

"Ken, was that sufficient?" she asked.

Operator Furgis dared not smile with excitement and answered quickly, "Thank you, Acela. I appreciate it." Raynor initiated the solar news.

The 3-D image of Acela disappeared, leaving the image of Operator Furgis as the narration continued. "And of course we must give our congratulations to Raynor and Kennith on their wedding." The spectators stood once again, applauding and cheering.

Sam turned to his father. "What's with that, Pops?"

Raynor was quick to lean forward with a response. "Sam, you should know how it is on a station with a lot of traffic."

Sam shook his head with disbelief. "I just don't like how everything is known; it seems no matter what precautions we take, everyone knows."

Sam's father laughed. "It's not like our wedding was classified."

A 3-D image of an Eastern Empire destroyer in orbit around Neptune One replaced Operator Furgis's image, and the news broadcaster continued the narration with skepticism in his voice. "On a more serious note, the Eastern Empire has accused the Solar Counsel of secret tests on the popular entertainment station." The image of Dr. Gerlitz was overlaid on top of the Eastern Empire's warship and Neptune One. The Delphi dome was silent with surprise as the narration continued once again. "The Eastern Empire has stated that they have proof that Dr. Niclas Gerlitz is conducting new weapons research based on Mortelis power." The 3-D image of a crude Mortelis cannon appeared, and the crowd oohed and aahed with several boos.

Operator Furgis was very agitated; he activated the main vid com in his sky box; not waiting for any chime or voice he instructed the transmission to be immediately connected with the security booth. Supervisor Stykes answered quickly with assurance in his voice. "Boss, I know what you're thinking, but we knew when the Essex linked with the shuttle, they would use it to cause trouble."

Operator Furgis calmed slightly. "Yeah, but this is getting ridiculous." Supervisor Stykes refrained from displaying humor.

Operator Furgis activated his ear com piece after shutting down the vid com and announced, "All senior staff to report to Operator Furgis's office following the match." Then he activated the main vid com in his sky box to contact the engineering booth, and after a brief pause Chief Tylor appeared in 3-D. Operator Furgis spoke quickly. "Chief, I assume you got my message."

"Of course, I'll be there."

"No, Chief, if the cat's out of the bag, then get with Dr. Gerlitz and schedule some tests. I want that main MC on my station ready as soon as possible."

"Yes sir."

"And tell him to finish installing the lighter MCs on the shuttles."

The solar news continued as the projection of the SS *King David* appeared, slowly approaching Neptune One. Pastor Murray was listening to Huiling explain the wanted situation with Acela but lost focus when he saw his ship displayed in 3-D above the arena floor. Pastor Murray looked back at Huiling with a smile and turned quickly to Acela. His look was as gentle as his voice. "We're going to ask the Father for justice in this matter; you have nothing to worry about." He looked out the dome at the actual SS *King David* before smiling wider and focusing on the 3-D image.

A large image of WH-12 appeared in the distance as the fight droid took the view from the SS *King David* through the Kuiper belt region, rotating around several astro bodies of interest before stopping a slight distance from the wormhole. WH-12 was small until a small droid flew past the image and entered the event horizon of the wonder; the light from the wormhole appeared quickly, slightly longer than a flash, and briefly blinded the spectators. As the light faded, a cloudy mix of white and blue swirled into a funnel with deeper colors in the center. The spectators' excitement grew, and the murmurs escalated to loud chatter. Wormholes were proven to exist, but this one was close to home and piqued everyone's curiosity.

"Are you ready, Hui Yan?" Pastor Murray asked with a wide grin.

Huiling's sister stared at the wormhole with a smile, in deep thought. Huiling turned to her sister. "Sis, you all right?"

Hui Yan awoke from her daydream. "I was just thinking about what the Father has beyond this beauty!"

Pastor Murray chuckled. "We'll find out when we get to Eos." He stared at the image of the wormhole and watched the SS *King David* approach.

Acela Vega joined the excitement and looked over at her friend Huiling. "Maybe they'll send us a vid card."

Huiling laughed as she turned her attention back to the broadcaster:

"As the magnificent *King David* approaches the wormhole, it will most likely encounter turbulent forces; however, the authorities believe the research vessel will have no trouble traversing one of the universe's marvels." The 3-D image of the SS *King David* approached the wormhole slowly as the broadcaster went on with his narration. "Who knows how long it will be before our glorious conquests and our conflicts settle in a new world." The image of the wormhole projected above the arena floor opened up, allowing the SS *King David* to slowly and gracefully enter the WH-12; the wormhole quickly closed, leaving stars projected in the vast distance.

The image quickly changed to the wormhole opening up on the other side and the SS *King David* slowly emerging from the center. The fight droid's projection panned out, showing the wormhole growing smaller along with the SS *King David,* and turned quickly to face a star not too far off in the distance. The broadcaster spoke with excitement:

"The Solar Counsel has authorized the following announcement. When the *King David* arrives, she will start settling the planet Eos and possibly one of Eos's habitable moons. May God travel with the crew of the SS *King David* and their new adventures." The 3-D image of Eos was projected, and the news broadcaster smiled and nodded his head.

As the credits for the solar news broadcast were projected above the arena floor for all spectators to witness, Operator Furgis looked over at Duncan Jennings with a grin and friendly sarcasm. "When are you going, Dunc? I got a shuttle waiting."

Everyone in Operator Furgis's sky box laughed at the two friends teasing. Duncan elbowed Dr. Cole as he responded to Kennith. "You should know that's for the young-hearted."

Raynor laughed. "We know that's not Ken."

Operator Furgis was slightly defensive. "We'll see about that later," but his voice grew erotic in mid-sentence. Sam turned, looking over his shoulder at his father with a disapproving glare. "Come on, Pops, we don't need to know about such things, all right?" His mother started laughing until complete darkness came over the Delphi dome.

After several minutes of chattering from the spectators sitting in the dark, with only Supervisor Stykes watching a very detailed and bright 3-D image of the stadium on the security booth's vid com, the fight droid suddenly projected the name Arina Petrov with a very large welcome above, lighting up the stadium and causing the chatter to quiet down to a slight murmur. The image changed from Arina Petrov's name to vid com recordings of her previous performances as the entire stadium in the Delphi dome became silent with anticipation. The image continued to change as the location of each performance was described, highlighted above her vid com recordings. The crowd's cheers would grow slightly up and down according to the individual location.

The stadium once again went dark, with only slight movement seen in the middle of the arena floor, where the lift for the fight droid would open and close, and a silhouette could be seen ascending from the dimly lit area. Supervisor Stykes watched the data flow across his transparent touch screen console as he worked the controls. He activated his ear com piece to contact Chief Tylor, who was quick to respond. "Yes, Leaf?"

"We're all set here, Chief. How's your end?"

Chief Tylor remained calm; he was always very hard to excite. "We're good to go, Leaf," and the ear com fell silent.

Stykes instructed his ear com to transmit to Operator Furgis next, who was slightly more excited as the opening ceremony was about to begin.

Chapter Seven

Operator Furgis's ear com chimed, followed by a vocal acknowledgment. "Incoming transmission." He already knew the source and accepted immediately. Operator Furgis's guests could faintly hear Supervisor Stykes in the ear com piece as he spoke with excitement. "We're ready to go, boss."

"Give it a moment, Leaf, and I'll let Acela know. When you hear her announcement, you can start." The ear com shut down, and Operator Furgis was quick to place an ear com transmission to Acela; he was also anticipating the start of the ceremonies.

Acela Vega sat next to Huiling and stopped in mid-sentence to answer her ear com piece.

Operator Furgis spoke quickly. "Acela, it's all yours."

Huiling could see the smile grow on Acela's face as she answered, "All right, Ken, I'll start now." She turned to Pastor Murray. "You're really going to enjoy this, Pastor." Acela stood and turned back, facing the vid com in the sky box. She instructed the device to project a 3-D image broadcast, and the spectators in the stadium grew excited as her image appeared standing in the middle of the arena floor. Most of the spectators clapped and cheered while several others offered cat calls and whistles for the attractive Spanish woman adorned with large diamonds.

The spectators quieted down as Acela Vega's sensual voice could be heard throughout the stadium. "Ladies and gentlemen," she paused for a brief moment, "and miners." The spectators started laughing. Acela let the crowd enjoy their laughter for several moments before continuing. "We have asked Arina Petrov to honor us once again with another visit." The crowd stood and clapped as Acela continued. "As soon as she heard of the Furgis's wedding, she adjusted her schedule for a very special appearance." Acela motioned with her hands for the crowd to calm and remain seated.

Operator Furgis looked at his wife and could see the grin growing into a very large smile as he rubbed the back of her neck. "Congrats, Ray." Sam looked back over his shoulder in time to see Raynor turn and hold his father by the face while she passionately kissed him.

Engineer Trently looked over from his engineering console at Chief Tylor; Trently was as excited as the spectators. "Chief, I hope she uses her new ESIC." Chief Tylor grinned at his engineer, ready to ask about this new instrument when Acela's announcement interrupted.

"We have the honor of being the first to hear Arina's new instrument." The crowd's cheering grew very loud, and the 3-D image of Acela in the stadium imitated her actions in the sky box as she turned to Pastor Murray. "Are we ready?" The crowd chanted Arina's name.

The 3-D image of Acela standing in the middle of the arena floor shouted, "Then give a warm welcome to Arina Petrov!" The spectators in the stadium stood, clapping and cheering with great excitement. Then the stadium grew quiet after a loud gasp as they watched a round wall of fire replace Acela's image. The flames were thick, shooting straight up past the fight droid hovering far above the arena floor. The peaks of the flames danced around without control, and the round wall of flame surged with brightness. The spectators in the sky boxes joined the general seating spectators in their arousal as they too stood in awe.

Operator Furgis was worried. "Those flames do not look projected!"

Sam turned to his father with a wide grin. "They are but there's no need to worry, Pop." He pointed at his bio eye, which his father had forgotten about.

After a brief moment Arina Petrov walked through the circle of flame, which quickly vanished, and the spectators grew even more excited at the new scene. Arina remained on fire. She was completely engulfed with the flames until she spun quickly and used her voice to extinguish them. She came to a stop with both hands open in the air, followed by a graceful bow. Operator Furgis was concerned for her safety until the sequence of events quickly ended, leaving the lovely Arina Petrov standing in the middle of the arena floor with the fight droid shining a slightly orange-colored light on her position. Supervisor Stykes was taken by surprise and now could feel the vibration from the spectators stomping their feet, his hand on the transparent touch screen controls of his security console. He relaxed as he watched Arina Petrov hold one hand up, taking control of the spectators and quieting them as she started speaking.

"Wan shang hao." The spectators murmured in approval as she continued. "Yuan Shang De zhu fu xin niang he xin lang." The tall, blue-eyed woman from the old Russian area of Earth's past stood like a princess in a dress that changed colors and flowed gently to the floor of the arena. Her beauty was mesmerizing, and the spectators offered only slight murmurs waiting for the well-loved singer to perform. Arina offered a pure, bell-like voice that impressed all her audiences. She smiled at the spectators before continuing. "Brothers and sisters." Arina twirled her arms, causing a quick burst of flame. "I have received a special request from a good friend, so please join me in a moment of silence before we begin."

Operator Furgis looked at his smiling wife, thinking, *Begin*. Arina was already impressive.

The Delphi dome was lit from outside as the SS *King David* fired light tracers around the domed area of Neptune One, and Arina Petrov clasped her hands together, looking into the crowded stadium. "And God is able to make all grace abound to you, so that having all sufficiency in all things at all times, you may abound in every good work." She stepped back and bowed her head. The light show from the *King David* stopped, and the Delphi dome became completely quiet as Arina stood in the light projected from the fight droid high above her head, which remained bowed.

Acela Vega looked quickly around the sky box and could see her companions focused on the arena floor with watery eyes.

Both Operator Furgis and Director Furgis held their partners' hands in anticipation. They did not have to wait long. The arena floor woke up in cloudy colors swirling underneath Arina Petrov as she raised her head to the sound of whales and seagulls that thrive on Mother Earth. Everyone gasped as they watched Arina open her mouth and her distinctive, beautiful voice started one of the most famous songs in human history. "Amazing grace, how sweet the sound that saved a wretch like me!"

Supervisor Stykes held his hands up from the touch screen console to make sure he would not accidentally interfere with this spectacular display of spiritual tribute.

Seth Adams looked over at Dr. Avers, witnessing the tears of bliss trickling down her cheeks. He leaned over and gently rested his hand on her shoulder. "She's really good, huh, Doc." Dr. Avers nodded with a smile as she wiped her eyes. Marco De Luca and Chayton both turned, smiling at Dr. Avers. Marco said, "Absolutely one of the best I have ever seen, Doc." Chayton was nodding with a grin. Seth's guests did not look away for very long as Arina's voice demanded attention and the lights added to the awe of her pure, innocent voice.

Engineer Trently's hands flowed across his transparent touch screen controls on the engineering console. Chief Dan Tylor stood behind his engineer in the engineering booth. The fight droid was given command programming for the entire event from Engineer Trently and Supervisor Stykes, but the small hovering device was linked to both the engineering console and the security console. Stykes appeared in the vid com projection of the engineering booth. "Chief, Arina is almost done with 'Amazing Grace.' The security monitors are a go."

Trently looked up at Chief Tylor with an approving nod, and the chief relayed to Stykes, "We're a go here as well, Leaf. Keep the droid active." Engineer Trently relaxed as he monitored his engineering console and turned to the chief with a smile and excitement in his voice. "I think she will use the ESIC next!"

The chief smiled. "I hope so, I've been hearing a lot about it," and both refocused on the arena floor.

The stadium grew very dark once again as Arina Petrov ended her performance of "Amazing Grace" with a gentle bow; the silhouette of a small lift behind her opened and a stand rose above the floor.

The first light to illuminate the Delphi dome appeared shooting from the SS *King David* as Supervisor Stykes continually linked the fight droid's event programming to the weapons officer's console on the *King David*. The massive ship threw volleys of ordinance over and around the Delphi dome for a brief moment before the fight droid projected spinning lasers that illuminated Arina and circled the beautiful blonde singer sitting on a transparent floating stool top as she held her new instrument. The chatter and applause from the spectators grew quiet, and they sat in their seats in anticipation of the next performance.

Operator Furgis chuckled when Duncan Jennings turned with excitement. "This will be good. I watched her practice on Earth." Raynor was curious. Duncan watched the look of curiosity grow on his companions' expressions before answering, "Who do you think gave her that fine instrument?"

Operator Furgis activated his ear com, and heard Acela Vega's sensual voice. "Ken, how are you guys enjoying the performance?"

"Everyone here is flabbergasted. Arina's been sitting in her laser circle for a while now. Is everything all right?"

Acela's laugh was reassuring. "Everything is fine. It's my understanding that Arina will not start until she feels completely connected to the instrument," and the ear com went quiet as Operator Furgis leaned back and relaxed.

The fight droid raised the lasers circling Arina Petrov so that they continued to move in a circular pattern, except the ends now extended outward at an angle over the spectators. Arina stood and slowly stepped forward; her head was bowed as the stool top disappeared. The ESIC hung from her neck like an old-style instrument except with no straps; it floated gracefully in front of her and at her command. She raised her right hand and gently floated her moving fingers over the larger sphere on the base of the instrument, while her left hand gently floated over the three semicircular bubbles on the neck of the instrument. These spheres, designed for empaths, would change colors of the gases inside as the empath connected with the instrument.

As Arina moved her hands over the spheres of her ESIC, the musical impressions in her mind would transfer to the converters of the instrument, creating the music only well-disciplined empaths could control. The sky boxes were secure and would not feel the entire benefit of the converters from the ESIC.

Operator Furgis watched as a slight wind flowing over the spectators caught their undivided attention, and they murmured in awe. All of a sudden, lightning flashing from the upper dome that could be seen by the SS *King David* flew quickly across, accompanied by the sound of light rain. The wind stopped abruptly and was replaced by Arina Petrov in a soprano with synthesized music from her ESIC; the sounds of flutes, harps, drums, keyboards, and various other instruments were joined together with a loud wolf howling in the background. The sound of the wind once again joined the empathically synthesized music in exhilaration of emotion from Arina as her soprano continued to mesmerize the Delphi dome and the SS *King David*. When she switched to vocals, the accent from her homeland enhanced the beauty of her music. She was joined by several sopranistas for a background that brought tears to most of the spectators, including the miners and Easterners. One of Arina's favorite songs was called "Daughter of the Cosmos," where her voice could reach the tenth octave.

As Arina's voice settled lower and became silent with her head bowed, the fight droid slowly brought the laser lights into an emerging single beam, illuminating her in changing colors. Arina was still for several moments before the spectators heard a gentle female voice broadcasted from the fight droid. "Father God, thank you for this gift. I sing in your honor, Father." Arina stood and opened her arms. The spectators rose to their feet in applause, and the Delphi dome was loud as the clapping filled the stadium.

Operator Furgis leaned over and hugged his wife tightly, and Raynor tried to refrain from smiling as she watched Kelly hug Sam too. But she could not resist and gently rested her hand on the back of Kelly's shoulder. Sam glanced over Kelly's head at his mother and without words said thank you.

Engineer Trently jumped from his chair quickly and turned toward Chief Dan Tylor. He could see his boss's watery eyes. "Chief, you all right?"

Chief Tylor looked at Trently, wiping his eyes, and replied, "It's a little smoky in here; increase the circulation." Trently grinned; he had seen his boss in rare form.

Pastor Murray leaned forward and grabbed Acela's hands. "Thank you, Acela, for that blessing."

Hui Yan added, "Acela, that was so beautiful. Can we meet Arina?"

"Yes," said Acela, "after the Grav ball match I'll ask her."

"Bless you, Acela."

They were interrupted by the vid com chiming, with a transmission from Operator Furgis.

Pastor Murray smiled. "Ken, what do you think?"

Operator Furgis did not hesitate. "Amazing. Acela, do you think Arina would like a permanent suite on Neptune One?"

"I think it's a good idea," she replied, "but I think she would have to refuse." The 3-D image of Operator Furgis nodded. Pastor Murray was ready to continue the conversation but realized Arina was about to start the Grav ball match with the Earth planetary anthem. "Ken, don't forget about grief share," he said, and Operator Furgis laughed as both vid coms shut down.

The fight droid illuminated the center of the arena in a soft white light where Arina Petrov stepped forward and stood facing the spectators in the stadium. Operator Furgis leaned forward slightly, anticipating the Terran Tribune's chosen song for Earth's anthem. Everyone in the stadium and skyboxes stood as Arina lift her open-handed arm high. "May the Father bring peace and blessings to the system." She gently lowered her arms as she started the song of tribute. Arina's voice captured the spectators instantly as she sang about the features of Mother Earth, the blue skies, and the different birds that enjoyed their freedom as they gracefully soared high above, the oceans with all the creatures that swam in the deep blue of Earth, and finally the land features with the marvelous animals that called Earth their home.

As Arina slowly became silent, her head bowed with honor, and the accompanying synthesized music for Earth's planetary anthem broadcasted from the fight droid ended soon after. The spectators stood and applauded once again for her magnificent performance.

Pastor Murray continued to applaud as he nodded at Acela with a very wide smile. Acela was pleased. "Pastor, was that not some of the most beautiful music you ever heard?" Hui Yan Li stood next to Pastor Murray and quickly answered for him in a louder volume to overcome the noise level from the applause. "She is surely gifted by the Father." Huiling winked at Acela but had no time for response as they watched Arina Petrov turn and walk to the center of the arena floor.

The vid com in Acela Vega's sky box chimed on, and Operator Furgis's name was 3-D projected above its base. Acela answered quickly. "Did everyone in your box enjoy the performance, Ken?"

Operator Furgis's 3-D image was projecting a very wide smile. "Absolutely, Acela, this woman is gifted," and Acela chuckled. "However, it's time for the match."

As Arina stood in the middle fight droid lift, the 3-D image of Acela appeared, and the spectators switched their attention back and forth between the two lovely ladies. Acela's 3-D image quieted the crowd as she raised her open hands. "Brothers and sisters." She paused to allow the noise level to drop even further. "One more time for our honored guest, Arina Petrov." The crowd was already standing as they erupted into a very loud cheer and applause. Arina blew several kisses to her fans before the fight droid broadcasted her voice loudly over the excited crowd. "Shang De zhu fu, Shang De zhu fu," and Arina continued the blessings until the lowering lift took her under the arena floor and out of sight.

The fight droid illuminated the arena floor with a dim, soft white light as the image of Acela continued. "Brothers and sisters, it gives me great pleasure to introduce this Grav ball match's commentator, Marco De Luca." The stadium applauded lightly.

Pastor Murray activated the vid com to contact Operator Furgis. Acela and Huiling turned to look at Pastor Murray, who was sitting back in his seat with a serious expression. Hui Yan Li, sitting next to Pastor Murray, was smiling. Operator Furgis took command of their attention as his 3-D image appeared in front of them "Pastor Murray, are you ready to see the Poseidons teach the Rovers how to complete a successful Grav ball match?"

Acela and Huiling started laughing and could be heard in Operator Furgis's sky box. Pastor Murray enjoyed the friendly rivalry and was quick to laugh with his response. "The Rovers will prevail; they are the chosen team, Ken. Remember Psalm twenty-three," and the vid com shut down.

The 3-D image of Marco De Luca appeared above the arena floor, and Furgis looked at his wife curiously. "What's twenty-three, babe?"

Raynor Furgis chuckled. "I think it's the valley one. Ask Sam." Operator Furgis leaned forward, putting his hand on his son's shoulder. Before he could inquire, his son held his pocket pad above his shoulder for his father to take. Ken squeezed his son's shoulder before grabbing the pocket pad. He leaned back in his sky box's command chair and started scrolling through the pocket pad, and he was quickly interrupted by his wife. "Read out loud." Duncan Jennings and Dr. Cole joined in unison, "Yeah, let's hear it." His son sat quietly smiling with Kelly Brown.

Operator Furgis looked around the sky box briefly and nodded. "Very well, guys."

"Kel, this ought to be good," said Sam. Kelly joined Raynor in a laugh. After everyone had quieted, Operator Furgis looked at the pocket pad and started to read aloud.

"The Lord is my shepherd; I shall not want. He makes me lie down in green pastures. He leads me beside still waters. He leads me in paths of righteousness for his name's sake." Operator Furgis stopped there with slight agitation. His wife was amused. "Keep going, you're not done." Raynor enjoyed watching her husband read scripture, knowing how reluctant he was to a strong belief. Operator Furgis looked around at the smiling faces in the sky box, wondering who was enjoying the reading or who was enjoying him reading.

He reluctantly continued in a lighter tone. "Even though I walk through the valley of the shadow of death, I will fear no evil, for you are with me; your rod and your staff, they comfort me." Operator Furgis held the pocket pad over his son's shoulder. "That's enough, Marco's starting his match introduction." Sam could hear slight laughter in the sky box as the large 3-D image of Marco De Luca started his commentary.

The forty-two-year-old man, born in the old Italian region of Earth, was wearing one of his finest suits. Marco De Luca was usually very humorous, but he started with honoring Arina Petrov. "Ladies and gentlemen, one more time for the lady with an angelic voice." The spectators stood quickly, almost jumping to their feet as they started applauding once again. Operator Furgis could feel the vibration of the stadium as the spectators grew excited and stomped their feet. He knew Supervisor Stykes had adjusted the grav net for this effect.

Marco held his hands up in a closed fist that brought silence to the stadium after several moments. His voice was cheerful and slightly teasing. "Are we ready for the match?" The spectators worked into a controllable state of frenzy, and Marco shook his fist in the air even harder as he repeated, "Are we ready?!"

Acela Vega shook her head with a laugh at Marco's performance. Huiling looked over at her, sharing a light laugh with her friend. "Marco knows how to deliver."

"He sure does," said Pastor Murray.

Marco continued. "The visiting GBers!" The spectators remained standing, cheering and chanting. "The Mars Rovers!" and more than half the spectators cheered even louder with an occasional boo as the fight droid illuminated the opening lift door on the arena floor. Red light shot up through the opening, overcoming the white light projected from the fight droid along with red sparks flying up into the dome of Delphi. A pyramid formation of Grav ballers flew straight up and hovered several meters off the closing lift door, the sparks from the grand entrance slowing as the door slid closed and the three individuals hovered in their grav suits awaiting introduction.

Marco De Luca was quick to increase the volume of the fight droid as the spectators roared with excitement. "Number three position for the Rovers, Yasin Jabir." The fight droid projected previous Grav ball matches with Jabir highlighted. Marco De Luca's projection was behind the highlight of Yasin

Jabir, and the spectators could see him smile in excitement as he continued. "Yasin Jabir, a former droid racer, is twenty-one years of age, five foot eleven, and weighing in at one hundred and sixty-five." As Marco introduced the number three Grav baller, Yasin Jabir used his Grav ball suit's gravity controls and miniature thrusters hidden in his suit to ascend straight up and slightly forward, and the spectators filled the Delphi dome with the sound of their applause.

Marco allowed the crowd to settle slightly before he started the next introduction. "Number two for the Rovers is Peter Robins. Robins is twenty-three years of age, six foot, and weighs in at one hundred and sixty." The fight droid had already replaced the highlights of Yasin Jabir with the 3-D projection of Peter Robins' Grav ball accomplishments. Robins flew straight up and joined his fellow Grav baller as Marco continued. "As a veteran of Grav balling, Peter Robins will bring a challenge to this match." After the spectators' excitement had died down slightly, he said, "Finally, we have number one for the Mars Rovers, Lewis Rogers, a twenty-four-year-old weighing in at one hundred and eighty-seven with the height of six foot two." The highlighted projection changed to a large black man in action during a previous Grav ball match. As the fight droid projected three highlights of Lewis Rogers, the Grav baller flew straight up in spinning in acrobatics; this caused the crowded stadium to erupt even louder in applause and chatter. Rogers gracefully stopped slightly above and in front of his fellow Grav ballers and started a slow descent until gently landing on the arena floor in formation.

The large 3-D projection of Marco De Luca hovered over the Mars Rovers like a giant moving statue. His arms were wide with open palms as he said, "The Mars Rovers," and the stadium went into a frenzy once again. Marco clasped his hands behind his back and smiled as he waited for the spectators in the Delphi dome's stadium to calm enough to continue. The fight droid illuminated another lift in white light opposite of where the Rovers stood, and the light from the sliding lift door that was opening illuminated straight up in a deep blue color. Lightning bolts shot straight up out of the widening opening of the sliding lift door, and the pyramid formation of three Grav ballers immediately appeared, quickly rising until they were high above the arena floor and in the middle of the lightning bolts, which slowly came to a stop as the lift doors started sliding closed.

The spectators vibrated the Delphi dome again with their excitement as they continued with cheers and loud chatter. The three new grav ballers hovered in the air, their Grav baller suits hiding the miniature thruster packs and anti-gravity devices that allowed them to fly in their formation. Marco was already gesturing with an open hand toward the three new Grav ballers who entered the arena in a magnificent display of showmanship, and his voice grew excited and louder to overcome the spectators. "Neptune One's Grav ballers." Marco paused once again to allow the spectators to enjoy the moment. "The Poseidons." The spectators cheered continually as the Poseidons hovered above the arena floor.

Marco started the individual introductions along with the changing scenes of each Grav baller's prior matches. His voice was loud and exciting, causing the spectators to maintain their own excitement. "Number three for the Poseidons— Ron Curtis, a former GB'er from Lunar One, now defends the honor of Neptune One." The highlighted scenes from Ron Curtis's prior matches started with his Lunar One matches before his Neptune One matches, but the excitement level didn't change with the different uniforms.

Marco continued. "A twenty-three-year-old weighing one hundred and seventy at the height of six foot one, Ron is definitely ready for this match." Curtis, a dark-haired white man, ascended higher with a quick burst before slowly lowering to a height right below his fellow Grav ballers. The fight droid quickly changed the highlights of previous matches projected in the air above the arena floor to the next Grav baller for Neptune One's Poseidons. A medium height and medium built black woman was projected in front of Marco's projection; this woman was very forceful and the spectators would add oohs and ahs to when the scene revealed some very aggressive moves.

The crowd joined Marco in a stunned vocal outburst as the projection showed the woman shoulder slam an opponent from slightly below their level and intercept the three-inch-diameter metal grav ball.

"We all know this will be a very exciting match when Poseidon's number two joins the fun," Marco continued. One of the most famous Grav ballers flew straight up and stopped slightly higher than Ron Curtis's previous level. She was graceful, and her arms went straight up as she stopped with open palms. The toes of her Grav boots pointed down, causing the thrusters of her feet to display a vapor distortion. The stadium was in a frenzy as she descended.

"Ladies and gentlemen, Nora Jackson—or, as some like to call her, Juno Jackson." Marco continued as the crowd slightly settled. "At twenty-two years of age, one hundred and fifty-one pounds, and a height of five-eleven, this young lady will bring some moves to this match." Nora Jackson bowed.

Raynor Furgis leaned sideways. "Babe, that woman will cost you the match." Her husband continued to watch the arena floor with a smile.

"What's with the Juno thing, Pops?" Sam asked, but before Ken could answer, Raynor laughed. "It's supposed to be some Nubian queen thing."

Dr. Cole turned and said, "Sam, it's the name of Jupiter's wife and the goddess of marriage."

"Knock it off," said Ray. "There are no Jupiter gods or other mythical chariot gods flying through space or whatever."

"Right on, Mom, GF," said Sam. His mother nodded with a grin.

Dr. Cole asked Duncan Jennings, "What's GF?" and Duncan shrugged his shoulders.

Raynor leaned forward. "God first, the One true God."

Operator Furgis smiled, shaking his head. "Guys, Marco's almost done," and they turned their attention back to the arena.

Marco had already started the final introduction. "Ali Fisher." The fight droid changed the 3-D highlighted projection to Ali's previous matches. "At twenty-six years of age, five foot ten, and weighing one hundred and forty-six, do not let this young lady fool you. She is a veteran of Grav ball, the best number one the Poseidon's ever seen." The green-eyed white woman flew straight up, spinning around and stopping with a somersault. The crowded stadium erupted even louder with cheers and an occasional boo as Ali Fisher finished her display of gravity flying and slowly descended to the arena floor; her fellow Grav ballers joined her descent as she slowly passed them.

Both Grav baller teams stood in a triangular formation, each facing each other at their ends of the arena, where the goals would be projected and moving in an erratic pattern. The 3-D image of Marco De Luca waited for the Grav ballers to turn and face the VIP sky boxes. "This match's statutes will be addressed by Operator Furgis," and his image disappeared.

Operator Furgis stood and approached the main vid com in his sky box, while his 3-D image appeared standing in the middle of the arena. He spread his arms wide with open palms. "Ladies and gentlemen, guests of Neptune One, I welcome the Rovers. They honor us with their outstanding Grav ball skills." The Rovers glided forward, using their thruster suits, and all three floated slightly off the arena floor in their deep red uniforms, with the shield and arrow symbol of the Roman god of war on the upper left chest hiding the anti-gravity and thruster devices needed for Grav ball.

Operator Furgis gestured to the Poseidons to move forward, and the station's three Grav ballers rose slightly off the arena floor and started a slow move toward the VIP sky boxes. The crowded stadium cheered and chanted for the Poseidons in their deep blue uniforms with a large pitchfork on the left chest. The forks on their uniforms were curved, unlike the pitchfork symbol of Neptune One with straight forks. As they came to a stop and bowed, Operator Furgis continued. "If both teams would please take their positions…" His hands turned into fists with bent elbows followed by a very loud "…it will begin!" The crowd went wild as the Grav ballers shot straight up and over to their starting positions.

Both sides hovered in their assigned positions of one defensive GB'er and two offensive, and Operator Furgis started the traditional rule countdown. "This cycle's regulations are as follows. The droid chose to shorten the arena to fifty meters." The crowd responded with shouts of approval. A shorter arena meant more contact between GB'ers.

Operator Furgis continued. "The target ring chosen will be four feet," and the fight droid projected a floating projection of a four-foot-diameter ring changing colors at random. "The travel of the target ring was chosen to be fifty feet." The target rings started moving randomly in a fifty-foot circumference.

The spectators were growing restless as they watched the Grav ballers exercising their Grav baller while hovering in their own anticipation. Operator Furgis continued without delay. "The Grav ball chosen has a five-second motion detector delay and a hit button delay of ten seconds. There will be some quick passing in this match."

The steel antigravity ball, with colors shining from the seams, would stand still for five-second intervals, allowing a GB'er only a brief moment to grab it; the color would change to the controlling team's color. As the GB'er passed the Grav ball, it would remain in flight for ten seconds before reactivating the motion detector and traveling on its own random course away from GB'ers. Operator Furgis looked down at the arena floor as a round hole appeared, and a Grav ball shot straight up and hovered for a brief moment, switching between the team's colors. It quickly turned red and traveled toward the Rovers, then swung around the team quickly before turning blue and shooting across the arena toward the Poseidons. As the ball swung around the Poseidons, Nora Jackson made an unsuccessful reach, and the Grav ball dodged her attempt, creating a mix of laughter and cheering.

The Grav ball returned to the center of the arena and hovered in front of the large 3-D image of Operator Furgis as he continued. "Are the Rovers ready?" The cheers from the spectators grew even louder as they watched the Rovers spread out. Yasin Jabir quickly backed up and kept steady pace with the moving target ring. Lewis Rogers and Peter Robins moved slightly forward and spread out to cover their territory, their knees bent along with their elbows in a stance ready for competition.

Operator Furgis turned toward the Poseidons. "Is Neptune One's team ready?" Ron Curtis flew backward in a somersault and stopped in front of the moving target ring. The crowd could not get any louder in their excitement.

Ali Fisher and Nora Jackson quickly spread out to face their opponents; their stance was quite similar. Nora was hitting her fists together as she hovered.

Operator Furgis threw his opens hands up in the air and held them steady for several moments until the spectators quieted down. "Ladies and gentlemen, I have asked Acela Vega to randomly choose tonight's victory setter." The spectators erupted again as the gorgeous Spanish woman appeared next to him. Operator Furgis laughed for a moment before holding his hands up again. "Acela, do we have an honored Grav ball fan to choose our victory set?"

"Yes, we do, Operator Furgis." Acela paused to glance at her data pad. "Tonight's victory setter is Polly P." The crowded stadium cheered, but the fight droid could not locate Polly P in the stadium.

Raynor leaned forward and spoke softly to her son. "We know where she's at," causing Kelly to laugh.

The fight droid turned red for a brief moment, with a chime that echoed throughout the Delphi dome. Operator Furgis turned once again to Acela Vega. Her 3-D projection smiled over the stadium. "Polly P is not present." Acela glanced at her data pad as the chatter from the spectators quieted. "Therefore we have another victory setter." She looked over the quiet stadium with amusement. Marco De Luca was not the only senior staff member who knew how to create a grandiose delivery. Acela allowed the suspense to build before she provided the much anticipated answer: "Kelly Brown!"

The fight droid's lights flew across the stadium in different directions, stopping to illuminate Operator Furgis's sky box, where Kelly sat in surprise. Acela introduced Kelly, and the image of Operator Furgis disappeared from the arena.

"Kelly Brown is visiting us from the Red planet, and we hope that she is enjoying our hospitality. It is our honor to bestow her with the choice of this match's victory set." Acela aroused the crowded stadium as she lifted her arms into the air and looked around. Operator Furgis returned to his seat and gestured to Kelly to step into view of the sky box's vid com. "You're on, Kelly." Sam Furgis nodded with a wink at Kelly as she nervously stepped into the active view of the vid com.

Chapter Eight

The standing spectators started clapping as the large 3-D image of Kelly Brown appeared next to Acela Vega's image towering over the floor of the arena. The twenty-one-year-old woman stood nervously with a slight smile as the spectators continued to clap. Acela turned to Kelly. "How is your visit, sweetheart?" The crowd quieted down to a murmur and chatter.

Kelly spoke softly. "It's okay."

Acela laughed. "Are you enjoying the astro tourney?"

"No ma'am, I'm here visiting a friend."

"Well, I hope you enjoy your stay!" As Acela looked around the stadium, Kelly answered quietly and with respect, "Yes ma'am."

Acela held her open hand out, gesturing to the hovering fight droid. "If you're ready for the victory set, just activate your data pad."

Kelly activated the transparent touch screen controls. While the data pad linked to the fight droid, Acela looked at the nervous lovely lady dressed in a button-up sweater that changed assigned colors at random. "Are we ready?" Kelly nodded and Acela repeated louder, "Are we ready?!" The crowd went into a chant. "Set, set, set." Acela winked at Kelly and nodded toward the data pad. Kelly glanced at it quickly and activated the victory set command for the fight droid. The floating sphere high above the arena floor started spinning quickly as it lowered into the center of the arena. It came to a sudden stop, and sparks flew in every direction, leaving a gigantic 3-D number projected in midair.

Acela Vega was excited and turned to Kelly. "Brothers and sisters, let's give Kelly Brown a hand for a job well done."The crowd was less enthusiastic in their applause; they thought the victory set was inadequate. The image of Kelly disappeared and she deactivated the vid com and went back to her seat in Operator Furgis's sky box. Sam laughed and teased as she sat down, but she was surprised at his mother resting her hand on her shoulder. "Well done." Raynor received a smile from her son.

Acela Vega smiled with her arms spread, palms up. "The victory number is set at three," and the spectators chattered with some booing because the followers of Grav ball knew if the victory set was high, the match would last longer.

Acela continued trying to spread more enthusiasm. "With a low victory set, this match will be more aggressive than ever as each team fights quicker to reach their victory goal of three." She was quick to keep the excitement alive. "Are we ready?" The spectators started the ranting and foot stomping throughout the stadium. "Then let the match begin!" Her 3-D image disappeared, along with the large projection of the number three when the fight droid rose higher above the arena. The grav ball's seams streamed with colors, alternating from blue to red like an ancient neon sign, and with incredible speed shot under the Rovers in a brief hover. The spectators went into another frenzy of cheering.

Pastor Murray stood quickly as he watched Lewis Rogers shoot forward with thrusters from his grav suit and make a quick capture. "That was quick!" Lewis Rogers hurled the grav ball forward in a pass toward Peter Robins. With thrusters from his grav suit, Robins quickly moved forward while turning sideways in an attempt at capturing the ball. The spectators roared, some with cheers and others with disappointment, as the ball flew past his grav suit's capture glove. Pastor Murray sat back in his seat with slight disappointment at the missed capture. The grav ball flew past Robins and regained its control as the ten-second hit button on the device delaying the motion detector reset.

Under its own control again, the ball randomly flew around the arena, dodging players as they tried to recapture and control it. As the ball turned and traveled directly toward Ali Fisher, the young woman shot forward, knowing the grav ball would change direction in an evasive attempt. She was a veteran and knew how to herd the ball, which turned in its evasion and traveled toward Nora Jackson. The very aggressive young GB'er grabbed the grav ball and spun right as Robins charged with thrusters full. The fight droid watched every detail as the mechanical device started the ten-second capture countdown. Jackson came out of her defensive spin and released the ball in a hurl toward her fellow grav baller, Fisher.

Lewis Rogers, in full flight, reached the speeding ball first and captured it as the spectators chanted his name. The fight droid reset the countdown, but it was not long before Robins flew past directly in line, giving Rogers the opportunity to pass the speeding metal ball, now glowing red to indicate the team's possession.

Operator Furgis was standing in his sky box along with his companions, and his shouts of disappointment were louder than his wife's cheers. Sam Furgis enjoyed Grav ball but found his mother and father's rivalry just as entertaining.

Nora Jackson flew in quickly and nudged Peter Robins aggressively. The fight droid followed high above, watching for fouls, and quickly determined no foul intents was displayed; however, the nudge caused Robins to change course, allowing Jackson to acquire the grav ball. She dropped down below Robins as he recovered quickly, and she shot the ball forward where Ali Fisher was quickly approaching. The ball quickly changed to the color of blue as the Poseidons took control. Fisher was quick in her capture of the floating metal ball and was just as quick to hurl it slightly backward and at a high angle as Jackson shot straight up and captured it.

Operator Furgis joined the spectators in an excited outburst. Nora Jackson spun and recovered in a horizontal flight, releasing the grav ball on a trajectory toward the target ring, estimating the travel of the target rings' movement. The crowd roared in anticipation of the first score.

Officer Armela stood and yelled, "Yes!" but both he and Supervisor Stykes were quickly disappointed as Yasin Jabir appeared in front of the speeding ball. It was a spectacular capture. The grav ball was now red as the delay forced Jabir to make a quick decision. He heard Peter Robins through his uniform's headgear, "Straight through," and Jabir moved sideways to his left, releasing the ball with his arm extended out from his side. The grav ball traveled in a left arc, and Fisher was already traveling toward her target ring with Lewis Rogers ahead and out of reach. Nora Jackson's attempt at first score took her far from her position, allowing the grav ball to travel to Peter Robins unobstructed; the only obstacle was the ten-second delay.

The spectators watched in awe as Robins captured the grav ball, still displaying the color red to designate control. He quickly released it on a course directly in front of Lewis Rogers and close to the Poseidons' target ring. Ali Fisher was horizontal in full thruster mode, struggling to close the distance between Rogers and her target ring; however, there was not enough time. The spectators gasped and grew slightly more restless as Lewis Rogers came out of a controlled flip and remained inverted as he released the grav ball. His show of skilled acrobatics was successful; Ron Curtis misjudged the ball's trajectory and made a desperate attempt at capturing it. But the crowded stadium cheered as they watched the red ball speed past Ron Curtis and fly through the Poseidons' target ring, which lit up with the color red. A loud horn was heard, followed by ancient, fast-paced organ music throughout the Delphi dome.

The grav ball slowly traveled to a position in front of the target ring and Curtis. It turned blue with a large red number one projected in 3-D floating high above the middle of the arena floor. The spectators were cheering and chanting Roger Lewis's name through the Delphi dome.

Ali Fisher and Nora Jackson slowly returned to their positions in formation, and the three Poseidon Grav ballers hovered motionless, facing their opponents. They touched the forehead of their headgear with the first two fingers of the right hand and bowed their head slowly as their two fingers extended outward in a gesture to honor their opponents' score.

Pasture Murray shouted with excitement and activated his ear com piece quickly, not waiting for a reply or acknowledgment. "First one's ours."

After a brief moment he heard a response from Operator Furgis with shouts and laughing in the background. "Well done, Pastor Murray, the first one belongs to the Rovers."

Pastor Murray put his hand on Huiling's shoulder as he stood slightly higher and behind her. "Thank you for inviting me." Huiling looked over her shoulder with a smile and rested her hand on his. The spectators settled down slightly at the quick burst from the horn. They knew the action was just starting and the Poseidons would intensify their determination. Operator Furgis smiled at his wife, and she looked quickly at him twice, not sure what type of smile he was wearing. The smile on his disappeared as the second quick burst from the horn was heard through the Delphi dome.

Ali Fisher quickly sped forward in a horizontal position, allowing her thrusters to shoot her forward on a direct path toward Lewis Rogers. Nora Jackson traveled quickly on the right side facing Peter Robins; she stopped abruptly and spun around to capture the grav ball illuminated in blue. With the delay timer activated, she needed to quickly release the device before it went into motion evidence mode. Her thrusters steered her to the left and around Peter Robins, requiring a half spin to face Ali Fisher's position, but Poseidon's number one was not there. Fisher traveled to her right side as Rogers spun backward to intercept; the fight droid sounded a horn, and the grav ball illuminated white.

The noise level intensified as the spectators stood with

cheers and boos. Engineer Trently shook his head and turned to Chief Tylor. "Penalty already?"

The chief grinned. "It is early in the match. What surprises me, Shaun, is that it's posted against the Rovers." He watched the look of realization appear on Engineer Trently as he shrugged.

The grav ball flew to a stop in the middle of the arena and hovered; the fight droid sounded the horn and projected the words "prohibited move" in 3-D above the arena floor. The words were red, and so was the name "Lewis Rogers," which appeared under the prohibited call.

Kelly listened to Raynor, who was sitting directly behind her. She leaned into Sam and spoke softly. "I don't see the issue. Lewis Rogers turned to close and blocked with thrusters. It's prohibited."

Sam laughed. "It's not only prohibited, it's also dangerous. What surprises everyone is the fact that Nora Jackson was not the first to receive a prohibit call."

They heard Duncan yell at Dr. Cole, "The wager was if Jackson got called first period, not what prohibit she got called for."

Raynor interrupted as her husband watched with a large grin. "Guys, guys…" She extended her hand, snapping her fingers. "Knock it off." They started to talk in unison but Raynor hushed them both. "I'll make a deal with both of you. If the Poseidons are victors I'll double both your credits, and if not, your wagers are void."

Duncan and Dr. Cole nodded in agreement. Raynor looked at her husband and said, "Kids." Operator Furgis's laughter was short-lived, and the fight droid sounded the horn that echoed through the Delphi dome. Instantly Ali Fisher shot from her position in the middle of the arena and captured the grav ball before the five-second evasion detector took control. The spectators roared as Fisher sped forward. The direction she chose was forward of the Rovers' target ring and slightly lower.

Yasin Jabir accelerated quickly in an intercept course, watching both the speeding Grav ball opponent and the direction of the target ring. Fisher suddenly switched course as she watched the target ring climb higher instead of the anticipated lower corner of the arena. This caused Jabir to stop instantly and change his direction; however, it was too late. Ali Fisher was close to her delayed time limit and released the grav ball in a direction just in front of the Rovers' target ring. Her task was complete, and she came to a hover in front of the Rovers' target ring area. She was still as she watched the first of the two factors needed to complete a score.

Jabir was quick but not quick enough as he reached out to capture the grav ball and with great frustration watched it speed past slightly out of reach from his capture glove.

The spectators roared with cheers and started chanting Ali Fisher's name as the grav ball flew through the traveling target ring, causing it and the target ring to turn blue. The scoring horn and the fast-paced organ music followed. Fisher returned to her formation's position, as did the other grav ballers. The fight droid projected an image of the number one in red on the Rovers' side and the number one in blue on the Poseidons' side.

Pastor Murray activated his ear com and contacted Operator Furgis, who said, "It's even, Don, and I think we'll get the next two scores for a complete victory."

Pastor Murray chuckled. "We'll give you that one because of the prohibited move, but I think you're going to be disappointed, Ken. Remember grief share." Operator Furgis laughed and both individuals returned their attention to the arena.

The Rovers stared at the Poseidons, both teams in formation, and the crowded stadium started cheering louder when they witnessed the three Rovers touch their foreheads with two fingers and then raise the same fingers high in a salute.

Hui Yan turned to Pastor Murray. "Pastor, why do you use your assigned ear piece when you have the new ear com implant?"

"Just being courteous, Hui Yan. I'll reactivate the implant when we're back on the *King David*." Pastor Murray looked back at the arena as the grav ball started spinning. All six grav ballers leaned slightly forward with bent knees, knowing the spinning ball would start moving quickly when the spinning came to a stop. The spectators watched in anticipation, and the grav ball stopped and shot sideways before making a ninety-degree turn toward Ali Fisher.

Fisher used her thrusters to quickly move sideways, with her capture glove extended in anticipation; however, the spectators roared as the grav ball's motion detector evaded the grav baller and turned with an upward motion to shoot above Nora Jackson. The ball was now on a direct course toward Peter Robins, who decided to use the herding tactic and give his teammate Lewis Rogers a chance. Robins was quick to fly toward the left side of the quickly approaching ball, causing it to change course toward the right side where Lewis Rogers was waiting. He quickly extended his capture glove and gained control of it. Rogers released the red ball in an attempt at passing to Peter Robins.

The grav ball's hit button was activated by Rogers' capture glove, which caused the start of the ten-second delay and allowed a successful pass to Robins. Nora Jackson realized before the pass was completed that she was too far out of range for an interception and used her thrusters to move backward in a defensive mode. She glanced over at Fisher and said, using her helmet's intercom, "Ready, Ali? Peter's going to try an under pass." Fisher was ready, with elbows bent and eyes watching both Lewis Rogers approaching fast and Peter Rogers spinning around Nora Jackson on the far side. Robins changed the direction of his spin abruptly and emerged facing toward Rogers; he hurled the grav ball straight for his teammate. The spectators were awed by the velocity; it seemed as if time slowed, leaving a red trail behind the grav ball. The illusion did not last long as Ali Fisher appeared quickly in front of Lewis Rogers and intercepted it.

Dr. Avers was not a Grav ball fanatic as much as her companions, and her scream of excitement shocked everyone. Seth turned to her with a laugh. "Not yet, Doctor, wait until she puts the GB through the target ring."

Dr. Avers was quick to put her hand out in front of Seth. "Okay, okay." Her attention was never diverted from the arena as she watched Ali Fisher move quickly toward the Rovers' target ring. Chayton and Marco De Luca leaned forward on the edge of their seats, cheering Fisher as she quickly released the grav ball; they watched Nora Jackson with a distortion in the air behind her as her thrusters used full force to propel her rapidly down the right side of the arena.

Jackson captured the grav ball and changed course for the center of the target rings' travel zone; she was quick to release the ball in a direction across the arena toward the left side as Yasin Jabir appeared in front of her. The false intent worked well. Fisher was moving quickly up the left side, followed by Lewis Rogers in an attempt at catching his opponent. The grav ball flew directly in front of Fisher, giving her the perfect opportunity to challenge the target ring. Her body became upright quickly and went into a spin. The grav ball was struck by Fisher's command glove, forcing it to change direction at an incredible rate of speed, heading for the center of the Rovers' target ring.

Yasin Jabir shot forward in a horizontal position, both his capture glove and his command glove extended in a desperate attempt at stopping the grav ball from entering his team's traveling target ring. He was too late as the grav ball sped by at an alarming rate; his body, in the horizontal position, rotated to watch the passing blue ball. As Jabir returned to the vertical position, he watched the grav ball fly through the outside part of the target ring and turn white as the floating device took control of its own direction. The spectators ranted and chanted with cheers and boos.

Operator Furgis was not pleased. He looked at Duncan and Dr. Cole and said, "Darn it, we almost had another."

Raynor grabbed her husband's arm. "Sit back down. You knew it was not going to happen."

Operator Furgis gave his son a friendly smack in the head to stop his laughing.

The grav ball, displaying white lines at the octagon seams,

traveled quickly and closer to the center of the arena as it evaded both the Poseidons and Rovers, coming to a complete stop. The closest Grav baller was Lewis Rogers, who was closing the distance, causing the motion detectors programmed into the grav ball to move with evasive tactics. It flew across the arena and was captured by Peter Robins with a burst of speed that shot him straight up into the grav ball's path. Robins quickly hurled the ball in front of Lewis Rogers's path as he informed him of his move through his helmet's ear com.

Ali Fisher was in full flight, shooting across the arena toward her opponent Lewis Rogers; she was far behind but traveling fast, knowing both Rovers were closing on Ron Curtis. Rogers knew Fisher was approaching quickly; the red indicator dot designating an opponent was flashing rapidly in his heads-up display. There was no ear com requirement between Lewis Rogers and Peter Robins; they knew each other's style extremely well, and instinctively Rogers released the ball toward Robins' flight path. Nora Jackson called out, "Ron, I'm coming up the right!" She was aggressive, causing Robins to capture the grav ball and move sideways toward the right where Ron Curtis was waiting.

The crowded stadium roared with excitement as Robins released the ball at an incredible speed toward the anticipated path of the Poseidons' traveling target ring. The ball instantly changed from red to blue as Curtis easily extended his capture glove and acquired the steel ball. The spectators once again roared with excitement, chanting Ron Curtis's name. Curtis hurled the grav ball toward the right side of the Rovers' target ring travel area. Curtis was allowed an extended capture time but decided to keep the ball in action as he witnessed Nora Jackson traveling quickly face-up toward the Rovers' score zone.

Peter Robins attempted to recapture the grav ball, but there was too much distance and he was forced to watch the ball pass toward Nora Jackson's position. With his thrusters in full force, he was determined to catch up with the action. Jackson captured the grav ball and without hesitation release it toward the flight path of Ali Fisher. Lewis Rogers was traveling in the horizontal position above and slightly behind Fisher, both pushing the limits of their Grav ball suits as the ball shot directly in front of her for an easy capture. Rogers watched the white dot in his helmet's display emerge with the blue dot designating Ali Fisher as she quickly vanished from his line of sight.

Fisher captured the grav ball with precision, she rolled up and over the quickly approaching Rogers, and straightened into a horizontal position. She wasted no time and released the ball on a direct course for the Rovers' target ring that was close to her side of the travel zone.

Operator Furgis jumped out of his chair, joining his companions in their excitement. "Yeah!" He grabbed his wife's shoulder a bit too hard, and Raynor pulled his hand off her shoulder as she watched the blue sphere quickly travel toward the opening of the Rovers' target ring.

With a burst of speed, Jabir appeared, traveling fast to intercept the grav ball; the spectators grew almost silent with the fast-paced action of the match, almost freezing in time as Jabir's capture glove struck the ball.

Operator Furgis's mouth was open in disappointment, and his wife held his shoulder tightly as they watched from their sky box with their companions, also caught up in the excitement.

Nora Jackson appeared a slight distance in front of Yasin Jabir, and with a quick display of acrobatics, she spun, striking the grav ball and changed its direction in an instant. The ball quickly sped past Jabir, slightly out of reach, and the spectators roared as they watched it close the distance toward the Rovers' target ring.

Jabir was in the horizontal position, extending both his capture glove and his command glove toward the grav ball. Operator Furgis joined his companions and the roaring crowd as they watched the ball enter the target ring and fly through the center, the ball displaying the color blue through its seams, turned white. The fight droid following the action of the match high above, close to the star-filled, transparent dome, sounded the horn designating the score.

The organ music started playing and echoed through the Delphi dome as the Grav ballers returned to their formation positions. Raynor grinned and shook her head as she watched her husband display his pleasure with the Poseidons' score, Operator Furgis tapped his ear com piece and stared at Dr. Cole and his good friend Duncan Jennings while he connected with Pastor Murray.

"Good shot from Nora Jackson, Ken." Furgis could hear the pastor's enjoyment in his voice.

"One more, sir, and the Poseidons win."

Pastor Murray replied with enthusiasm, "We'll see," and the vid com shut down.

The grav ball returned to hover in the center of the arena as the organ music stopped and the fight droid projected the 3-D image of a number two in blue on the Poseidons' side and a red number one on the Rovers' side. The Rovers extended the traditional honoring of a scoring opponent.

The horn sounded and the grav ball, displaying white, raced across the arena toward the Poseidons, dodging Ali Fisher with a course change that took it directly toward Ron Curtis. His capture glove extended and quickly secured the octagon sphere, which now turned blue. He hurled it in front of Nora Jackson, who flew forward with her thrusters on full; she stooped quickly as she captured the grav ball and spun around, watching the red dot in her helmet's heads-up designating Peter Robins' quick approach. Jackson called out, "Back!" and slung up above Robins, their helmets almost touching. She released the ball on a backward course and straightened out from her maneuver.

Ali Fisher was already in position, traveling quickly toward the grav ball in a race with the ten-second delay and Lewis Rogers. The blue ball entered Fisher's capture glove, and she used her thrusters to move sideways, evading Rogers and accelerating quickly toward the Rovers' score zone. The spectators cheered loudly, aware that the next score from the Poseidons would be a victory set and end the match.

Fisher released the grav ball toward Nora Jackson, who was on the right side of the arena and rapidly approaching the Rovers' target rings travel zone. Yasin Jabir watched his heads-up display, acknowledging the position of his opponents as the ball shot from Jackson's command glove with fury.

Lewis Rogers flew around Ali Fisher as they struggled for position, Nora Jackson back flying toward her quickly approaching opponent. Yasin Jabir did not make the same mistake that cost the Rovers the last score; this time he took complete control of the grav ball as it came to a stop and rested in his capture glove.

The spectators sounded disappointed at the capture, along with Operator Furgis. Raynor Furgis, however, was excited. "Yes! That's my man!" causing the people in the sky box to quickly look at her with a surprised expression. Raynor put her hand on the back of her husband's head and spoke softer. "You know what I mean." Operator Furgis was about to respond, but the action in the arena took precedence as he watched Yasin Jabir.

The grav ball shot from the Rovers' score zone toward Nora Jackson as she traveled backward, watching the ball. Jabir was instructing Peter Robins on his direction of release. Robins was already extending his capture glove, knowing almost immediately the grav ball would be in reach for capture, but he was forced to fly sideways as Jackson spun to face the direction of her flight and hit him on the side. The ball turned white at the octagon-shaped seams and stopped in a rapidly spinning hover. The fight droid sounded a horn and projected "prohibited maneuver" in blue and then switched to Nora Jackson's name. The spectators in the stadium roared with chatter and boos. The grav ball stopped spinning and slowly traveled to the center of the arena, followed by both the Poseidons and Rovers entering a formation for a penalty shot.

Raynor leaned over to her husband. "I told you Jackson is too aggressive." Operator Furgis chuckled. "It's all right," he replied, "Ron Curtis is the best." He motioned at the arena with his hand.

Peter Robins took his position to attempt the penalty score against Ron Curtis; his helmet displayed the indicators of all Grav ballers, and he knew if he did not score, Ron Curtis could put the ball into instant action toward the Rovers' target area. The fight droid sounded the horn, and Robins shot forward after a quick capture of the grav ball, now displaying the color red. Curtis watched Robins carefully and matched his moves; his heads-up display indicated the position and direction of travel of the Poseidons' target ring. Robins tried several false moves to evade Ron Curtis, but the ten-second delay was started immediately after capture of the ball.

The red ball shot toward the Poseidons' target ring at incredible speed as Robins released it. He shot backward, his suit's thrusters in full, knowing that Ron Curtis would not delay sending the octagon sphere toward Ali Fisher or Nora Jackson.

Operator Furgis jumped up out of his chair, joining his companions and spectators in the excitement. "Yes, send it to Nora!" His wife joined in. "Lewis, get over there," and the others ranted and raved but were not heard over the senior Furgises.

Ron Curtis called out, "Nora, go far!" He knew Peter Robins would need time to recover from his shot, and in the fast-paced action of Grav ball, that small amount of time could cost.

The blue ball flew down the right side of the arena on course to Nora Jackson and a prepared Yasin Jabir. Jackson watched her heads-up display and twisted at the precise moment to capture the grav ball before the timer allowed it to regain control of its own course. Jackson straightened out and flew in a horizontal position toward the waiting Grav baller in the Rovers' score zone, and with the ten-second timer almost elapsed, she spun and shot the ball back to Ali Fisher.

Lewis Rogers struggled to close the distance with Fisher but continued to stay an arm's reach behind. Nora Jackson was already in position in front of the Rovers' score zone, watching her display and listening for Fisher. "Straight up, Nora, take it home!" The dot in Jackson's helmet turned white as it approached her quickly. She spun with her capture glove extended and continued to spin as the grav ball landed in her capture glove; in mid-spin she switched the ball to her command glove and hurled the it toward the anticipated target ring as she came out of her spin. The spectators roared once again, but Yasin Jabir now commanded their attention as he swiftly flew directly in front of the target ring and caused the grav ball to switch to the color red as it entered his capture glove.

Ali Fisher now struggled for position with Lewis Rogers as he caught up to her position, both in a backward thrust. The spectators started cheering for their different favorites, causing a distorted chant as they waited to see what Yasin Jabir would do with the grav ball. Peter Robins shot into the unobstructed opening in the middle of the arena and was followed closely by Nora Jackson. Robins called out, "Open" and watched the grav ball shoot directly at his position as it was quickly released from Jabir's command glove.

Operator Furgis was standing next to his new wife, and both were shouting at the action until Operator Furgis lost interest and grew completely serious. The sky box's vid com lit up in red, projecting the 3-D letters "station emergency." He sat back in his command chair and linked his ear com piece with the sky box's main vid com. Everyone in the sky box sat quietly, aware that Operator Furgis now had an emergency transmission. Furgis stated, "Nature of emergency," and waited briefly in suspense for his answer: "Collision, docking sphere E." He stood quickly, switching to his ear com's general announcement. After the quick chime he contacted "engineering and security."

"Leaf, Dan, we have a collision at docking sphere E." Operator Furgis had already implemented the emergency exit procedure from the arm of his command chair and was waiting to exit.

Before Chief Tylor or Supervisor Stykes could respond, everyone in Furgis's sky box insisted on joining him, but Furgis only allowed Duncan and Dr. Cole to accompany him.

Chief Dan Tylor chimed in on Operator Furgis's ear com piece first. "Sir, Engineer Trently will be there. I'll handle the match." He knew Trently was younger and the Grav ball match was important to Neptune One's offerings of entertainment.

Leaf Stykes followed next. "Boss, I'll be there quickly. Armela will stay in the booth." The ear coms went into emergency standby mode as Dr. Cole and Duncan Jennings followed Operator Furgis into the lift. They entered the glide tube station; the claxon was sounding and the emergency lights were already flashing with the announcement for the guests. Furgis quickly approached the nearest enforcer. "Officer, these alarms are making my guests nervous. Let's get them off before we have another situation down here," and without waiting for an answer, Operator Furgis entered a waiting glide tube car. Other enforcers from Supervisor Stykes' department were already on the scene helping out. The glide tube car's door closed with a hiss, and everyone fell into seats as the car accelerated forward. Operator Furgis was on the right side of the car, and as the stars that lit up the vast universe emerged into sight from the transparent top of the docking tube, he looked out, struggling to see the area that was in trouble.

The glide tube car swiftly came to the docking spheres at the end of the docking tube, and Operator Furgis caught a glimpse of a ship with an occasional spark coming from its hull. Before the glide tube came to a complete stop in docking sphere E, the individuals in the car were already standing and waiting for the door to open. Operator Furgis did not wait for the door to completely open; he jumped from the arriving glide car quickly and headed for the sphere itself. He was impressed when he saw Dr. Brook Avers and Dr. Niclas Gerlitz's assistant standing in front of the sealed door to the docking sphere. Dr. Avers greeted him with a sigh. "Thank the Lord, Leaf just reported no injuries or fatalities, Ken." Operator Furgis answered with a sigh of relief.

Dr. Avers stepped behind Operator Furgis and quickly nodded at Duncan Jennings before hugging Dr. Cole. Furgis watched with a quick smile before returning to his serious disposition. "What is Dr. Gerlitz's assistant doing here?" Everyone grew quiet, and Dr. Gerlitz's assistant was surprised at the harsh tone. Operator Furgis held his hand out and quieted his tone slightly. "Well, sir?"

Dr. Gerlitz's assistant shook Furgis's hand and replied, "Dr. Gerlitz has a colleague on the SS *Star Traveler* who was supposed to report to Pastor Murray." It was Operator Furgis's turn to show surprise. The airlock doors hissed open quickly, allowing Engineer Trently and Supervisor Stykes to enter from the docking sphere. Operator Furgis ignored Dr. Gerlitz's assistant and looked at his two staff members now approaching. Supervisor Stykes was senior and spoke first. "Hey, boss, no injuries, and no fatalities; however, the report of a transport ship was wrong."

"Yeah, it's the SS *Star Traveler*." Supervisor Stykes did not look surprised.

Engineer Trently spoke quickly. "Sir, we have major damage to the docking sphere, and the chief has already assigned a repair team."

"What about the *Star Traveler*?" Furgis asked.

"The captain said he has minor damage and put in a repair request already," Trently responded.

Furgis chuckled and turned to Stykes. "Now for the *what happened* question."

"The guide module was defective," interrupted Trently. "I need to check out why the backups did not override."

Operator Furgis nodded. "All right, get on it." He turned to Dr. Gerlitz's assistant. "When you get back down to your lab, tell Gerlitz I want to see him, and please do not make me chime him either." He turned toward the glide car station.

As the Neptune One's docking tube returned to normal, allowing its four other docking spheres to carry the load of arriving and departing visitors, Operator Furgis joined his staff members in their wait for a glide tube car. Supervisor Stykes deactivated his ear com piece and turned to Furgis. "Boss, as soon as docking sphere D is clear, the *Star Traveler* will dock," and he turned to watch a glide tube car enter the station.

Operator Furgis allowed the doctors to enter first and followed behind. "Now for the big question."

Supervisor Stykes finally had to ask, "What is that, boss?"

Furgis continued to grin.

They could hear the glide tube car's air thrusters and feel the slight forward motion of the glide car. Operator Furgis looked at his security supervisor. "No need to check. I already know the Poseidons were victorious." His grin grew into a full smile.

The stars emerged through the transparent top of the station's long docking tube, and Stykes knew the SS *King David* could not pick up the noise from the glide tube car. But he wondered if they could focus on the vibrations from Operator Furgis as Stykes informed him of the final score.

"Boss, Officer Armela just informed me that the Poseidons remained at two, and the Rovers took the match."

"What?!"

The glide tube car was quiet as it arrived in the station.

Operator Furgis followed Dr. Avers out of the docked glide tube car, shaking his head with disbelief. "It was two to one. I can't believe it!"

Dr. Avers started laughing. "You know Pastor Murray will tell you to go to grief share at Huiling's church."

Operator Furgis frowned. Before he could answer, he heard his good friend Duncan laughing as he exited the glide tube car. Furgis looked at him with friendly aggression. "What are you laughing at? You wagered on the Poseidons."

"That's nothing compared to watching you speak with

your wife." Jennings rested his hand on Furgis's shoulder. "I'll be there for you, brother."

Operator Furgis laughed and shrugged his shoulders. He watched his companions exit the glide tube station before asking, "Duncan, are you joining us at the Solar House?" and Duncan nodded quickly with a smile. "Right behind." Furgis and Jennings left the glide tube station.

Chapter Nine

Raynor Furgis waited at her table in Seth Adams' restaurant along with her guests, waiting for Kennith Furgis to arrive. The chatter over the Grav ball match was loud, and Supervisor Stykes' enforcers patrolled the station and the crowded Solar House. Raynor looked across the table. "Pastor, what do you think about the match?"

Pastor Murray answered with his own smile, "Excellent match. I'm interested in what your husband thinks."

Huiling said, "Kelly, you were so beautiful with the victory set!"

Kelly Brown was startled, but she smiled. "Yeah, that caught me by surprise." Her companions joined in her laughter, allowing Kelly to relax.

The server arrived with the drinks ordered from the table's vid com. Hui Yan asked, "Raynor, when will you be leaving?"

Raynor looked distant for a moment. "I'll probably travel on the *Jupiter Queen*."

"It's a shame you're heading the opposite way," said Pastor Murray. "We would have enjoyed your company on the *King David*."

Raynor laughed. "WH-12 is a little bit out of the way."

Sam laughed too. "Mother, you would make a good regent

for Eos."

Kelly held her drink up high. "Here's to the Rovers!"

Raynor was quick to initiate another toast before the drinks went back on the tabletop. "Here's to the *King David*." Pastor Murray finished first and set his glass on the table, looking at Huiling with a large grin. "I see you have the station hooked on Dou Zhe." Huiling nodded at the smiling senior pastor.

Operator Furgis and Duncan Jennings approached the table followed by the two doctors; Operator Furgis sat next to his wife and watched his other companions around the table. Raynor looked at her husband with curiosity. "Where's Leaf?"

"He's in engineering with Dr. Gerlitz and Marshal Scoop." Operator Furgis paused to adjust his chair. "Where's Acela?"

Sam Furgis was quick to answer. "I asked her to continue the astro tourney."

Operator Furgis nodded in agreement, knowing he had placed his son in charge as director. He looked over at Senior Pastor Murray with a wide grin as the server placed fresh drinks in front of everyone. "Well done, sir, congratulations."

Pastor Murray nodded with a smile as he returned the gesture. "I hope you watch the vid com recording; it was a lucky break for the Rovers." Each picked up their drinks in a toast.

Operator Furgis set his drink down in front of him gently. "Don, I met Dr. Gerlitz's assistant at docking sphere E, and he said he was waiting for a colleague of the good doctor to arrive and speak with you."

Everyone at the table became tense as they waited in anticipation for Senior Pastor Murray's reply. They did not wait long as Pastor Murray remained relaxed and set his drink down. "He was supposed to report directly to the *King David*, not visit his cousin."

Operator Furgis chuckled and looked at Duncan. "That explains the resemblance."

Pastor Murray said, "Ken, the Terran Tribune decided to install Dr. Gerlitz's new weapons on the SS *King David,* and the Solar Counsel has authorized the install."

Operator Furgis nodded.

Sam Furgis spoke to Kelly Brown. "Terran Tribune, Solar Counsel—two heads to the same serpent." He looked around the table when he heard the laughter.

Pastor Murray leaned forward and rested his elbows on the table. "Son, serpents or not, they are the appointed authority and set the rules." He held his hand up to stop Sam's comment. "If you have a problem with this, just remember who you're really serving and what his commands are."

"Well said, Pastor," said Raynor as she hugged her son with one arm.

Operator Furgis nodded. "Very well, Pastor, I appreciate your honesty; however, I need to inform you that Dr. Gerlitz is busy upgrading Neptune One."

"There will be no burden on your station, Ken. Dr. Hans Gerlitz will perform all the necessary work."

The mood around the table started to relax. Operator Furgis was curious. "Don, does your Gerlitz know about the Eastern Empire's attempts at stealing the Mortelis cannon? Do you need more security? I can ask."

"No need, sir, the *King David* is aware and taking precautions."

Raynor laughed as she leaned toward her husband. "Ken, I have a feeling the *King David* could put the *Essex* or the *Staton* to shame at the same time." Operator Furgis nodded and picked his drink up for a toast.

Engineer Trently walked down the docking tube and entered the newly refitted *Research One* shuttle; he looked around at the new equipment and the crew of the small vessel. Dr. Gerlitz and his assistant were in the cockpit while an engineer, Marshal Scoop, and Supervisor Stykes were at the engineering and weapons station. Engineer Trently walked up to Supervisor Stykes and said softly, "I still can't believe the chief authorized a close test like this."

Stykes turned to answer but was interrupted by an excited Dr. Gerlitz from the cockpit. "He did and we are, so get ready, Engineer Trently. I could use your help on this one."

Marshal Scoop laughed. As Trently relieved his fellow engineer, Scoop exited the small vessel. Stykes patted Trently on the shoulder. "We'll be in operations if you need anything." Trently frowned as Stykes followed Marshal Scoop out of the craft.

The hiss of the airlock sealing behind the departing personnel from *Research One* was heard loudly through the small vessel, and the caution lights could be seen through the cockpit window as the systems of the research shuttle came to life. Dr. Gerlitz swung his navigations chair around to look back into the interior of the research shuttle. "Engineer, are we ready?"

Engineer Trently responded immediately, "Yes sir, all systems ready."

Dr. Gerlitz turned his navigations seat forward. The sound of the docking tube releasing its hold on the small vessel echoed through both compartments. The pilot activated the navigation thrusters, causing the small vessel to lift slightly and allowing the landing struts to retract into the under hull of *Research One* .

The cautionary lights were more visible and the warning sound was heard as *Research One* floated at its berth; the small vessel hovered as the crew adjusted the systems. The pilot worked the transparent touch screen controls, instructing the small craft to move sideways and align its course with the opening hangar bay doors. Dr. Gerlitz was always slightly nervous; however, the sixty-seven-year-old man from the old German country was more so on this trip. Trently sat at his engineering console and watched the scientist instruct the pilot with hand and arm movements. The pilot acted like Dr. Gerlitz was not in the cockpit as he worked the touch screen controls, instructing the small vessel's thrusters to propel the research shuttle slowly forward. Engineer Trently returned his attention to his console as *Research One* lifted higher and its nose lowered slightly.

As *Research One* slowly increased speed, the hangar doors became larger through the cockpit window, and Dr. Gerlitz's assistant maintained an accurate speed, allowing the opening doors that parted Neptune's pitchfork time for safe passage. Trently remain somewhat concerned for this experimental test; he knew if the light armor on *Research One* was struck by discharge from the Mortelis cannon, the shuttle may not survive. Several other smaller and medium-sized ships were seen through the porthole as *Research One* neared the opening hangar bay doors; Engineer Trently was entranced by stars shining through the growing passage. The chime of the vid com on his engineering console snapped him back to reality as a small 3-D image of the chief appeared.

Engineer Trently had always respected Chief Tylor, a fifty-seven-year-old man with the same ancestral roots. He could not help but grin after noticing the chief had gained some weight.

"What's so funny, Engineer?" said the Chief. "Get serious out there."

Trently lost his grin instantly and replied in a more serious manner. "Yes sir."

The chief continued. "I'm joining Supervisor Stykes and the marshal in operations. There's a small asteroid slowly making its way into an approach zone."

"No need to send a team out, Chief. We'll take care of it."

The chief nodded as the vid com shut down.

Dr. Gerlitz spoke loudly over his shoulder. "Tell the chief I'll take care of his rock."

Engineer Trently looked at the pilot, grinning as *Research One* exited through the hangar bay doors into the Neptune sector of the solar system. *Research One* climbed steeply and turned slowly toward the side of the station. Dr. Gerlitz grew a little concerned, "Take it easy," and Trently knew the pilot wanted to stay close to the station and rise above the Delphi dome in order to check for any ships not on the flight schedule. As the small research vessel climbed, the view of the big blue planet was breathtaking.

Dr. Gerlitz chuckled as he spoke into his vid com. "Remember those trips, Trently?" Engineer Trently's attention became more in tune with his surroundings as he recalled the flights into Neptune's atmosphere with Dr. Gerlitz.

Several ships were docked with Neptune One's docking spheres, including the SS *Star Traveler,* and Trently could see the engineering repair crew working alongside the maintenance droid on the damaged docking sphere. Even more impressive were the massive rings suspended around the giant blue planet. Close by was one of the giant satellites. Triton was a lucrative mining colony and provided different types of ore and precious metal. Engineer Trently activated the troposcope for a long-range sweep of the sector; the vid com interpreted the data from the troposcope and displayed the information on the now active transparent touch screen console in front of him. Trently called out the findings. "We're clear, Dr. Gerlitz. The chief's rock is in the approach zone but no traffic in the area." The only response he heard was a small grunt as the shuttle turned and commenced a slow nose dive.

Research One started a slow spiral down as it steadied into a pitch toward the bottom of the station where Dr. Gerlitz's Mortelis cannon was previously installed. As the small research shuttle approached its final destination, Engineer Trently passed his hands over the touch screen control console and initiated the link between *Research One* 's main vid com and the MC. The engineering station's vid com chimed and the 3-D image of Chief Tylor was projected on the engineering station's vid com. The chief's heavy English accent demanded immediate attention.

"Shaun, we're clear up here."

Engineer Trently turned his head to look up into the cockpit, his English accent not as heavy as the chief's. "Dr. Gerlitz, we have a test link, and the chief authorized the rock for a test target." He waited.

After watching the back of Dr. Gerlitz's navigation chair, Trently was rewarded with a chuckle as a fist with a thumb up appeared. The cockpit and rear cabin of *Research One* turned yellow with cautionary lighting as the small vessel very slowly started to back away from the large bluish-white dome attached to the very bottom of Neptune One. Engineer Trently instructed his chair to face forward and watched the MC gain slight distance from the small vessel. "Dr. Gerlitz, your MC can put out a very high amount of electrical calories. Don't you think we should increase our distance?"

"No need, Shaun, we're only testing at half power."

Engineer Trently activated the research shuttle's vid com on the engineering console to contact Chief Tylor, who asked, "Shaun, how's it look out there?"

Trently replied, "Everything's a go, Chief."

The chief was silent for a moment before replying, "Ops shows *Research One* a little close."

"Dr. Gerlitz said we're only testing at half power." Trently could see the look of concern on the chief, who looked down at a data pad and said, "All right, Shaun, but I want you to check the plating on the shuttle. If you get hit with a partial discharge, you'll have approximately three million large calories striking the shuttle."

Engineer Trently nodded. "Ten-four, Chief. I'll let you know when the check's done." The vid com deactivated.

Dr. Gerlitz turned his chair around impatiently. "Engineer Trently, are we ready yet?"

Trently looked forward from his engineering console. "No sir, I need to check the armor plating first, or you need to give me more distance."

"The station's trop is showing long-range traffic coming our way." Dr. Gerlitz returned his chair to face forward with forced patience. After a brief moment he received the answer he was waiting for, and Engineer Trently called out loudly, "Armor plating is good, engineering is all set; on your command, Doctor."Trently did not have to see Dr. Gerlitz directly to know he was grinning with pride.

Dr. Gerlitz worked his touch screen controls carefully to acquire the large rock slowly moving into the approach zone; the target was still beyond visual range. *Finally,* he thought.

Dr. Gerlitz smiled at his assistant and looked down at his touch screen console; he activated the initiation command and "fire" echoed through *Research One* . Inside, the small research shuttle lit up brightly as a bluish-white cloudy ball shot from the dome at an incredible speed. The crew of *Research One* felt slight heat from the discharge but were hypnotized by the incredible sight. The glowing cloudy ball traveled quickly, almost instantly, to its designated target, leaving a slight sparkle in its path that quickly faded. The energy discharge impacted the large rock with fury.

Several small rock fragments emerged from the bright light where the large space rock was slowly traveling, and sparks erupted in all directions as the explosion expanded instantly on impact. After a brief moment Dr. Gerlitz called back to Engineer Trently, "Data," and Trently shook off the awe he was enveloped in. Turning back to his engineering console, he quickly worked the touch screen controls, sending the incoming data to Dr. Gerlitz's navigation console. Dr. Gerlitz's assistant piloting *Research One* hovered the small shuttle behind the Mortelis cannon as Dr. Gerlitz looked over the data. He spun his chair around and looked at Engineer Trently with a questionable look.

Engineer Trently finished working his console and turned to see the doctor staring at him. He shrugged with his own questionable look. "What is it, Doctor?" and Dr. Gerlitz smiled before answering.

"Engineer Trently, why do you think this particular rock was volatile?" He watched Engineer Trently think.

It did not take very long for Trently to analyze the question. "The rock was BVR, so without a visual inspection and only relying on the results of impact, I would say the rock held traces of magnesium four."

Dr. Gerlitz continued his questioning. "And where is it possible a rock containing mag four came from?"

Engineer Trently thought. Suddenly he blurted out, "The Kuiper belt!"

"And why would a large rock with mag four reach our sector, Engineer?"

"They hit a large amount on a larger rock and demoed; this one probably got away in the explosion." Engineer Trently was interrupted by the vid com chime. He was quick to watch the data and did not bother to turn to Dr. Gerlitz as he relayed the information. "Dr. Gerlitz, the trop is done collecting and analyzing, sir. I'll send it to your navigation's vid com."

Dr. Gerlitz nodded as he watched the data appear on his touch screen console. "Thank you, Engineer." He continued to study the data. After a brief moment he looked up at his assistant. "Laying in a course for the KD...sorry, I mean the *King David*."

His assistant laughed. "Yeah, they get touchy over the name of their ship."

Without warning Engineer Trently felt the small shuttle's

movement. He turned his engineering console's chair to face forward and said, "Sir, we're expected back in the hangar bay. Why are we headed for the *King?*" He waited as *Research One* turned toward port and slightly rose until the SS *King David* appeared in the distance through the cockpit.

Dr. Gerlitz was quick and sharp in his answer. "I have someone I need to speak with. Let ops know we'll be delayed." Engineer Trently stared at the SS *King David* through the cockpit in silence. Dr. Gerlitz turned to his assistant, "Make it a slow approach," and activated his ear com piece. "Dr. Gerlitz, SS *King David,*" and another quick chime was heard. He watched the SS *King David* grow larger as they slowly approached the rear of the massive ship. He was ready to bark more orders at his assistant when he received a reply from his ear com piece. "Niclas, is that you flying around out there?"

Engineer Trently sat quietly watching as Dr. Gerlitz returned the greeting with passion. "Hans, it's been too long." The smile grew larger on his face. The pilot of *Research One* nodded and pointed at the rear of the SS *King David*. Dr. Gerlitz returned the nod. "Hans, we're approaching the rear, and I have a small gift for you."

"You're cleared, Nic." The pilot maneuvered above an opening door on top of the SS *King David*. *Research One* slowly lowered into the opening on the back of the SS *King David*, and the red lights from the hangar deck lit up the inside of the small shuttle. As *Research One* hovered and the landing struts extended, the small vessel set down with a docking tube extending to the air hatch, and the lights were now flashing yellow. Dr. Gerlitz swung his chair around quickly without the use of the chair's mechanical controls. He faced a very curious and concerned engineer, and before Engineer Trently could ask, Dr. Gerlitz stood and moved to the rear cabin of *Research One* . He put his hand on Engineer Trently's shoulder as he tried to rise from his engineering chair. "We'll wait here." The doctor moved to the airlock touch screen control panel next to the hatch way. A loud chime was heard, followed by a female voice, "Request entry." Dr. Gerlitz did not hesitate and worked the console, allowing the entry hatch to open.

Engineer Trently watched an older man he estimated to be in his mid-sixties enter the shuttle. The man hugged Dr. Gerlitz quickly before offering his greeting. "Nic, how long has it been?"

"Hans, it's been too long."

Engineer Trently noticed the old German accent became more heavy as the two almost identical men spoke. Dr. Gerlitz moved back slightly and gestured with his hand. "Hans, this is a friend, Engineer Shaun Trently."

Dr. Hans Gerlitz extended his hand. "How do you do, sir?" and as Trently accepted the offer, Dr. Niclas Gerlitz continued. "Shaun, this is my cousin, Dr. Hans Gerlitz." Trently returned the greeting. "Very well, sir, and yourself?"

Hans looked at his cousin. "Not sure yet," he said and waited.

Niclas handed a data pad to his cousin. "I think you're doing fine, Hans. Install these commands and you're all set."

Hans nodded with a smile as he looked up at the cockpit. "Hey, young man, how are you doing?"

Dr. Gerlitz's assistant was already watching the individuals in the rear cabin. "Very good, sir." Engineer Trently thought this was weird; he was younger than Dr. Gerlitz's assistant. Hans turned in the entry hatch. "Nic, when we go through the

Kuiper belt, I'll say hello to Terry for you."

Niclas was amused. "Tell him he still owes me from the last poker match," and Hans laughed before shaking his head and exiting the shuttle. "You still remember that!"

Dr. Niclas Gerlitz activated the airlock's touch screen control panel and the hatch slide closed. The inside of *Research One* was bright from the yellow flashing warning lights, and his assistant worked the control panel and prepared the small shuttle for launch from the SS *King David*.

Engineer Trently waited until Dr. Gerlitz was strapped into his chair. "Are we heading back to Neptune One, sir?"

Dr. Gerlitz could hear the concern in his voice. "Yes, we are, Engineer, and if your superior has any questions about our delay he can ask Governor Davis. This trip was authorized by Dr. Bauer from the Terran science council." The inside of *Research One* turned red as the hangar doors on the SS *King David* slid open. The shuttle gently floated off its skid pads, allowing them to retract inside the small vessel's hull, and Engineer Trently sighed as he felt a slight tilt of the ship and watched the scenery pass the cockpit window as they lined up for a vertical exit from the massive ship.

Trently turned his head once again to watch the stars emerge into view as the shuttle exited the hangar bay. The pilot initiated low power to the thrusters, causing the shuttle to move forward at a degree, steering clear of the numerous coning towers of the SS *King David*, Neptune One appearing in the far distance from the SS *King David's* elliptical orbit. The station was discernible even from this distance. The pilot increased power to the thrusters to gain more speed, but slowed the acceleration slightly as Engineer Trently called out, "Contact on the troposcope, fifteen degrees port." He watched Dr. Gerlitz speak to the pilot but could not hear the conversation. *Research One* veered to starboard and increased speed; the other vessel was now in visual range. Trently relayed the data from his engineering console. "A medium transport cleared for docking with the cargo sphere," he said and leaned back in his chair.

The vid com chimed on the engineering console, and Trently wondered why it took so long to hear from his superiors. He smiled and accepted the transmission from Chief Tylor. "Shaun, how's it going out there?"

"Good, sir, we had to make a small visit to the *King*."

"Yeah, don't worry about that, Operator Furgis is aware. I'll talk with you when you get back." The vid com shut down.

Trently could see the data from *Research One* 's troposcope displayed on his console; the small vessel was quickly approaching Neptune One and lining up for entry through the large opening in the hangar bay.

Dr. Gerlitz's assistant slowed the speed of the small shuttle as they approached the bay. The pilot was receiving instructions from the hangar bay control room that oversaw the operations of the massive repair facilities. *Research One* glided slowly through the doors and traveled toward the center of the bay, where it turned with a slight tilt. The vapor distortion from the thrusters was visible from the hangar bay and its control room; the small vessel moved sideways slowly toward the docking tube at its assigned berth. The landing struts already extended, the pilot worked his controls with ease, his fingers gliding over the commands and instructing the shuttle to gently lower onto the landing struts and the thrusters to power down as the docking tube moved into position to greet the crew of *Research One* .

Engineer Trently stood in front of the chief's office in anticipation as he reached out and activated the door panel. When he was granted entry, he walked in and stood in front of the chief's desk. Chief Tylor gestured with an open hand. "What are you waiting for, Trently? Sit down." He did not give Engineer Trently a chance to speak; he held his hand up, stopping him before he started. "No need to worry, Shaun. This Dr. Bauer granted assistance to Pastor Murray with the *King David*. Dr. Gerlitz on the *King* has installed Mortelis-based energy weapons and required assistance from our Dr. Gerlitz with the command systems. How's *Research One* check out?"

The chief leaned back in his chair, looking at the data from his pad. Engineer Trently was more relaxed. "The shuttle checks out, and the armor plating held up pretty well to the radiation and heat from the MC." He stood and started to walk toward the chief's office door, then turned quickly back to face his superior. "Chief, I overheard Dr. Gerlitz talking with his assistant about the armor plating."

"What did you hear, Shaun?"

"His assistant said something about not requiring armor plating on *Research One* soon."

Chief Tylor chuckled, which was unusual for him. He leaned back in his chair and pointed at the empty chair in front of his desk again with an open hand. Engineer Trently accepted the invitation to sit and waited patiently, not knowing what the new information the chief offered was about and what his role would be.

"Shaun, this cannot leave my office. I was going to discuss this with you later because you will be working with Dr.

Gerlitz's assistant. You and Operator Furgis are the only others at this time aware of this." Chief Tylor quickly leaned forward and slid a data pad in front of Trently, allowing him time to study the pad. He watched Trently grin numerous times before setting the data pad back on his desk.

"Shaun, what do you think?"

Engineer Trently looked at the chief for a brief moment before replying, "Wow. Is it possible? I mean, can enough energy stop a missile's penetration even if it detonates the missile before impact?" The chief nodded, leaning back in his chair. Suddenly Trently said, "You said Dr. Gerlitz's assistant came up with this."

"He's not just his assistant, Shaun. I thought you would have figured that out by now. In any case, his assistant has developed a way to create energy shields from Mortelis, and you are to assist him."

Engineer Trently grew excited. "In any way I can. I'll talk with him immediately, Chief."

The chief nodded as Engineer Trently stood and turned toward the office doors.

Operator Furgis approached the glide tube station with his friend Duncan Jennings; they both noticed Pastor Murray and his companions speaking with Raynor and Operator Furgis's other staff. As Operator Furgis slowly approached, Pastor Murray smiled with a greeting. "Ken, I'd like to tell you what a wonderful stay we had on your station."

Operator Furgis returned the smile. "It was our pleasure, Don," and he held his hand out for final good-bye. Huiling Li released her twin sister from a hug, and with watery eyes she moved to her mentor, Pastor Donald Murray. "Pastor Murray,

I am going to kiss you with all my heart."

Pastor Murray's smile widened as he gently touched the side of her face. "It was good to see you again." He turned to enter the glide tube car after Hui Yan and then paused. He turned around quickly and approached Huiling. "I want you to have this." Pastor Murray removed a necklace from under his suit shirt and placed it around Huiling's neck.

Huiling held the crucifix in her hand as it hung from her neck. "Pastor, there's no need for this gift."

Pastor Murray turned as he entered the glide tube car. "It's made from acacia wood; hold onto it for me," and he winked before the sliding doors hissed closed.

Raynor stepped closer to Huiling. "It's beautiful. What did he say it was made from?" She held the cross, inspecting it closely.

Huiling smiled as she watched the glide tube car leave the station and start its journey down the long glide tube to the docking spheres. "Acacia wood," she said. "It's one of the Father's favorite woods." Huiling tucked the cross under her high neckline purple shirt.

Operator Furgis walked to his wife and kissed her passionately. Raynor was slightly surprised. "You usually don't do that in public," and Operator Furgis leaned into his wife's ear. "It's better than wood." Raynor started laughing. Operator Furgis looked around before asking his wife, "Where's Sam and Kelly?"

"They said they were needed in our suite."

Her husband looked at her with puzzlement. "You didn't think that was odd?"

"That's our son," she snapped. "What, you think he's

putting a surveillance droid in our rest chambers or what?"

Operator Furgis's voice softened. "No ma'am, I just thought it was odd that Sam and Kelly did not want to see the senior pastor off."

Raynor laughed. "Ken, did you or did you not assign the Mech Fight match to Sam?"

Operator Furgis nodded. "You're right, I did." He paused before looking at Duncan and shrugging his shoulders. "I just thought we had a little more time."

Duncan returned the shrug. "Don't look at me, I'm just a guest."

Operator Furgis turned to Huiling. "It's a shame Pastor Murray could not stay for the Mech fight."

Raynor Furgis joined her husband in a nod. Huiling smiled. "Pastor Murray wanted to, but the *King David* is scheduled to pick up Terry Pines, a friend of his."

Operator Furgis smiled. "We all have our responsibilities, I suppose, and speaking of which, I need to get to my suite and see what Sam's up to."

Raynor winked at Duncan quickly. Duncan grabbed his friend by the shoulder and squeezed. "We need to get to the solar pit first and see who won Acela's astro tourney."

Raynor spoke quickly. "Yeah, Acela's getting ready to announce the winner," and the three followed Operator Furgis out of the glide tube station.

Acela Vega stood at the solar pit's podium operating the touch screen display from the vid com. The noise in Neptune One's casino area was loud, and Acela did not hear Operator Furgis enter the pit and stand behind her. He put his hand gently on her shoulder, and she was slightly startled. Acela completed the data entry on her display and turned to Operator Furgis; she noticed Raynor was standing behind him, but Duncan was sitting at an old-style blackjack vid com table. A surveillance droid revealed itself high above the solar pit podium. Acela Vega reached her ear com piece and activated the device. "Ladies and gentlemen." The droid was loud and the crowded casino's chatter grew quieter. "We have the results of the first Astro Tournament. Would the second winner of the tourney please approach?" She paused to create more excitement before continuing. "Mrs. Alberts." A shout was heard from the crowd. Acela turned around and handed a data pad to Operator Furgis, who looked it over as a gentle older woman approached the solar pit. Operator Furgis activated his ear com piece quickly. "Mrs. Alberts, I am very pleased to present you with the astro tournament's second place award." The droid projected a 3-D image of Operator Furgis and Mrs. Alberts.

Mrs. Alberts was excited as she received the data pad from Operator Furgis; the crowded casino area started applauding with several whistles. Operator Furgis was caught off guard at Acela's push into a presentation of awards. His projected image smiled as he held his hands up to quiet the crowd. "Mrs. Alberts, would you be so kind as to inform our guests of the award?" The crowd cheered.

"Yes sir." Mrs. Alberts started reading from the data pad. "A credit-free queen suite accompanied by credit-free meals at the Solar House for my entire stay."

The droid broadcasted Acela's voice once again. "Mrs. Alberts, would you please tell us, from your data pad, who the winner of this solar year's astro tourney is?"

After a brief moment Mrs. Alberts called out a name with excitement: "Bruno Marvelous!" The crowd cheered and murmured loudly. Operator Furgis turned to look at Duncan Jennings and noticed three enforcers standing behind him. Supervisor Stykes stood next to Marshal Scoop, and Officer Armela was smiling at Mrs. Alberts. A large man easily moved through the crowd toward the solar pit. Bruno Marvelous was six foot one, thirty-six years old, and of Spanish descent. The mining supervisor was also the nephew of Ambassador Davis.

Bruno approached the solar pit quickly and stood next to Mrs. Alberts; Huiling Li was standing close to Officer Armela and watched the large man grow very concerned as the large miner hugged the smaller older woman. Bruno Marvelous was very large and strong, but he treated Mrs. Alberts very gently. He picked her up in a loose hug before setting her down. Operator Furgis moved closer to both of them nervously. Everyone grew less concerned as Bruno received the data pad from the older woman. "Congratulations," she said, and she reached up and patted him on the cheek. Bruno stepped slightly away from Mrs. Alberts and Operator Furgis, the droid now projecting the image of him holding the data pad high, causing the miners in the casino to chant his name.

Acela looked at Operator Furgis with a smile as she shook her head. She allowed Bruno to enjoy his victory for several moments before broadcasting from the droid, "Ladies and gentlemen, the winner of the Astro tourney: Bruno Marvelous!" The noise in the casino area was too loud to notice a change. "Bruno, could you please tell us what your award is?" The crowd quieted enough for Bruno to speak as he lowered his hands and data pad.

"Credit-free stay in a suite, all meals throughout Neptune One are credit free, and entrance to Grav Zero is credit free and includes all drinks." Bruno paused as the crowd watched, his eyes growing wide before continuing with a louder voice. "And a credit-free cruise on the *Jupiter Queen!*" The 3-D projection of Bruno looked up from the data pad with a wide smile.

The droid projected the image of Acela Vega, which brought whistles and several calls as the crowd saw the very large diamond necklace covering her cleavage. As the calls and whistles quieted down, Acela addressed the crowded casino. "This tournament has been successful mostly due to your participation, and the staff of Neptune One thanks you." The crowd in the casino area started applauding. "Everyone is a winner in this tourney, so if you would please link your data pads or pocket pads to the nearest vid com, your credits will be tallied. Please continue to enjoy your stay with us here at Neptune One." The droid stopped the 3-D projection and initiated its stealth mode once again.

Operator Furgis gently hugged Mrs. Alberts and shook Bruno Marvelous's hand. As the two winners of the Astro tournament left the solar pit, Operator Furgis approached Acela with slight sarcasm. "Thanks for the warning, Acela."

Before Acela could reply, Raynor grabbed her husband's arm. "You were fine, Ken."

Acela added, "I thought you should announce the winner. You're very good at it, sir."

Operator Furgis snickered. "Yeah, all right, I see a conspiracy somewhere in this," and both women laughed.

Raynor looked at Acela. "Would you like to join us at the Solar House?"

Acela shook her head. "I wish I could; my other pit bosses are busy."

"It's all right, I need to see Sam in our suite anyway," Operator Furgis said. He turned to leave the solar pit.

Raynor quickly looked over at Duncan Jennings nodding at her with a smile. "All right, Ken, we'll see what Sam's up to."

Operator Furgis looked at his wife curiously before walking by Duncan and smacking him on the back. "Let's go." The enforcers watched the three individuals walk slowly toward the lifts.

Supervisor Stykes and Marshal Scoop laughed, shaking their heads at Acela; she returned the gesture with a slight smile as Huiling and Officer Armela entered the solar pit. Supervisor Stykes turned and nodded at Marshal Scoop, knowing he was required to meet Dr. Gerlitz in his lab. Stykes himself needed to complete a lot of reports for Director Furgis in his office, so they both left, slowly walking and conversing toward the lifts.

Huiling was excited. "Ken has no idea, does he?"

Officer Armela and Huiling waited for the smiling senior pit boss to answer. Acela Vega smiled. "None whatsoever."

Operator Furgis approached his suite's entry door and followed Raynor and Duncan inside. He stopped quickly in surprise. His son approached with a large smile, and Chief Tylor and Kelly Brown stood in front of a curved panel that encompassed the entire far walls of his recreation quarters. Sam snickered with excitement and rested his hand on his father's shoulder. "You like it, Pops?"

Operator Furgis looked around the room before answering. "What is it?" He walked toward the middle of the quarters.

Chief Tylor handed Operator Furgis a data pad. "I think I

have it programmed correctly."

Operator Furgis took the data pad and sat in his recreational chair. "Well, try it out, Pops," Sam said, and his father looked up at him curiously. "You still haven't told me what it is."

Kelly was soft spoken and Operator Furgis struggled to hear her. "Sir, we spotted this while checking for a new vid cam. Sam wants to start vidgraphy, so we were looking for new equipment. We got this old-style vid display from the solar net, and Sam thought it would be a great gift."

Operator Furgis chuckled, shaking his head and nodding at his son. He stood quickly and roughly grabbed Sam for a very heavy hug, and he held the back of his head.

Raynor was thrilled to see her husband and son in an affectionate display. She moved closer to Kelly and spoke softly. "Very well done."

Kelly looked surprised. "It really was Sam's idea."

"Girl, take a compliment when you can," Raynor said and walked closer to her husband as he released their son.

Sam looked into his father's watery eyes. "Kelly spotted it and asked me what it was for. I then asked the chief if he could install it in your suite."

Operator Furgis turned to the chief with a grin. "Thank you, Chief."

Sam quickly continued. "The next two obstacles were easy with the help of Duncan and Seth. I could not use station credits or you would have questioned the expense, so I asked Duncan for a favor."

"Not a favor, a gift," Duncan said quickly, and he moved to the dispenser as the chime indicated his drink was ready.

Sam continued. "The next thing I needed to do was transport this beast to the station and up to your suite."

The chief interrupted. "We thought about breaching the hull and bringing it in from outside."

Duncan walked around the room with a transparent tray handing out drinks. "Cheers," he said as he handed the last drink to Operator Furgis. "That's where your good friend Seth helped out with his transport contacts."

Operator Furgis laughed. "You mean black market transportation."

His wife decided it was now her turn. "And getting it up here to the chief without you knowing was my job."

"And you're very good at your job. Thank you all." Ken Furgis raised his drink in a toast. He returned to his recreation chair with enthusiasm. "Let's see if we can get this thing running." He leaned forward and said, "Vid display on." He was confused as he stared at the blank panel that wrapped around the two far walls of his recreation quarters.

Chief Tylor picked up the data pad next to Operator Furgis and handed the communications device to his boss. "Sorry, sir, we haven't got the voice recognition set up yet."

Furgis laughed. "Old school." He took the data pad from the chief and set it into the communications dock on his recreational chair. "Link." After hearing his chair chime, he was anxious to test his new device. "Vid display on," and the wraparound video display screen came to life displaying commands from his data pad.

The quarters were silent; his guests were impressed with his technique used to operate his new device. Furgis quickly chose a command, "Display four," and an ancient broadcast appeared on the display as his colleagues sat in the various chairs throughout the quarters. Several of his guests started laughing at the broadcast, and Duncan commented, "These three guys are stupid. What did they call this, silly humor?"

Sam found this more entertaining than his father's favorite old-time classic broadcast. "Slap stick, Duncan."

Operator Furgis looked around with a smile, comforted with his family and friends as he enjoyed his new device. He looked at his son, sitting next to Kelly and holding her hand, and said, "Sam, this broadcast was not meant to be streamed in color."

"I don't think they streamed transmission back then," Raynor said.

Ken looked up into his wife's eyes. "It's still better in black and white." Raynor was ready to respond, but the main vid com chimed. Ken quickly responded with "Pause," and the display panel froze the broadcast as he continued. "Source of transmission." The vid com voice answered almost immediately. "SS *King David*." He stood and approached the vid com close to the entry door. His family and friends walked to the large observation window, where Raynor said, "Allow view," and the observation window became transparent, showing the SS *King David* slightly off in the distance. Sam smiled as he watched the thrusters of the massive ship glow and start the SS *King David* on its journey. Kelly pointed to the front of the ship. "There's your symbol," and Sam nodded with a smile.

Duncan felt like he could step out into the vacuum of space and float toward the SS *King David*. After a moment he asked the chief, "What symbol are they referring to?"

"Do you see the large circle on the first conning tower?"

Duncan focused before nodding. "Yeah, it has a large G and a large F inside."

Kelly, in a slightly louder voice than usual, said, "God first, Duncan." She was holding Sam's arm and did not look away from the magnificent view of the planet Neptune, the stars, or the SS *King David* now in full thrusters.

Operator Furgis stood in front of the vid com to receive a transmission from Pastor Murray. "Thank you again for your hospitality, Ken, and your assistance with the *King David*."

Operator Furgis was pleased to have a new friend, even though he was not sure about his own beliefs, and he quickly responded. "I wish you could have stayed longer, Don. The Mech fight with Taby is almost ready to start."

"I wish I could have. I bet it will be a great challenge, but my responsibilities are required elsewhere."

Raynor joined in. "Sir, the Mech fight may be over before you enter WH-12; we'll send it to you via droid."

Pastor Murray smiled and held his hand up. "We'll be silent until we enter, Raynor, but God bless you and thank you. Ken, you take care of that family you call Neptunians, you hear?" and the vid com shut down.

Sam looked at his father. "Neptunians?"

His father smiled with a nod. "It's a hint about my faith, son," and he activated his ear com piece to contact Supervisor Stykes.

"Yeah, boss?"

"Leaf, tell Acela and the others I'll watch the Mech fight from my suite." Supervisor Stykes acknowledged the order, slightly disappointed.

Raynor was surprised. "What's up with you? You don't

want to watch the fight in the Delphi dome?"

"I plan on enjoying the fight right here with this new display," he said. "You guys can join me if you want."

Duncan and approached the dispenser. "If we're going to watch the fight in old school, then we need refreshments."

Raynor laughed. "Pass them out, Dunc."

Chapter Ten

Captain Justin Drake activated his ear com while waiting for his daughter to emerge from her armor warrior room in the Earth dome. He spoke softly. "Mela."

His first officer, Commander Mela Finch, responded to her captain from the bridge of the SS *Hammerhead* immediately. "Yes sir."

The transmission was clear, but Captain Drake knew it was not as secure as a vid com. He looked in both directions of the hallway leading to the armor warrior's room. "Mela, what's the sitrep?"

"Sir, we have four friendlies and eight guests." She paused. "Sir, the transmission is bad; is everything okay?"

"Yeah, I'm under Earth dome waiting for Taby." Captain Drake could hear people coming around the other corner of the hall.

Mela called out, "Hound dog," and Captain Drake smiled as he replied, "Let him go." He deactivated his ear com piece as the door to Tabitha Drake's room hissed open. The captain turned to the open door and watched his daughter emerge. Tabitha was a short blond woman in her late twenties, and she was very feminine; however, the muscles on her were noticeable. Captain Drake was proud of his daughter and felt lucky that she resembled her mother. After a quick hug, Tabitha said, "Dad, I'm ready for the pre-match. Karl said he would meet us there before we go in." Captain Drake nodded with pride as he escorted his daughter to the Earth dome chambers.

He followed her out of the lift and turned down the corridor toward the Earth dome chamber. The hall was busy, with an occasional solar net droid hovering by. Tabitha noticed Karl Hobbs in the distance, leaning on the wall next to the chamber's entrance door. The tall black man, now in his early thirties, respected Tabitha and had volunteered to accompany her during these next two fights as an advisor and promoter. He had already informed the solar news that she would be on the pre-match segment. Karl turned and smiled as the attractive young lady quickly moved through the individuals in the corridor, and he stepped into the middle of the corridor to receive a friendly hug as Captain Drake slowly approached.

Captain Drake sighed with a grin. "Karl, is everything all right?"

Karl took an extra moment to stare at Tabitha before turning his attention to her father. "Everything's fine, sir. I was told we'll be called in shortly."

"What's the holdup, Karl?" Tabitha asked.

"Taby, you were behind schedule again, so the commissioner decided to speak with Ben first." Karl noticed Tabitha was annoyed and offered a light chuckle. "I know the commissioner usually speaks to both armor warriors together, but I was told this cycle's match is different."

Captain Drake interrupted quickly. "In what way?"

Karl turned to Tabitha's father. "Something about the military." The sound of the door hissing open interrupted the conversation.

The commissioner's assistant walked through the door and stood in front of Tabitha. The older, gray-haired woman's voice was snappy. "I presume you're Tabitha Drake."

"Yes, I am—and you are…?"

"The one calling you in," and she stepped to the side of the door with her open hand extended. Tabitha walked through the door and Karl gestured for her father to follow. As the three individuals entered the large room, they noticed pictures of events from Earth dome's historic matches. In the middle of the room was a large triangle-shaped transparent table with rounded corners. The three men sitting at the far side stared at them with serious expressions.

The tall, aging man sitting in the middle of the three spoke with authority as he glanced on occasion at his data pad. "Tabitha Drake, can you please have a seat?" and Tabitha nodded, "Yes sir," and sat facing the officials. The commissioner looked at Karl before looking down at his data pad; when he looked back at Karl, his voice was a little more curious. "And you are…?"

"Karl Hobbs, sir."

One of the commissioner's colleagues said, "Triton's Terror from the Neptune sector."

The commissioner looked back at Karl with a slight smile. "Oh yes, very well, please have a seat," leaving Captain Drake standing alone as Karl pulled the chair out next to Tabitha and sat.

The commissioner placed his data pad on the triangular vid table and leaned back in his chair as he stared at Captain Drake. He could only see a man in a military uniform standing in his meeting chambers, and he was annoyed. "And what are you, *sir?*"

Captain Drake felt no threat; he had learned to tolerate superiors through his years with the Western Empire's space fleet. "Captain of the SS *Hammerhead*, the finest cruiser in the Western fleet, *sir.*"

The commissioner did not receive this well. "I will have to ask you to leave; the military has no business here." Captain Drake snapped to attention and saluted before turning in military fashion toward the door.

Tabitha was ready to stand, but Karl grabbed her arm and whispered, "Relax, your father will wait." She relaxed in her chair as the vid com activated, showing a 3-D projection of her slowly turning in the middle of the table. The commissioner started reading out loud from his data pad. "Tabitha Drake, armor warrior known as Darkstar. Five-ten, twenty-eight years old, and sponsored by Neptune One." The commissioner leaned on the table after setting his data pad down. "Ms. Drake, we usually have both warriors here, but due to the growing hostilities, we decided it was best if we discuss the changes to this cycle's match separately; it also did not help by arriving on a warship." The commissioner leaned back in his chair.

"With all due respect, sir," said Karl, "Tabitha Drake can use any means."

"It would be wise to show that respect, sir."

Tabitha grabbed Karl by the arm. "It's fine, I got this," and she turned her attention to the commissioner. "Apologies, sir, no disrespect was intended." The commissioner gestured with an open hand. "Continue." Tabitha proceeded with caution. "I needed a transport to Earth dome and I realized this was an opportunity to also spend time with my father, sir."Tabitha noticed all three officials nod as the 3-D image changed to her Mech fighter.

The commissioner continued. "Tabitha Drake, we are allowing a small complement of long-range missiles, no stunners, but we also will increase the number of short-range missiles."

Karl Hobbs studied the data on the projected sidebar next to Tabitha's Mech fighter. "Sir, would this cause a problem for Earth dome?" Tabitha tapped his leg under the transparent table.

The commissioner took a deep breath and sighed with annoyance. "We will get to that issue in a moment, Mr. Hobbs. The usual customizable weapons are still permitted along with slightly longer lasting thrusters." The vid com changed to a 3-D projection of a desert landscape. "And to answer Mr. Hobbs' question," the commissioner paused to scowl at Karl before continuing, "the match will be in the Simpson Desert, and the spectators and solar news will be in hover stands." Tabitha Drake nodded, knowing for her it was more room to fight and less droid control. The commissioner was quick to add, "Ms. Drake, I suggest you look over the new governs of the match."

Karl held up his data pad. "We have them right here, sir."

The commissioner stared at Karl before looking directly at Tabitha. "I suggest you get to the solar segment on time, young lady." Tabitha grinned with a nod as she stood. Before Karl and Tabitha could get to the meeting chamber's doors, the commissioner made one final comment. "And Tabitha, I hope you fight like your mother."

Tabitha smiled as Karl followed her to the door.

Captain Drake waited patiently and turned quickly as he

heard the familiar hiss of the door opening. The commissioner's assistant escorted Karl and Tabitha out. Tabitha offered a one-armed hug to her father, who asked, "How did it go?"

His daughter chuckled. "All right, I guess. I can tell you he does not like the military."

Captain Drake laughed, and Karl asked, "What's humorous about that, sir?"

The three walked down the corridor under Earth dome toward the lift, and the captain adjusted his uniform's cap on his dirty-blond hair before answering casually, "I met the commissioner several times when Taby's mother was fighting. She was very young at the time."

Tabitha knew her father was sensitive about her mother's past, but she had never heard her father mention the commissioner before. "Dad, you never said you met the commissioner."

They approached the lift. "Twice before, and it was long ago." Captain Drake sighed before entering the lift. "It did not go well."

"What happened, sir?" asked Karl.

"The second time I met the commissioner was after your mother's death," the captain said, facing Tabitha. "He apologized but said that was the nature of Mech battles." He turned to Karl. "That's when I hit him."

Karl snickered. "I can picture it, sir, and I can see he had it coming."

As Captain Drake and Karl Hobbs exited, Tabitha grabbed her father by the arm. "Wait, you never told me that. I want to know more."

Captain Drake looked into his daughter's eyes and was reminded of the passion his wife once had. He rested his hand on the back of her shoulder. "Taby, let's step outside for a moment."

Karl followed with concern. "Not too long, sir, the solar segment will start soon."

This did not slow the father/daughter couple down as Karl followed them out onto a balcony overlooking an ocean view. For a brief moment the three relaxed in the ocean breeze; the smell of the salty air was something not offered on the SS *Hammerhead*, and the sound of birds flying overhead was even more relaxing.

Tabitha finally shook the feeling off and turned to her father. "Are you ready, Dad?"

Captain Drake took in one more heavy breath and exhaled deeply before answering. "Taby, your mother was killed in a Mech fight." His daughter nodded as she focused her attention on him. Karl was concerned for the scheduled solar news segment but was interested in Captain Drake's story as well and remained quiet.

Captain Drake continued. "The armor warrior your mother was fighting against for the Western Empire—I can't remember what territory it was for, but I do remember her opponent hit her with a small stunner missile on her Mech fighter."

Karl said, "Were stunners authorized for the territorial match?"

Captain Drake leaned on the rail of the large balcony watching the hover vessels fly by below. He took another deep breath. "No, they were not. Stunner missiles were a fairly new technology back then and quite small, not large enough for warships yet, and they were not expected to be seen in a Mech battle so soon." He stared across the ocean in deep thought.

"What did the commissioner say?" Tabitha asked.

"They did not rule on the issue of unauthorized weapons because there was no discussion in the chamber to place a ruling on stunners at that time."

Karl interrupted. "I would have slugged him as well."

Captain Drake laughed. "I'm lucky we were alone with no droids around." He held his hands behind his back in military fashion.

His daughter was not satisfied. "Dad, there's something you're not telling me."

Captain Drake grabbed his daughter gently by both shoulders and looked into her eyes with pride. "You're just like your mother, Taby." Karl moved closer but remained quiet to hear the secret. The captain looked across the ocean once again while taking a deep breath and slowly turned with his exhale, focusing on his daughter. "Taby, the armor warrior driving the Mech fighter that killed your mother was Andrew Swells."

Tabitha stared out over the ocean in deep thought as her father stood behind her. She felt rage at the thought that Ben Swells' uncle was the reason her mother was killed and that it was also from an unauthorized weapon on his Mech. She was also kind-spirited and struggled with the anger; her father could see the struggle and moved closer to offer a hug. She gently pushed herself from her father. "It's okay, Dad, I'll be fine."

Karl Hobbs spoke softly. "Remember it was Ben's uncle, not him, Taby." He rested one hand gently on her shoulder. "Are you ready for the solar news?"

Tabitha looked at her father. "I'm ready. Dad, I'm fine. I'm just a little more cautious and plan on checking all the commissioner's rulings on this match."

"That's my girl. Now let's get to the segment."

Karl followed both father and daughter back into the Earth dome administration section.

The commissioner's assistant stood in front of the door to the solar news chambers listening to her new ear com implant as Tabitha Drake waited along with her father and good friend Karl Hobbs. She nodded and turned to Tabitha. "You're up, honey," and she stood aside. Tabitha approached the doors as they slid open with the familiar hissing sound and revealed a small set of steps in front of her. The noise level was high with chatter and murmurings from close by. She slowly climbed the steps and looked around; she was standing behind three empty seats with the commissioner and his two sub commissioners on each side.

Tabitha looked to the other side of the long table past the commissioner, and her eyes grew tight as she watched Ben Swells laughing with his escorts. The noise from the room and several droids hovering by snapped her out of her deep thoughts; she sat and smiled, facing the crowded room. The lighting in the room flashed yellow several times along with a heavy chime, and the commissioner picked up a round transparent ball with a smaller globe of the Earth inside. The hovering droids broadcasted the noise of the impact as the commissioner hit the balvel on the striker base. The noise echoed throughout the large chambers, causing the chatter to quiet down to a light murmur. The commissioner was loud as the droids broadcasted his voice. "Ladies and gentlemen, there have been some minor changes to the regs regarding the match." He struck the balvel hard against the striker base as the chatter started again. As the room slowly grew quieter, the commissioner continued. "Please remain civil or this briefing will be held through vid coms only." He picked up a data pad off the vid table and activated the transparent touch screen; a hover droid glided to a position directly in front of the vid table and projected a 3-D image of a desert landscape. "The match will not be in Earth dome. The Mech fight will take place in the Simpson Desert of Australia. This will allow for long-range missiles and more short-range missiles."

The room grew noisy again and the balvel, held high in the commissioner's hand, came down quickly, striking the base. Sparks flew from the vid table, grabbing the attention of the entire room. "Hover stands will be provided for the Mech fight, and all other pertinent data for the addendums will be linked to the main fight droid."

The droid switched to a 3-D projection of a young man in an expensive suit. "Submit your questions through your data pad at this time if you have not done so already, and the vid com will ask them at random." The rotating sidebar displayed the names of the individuals linking with the vid com. The vid com avatar hovered in front of the assembly and turned to Ben Swells first.

"Ben Swells, call sign Cronus, six foot and twenty-nine years old, winning every Mech fight this solar season except one." Ben Swells smiled and shrugged his shoulders. The vid com started the interview. "How will the match's changes affect your fight, Cronus?"

"I believe it will give me an advantage. Tabitha Drake is used to matches that are more confined for her style of driving.

Don't get me wrong. Tabitha's a good Mech driver. I just think it would be a quick match."

The vid com's 3-D projection was emotionless as it continued the questioning. "In your opinion this match will be over quickly, and you're already prepared for Noyami Masoko in the final championship match."

The armor warrior leaned back in his chair with a smile. "Like I said, I admire Darkstar for getting this far, and I would be a fool to think this match will be taken easily; however, I am confident that Darkstar will not fight the Sword in the final match; she's good but not that good."

The vid coms around the meeting chambers switched to the 3-D projection of Tabitha Drake sitting at the table. She was tense but maintained her composure as she occasionally looked at Ben Swells.

The chambers erupted in chatter, forcing the commissioner to strike the balvel hard on the base, causing more sparks to shoot out from the vid table and vanish quickly. The noise and sparks quieted the room as the vid com's 3-D projection turned to face Tabitha. "Tabitha Drake, call sign Darkstar, five foot ten and twenty-nine years old." The droid displayed the specifics about Tabitha Drake on the sidebar. "Will the open arena of the desert affect your match?"

Tabitha was relaxed as she answered with less enthusiasm than her opponent. "Not at all. The freedom of more space will be to my advantage." She smiled at a few shouts of approval from the crowded chambers.

"What will the changes to the weapons do for your Mech?"

Tabitha laughed. "It will allow me to see Masoko that much quicker," and the chamber's noise level grew in laughter.

Ben Swells was smiling and nodding. Tabitha stood with her hands in front of her. "I will add...this will be an easy victory. After watching the vid cording of Cronus's last Mech fight, I've come to the conclusion that he is a sloppy driver and has luck for skills; he should retire to shuttle driving before he gets hurt."

Ben Swells stood quickly and faced his already standing opponent; he was not in a rage but was very defensive. "Darkstar, we will test that assumption in the desert, where your words mean very little."

"I can back my words up, *sir*."

The commissioner grabbed his balvel quickly. Ben was standing behind his chair, ready to respond to the insult, when the balvel struck its base with a force that vibrated the vid table, and the sub commissioners squinted as the sparks shot out from the balvel base. The droid discontinued the avatar projection and switched to the audio of the commissioner. "Enough. I told both of you this would be civil." He slammed the balvel onto its base before he stood and walked down the steps behind his chair.

Tabitha looked over at Ben with anger in her eyes; her father grabbed her by the arm and directed her toward the door behind them. Karl laughed. "That could have been better."

Tabitha waited for the sound of the door closing before replying, "I think it worked well."

Her father looked at her with puzzlement. "What are you talking about? The commissioner is red-faced."

Tabitha laughed. "Who cares about the commissioner?" She hugged Karl with one arm. "Napoleon once said, if you want a quick victory, make your enemy angry."

Her father laughed and shook his head. "I should have remembered, that was one of your mother's favorites."

At the lift, Karl said, "You guys get some rest for the match. I wanna check your Mech fighter out one more time." He winked at his fellow Mech fighter before the lift doors closed.

Tabitha removed her helmet from the transparent security podium; the vid com recognized her as the operator and depolarized the field. She slipped the last piece of her armor warrior suit over her head and initiated the heads-up display. "HUD activate." The transparent display of her helmet appeared in her helmet. Tabitha was very competent as a seasoned Mech fighter; she continued her helmet's operations check. "Bio stat," she said, and a low chime was heard before the helmet displayed the readout for her bio implants. The display instantly turned yellow, indicating a broken link to her Mech fighter, and after one final adjustment for her armor warrior boots and quick shake of her head to test the security of her helmet, Tabitha Drake turned toward the Mech hangar door.

Captain Justin Drake stood close to Karl Hobbs near a hovering maintenance module. After noticing the armor warrior door lights flashing, he looked over and smiled with pride as he watched his daughter approach. Her suit matched her Mech fighter exactly; red with gold trim and a slight gleam. Her visor was dark, but her father could see some of her features. She stopped and the visor disappeared altogether. Karl looked at her with growing excitement only a Mech driver could have. "We got some new features on Darkstar, Taby." Everyone looked around the Mech hangar as the lights turned green, indicating the boarding procedure would start. Karl looked back at Tabitha. "Look, the main change to Darkstar is the long-range missile launchers on her shoulders and a more intense flash bolt in the chest armor. Cronus is not aware of the flash bolt."

Tabitha nodded. She smiled at her friend and fellow Mech fighter. "Thanks, Karl, I'll be sure to give him the surprise." She turned to her father. "Dad, I will make it to the championship match on Mars."

Captain Drake looked at his daughter with a wide smile. "I know you will. Now go make your mother proud."

The time for talk was over as a four-passenger hover cart stopped next to Tabitha. Her helmet's visor went completely dark as she entered the hover cart and shot forward toward the giant Mech fighter in the hangar.

Karl stood behind Tabitha's father. "Should we get to the shuttle before it leaves?"

Captain Drake finally looked away from the hover cart. "We'll take my shuttle from the Hammer; everything we need to assist Taby is set up on board." He started walking toward the maintenance lift.

Karl was assured, knowing he could help with Darkstar's operations through the SS *Hammerhead's* equipment on one of its shuttles; the operations shuttle provided by Earth dome was generic for each Mech fighter. Karl could not resist asking, "Is Mela piloting the shuttle?"

"No," the captain laughed. "A command officer needs to stay with the *Hammer* at all times." Karl sighed with disappointment. As they entered the lift, Captain Drake said, "Son, you need to leave Mela alone; she is not a good match for you."

Karl scoffed, "I think she is."

Captain Drake called out, "Shuttle bay," and the lift started to move. He chuckled.

"What's so funny?" Karl asked.

The lift doors opened on the far side of Earth dome's shuttle bay, and the two men stepped out and waited for a hover cart. Captain Drake looked at Karl and said, "If you're interested in Mela, then you need to sign a disclaimer."

"Where do I sign?" Karl laughed.

When the hover cart stopped in front of them, Captain Drake instructed the vid com, "SS *Hammerhead*," and both men were pulled back in their seat by the motion of the hover cart. They struggled to hear each other as the hover cart sped down Earth dome's shuttle hangar; it would correct its course as other crafts created obstacles.

They came to an abrupt stop, allowing a shuttle to move into the launch lane of the hangar. This particular shuttle was of a military design and displayed the armor plating along with the accompanying weapons modules. Captain Drake stopped speaking in mid-sentence as the markings caught his attention. Karl had mixed feelings of curiosity and concern. "What is it, sir?"

They fell back into their seats as the hover cart resumed. Captain Drake looked at Karl with a scoff. "I had a feeling Kruger would be here."

Karl took one more look at the shuttle leaving the open hangar bay. "Who's Kruger?"

The hover cart slowed to turn into the berth of the SS *Hammerhead*'s shuttle. Captain Drake stepped off and looked at Karl with a smirk. "Kruger is captain of the *Essex*."

Karl shrugged. "And?"

After the captain cleared the hover cart, the small floating transport sped away. He and Karl stood by the opening hatch of the shuttle. "I never really met Kruger, but his reputation is well known throughout both sides; he is a great tactician, and the Essex usually leads in their attacks."

Karl smiled. "So the *Hammer* has no chance against the *Essex.*"

Captain Drake shook his head with a proud laugh. "That's not what I meant. If the odds were equal, Commander Kruger would try taking out the *Hammer* with liter vessels and maybe even sacrificing an equal cruiser." As he entered the shuttle, he stopped and looked back to see Karl standing at the bottom of the shuttle's entry steps. "What are you waiting for?"

Karl inhaled deeply several times before turning and climbing the steps. He stepped through the airlock hatch and exhaled. "I'll always miss the salty air of Earth's oceans."

Captain Drake started laughing as buckled into his seat. "You've got water on Triton."

After a brief moment of working his seat's safety devices, Karl replied, "Yeah, if you like a mix of manmade water and extracted water."

"At least with all those miners it's salty!"

Karl lowered his head with a smile. "Wrong type of salt."

They laughed as the lights turned red inside the shuttle cabin. They felt the lift of the shuttle and the vibration from the landing struts hiding themselves into the under hull of the shuttle. The SS *Hammerhead* shuttle slowly moved out of its assigned berth and turned to line up with the launch lane; the bow of the small craft lowered as the speed increased. The sunlight filled the rear cabin briefly through the cockpit before the pilot adjusted the tint of the cockpit window, and Captain

Drake could see the pilot and copilot conversing and chuckling. The shuttle turned slightly to port for a moment before straightening out, and the bow slightly above the horizon as the craft slowly gained altitude.

Captain Drake activated the main vid com in the rear cabin to contact the *Hammerhead*. Commander Mela Finch's 3-D projection appeared from the vid com base. "Sir, what's the stat?"

"On our way to the designated Mech fight area, sitrep."

Commander Finch's projection looked past Captain Drake, who could visualize his first officer looking down at the three-level bridge of his heavy cruiser; she returned her attention to him almost immediately. "Several transport ships approaching; the friendlies and guests are the same, sir." Captain Drake nodded as the vid com shut down.

He turned to Karl. "Now back to Kruger," and he waited for Karl's attention to catch up with his own.

Karl looked confused at first but he quickly realized the question. "You mean the strategy, sir?"

"Of course. As a Mech fighter in a battle over territory, how would your strategy play out?"

"Knowing Kruger will try to take out the *Hammer* first...I would send the *Hammer* through the center of his formation with fighter escorts."

The shuttle shook as it encountered some turbulence, but Captain Drake remained focused on Karl as the armor warrior looked through the small porthole window. "Karl, what would you do about his escort ships if the *Hammer* attacked forward?"

Karl leaned back thoughtfully. After another slight jolt, the shuttle calmed into a more graceful flight. "The *Hammer* would go through the front of Kruger's formation while the *Hammer's* escort ships covered the rear." He watched the smile grow on Captain Drake's face but could not resist asking, "What would the right action be?"

The shuttle leaned to its port side quickly and straightened as it completed a turn. Captain Drake activated his ear com piece and asked, "What's the problem?"

"Sorry, sir," said the pilot. "The closer we get, the more traffic we encounter."

Captain Drake replied, "Check the Tribune's transponder; let these guys know we're on Tribune business," and he deactivated his ear com piece before the pilot could respond. The captain turned to Karl. "If you left your escorts to protect the rear, what would happen to the *Hammer*?"

Karl grinned. "I see your point, sir, however, if you don't want to risk battle damage to the *Hammer*, then why go straight at Kruger?"

"Commander Kruger, I believe, is a controller, and he likes to set the battlefield to complement his style. His formation would divide our formation, creating support fire from both sides of his escort and only one side from ours; therefore, the *Hammer* would use her superior fire to split his formation down the middle."

Karl focused intently. "Yeah but the *Hammer* would be attacked from both sides and take heavy damage."

"You're right, of course, about the *Hammer* receiving too much damage to face the *Essex;* however, you have escort ships."

It did not take long for Karl to understand Captain Drake's strategy. "Use the escorts on each side as a wall with the fighters moving forward."

Captain Drake grinned as he listened to Karl explain the tactics. When Karl was slow, the captain could not resist taking the tactical explanation into his own words. "Karl, the fighters hit the front of his formation while the escorts stay tight to the *Hammer*. As the *Hammer* enters Kruger's formation, the escorts widen their berth from it, and the *Hammer* of course releases her arsenal against the enemy escorts and a frontal assault on any remaining ships in front." Captain Drake stopped to watch Karl think about this tactic. "Kruger may expect the *Hammer* to attack from broadside, and he will attempt to use stunner missiles. But with the *Hammer* bearing down his throat, it would be difficult to hit her with a stunner."

"Within a flash he will have the *Hammer* and the escort ships on each side," said Karl, excitedly. Captain Drake laughed, and Karl looked confused. "What's wrong with that?"

"The escort ships will go into a series of defensive and offensive maneuvers, leaving the heavy cruisers and/or battle cruisers to slug it out. It will be a close encounter, but I will instruct the other cruisers to launch mid-range missiles at multiple targets. This will cause the enemy to focus on more than one attacker at a time and with short-range missiles causing as much damage as possible."

Karl whistled. "The escorts will take a beating." He looked at Captain Drake with his eyebrows raised in a frown.

"Karl, a commander who is required to win a battle knows there will be losses; a lot of good men on both sides will lose their lives, and a lot of good ships will suffer. The *Hammer* will receive damage, but she will prevail," the captain said with pride.

"This is all speculation. There's no way that new guy on the

Eastern side wants all-out war."

Captain Drake chuckled. "How do you know what that young kid will do? I think the guy is crazy enough, especially after killing his father for power."

Karl grew more serious. "You actually think this chest-beating stuff will escalate?"

Captain Drake sighed. "I hope you're right, Karl, but I have a gut feeling, and with all the other skirmishes throughout the system…"

Karl interrupted. "…you believe war is coming."

"Either way it does not matter; my job is to have the *Hammer* and her escorts ready in a moment's notice. If we do go to war, the *Hammer* will make it a victory." Both men smiled.

Captain Drake heard the chime of the vid com from the cockpit and noticed the shuttle slowing down. He activated his ear com piece and waited for the acknowledgment. "Lieutenant, what's the stat?"

The pilot was respectful, but his attention remained forward as the shuttle continued to decrease in speed. "We're approaching the match area, sir."

Through the cockpit window both Captain Drake and Karl could see the increasing number of shuttles and hover stands.

The main vid com in the cockpit chimed and lit up the cabin in a 3-D display of the Simpson Desert. Captain Drake released his safety harness and moved to the navigation seat in the cockpit. Karl Hobbs unfastened his own harness to follow the captain into the cockpit and stand slouched over Captain Drake's shoulder. "It's getting crowded around here," the captain said as he watched the pilot focus on the flight path of the shuttle. Captain Drake reached into the vid com's 3-D projection and circled with his finger to enlarge an area of the projected desert. He scrolled through the zoomed image, "Ah, there it is," and looked at his pilot. "Set a course for here until we see Taby's LZ." The pilot glanced at the 3-D image as the shuttle slowly turned, and he flew the shuttle gracefully around the traffic of ships in the area.

The small shuttle from the SS *Hammerhead* traversed the desert with elegance; the turns were smooth as it approached a projection that was not clear from her present position. Captain Drake unharnessed himself from the navigation chair and turned to face Karl. "Is Triton's Terror ready?"

Karl snickered. "Is Hammer Strike ready?"

Captain Drake gave him a instant. "I like that. If I ever become an armor warrior, may I use it?"

Karl's snicker turned into a laugh. "I think it's fitting."

Captain Drake followed Karl to the rear cabin. The pilot called out over the vid com, "Sir, we're at the landing zone," and the massive 3-D projection grew in detail as the shuttle slowed to a stop. The image of Darkstar towered over the shuttle, and the pilot could not help leaning forward, looking up through the cockpit window.

Karl turned his operations chair to face the console that was starting to illuminate the rear cabin as the systems became operational. Captain Drake sat at the engineering console and activated the vid com. Karl spoke over his shoulder. "Are we linked?" and Captain Drake responded instantly, "Stand by." He heard the vid com's chime followed by "Ready."

"Darkstar," he instructed as he leaned back. The 3-D projection of Tabitha Drake appeared. "Hey, guys, are you ready?"

Her father was excited. "Just waiting for you to drop in."

Tabitha focused on her Mech fighter's controls for a brief moment before responding. "Going through some final checks while waiting for the drop ship to close."

"We're not going anywhere," said Hobbs and Tabitha replied, "All right, Karl, I'll be dropping in soon." The vid com flickered.

Captain Drake checked the systems quickly before turning around in his chair to face Karl. "No problem, the systems are linking." Karl nodded. "Taby, do you have our read-out on display?"

Tabitha checked the systems link between her Mech fighter and support ship. "Yeah, we're all set, Dad."

"Sir, the officials are requesting us to take our support positions and clear the LZ," said the pilot, and the shuttle vibrated slightly as its propulsion systems engaged. Captain Drake switched the 3-D projection from the vid com to the Simpson Desert and circled a destination. "LT, take us here and stand by." After hearing the pilot's acknowledgment, Captain Drake said, "Taby, we'll keep an open vid com. Have a good drop." A quick chime from the match officials was heard.

Chapter Eleven

Darkstar's HUD, illuminated in red, was accompanied by a chime, and the voice of the Mech fighter hangar bay boss was heard from Tabitha Drake's vid com. "Stand by for drop ship engagement." Tabitha double-checked the status of her Mech fighter's weapons systems. The hangar boss's voice, after the quick chime, said, "All checks completed, weapons powered down, engaging drop ship." Tabitha felt her Mech fighter vibrate. She was held still by the piloting control harness but could see her Mech fighter moving from the view of her heads-up display. The platform it stood on was turning as two shells slowly closed like a giant jaw engulfing her Mech. The only light illuminating it was her heads-up display, and the external lights from the Mech hangar bay faded as the drop ship closed in around her Mech.

Operator Furgis sat in his seat watching the three individuals on the wraparound display perform their slapstick comedy routine; Sam Furgis could not help laughing at the simplistic humor. Duncan Jennings lightly tapped Sam on the back of the head, and when he turned, Duncan held two fingers in front of Sam's face, imitating the sound the big bald man on the wraparound made. Kelly was not amused and smacked Duncan's hand quickly, causing everyone's eyes to widen. Raynor grinned as she watched Kelly's display of protection. She never really liked Kelly and knew she was a shy girl with only common intelligence, but Raynor was aware of the protective feelings she felt toward her son. Operator Furgis looked at Chief Tylor with a grin and was ready to offer humor when he was interrupted by the vid com chime and voice recognition. It was Supervisor Stykes.

"Hey, boss, we're ready at the dome."

Operator Furgis nodded. "All right, Leaf, I'll get back to you shortly." He instructed the vid com to change destinations. He contacted Dr. Avers, who asked, "Ken, are we ready to go?"

Operator Furgis chuckled. "Almost, Brook, I need to speak with Ambassador Davis first."

"Sorry, Ken, it's just Dr. Cole and Seth here."

"All right, Brook, tell everyone I hope they enjoy the match," and the vid com shut down.

Operator Furgis instructed the vid com once again, this time "Marco De Luca."

"Yes sir."

"Marco, is the ambassador with you?"

"Yes sir, along with Chayton."

Operator Furgis nodded with a smile. "Ask the ambassador if I could speak with him." After a brief moment Marco stepped aside, and the 3-D image of a short, fat Irish man wearing a rainbow tweed cap appeared. Operator Furgis wanted to laugh but only allowed himself a snicker. "Ambassador Davis, how are you?"

The ambassador was in a cheerful mood. "Excellent, Ken, what can I do for you?"

Operator Furgis could hear his wife laughing in the

background. He was not sure if Raynor was laughing at the three inane characters on the wraparound or something else. His attention refocused on Ambassador Davis. "Sir, would you like to address the dome before we start?"

The ambassador looked surprised and flattered. "Oh, I'm not really prepared, Ken. I was thinking about just watching Tabitha Drake win the match."

"All right, Ambassador, I'll take care of it," and the vid com shut down. Operator Furgis turned toward the recreation chamber. "Sam, are you guys ready?"

"Yeah, Pops," said Sam. "Let's start this."

Operator Furgis turned back to the vid com and reactivated the communications device. Everyone in his suite sat in front of the massive wraparound display as the scene changed from the three comedians to the arena of the Delphi dome. He glanced over at his wife as she smacked Duncan Jennings several times on the back. "You're not sitting on my lap. I don't care if you're an investor or not." Operator Furgis shook his head, laughing at his friends clowning around.

Supervisor Stykes turned to look over his shoulder as he heard the hiss of the Delphi dome's security booth door opening. Huiling Li and Officer Armela walked in, both smiling, and Huiling was holding Juan Armela's arm. Stykes chuckled. "Good to see you, Huiling." He gestured to a chair on the other side of the vacant security console's chair. Huiling let go of Officer Armela and sat down. Officer Armela winked at her as he sat in the vacant chair for the security console.

Huiling was excited. "The best part should be starting soon."

Officer Armela looked at Supervisor Stykes with

confusion. "Operator Furgis," said Armela, and before Stykes could reply, Huiling laughed. "Silly man, I'm talking about the pre-match entertainment."

Stykes laughed and Armela smiled as he leaned closer to Huiling. "Operator Furgis can be very humorous at times."

Supervisor Stykes interrupted. "I'm with Huiling and prefer some real entertainment." Officer Armela nodded in agreement.

Stykes grew serious. "All right, Juan, I have all droid systems up and ready for Furgis." The security console's touch screen lit up with data and control command prompts. She looked up in several directions and watched the fight droids circle around in a designated pattern.

Stykes activated the security booth's main vid com and stated his instructions clearly. The lasers projected a 3-D image of Engineer Trently, who said, "Supervisor Stykes, we're all set over here."

"Glad you're here, Shaun. I thought you might be stuck with Dr. Gerlitz's assistant." Supervisor Stykes knew Engineer Trently was one of the best engineers in the system, and Chief Engineer Tylor would be hard pressed to replace his skills and friendship. Officer Armela and Engineer Trently also had developed a more personal relationship through their tour on Neptune One. "Shaun, you actually made it."

Trently laughed. "Marshal Scoop gave me a hall pass while retaining my two new bosses."

Huiling smiled. "We're glad you're here helping, Shaun."

Before Trently could respond, Stykes' ear com piece chimed; he already knew it was Operator Furgis. "Hey, boss, are we ready to go?"

"Let's get it started, Leaf," and the ear com piece chimed off.

Supervisor Stykes looked at Officer Armela and the 3-D projection of Engineer Trently. "It's a go." Trently's image disappeared as the vid com shut down. Stykes and Armela worked the security console in conjunction and focused on the display of their individual consoles. The chattering from the spectators in the stadium grew louder as the Delphi dome's carbon electric glass slowly turned transparent, allowing the stars and blue planet to shine into the stadium.

The spectators were restless. The 3-D image of Operator Furgis was projected in the middle of the arena by the fight droid, and he held his open-handed arms up high and turned in every direction until he finally gained the spectators' attention. The noise level calmed to a low chatter as Operator Furgis addressed the crowded stadium. "Ladies and gentlemen, guests of Neptune One, the Terran Tribune has made a few changes to the match."

Acela Vega laughed as she looked over at Chayton. "This ought to go over good for the crowd."

Ambassador Bob Davis leaned forward and said, "The Tribune has their reasons. These fanatics will have to get over it." His rainbow tweed cap almost fell onto Marco De Luca.

Operator Furgis continued. "Guests, please allow me to continue. The match will not take place in the Earth dome. The match will take place in the Simpson Desert. I believe the Mech fight will be more impressive than usual, and the changes will allow for long-range weapons and less limits on their boundaries." There were shouts of excitement from the stadium.

The 3-D projection of Operator Furgis stood towering over the crowd with his hands clasped behind his back in military style; the fight droid regulated the volume of his voice according to the noise level of the stadium. Operator Furgis knew his next announcement would not be accepted very well. "Guests of Neptune, the bad news is the only pre-match entertainment will be the Earth Planetary anthem." He could hear the disappointment from the crowded stadium as the ranting grew louder.

Officer Armela looked over at Huiling with sad eyes; he could see the disappointment in her eyes as she returned his gaze. Officer Armela spoke gently. "I'm sorry, Huiling."

"That's okay, Juan, we accept what is meant to be."

Officer Armela knew why he felt love for this young lady. Supervisor Stykes nodded with a smile. "You ready, Juan?" and Armela returned his attention to his console.

Operator Furgis was quick to respond; he did not want the ranting to continue. "Guests of Neptune, please join me in Earth's planetary anthem." The projection of Operator Furgis disappeared as the lights from the stadium faded, allowing Neptune and the stars to illuminate the Dome of Delphi.

The spectators stood with fist over fist resting on their chests as the fight droid started the pre-vid com recording of the anthem. Operator Furgis instructed the main vid com in his recreation chambers to shut down, and he returned to his chair. He looked at his son. "Next time you take over."

Sam laughed. "I think you did great."

Raynor Furgis agreed. "Yeah, very good." She looked at Duncan, who was laughing. "What do you think, Duncan?"

"Ken, don't worry, you were outstanding. In fact the next

creditors meeting I have, you can be guest speaker."

Operator Furgis shook his head with a smile. "All right, enough, the match is ready to start." He picked up his data pad, causing the large wraparound display to project the same image of the Simpson Desert the Delphi dome was receiving in 3-D.

Armor warrior Tabitha Drake was strapped into her Mech fighter, tightly held by her harness, and she watched the illumination of her HUD turn red, followed by the Mech fighter hangar boss's voice. "Prepare for drop ship evac." She felt a slight vibration from her Mech fighter. The vibration increased briefly before the force of acceleration pulled on Tabitha, and the view from her HUD showed the drop ship rising past the Mech hangar levels. The vibration and force grew more intense as the drop ship quickly increased speed, accelerating through the Earth's atmosphere at a slight angle. She watched the troposcope's display in her HUD, knowing the red indicator blinking with details on the sidebar belonged to Cronus. Darkstar was not familiar with the transport procedures combat Mechs traveled in, but she realized the Mech lifts in arenas offered more control and a smoother ride.

Tabitha knew there were numerous differences between Mech fighters and combat Mechs, and one of those differences was the size. Combat Mechs required a Mech driver to sit in the head of the Mech, also called the headpit, and communicate with the squadron that fought as a team for their individual territorial disputes. Mech fighters, or the drivers known as armor warriors, fought in competition matches with Mechs sized to their physical traits, and they rarely worked in teams. Tabitha Drake's admiration and pride of her mother grew with this new understanding of drop ships, and she now realized why the larger Combat Mechs fought their battles in isolated areas, something she never really thought about until inside her own drop ship.

The drop ship would rock from side to side as it went through the atmosphere quickly. Darkstar concentrated on the troposcope and the red dot her indicator identified as Cronus. Her HUD also informed her that the drop ship had entered a low orbit of Earth as well as the sudden stillness of the flight, but it did not last long. Claxons sounded as her HUD turned yellow. Darkstar could see that the drop ship was slowly spinning.

Her vid com chimed. "Prepare for drop." She felt a large jolt rock the drop ship, and her HUD displayed the data informing her of reentry. She took a deep breath and called out, "Weapons activate." She heard the response from her vid com—"unauthorized"—and after checking the troposcope, she realized she was still too high for activation.

After a brief moment that seemed like cycles passing by, Tabitha called out, "Hammer One," and heard the voice of Karl Hobbs. "Taby, you finally made it; we were going to start without you." Karl grew more serious after hearing her heavy breathing. This was Tabitha's first drop ship match.

"Karl, I'm coming in fast."

"Relax, Taby. The drop ship will release soon, and your Mech fighter's thrusters will take over." Karl continued to watch her father as he nodded. Just as quick as Karl spoke to Tabitha, the split shell of the drop ship opened and released her into a free fall. Tabitha was scared and excited. "Hooyah!" was all they could hear from the vid com.

Tabitha's heads-up display in her helmet flashed yellow as she felt a sudden jolt and the sound of her Mech fighter's thrusters firing. Jump thrusters started slowing her descent automatically, but she initiated manual control of her jump thrusters after the red dot in her troposcope indicated her opponent was already landing. Karl yelled into the vid com as her father stood from his engineering console's chair and turned toward him. "Taby, slow down." They could hear heavy breathing through the audio feed of the vid com.

"No, Cronus is already landing."

Karl and Captain Drake watched the data on the projected screen. Tabitha focused on her HUD inside her helmet, and watched the altimeter reading and her opponent on her Mech fighter's troposcope.

Operator Furgis jumped up from his seat in the recreation chamber of his suite with excitement and concern as he watched the action of the Mech fighter match unfold on his wraparound display. Chief Tylor looked over at his boss. "That speed is very dangerous."

"She has no choice, Dan," Raynor replied. "Swells is already down."

Operator Furgis sat back down, on the edge of his seat. They were mesmerized and surprised as they watched Darkstar land hard on one knee with her right fist hitting the ground, and at the same time they witnessed flashes and streaks leaving the shoulders of Cronus. The display was broadcasting the Mech fight in great detail, allowing Operator Furgis and his guests to watch the missiles fly rapidly through the air.

Karl Hobbs yelled into the vid com, "Get up!" and at the same time Captain Drake yelled, "Countermeasures!" as

Hammer One's troposcope projected the data onto their console's display. Tabitha was quick in landing and used her drop thrusters for the entire procedure; the assembly was still engaged to her Mech fighter. Instead of dropping the jump pack, she decided to chance using the jump thruster pack as armor and stood in a squat with her back toward the approaching missiles. The time required for Cronus's missiles to traverse the distance to his opponent did not allow Darkstar a chance to change her tactics. The missiles roared in with gases, leaving a mild smoke trail. Darkstar was engulfed in explosions as the missiles impacted the entire area around her, leaving a cloud of smoke and debris from the Earth.

Kelly Brown's expression of surprise quickly turned to a frown as Sam jumped from his seat, almost knocking her off.

Raynor was slightly shocked as well. "Take it easy, Sam, she's in one of the best Mech fighters designed."

His father laughed with excitement, but he was aware of Sam's affections toward Tabitha Drake and felt the same in a different way. Duncan Jennings nodded with approval. "No need to worry—that Mech fighter is built with Jennings technology," and he smacked Sam hard on the shoulder while winking at his father. Everyone in Operator Furgis's suite relaxed slightly as the display showed Darkstar stand up through the cloud. Her jump thruster pack was sparking and fell from her Mech fighter as she released the damaged assembly.

Captain Drake called out to his daughter through the vid com, "Get in the fight!" and watched the bursts of flame shoot out the Mech fighter's thrusters as Darkstar rose straight up and spun in a 180-degree turn. Cronus was beyond visual range, leaving Darkstar with the choice of long-range missiles.

She locked in on Cronus using her troposcope and launched a volley of long-range missiles from her shoulder packs. The coliseum in the Delphi dome witnessed their counterparts standing and cheering in the hover stands as the fight droid's projection zoomed in and out of the many vessels hovering around the outskirts of the match. The fight droid was quick to return to the projection of Cronus skimming sideways with his thrusters on and launching countermeasures against Darkstar's assault of long-range missiles.

Several small projectiles shot from Cronus and struck the approaching missiles that would have impacted the Mech fighter; the other missiles struck the ground, causing flumes of Earth to rocket out. Cronus watched his HUD as the troposcope from the Mech fighter instantly uploaded the data acquired through the sensing device. Cronus was a seasoned Mech driver and could instinctively foresee Darkstar's attempts. He moved closer at an angle of approach on the left side as he watched the data in his helmet display Darkstar's advance on his right. Cronus watched the red blip flash in an indication of missile launching, and he spoke calmly through his helmet's vid com. "LRMs fire." He felt the jolt of his long-range missiles leaving his shoulders' missile packs.

Tabitha, having already launched a long-range assault with her Mech fighter's missile packs, now went into defensive mode. The spectators in the Delphi dome on Neptune One and occupying the hover stands near the assigned combative area knew how important an armor warrior's ability to switch between offensive and defensive maneuvers was. Darkstar waited briefly for the missiles to approach while to her right—"Counter fire"—and both her father and good friend

Karl could hear the heavy breathing through the linked vid com. Darkstar was now positioned directly in front of Cronus as the missiles from both sides flew past each other and several midair explosions lit up both Mech fighter's HUDs as the missiles struck each other.

Both fighters remained vigilant as they watched their individual counter missiles intercept the incoming flight of heavily explosive projectiles. Cronus sidestepped one of Darkstar's missiles that flew through his defensive barrage, and Karl and Captain Drake grew concerned as two missiles from Cronus locked onto Darkstar. Captain Drake yelled, "Get out of there!" but Tabitha made a quick decision of unorthodox use of weapons. She shot sixty-five-caliber rounds from her left arm cannon, creating a defensive wall of projectiles. One of Cronus's missiles exploded, causing Darkstar to stagger from the shock wave and leaving an opening for the remaining long-range missile. The missile impacted Darkstar's left upper leg, causing sparks and odd-colored, dark smoke. Captain Drake grabbed Karl tightly by the shoulder. "Damage?" and they watched flashing caution indicators throughout their transparent touch screen console.

Tabitha could hear her father's voice through her vid com link. "Taby, you all right?" She shook the shock of impact off quickly, responding while catching her breath, "Yeah, it seemed like a good idea at the time."

"Taby, you don't have much time. Move up in his heading; close the gap quickly."

Karl added, "He can tell through his trop you're moving slower and he will try to hit you with more long-range weapons."

They heard heavy breathing for a moment before watching Darkstar rise up with thrusters on full. Karl checked his console with a glance. "Sir, Taby's mix is off."

Captain Drake did not reply as he focused on his engineering console. After a brief moment he called out over the vid com, "Taby, adjust your secondary scrubs; your primaries are damaged," and he watched as several indicator lights on his console stopped flashing.

Cronus could see Darkstar moving closer at a fast pace, and he knew from watching several vid com recordings of Darkstar's previous matches that she was fierce in close combat. Cronus decided to veer right, leaving Darkstar's left side in front of his approach. Darkstar matched him move for move as they slowly closed the distance and continued to fight with troposcopes at long range. Darkstar spoke with more ease in her voice as her oxygen levels balanced out. "LRM launch, discharge packs." She felt the jolt of her missiles launching with an increase in speed as the long-range missile packs fell off her shoulders. Cronus was committed to the same tactic, knowing Darkstar could close the gap between them with the newly acquired speed of her Mech fighter. Cronus's shoulder packs fell from his Mech after launching the remaining missiles; he was quick in launching countermeasures against Darkstar's final long-range assault.

Darkstar sprinted with a limp from her left leg; she was determined to close the gap quickly as she watched for Cronus on her HUD and visually. Karl was loud but calm. "Taby, he should be in visual range soon."

"I know where he is. I can see smoke trails from his missiles."

Tabitha's father called out, "That's not him—he's using a

decoy droid," and he worked his console, trying to get an accurate location on Cronus.

The warning from her father was too late. Tabitha watched her helmet light up with warnings, accompanied by an alarm tone. She ducked into a right shoulder roll as two medium-range missiles flew over her back.

Darkstar spoke softly to herself. "This guy's good," and she heard her father's voice: "You're better. Switch to MRMs." Tabitha spoke loudly and her Mech fighter responded to her physical commands. Her bio implants created an instant link between her reactions and the Mech fighter, and her thruster lifted off her knees when she rolled out of her evasive maneuver and took her straight up while releasing a volley of medium-range missiles. Cronus was prepared for the attack and sidestepped with thruster assistance. He launched countermeasures along with another volley of medium-range missiles, and he could see the distance closing between himself and his aggressive opponent. His HUD showed her moving up on his left side in an attempt at a direct assault.

Tabitha remembered a decoy trick that Operator Furgis once talked about. She allowed several of Cronus's missiles to close in quickly before exploding them in a defensive counter missile projectile wall. After the explosion, which resulted in a cloud of Earth and missile debris, she released two skimmer missiles from her lower right leg arsenal. She also released a volley of medium-range missiles to accompany her skimmers; she was relying on the skimmers' ability to hug the Earth at a close distance and hide from Cronus's troposcope. The only way Cronus would know of the skimmers approaching from Earth level would be from visual acquisition. Darkstar was counting on her missiles to distract Cronus long enough to allow her skimmers to impact his lower legs.

The alarms in Cronus's HUD sounded with a display of incoming medium-range missiles; they had already locked on, becoming an immediate threat. Cronus acted quickly by releasing countermeasures and sidestepping to his right with thrusters firing. His Mech fighter lifted off the ground and moved with great speed. Darkstar's missiles were destroyed in Cronus's countermeasures, except one that impacted the ground in front of Cronus as his Mech fighter landed on its legs.

Tabitha could hear the cheering from her father and Karl through her vid com as the skimmer missiles shot straight through the debris of her missiles and impacted with great force on Cronus's lower legs. Cronus was taken by surprise as the explosions shot debris straight up in front of him. He watched the display of his HUD and heard alarms sounding as the damage to his Mech fighter was displayed, but he focused first on his troposcope. The debris caused by both the skimmer missiles and medium-range missiles removed his visual sight of Darkstar, and the red indicator on his troposcope showed a contact with Darkstar's data in the sidebar moving directly in front. Cronus now moved to his right without using his damaged thrusters; his tactic was to stay on Darkstar's left side and not get lured into close combat.

Darkstar watched her troposcope carefully at the distance read-out; she was closing slowly while maintaining a medium-range assault when her alarm canceled her thoughts of launching another assault. Her troposcope and threat alert indicated fire pods approaching rapidly, and she instinctively activated her previously damaged thrusters.

Tabitha heard Karl's voice through her vid com as she piloted her Mech fighter away from the assault of fire pods. "I wanted to save your thrusters, but good call, Taby." Darkstar knew that when a fire pod explodes in close proximity to a Mech fighter, the incendiary blast overheats the entire Mech fighter, causing a shutdown; the only other weapon worse than fire pods was the dreaded stunner missile. Darkstar rose above the massive fire ball engulfing the area she last occupied. She knew Ben Swells was very good at long-range and medium-range combat, but short range was in her advantage. Darkstar quickly shut down her thrusters and descended to the ground toward Cronus, her bio implants already with short-range missiles selected as she watched the distance read-out displayed in her HUD from the troposcope. "SRM fire." She could not feel the jolt from the launch as her Mech fighter was already in motion, preparing for a counterassault.

Darkstar slowed her speed down as she turned right to face her opponent; her HUD flashed briefly, followed by the vid com chime and voice: "Incoming transmission." She double-checked her HUD for contacts and responded, "Source." The voice of the vid com was instant in its reply: "Ben Swells." Tabitha was curious more than cautious, knowing it was rare to transmit during a match, but it was not unheard of. Tabitha was driving her Mech fighter hard in zigzag maneuvers, attempting to bring a close combat fight to Cronus, and she took a deep breath so she would not sound strained from the match. "Accept," she said, and the transmission offered static at first before Ben Swells' voice was clearly heard. "Tabitha, hold position for a moment. I got a hover stand that keeps closing in on my position. It's up to you, Tabitha," and the vid com transmission shut down.

Darkstar quickly switched her troposcope from a focused, medium-range scan to a general long-range scan; she could see in her HUD a green dot appear and disappear at random behind Cronus. She was ready to launch an assault but canceled. Darkstar stood still in the middle of the Simpson Desert waiting and watching. The vid com chimed once again and she did not wait for recognition. Ben Swells' unstressed voice was heard. "Thank you, Tabitha, you're a good opponent, and by the way, I like those skimmers you threw at me."

Tabitha chuckled. "I got some more if you like them so much," and she heard her opponent return her chuckle. "No thanks. In fairness it's your lead, Darkstar," and the vid com shut down the transmission.

Darkstar moved quickly to her left, knowing Cronus was attempting a flanking move on her damaged left side. Tabitha's bio implants controlled her Mech fighter with precision, allowing for a rapid launch of short-range missiles and a quick turn right before offering Cronus an opportunity to approach from her rear. Ben Swells was quick in his countermeasures and the use of his bio implants to control his Mech fighter. Darkstar watched Cronus evade her assault with a combination of maneuvers and countermeasures. She checked her weapons read-out on her HUD, selecting her preferred close-combat weapons; both armor warriors knew the time for hard steel to clash was approaching as the distance between them closed.

Ben Swells realized his attempt at slowing Darkstar's approach was in vain. He was hoping for more damage before engaging in close combat. He watched a volley of short-range missiles launch from Darkstar visually through his armor warrior's helmet as well as a green dot flickering on his HUD from the troposcope. Cronus was concerned knowing the hover stand was encroaching in his combat area, but the short-range missile assault was also a concern. Each Mech fighter was quick in their attempt at unloading unwanted arsenal onto their opponent's position, whether it was damaging or not. The loss of weight in close combat was strategic.

Darkstar watched with anticipation for Cronus's answer to her assault, and her troposcope lit up with an alarm and data, informing her of the approaching threat; she quickly launched low-yield Mortelis flares to decoy the volley of heat sticks from Cronus's arsenal. She drove her Mech fighter hard, attempting to evade the heat sticks. She knew the armor-piercing tips would not penetrate her Mech fighter's armor, but the design of the heat sticks was simply to embed itself into the armor of the Mech fighter and produce excessive heat. Tabitha Drake felt several impacts and watched the temperature reading in her HUD climb slowly. She could hear Karl's voice through the noise of her Mech fighter and the combat she was engaged in. "Adjust your temp with emergency cooling before your systems shut down and return the favor." Tabitha did not reply as she concentrated on her Mech fighter systems.

Cronus was moving up on her left flank once again, but he slowed as he drove his Mech fighter in a left turn, attempting to evade Darkstar's response. He was impressed not only with Tabitha's driving skills but also with her choice of weapons; he watched a barrage of heat discs streak toward his position with a target lock on his Mech fighter. It was too late for evasive maneuvers. Instead, Cronus launched defensive low-yielding Mortelis flares and dove forward, causing the massive mechanical fighter to lunge forward into a forward roll. Cronus could not believe the tenacity of Darkstar as his Mech fighter straightened out and stood facing his rapidly approaching opponent. Alarms sounded in his HUD as two heat discs that impacted his armor started emitting high temperatures. He watched the read-out of his HUD display damage information.

Cronus concentrated on evasive tactics while adjusting systems for heat dissipation; the temperature alarms continued to broadcast audibly in his helmet as he watched Darkstar move closer.

Darkstar watched her opponent struggle to recover from her assault and listened to her father's voice escalate into excitement as he shouted through the vid com, "Metal to metal—this is your fight!" Tabitha concentrated intensely on her bio implant, knowing she owned the advantage.

Operator Furgis and his son watched the wraparound in his suite, shouting cheers with wide smiles as they watched Darkstar move in for a Mech fighter slug match. Chief Tylor stood on the far end, focused on the display that zoomed in on the area where the two Mech fighters faced off. He was calmer than his companions but still offered excitement in his voice, "Protect your left," as he watched Darkstar move into striking range.

Cronus watched Darkstar appear quickly, and he knew she was very aggressive in tight combat. Cronus, with temperature alarms beeping loudly from his HUD, managed to straightened out before his opponent was in striking distance. He was impressed once again with Tabitha's speed as her right arm came directly in front of his Mech fighter's chest; he knew he if he wanted to survive this assault, he was required to escape and gain some distance to recover. Cronus concentrated on a defensive tactic and used his left arm to block her strike; however, this was an opportunity for Tabitha Drake. She chanced leaving her back open to a strike as she took advantage of Cronus's mistake; her left arm sprung forward into a powerful projectile as Cronus's torso turned in his blocking maneuver.

Both Mech fighters felt the jolt and heard the sound of the impact as Darkstar's left arm impacted Cronus's left shoulder. She could hear her father and Karl Hobbs cheering over her vid com as she watched sparks fly from Cronus's Mech fighter. Darkstar was feeling very powerful and was determined to finish this match quickly; she stepped forward to follow up on her assault and watched her opponent land on his right side. Cronus rapidly rolled into a kneeling position without pause and faced the approaching Mech fighter; he watched Darkstar approach with a slight limp on her left side. Cronus focused on the vulnerable spot of his opponent's Mech fighter as he spoke quickly. "Sixty-five gatling." A burst of sixty-five-caliber rounds from his left arm struck Darkstar's left leg, followed by a heavy blow from his right leg.

Darkstar staggered back. As she watched Cronus rise to his feet, she knew at this moment that he would not give up this fight easily. The alarms sounded as her HUD displayed the damage Cronus inflicted to her Mech fighter; she quickly diverted system commands and bypassed emergency shutdowns as the temperature rose. The vid com audibly crackled with static before Captain Drake's voice was heard. "Taby, I know you want to pursue, but watch that temp with your emergency shutdown procedure bypassed." Her father waited patiently for a reply as he watched Hammer One's engineering station's troposcope display Cronus slowly increasing the distance between the two Mech fighters.

Tabitha was pushing the design of her Mech fighter as she turned left, knowing Cronus would circle in a spiral course, increasing his distance slowly. She watched the temperature read-out from her HUD as she increased speed, and she now understood why the commissioner of Earth dome wanted this fight in the Simpson Desert. She increased emergency cooling when she noticed the ambient temperature rising slowly; her HUD also displayed the heat signature of Cronus slowly increasing. Darkstar spoke softly into her helmet's vid com. "Heat discs fire." And she felt the small jolt as the heat discs shot from her Mech fighter and rapidly traversed the distance toward Cronus. All four of her heat discs flew by her opponent; at close distance they were not successful at acquiring a target lock on her opponent.

Cronus turned sharply to his left to face his opponent with the same determination of finishing this match quickly. He turned sharply right once again with his torso remaining left and facing his opponent. His choice of weapons was different. "SRM fire."

Darkstar watched smoke rise from Cronus's chest. She did not need the troposcope to know what was rapidly approaching in an assault course toward her, and she quickly responded, "Counter fire, heat rounds." She raised her right arm toward Cronus and fired off a short burst of sixty-five-caliber rounds as her Mortelis flares distracted the short-range missiles.

Cronus also bypassed his emergency shutdown procedure

and increased speed and watched his temperature read-out. The incendiary round struck his left side, and his torso straightened with his direction of travel. The temperature level increased in his Mech fighter as Darkstar's incendiary rounds exploded on contact. He wondered why Tabitha never made it to the semifinals before after experiencing combat with her as an opponent.

The temperature increase forced Cronus to decrease speed, allowing Darkstar to gain speed; the limping Mech fighter was persistent in demanding a close combative match with her opponent. Cronus watched his HUD carefully. His troposcope also informed him of the ambient temperature rise, and he turned his torso left toward Darkstar while keeping his course straight. "Heat pods, fire." His Mech fighter staggered to the right as large heat pods launched from his chest weapons pod.

Darkstar's proximity alarms sounded, alerting her to the danger of heat weapons. She raised her left arm quickly, "Fifty cal high yield," and fired a short burst from her left arm's arsenal. A massive explosion resulted from her evasive tactic, causing a slight shock wave to hit both Mech fighters. Cronus shrugged off the disappointment and continued on an outward spiral course.

Operator Furgis sat on the edge of his seat. "Yeah, Taby!"

Raynor chuckled. "Woo, that girl is good!" She smiled and watched the others nod in agreement.

Duncan Jennings was quick to join in on the critique. "She could go further—that Mech fighter will take the heat."

Chief Tylor disagreed. "It's best if she holds the temp down until she's sure Swells is vulnerable."

"Absolutely," said Furgis. "Wait until he's overheating and

then hit him with some more incendiaries."

Duncan laughed. "I tell you she can do both." Raynor patted him on the shoulder and pointed at his seat.

Cronus ignored his temperature read-out along with his support crew's warning from Earth Dome One shuttle and increased speed. He spoke softly and instructed his vid com to select his next choice of weapon: "Incendiary grenade." Darkstar was closing on a direct heading toward Cronus; he waited, allowing her to believe his Mech fighter was overheating and slowing. Cronus watched the distance read-out carefully for the right timing. "Fire!" And he instructed his Mech fighter's speed to increase as the grenade launchers from his upper torso catapulted incendiary grenades rapidly into the air above Darkstar.

Tabitha was surprised but not unprepared; "Thrusters," she commanded, and the massive mechanical fighter rose quickly above and beyond the area of impact, her troposcope showing very large heat signatures of the impacting grenades. She shut down the thrusters quickly and heard Karl's voice through the vid com audio transmission. "Good call, but save your thrusters." Her Mech fighter landed hard but upright in close proximity to Cronus, who realized quickly that he was in a perfect position to strike at his opponent. He chose his weapons fast, "Sixty-five-cal incendiary," and raised his right arm toward Darkstar. Instinctively she raised her left arm and fired her high-yielding fifty-caliber rounds and crouched into a defensive position. The explosion of the two arsenals colliding was felt throughout the match area. Hammer One rocked when the shock wave from the blast struck the shuttle.

Captain Drake held on to his engineering console, and

when the shock wave passed, allowing Hammer One to become more stable, he called to his daughter with great concern, "Taby," but only heard static from the vid com. As the crackle subsided and static cleared, Captain Drake felt relieved to hear his daughter's voice. "All right, Dad, I had some systems shut down, including my trop, but they're coming back on line." He could hear heavy breathing as his daughter continued. "I managed to get above the worst of it, but I have no visual on Cronus."

Slight static returned. Her father turned around in his chair. "Karl, where's Cronus," and he watched Karl work his operations console with determination. After a moment Karl responded calmly, "Taby, he's moving away on your left." Before either man could speak, they heard Tabitha's voice clearly. "I got him and he looks damaged." Karl was quick to reply as he swung his chair around to work his controls. "Yeah, Taby, he has some residual heat dissipation; however, he'll be picking up speed soon, so get in there." They kept an eye on the readout of Darkstar's Mech fighter as she pursued her opponent.

Cronus watched Darkstar closing the distance quickly on his HUD as he heard the temperature alarms sounding off; he quickly silenced the alarms and turned to face his opponent. He knew it was inevitable that she would be in close-combat range within moments. Cronus selected close-combat weapons as he visually watched Darkstar approach; he was also aware of the green dot that would occasionally blip on his troposcope.

Duncan was standing behind Sam Furgis as they watched the match unfold on Operator Furgis's wedding gift, and he was excited. "That is a well-built fighter."

"Very well designed," Chief Tylor responded. "However, the next design needs more heat sinks."

Duncan frowned with a quick nod. "Absolutely correct, but no one said anything about desert fighting."

Sam agreed. "I think you need to include some of those grenades as well," and Operator Furgis laughed. "Yeah, that as well."

Cronus watched the green blip on his HUD grow steady, while smoke trails appeared from Darkstar's chest followed by proximity alarms indicating the threat of heat weapons approaching. His HUD continued to sound the alarms as well as a steady green dot. With the data of the hover stand closing, Ben Swells made a decision from his conscience and changed course. He turned straight into the incoming barrage of short-range incendiary missiles. He knew if one was to fail in its target lock on his Mech fighter, it would bypass with the possibility of locking on the hover stand. Cronus launched countermeasures and released a barrage of sixty-caliber incendiary rounds on both sides; he was not worried about his Mech fighter as much as creating a wall between the hover stand and the incoming ordinance.

Tabitha activated the thrusters on her Mech fighter using the last of her Mortelis fuel, and the ground erupted in a cloud as her thruster forced her fighter into the air. She rose quick and high while releasing a short burst of her flash bolt aimed directly at Cronus. She could feel victory as she gained altitude and closed in on Cronus. Her father and Karl both shouted in the vid com, "Taby, no!" as they became aware of the hover stand, but it was too late. Darkstar could not hear over her own shouts of victory, "Death from above," and the two individuals in Hammer One watched in shock as Cronus aimed his left arm toward the incoming incendiary short-range missiles. He was aiming toward the missiles he knew would fly past without a target lock and ignored the threat to his chest.

Operator Furgis and his companions jumped up from their seats with excitement, cheering for Tabitha Drake as the wraparound display showed the Mech fighter rise into the air after firing a round of missiles at her opponent, followed by a bright light designed to temporarily blind the Mech fighter. Flash bolts were designed not only to blind the armor warrior but also to interrupt the troposcope the driver relied on for their HUD. Raynor was the first to shout with horror, "No," as she watched the display change into a wider view. Operator Furgis's chamber grew quiet as the guests stood watching Darkstar rise above Cronus. Sam broke the silence. "She does not see them." Then he felt Kelly Brown leaning on him and squeezing his shoulder tightly.

Cronus was ready to release his sixty-five-caliber incendiary rounds at the approaching missiles that reacquired a new target, but the impact of the missile strikes on his chest caused his troposcope to lose targeting lock. His right arm pointed straight up and released a barrage of sixty-five-caliber rounds that struck Darkstar, and the missiles Cronus attempted to intercept raced past quickly. The rounds from Cronus's right arm struck Darkstar as she was landing without thrusters, and the heat from these rounds was extensive, causing most of her systems to shut down. As Cronus fell back, landing flat on the ground, he could visually see Tabitha's Mech fighter blocking the sun. Darkstar landed on top of Cronus without thrusters, and the heavy Mech fighter's legs impacted him with a fierce, crushing blow, causing tremendous damage to the already damaged Mech fighter.

Most of Darkstar's systems were shut down as she completed her death-from-above maneuver, and the impact caused her to lose footing and fall to one side of Cronus. She was dizzy from the impact, and as she shook the feeling off, the veteran armor warrior realized her Mech fighter's left foot was on Cronus's chest and her right knee was beside his head. She also noticed Cronus was not moving. A bright flash appeared, causing her helmet's visor to darken; she looked toward the source of the intense light but could not believe what she was watching. Her systems started to regain functionality, and through the alarms sounding she could hear the vid com. "Taby, Taby!" She responded with haste. "Dad, my troposcope is down, what's happening?" She waited for her father's response as she checked the systems of her damaged Mech fighter.

Darkstar's vid com was fully functional once again, and she could hear her father clearly. "Taby, get off Cronus and come to a lockdown position; the fight droid is approaching rapidly and will shut you down if you don't comply."

Darkstar could see the fight droid approaching as her HUD started receiving data from her troposcope. As her Mech fighter struggled to rise to its feet in a standing lockdown position, she watched other contacts appear quickly on her HUD. "What's happening, Dad?" Her father was slow to answer as he checked Darkstar's systems through his engineering console on Hammer One. Karl replied, "Taby, there's been an accident," and he continued to work his transparent touch screen console.

Tabitha waited patiently in silence as her HUD displayed

the carnage of the blast area, and the voice of her father snapped her out of a slight trance. "Taby?" She shook the unfocused feeling off as she quickly returned her thoughts back to the situation she was in. Her father could hear the worry in her voice. "Dad, my HUD is showing a lot of damage." Her father interrupted her with a calm tone in his voice. "Don't worry about that, Taby, the match is over."

Tabitha was insistent and repeated, "What happened, Dad?" She paused for a moment, watching the fight droid through her HUD.

Captain Drake remained calm. "One of your incendiary missiles impacted on a hover stand that was too close to the match area."

Tabitha's voice was shaky as she asked a question she already knew the answer to. "Is everyone all right?"

"Taby, the hover stands have no defensive platforms; they were designed to operate in Earth dome under a more controlled environment."

"What's the damage?"

Captain Drake could hear the concern and grief in her voice. Karl said, "Not sure, Taby. The stray missile impacted in the middle of the HS, causing major damage. Most likely there will be a lot of casualties."

"Dad, the rescue shuttles are here, and the fight droid is requiring I enter the drop ship." Karl Hobbs nodded at Captain Drake as he watched the area grow in traffic on his vid com display. Captain Drake responded, "Taby, we'll see you back in the Mech hangar," and he waited for his daughter's acknowledgment.

The fight droid released Tabitha's Mech fighter in transport mode only, allowing her to enter the drop ship; as the rear hatch of the drop ship closed, her father could hear the grief in her voice. "I'll see you guys back in the hangar," and the vid com shut down. Captain Drake swiveled his chair quickly to face the cockpit. "Follow that drop ship, Lieutenant." He did not hear a reply—only a slight salute of his hand, a nod of the head, and a quick motion of Hammer One as it lined up with the course of the drop ship.

Chapter Twelve

O perator Furgis stood and looked around his recreation chambers. He was feeling grief and knew from the look on his guests that they too were grieving. "I guess I need to address the dome." He walked over to the main vid com. His wife and son followed and stood on the side out of view of the communications device, and Operator Furgis spoke softly. "Delphi dome link, authorization Furgis," and the vid com flickered with a chime and acknowledgment.

Supervisor Stykes looked over at Officer Armela and Huiling Li. He could see the same grief on their faces as he felt inside. "Juan, Operator Furgis is linking in." Officer Armela let go of Huiling's hand to work his touch screen control console.

The spectators were loud as the large 3-D projection of Operator Furgis appeared in the middle of the arena floor. They quieted down into a murmur as the Delphi dome started closing and the carbon electric glass dome switched from transparency to a projection of an Earthen sunset. Operator Furgis held up both arms with his palms open; he was soft-spoken. "Ladies and gentlemen, guests of Neptune One. Thank you for your attention. As we all have seen during this Mech fight, there has been a tragic accident. We do not know the extent of the damage, but what we do know is that this accident has caused severe harm to our brothers and sisters, and our hearts go out to everyone." Operator Furgis listened for a moment as the murmur grew into slight chatter. He held his open palms up once again. "Ladies and gentlemen, please allow me to continue. For our guests who have family and friends on Earth attending the fight, please input your data into the nearest vid com, and we will do our best to get you the information you deserve." He was interrupted by the chime on his ear com piece.

Operator Furgis reached up and activated his ear com piece while holding his other palm up in a display of pause. After a moment, he spoke to his guests calmly. "Pastor Li has informed me that she will be contacting the Christian ministries of planetary relations, and a service will be held directly for those who choose to attend. May God bless you all," and the 3-D projection of Operator Furgis disappeared.

The vid com in his chambers shut down, and he turned to his guests. His wife held his arm tightly. "That was good, Ken," along with support from his son. "Yeah, Pops, you did good."

"Ken," said Raynor, "I need to use the vid com in the rest chamber. I got a data message from Mars City Central." She walked away.

Sam Furgis activated his ear com piece to contact Supervisor Stykes, while his father watched with pride and gratitude, knowing his son had turned into a successful administrator. He approached Chief Tylor. "What do you think happened, Chief?" and waited patiently as the chief thought for a moment.

"My guess would be the pilot of the hover stands grew reckless and entered the fight zone."

"Will Tabitha be held responsible?" Kelly asked.

Sam stood behind her and gave her a slight startle as he held her shoulders. "Absolutely not—there's no way they can hold Taby responsible."

Operator Furgis decided to check. "Time to find out from the *Hammer* what's really happening." His guests gathered around as the vid com flickered for a moment before displaying a projected 3-D image of Commander Mela Finch. The short blonde woman, dressed in her Western Empire commander uniform, sat in the command chair on the bridge of the SS *Hammerhead*. "Ken, how's that floating vid slot?"

Operator Furgis chuckled, knowing this was what Captain Drake always said. "Mela, how's Taby?"

"Not sure, Ken—all Captain Drake told me was that Tabitha was required to remain in her assigned chambers until called for. Sorry, Ken, that's all I know."

Operator Furgis sighed heavily. "All right Mela, let Justin know that I was looking for him." He looked at the chief with disappointment.

"I'll let him know, Commander," and the vid com shut down.

Raynor emerged from the rest chamber. "She still calls you commander," and Operator Furgis laughed. "It's better than what you used to call me." Before either could comment, the vid com chimed and displayed the name of Supervisor Stykes.

"Hey, boss, got some good news I think."

"Let's have it, Leaf."

"Edwards and the rest of the Easterners are leaving for their ship, boss." Operator Furgis knew this was good news to his security supervisor. "I'll keep an eye on them and let you know when the *Staton* leaves orbit."

Operator Furgis nodded. "Thanks, Leaf. Let the senior staff know we're all meeting in the Solar House for the next meal period." He was ready to end transmission but noticed his security supervisor was waiting for more. "All right, tell them it's on me." After a quick smile from Stykes, the vid com shut down. Operator Furgis turned and watched the smiles on his friends grow after hearing the offer—everyone except his wife.

Raynor looked disappointed. "Ken, that's what I wanted to discuss."

"What's the problem?" Sam moved closer to his mother in concern. Raynor chuckled. "The timing is bad. Derek said Mars City Central is growing in its anger over the championship Mech fight."

"What's the problem with the Mech fight being in City Central?" asked Sam.

Raynor looked quickly at her son before speaking to her husband. "That's the problem, Ken, the match was set up for the Mariner Desert, but with the issue Mother Earth caused..."

Operator Furgis nodded and interrupted. "...the Martians want the fight to be held in City Central."

"Yes, the citizens of Mars are concerned with the match as well as the Eastern Empire's presence." She glanced over at Duncan Jennings.

Duncan snickered. "I'll be leaving shortly; if you hurry I'll give you a lift," and Raynor looked at her husband hopefully.

Operator Furgis wanted more time with Raynor but understood the responsibilities of administration. "All right, Ray, we gotta do what we gotta do." Before either his wife or son could reply, the vid com chimed. The incoming transmission said, "Earth, Drake."

Captain Drake was in his daughter's assigned chambers and spoke somberly. "Ken, what's the word?"

"Justin, is everyone all right? How's Taby doing?"

"She's kinda shaken by the accident, and she's blaming herself for the destruction of the hover stand."

Raynor Furgis stepped into view of the vid com. "Can we say hello, Justin?"

Captain Drake looked behind him quickly and turned back with a frown. "She's resting, Ray. When she comes out, I'll tell her you were asking for her."

Karl Hobbs appeared in a 3-D projection behind Captain Drake. "She's been through a lot and needs to rest; the commissioner will most likely be rigorous in his interrogation."

Sam Furgis did not like this news. "What do you mean interrogation? She's not responsible for all those people."

Operator Furgis turned to face his son and calmed him with a soft hold on the shoulder. Raynor shook her head in disbelief. "How many injured, Karl?"

The tall black man known as Triton's Terror frowned with before answering. "Poor choice of words, Sam. I should have said 'investigation.'"

Operator Furgis said, "No, Karl, I think you had it right the first time," and he could see his former commander nodding in agreement.

Raynor asked again, "How many, Karl?" and Karl sighed heavily. "At this time they say two hundred and eighty-three dead and twelve seriously injured."

There was silence until Operator Furgis heard Chief Tylor

speaking to Duncan. Captain Drake watched Operator Furgis turn and talk to the background before returning his attention to them. "The chief wants to know if they're investigating the troposcopes yet or if they're focusing on driver error."

Captain Drake shook his head. "No, they're focusing on operator error, Chief." Operator Furgis immediately heard a slight grunt from behind him.

"Justin," Raynor asked, "when are you leaving for Mars? Not to sound gruesome, but she did win the match, and I look forward to seeing you guys."

"Mom has a point," said Sam. "Taby won and has the right to the championship."

"If they let us leave," Captain Drake added.

Operator Furgis held his hand up as he looked around his chambers, confirming everyone was quiet. "Just hold on for a moment." He turned to the chief. "Any worms?"

Chief Tylor pulled his data pad out of its holster and activated the transparent touch screen; his hands and fingers glided over the commands of the device before he looked up. "This should secure the transmission, sir."

Operator Furgis turned to face the 3-D projection of the vid com as it turned yellow and flickered for a brief moment. "We're all set, Just. Now what's up back there?"

Duncan and the chief crowded in behind Raynor and her son. Captain Drake looked around Tabitha's assigned quarters. Karl Hobbs was working his data pad and suddenly stopped. "You're clear, sir," he said to the captain and re-holstered his data pad.

Captain Drake spoke softly. "Ken, the Eastern Empire is attempting to connect Taby to the Western empire. They're using the fact that Taby used the *Hammer* as transportation, and the *Hammer* has support ships in Earth's orbit."

Sam was not amused. "That's absurd—everyone knows you're her father."

"Sam," said his father, "political wars are started by petty insinuations like this."

"Yeah, but to say…"

His mother interrupted. "Sam, your father's right."

Operator Furgis started laughing. "Sam, it's real easy to fight an actual war with ground troops, space marines, and large solar ships; the challenge is the political war of words and accusations that rally alliances."

"Sam, you could learn a lot from your father," Duncan Jennings offered.

Operator Furgis frowned, not knowing if this was a joke about his political insight or a compliment on his administration skills. Sam grew calmer. "So what's the plan, Pops?"

"I'll check with Ambassador Davis and see if he can help." Operator Furgis paused before turning his attention to his 3-D projected guests. "What about you, Just? What do you have in mind?"

Captain Justin Drake looked around the room with a nervous gaze. "Karl, are you sure there's no stealth droids around?"

Karl lifted his data pad out of its holster and studied the read-out briefly before handing the device to the captain. "I don't think so, sir."

Captain Drake took the device and studied the data carefully. "Ken, either way my daughter is leaving with me when we head for Mars," and before Operator Furgis could reply, Karl interrupted. "The commissioner will be sending for

Taby soon."

Raynor said, "Just, let me know if I can do anything. I'm catching a ride with Duncan as soon as I pack."

"All right, Ray, we'll keep in touch," and the vid com shut down.

Operator Furgis turned and held his wife's hands before pulling her in for a hug. He whispered into her ear, "I'll miss you," and he released her as he stepped slightly back. "Now get your stuff ready. I'm sure Dunc needs to get back to his office."

The smiling Duncan followed Raynor into the rest chambers to help her with her luggage. Operator Furgis looked at the chief. "Get everyone together and meet us at the Solar House."

"Yes sir," the chief replied as he activated his ear com piece and exited Operator Furgis's suite. It was not long before Raynor and Duncan emerged with Raynor's luggage. She walked to her son, who was already grabbing her bags. "I'll get that, Mom," and Raynor held her son by the back of the neck and kissed him on the forehead.

Operator Furgis chuckled. "Sam, ask Marco to send someone up to get those."

"No need, Pops, we got them," said Sam.

The entry door slid open with a hiss, and everyone gathered in the hall. Sam and Duncan followed the newlyweds down the hall to the lift, and Duncan said, "Wish we had more time for the casino."

Raynor laughed. "You know, we have casinos on Mars."

"Yeah, but nothing comes close to Neptune One."

The lift came to a stop on the hotel lobby level, and the group exited. The lobby was very loud and full of guests arriving and leaving the massive station. Duncan looked around slowly before looking at Operator Furgis. "I look forward to seeing your reports, Ken."

"Between accommodating for the matches in the Delphi and Acela's everlasting tournaments, we're doing great," Operator Furgis said with a very wide smile.

Raynor snickered and held her husband's upper arm. "I guess I'll have to entice Acela to move to Mars."

They started walking toward the glide tube station and saw Marco and Chayton rapidly approaching.

"Why so soon, Ray?" Marco asked, and before she could answer, Chayton interrupted. "Join us at the Solar House first."

Duncan started laughing. "Sorry, Charlie, we need to leave right away."

Operator Furgis grinned at both of his staff members. "I wish she could stay as well, but duty calls. Is everyone else meeting you at the Solar House?"

Operator Furgis did not have a long wait as his attention was captured by his friend and front desk supervisor. Marco De Luca adjusted his expensive jacket and looked up and down at Chayton as he spoke. "Seth has one of his large tables waiting for us. I'll let him know you'll be arriving soon." He gently hit Chayton on the upper arm and said, "Time to go," and he turned to Raynor with open arms. "We're all going to miss you, Ray."

Operator Furgis smiled at his wife as he watched her release Marco from his hug and move to Chayton. Raynor was fond of the tall, slim, and well-dressed man from the ancient Americas. She hugged Chayton tighter. "I'll miss ya, Chay," and released him quickly. Chayton smiled at her. "You have a safe trip, Ray, God speed" and he held his hand out to Duncan.

Duncan Jennings leaned forward and shook their hands. "It was a pleasure, gentlemen. If you're ever on Mars, stop in at the Hotel Cartago."

"Between you and my wife, I won't have any senior staff left," joked Operator Furgis.

"I'll be here for ya, Pops," his son joked and patted him on the shoulder. Chayton and Marco entered the lift, and Raynor looked at Duncan with a teasing stare. "We need to put father and son on the side of this tin can." Duncan could not refrain from laughing. Operator Furgis shook his head with a smile as he looked at his son. "Now you know why I love her." Kelly Brown attempted to sound serious as she interrupted. "Sam, I think it's a great idea," and Sam agreed. "I do too, Pops." Operator Furgis chuckled as he grabbed his son by the back of the neck tightly. "It's already a father-and-son operation," and he gently pushed him toward the crowded lobby.

Raynor watched the glide tube car's doors slide open and heard the familiar hiss over the chattering from the crowd that was arriving and departing. Duncan hugged his good friend. "Ken, if you need anything…"

Ken Furgis interrupted. "I love ya like a brother, Dunc," and he let go of his good friend. Duncan turned and hugged Kelly. "Take care of Sam." He then turned to his adopted nephew. "I'm proud of you, Sam; you came a long way from where you were on Mars." Sam smiled as he watched Duncan enter the glide tube car.

Raynor paused with a slight frown at Kelly Brown; she studied the young woman before reaching out and offering a one-armed hug. "I can see that you've come a long way as well," she said, and Kelly replied, "Thank you, ma'am."

"You want to thank me, then take care of my son," Raynor said, and Kelly respectfully replied, "Yes ma'am."

Raynor turned to her son with tearful eyes. "My boy, look at him, all grown up." Sam tried to interrupt, but his mom pulled the tall young man into her for a very large and loving hug. When she finally released her son, she said, "I love you, Sam."

Sam was feeling slightly embarrassed as she kissed him on the cheek, but he loved her as any son loves his mother. "I love you too, Mom." Kelly moved closer to Sam as his mother turned to her husband.

Ken looked at his wife with a large and loving smile. "I know you're going to give me more than that," and he held his arms open. Raynor rested her head on her husband's chest as they hugged tightly before offering a very passionate kiss. Sam looked around the glide tube station and smiled as he witnessed several other couples in lasting hugs and kisses; he wondered if they were employees of Neptune One. Operator Furgis released his wife and she reluctantly pulled away. "I love you, Kennith Furgis," she said, and he returned the loving stare into her eyes. "I love you too, Mrs. Furgis. Now take care of business so you can get back here for our honeymoon, which was taken..."

Raynor laughed through her tears. "You mean *postponed*, and don't worry because good things come to those who wait." She smiled and turned to enter the glide tube car. Before the doors could close, she added, "And when we do get our honeymoon, watch out. I'm gonna rock your shuttle."

Sam grew slightly embarrassed. "Mom, get in your seat!" He turned to Kelly with a laugh. "I hope you're never that bad," and his father interrupted, "Yes you do."

The doors to the glide tube car closed, and the car hissed from the compressed air drive as it quickly increased speed in the direction of the docking spheres.

Operator Furgis, his son, and Kelly Brown made their way toward the Solar House. Sam smiled when he saw several guests stand in front of Pastor Huiling Li's church and watch her announcements on the vid com display projected in front of the church's entrance. The entry door was translucent with the capital letters GF projected in a circle and "come as you are" displayed in old-fashioned writing above. Operator Furgis entered the Solar House and waited with his companions for Seth Adams to walk them to the large table where his senior staff waited.

Seth greeted him with excitement. "Ken, where is your lovely wife?"

Operator Furgis replied with his usual calm demeanor, "Seth, she needed to get back to Mars right away, so she hitched a ride with Duncan."

"Ken, I just got another shipment of strawberries off the transport if you're interested."

"Send them to my quarters, Seth," Operator Furgis said, and Seth replied with a nod of his head. The senior staff stood once Operator Furgis reached his seat. He held out his left hand and said, "Stay seated," then pulled out the chair as his staff sat back in their seats.

Acela Vega looked across the table at her boss. "Ken, I'm sorry Raynor had to leave so early."

Operator Furgis snickered. "No need to apologize, Acela, Ray and I both know the responsibilities of administration."

"Well, tell Ray that we all miss her."

Kelly squeezed Sam's hand hard under the table as she watched Acela wink at him.

Dr. Brook Avers was wearing a beautiful dress, and most men found her to be extremely attractive. The tall, blue-eyed blonde raised a glass. "A toast to Mrs. Furgis." The senior staff picked up their glasses and waited for Operator Furgis. He looked at Brook as he raised his glass. "To my wife," and he heard the men sitting around the table: "Here, here."

Sam shook the taste of the drink off with surprise on his face, and Kelly grabbed his arm. "What's wrong?"

"I didn't expect Dou Zhe. I thought we were having something a little stronger."

"You don't think we're a bunch of drunks floating around in space, do you?" joked Supervisor Stykes.

Sam laughed. "Not at all," and he remembered the last recovery celebration meeting he attended with Dr. Avers as she winked at him.

Operator Furgis looked around the table slowly and raised his glass. "Here's to the best crew in the system." He watched Supervisor Stykes closely. Seth's waiter stood patiently with his data pad ready to input their orders, and Furgis casually looked up. "The usual please." He then turned his attention to Supervisor Stykes and Chief Tylor. Stykes noticed his boss gazing between him and the more private and dimly lit table in the corner. "What's up, boss?"

Operator Furgis looked at Chief Tylor and asked, "Chief, where is Engineer Trently?"

"Engineer Trently is with Dr. Gerlitz's assistant working on that project you requested, sir."

Operator Furgis nodded. "That's acceptable." He looked back at his security supervisor. "However, I see Officer Armela sitting in the corner with Pastor Li." All his senior staff turned to look over at the couple. It was hard to see due to the lighting, but they could see Officer Armela leaning across the table. The very large, muscular security officer with origins from old Mexico was holding the hands of the petite Chinese woman; they laughed and stared into each other's eyes, not allowing any distractions to interrupt their pleasure.

Leaf Stykes turned back to face Furgis. "Boss, Officer Armela asked if he could have a private meal with Huiling."

Sam laughed as he looked at Kelly. "We need to make a vid story about this station." He turned to his father. "Come on, Pops, with all the stuff happening on this station? Just think, you can read the sidebar of any character and choose the one that most intrigues you."

His father laughed. "Yeah, I can play your role and you mine; then you'll know what happenings intrigue me."

The entire table started laughing except Kelly Brown. She leaned into Sam with a smile. "No one plays my role because you're all mine." The table quieted to a slight chuckle.

Officer Armela gently held onto Huiling's hands while he stared into her eyes with passion. "Huiling, you're an angel," and Huiling responded with a shy laugh. "Thank you, Juan, praise the Lord he let us come together like this. You have helped me in so many ways. Sheng De zhu fu ni." Officer Armela's smile grew wider. "Blessings of Abraham," and he stood. Officer Armela walked to Huiling's side and kneeled beside her; at first Huiling looked at him confused until she noticed the small black box with silver inset studs he was holding. Armela opened the very small box with the contents facing Huiling. She looked inside and saw a red glare from the Martian diamond. Officer Armela looked deep into her eyes. "Huiling, walk with me in this journey. As the Lord is my witness, I shall love you forever." Huiling squealed with excitement as Juan put the ring on her finger and she stood quickly.

Everyone in the Solar House became silent as they turned to see where the squealing was coming from; Operator Furgis's table was stunned to see Huiling jump into the arms of Officer Armela as he stood up. His companions followed his gesture as he stood and clapped; he knew a proposal when he saw one. Huiling could not contain her excitement as she ran to Dr. Avers and embraced her in a very large hug. "Look at it, Brook," and she held the large Martian diamond up. Dr. Avers held Huiling's hand as she inspected the ring and then turned to Acela with happiness in her voice. "Lady Diamonds has some competition."

Acela Vega stepped over and put her hand on Dr. Avers'. She pulled both Dr. Avers hand and Huiling's hand higher and closer to study the ring. "Very beautiful, Huiling," and she turned to look at Officer Armela slowly approaching.

Kelly ran to the other side of the table to hug Huiling while the men stood and walked to the approaching security officer; his smile could not be matched as his boss offered a rare hug. Supervisor Stykes let go of Officer Armela quickly as he watched Marco De Luca and Chayton approach curiously.

"What's all the excitement here?" Chayton asked, and before anyone could answer, Sam held up a glass and started tapping the side with his utensil, bringing to the Solar House. "Ladies and gentlemen," Sam held up his glass, "here's to the happy couple, my good friend Juan and my very special friend Pastor Huiling." Cheers and chatter erupted throughout the Solar House.

Marco and Chayton pulled up chairs to the large table, and Marco asked Huiling, "Are you joining us?"

Before the polite young woman could answer, Officer Armela responded in a loud and deep voice. "We would like to, Marco, however at this time we prefer some privacy," and he wrapped his large arm around Huiling. Acela laughed as she stared at Marco. "Good grief, let them have some time together."

As if on cue, Supervisor Stykes turned to Officer Armela with a smile. "Juan, you've got the rest of the day off." Officer Armela smiled and nodded at Supervisor Stykes with appreciation.

Chief Tylor activated his ear com and stated his destination with haste. "Engineer Trently." Engineer Trently was walking down the corridor with Dr. Gerlitz's assistant and Marshal Scoop when his ear com chimed. "Incoming transmission." He slowed as he answered and smiled as he heard the excited voice of the chief. "Shaun, got some good news." Trently stopped at the entrance to the docking tube for *Research One* . "What's the news, Chief?" Marshal Scoop and Dr. Gerlitz's assistant stood by with curiosity.

"Shaun, Officer Armela just proposed to Pastor Li."

Engineer Trently laughed. "Did he take my suggestion and get the red diamond?" Trently's companions watched the smile on his face grow wider. "Tell Juan we'll be up there shortly; we just have a few checks on the engineering console in *Research One* to complete." He reached for the docking tube's control panel. The doors for *Research One* hissed open, allowing Engineer Trently and his companions to enter, and Trently explained how he had assisted Officer Armela with his choice of wedding rings. His explanation was interrupted by the sound of a door hatch opening.

Dr. Gerlitz's assistant and Marshal Scoop also stopped as they too heard the hiss of *Research One* 's hatch opening and saw a man dressed in the same coveralls an emergency engineer would wear step out of the shuttlecraft. Trently was concerned; he did not recognize the individual wearing a Neptune One uniform and knew this vessel was off limits. He called out to him loudly, "Hey!" and watched in horror as the tall, dark-haired man lifted a Tobine repeater pistol and tried to step backward returning to the shuttle. The intruder was too slow. Marshal Scoop was behind Engineer Trently and Dr. Gerlitz's assistant; he pushed himself between his companions and quickly raised his air pistol and fired two rounds. They could hear the plastic metallic projectiles whiz by their ears as they sidestepped in a sloppy maneuver to get out of his way, landing on their knees they looked down the docking tube.

Engineer Trently felt like time slowed to a crawl as he watched one projectile penetrate the intruder's forehead while the second projectile penetrated his chest. The motion detectors from the vid com operating the docking tube sensed the discharge from the weapon and initiated emergency lockdown procedures, along with an intruder alert. Trently stood quickly and ran down the docking tube, followed by Dr. Gerlitz's assistant. Marshal Scoop was already checking for the intruder's identity. He pulled a pocket pad out of the man's coveralls but could not get the device to activate. He shook his head as he handed the device to Engineer Trently.

Dr. Gerlitz's assistant watched over Engineer Trently's shoulder as he tried to gain access to the pocket pad, and after a brief moment he handed the device to the assistant and looked at Marshal Scoop. "No good, it has a worm virus. If we attempt to access without a decoder, it will wipe clean."

Dr. Gerlitz's assistant stepped back. "Marshal, we have a grade four decoder in the lab."

Marshal Scoop reached up and activated his ear com piece quickly.

Supervisor Stykes and his companions heard the emergency alarm over their ear com pieces. Stykes accepted the transmission from the marshal as Officer Armela approached the large table.

The marshal's tone was calm. "Leaf, we got a situation in the hangar bay."

Stykes looked across the table at his boss and said, "Sitrep, Marshal." He nodded at Operator Furgis as he reached up and issued the link command for his ear com piece; Operator Furgis listened to the situation report intently.

"We have an intruder down in front of *Research One* ."

The marshal was quickly interrupted. "Marshal, this is Dr. Avers. Do you need a med tech?"

"No ma'am, the intruder is neutralized; all we need is a pickup." The three individuals in the docking tube stood around the growing red puddle on the floor.

Operator Furgis could not wait. "Marshal continue."

"We have no ID, sir. Trently says the pocket pad from the intruder's coveralls has a worm virus."

Chief Tylor was quick to ask, "Shaun, is the shuttle breached?"

Engineer Trently replied, "Not sure, sir. We were just arriving. I think we surprised him on his way out."

Operator Furgis ordered, "Trently, I want you three to meet Leaf and Armela in Gerlitz's lab. I want that pocket pad decoded immediately," and he started to walk toward the exit of the restaurant.

Operator Furgis stopped and turned quickly causing Supervisor Stykes and Officer Armela to walk around him. He looked at his son as he started to follow. "Sam, I need you to stay here with the others in case we have other issues elsewhere." He turned to Dr. Avers. "Doctor, please remain here; we'll let you know," and again he started walking away. "Keep an open com."

Chayton stood next to Kelly and Sam. "I thought Gerlitz finished his experiments."

Marco rested his hand on Sam's shoulder as he watched the look of concern grow on the young man.

Operator Furgis and Chief Tylor entered the restricted docking tube for *Research One* and saw the med techs cleaning the red liquid off the floor and the spray from surrounding walls. The intruder was already inside a med tube. Operator Furgis stood back to the side of the entry hatch for *Research One* . "All right, Chief, do it," and Chief Tylor lifted his data pad from its holster and linked with the hatch's control panel. Furgis heard the air being drawn out of *Research One* and said, "That should be long enough to knock anyone out. Check for stealths."

As soon as the Chief looked up from his data pad, Operator Furgis nodded, and instantly the hatch slid open with a hiss and the rushing of air. Chief Tylor entered first and proceeded directly to the pilot's seat. Operator Furgis followed quickly and sat in the engineering console's seat, and both men activated their individual consoles. Chief Tylor turned to face Operator Furgis. "He wasn't trying to take the ship, sir."

"No, Dan, I think he got what he wanted from the engineering vid com." Furgis reached for his ear com piece to switch to a secured transmission and connected to Supervisor Stykes.

"Yeah, boss?"

"Leaf, I need to know what's on that pocket pad."

"We're almost at the Dr. Gerlitz's lab, boss."

Supervisor Stykes and Officer Armela were huffing as they moved quickly to reach the lab.

Chapter Thirteen

The door on Dr. Gerlitz's lab slid open with a quick hissing sound, and Supervisor Stykes and Officer Armela walked in. The two enforcers approached Marshal Scoop while Officer Armela looked at his friend Engineer Trently with his eyebrows raised. Supervisor Stykes took a breath and exhaled deeply. "Did we find anything yet?" He watched the marshal's expression turn to frustration.

"Nothing."

Engineer Trently interrupted. "There's something there, we just have to proceed slowly so we don't wipe it," and everyone grew quiet, allowing him to manipulate the controls on his data pad. The rear entry hatch to the lab slid open, but Trently remained focused on his data pad. He knew the voice of the man entering the lab.

Dr. Gerlitz was loud with concern. "What did they get?" He quickly approached his assistant and grabbed the data pad from his hands. Dr. Gerlitz's assistant held his hands up and stepped back. The young engineer looked up at Dr. Gerlitz briefly before continuing with his study of the pocket pad linked to his data pad. Marshal Scoop glanced at Supervisor Stykes with annoyance and gestured with his hand not to interfere. Dr. Gerlitz looked across the transparent vid com tabletop where the pocket pad was placed and yelled, "Trently, you almost wiped it!"

Engineer Trently lowered his data pad. He had assisted Dr. Gerlitz on Neptune One for a long time and was used to his slightly abusive nature. "I was trying to infiltrate with your decoder grade four protocol."

This agitated Dr. Gerlitz. "Not with a worm decoder four." Trently shrugged, while Dr. Gerlitz's assistant shook his head and walked closer to Engineer Trently. He spoke very softly. "I'm glad that doesn't run in the family."

Trently gave him a puzzled look. He had already met Dr. Gerlitz's cousin on the SS *King David*, and his personality was the same.

Suddenly Dr. Gerlitz said "Aha!" and he looked up from his data pad and stared at Engineer Trently for a moment before walking away.

Trently looked at Marshal Scoop with a blank stare, and in return Marshal Scoop chuckled. "Don't ask me."

Dr. Gerlitz's assistant laughed. "He always has a solution," and he rested his hand on Engineer Trently's shoulder.

Supervisor Stykes grew anxious. "I'll go back and see if the good doctor is okay," but Marshal Scoop stopped him with a hand on his shoulder. "No need—his office has only one entrance, and this whole lab is secure from stealth droids." Marshal Scoop smiled with a nod of his head and then heard the faint chime of Supervisor Stykes' ear com.

Operator Furgis was slightly agitated. "Leaf, what do you guys have?"

"Hey, boss, sorry about the delay, but Dr. Gerlitz came out and put a stop to everything and went back in his office."

After a brief moment of silence, Stykes once again heard his boss's voice. "Leaf, stand tight. I'll find out what's with our boy," and the ear com piece shut down with a quick chime.

Dr. Gerlitz sat at his desk and rustled through a stack of data pads. He growled loudly and threw one data pad off his desk when he heard the vid com in his office chiming with an incoming transmission. It was Operator Furgis. Dr. Gerlitz stopped moving data pads around as he stared at the vid com and took a deep breath. "Ken, what can I do for you?"

"Dr. Gerlitz, I need to know what the intruder was after and if he got it."

It was not long before Dr. Gerlitz leaned forward, resting his elbows on his desktop. "I was in the middle of looking for a worm decoder grade five. Engineer Trently is good, but he almost wiped the pocket pad clean."

"Grade five? I thought grade four was the highest a worm decoder would go."

Dr. Gerlitz was not egotistical, but he did have pride in his work and was not afraid to show it. "Only if you design one yourself," he said proudly. "I designed a sophisticated worm decoder that will penetrate the pocket pad with ease." He leaned back, picking up another data pad. "Ah, here it is. I call it a scarab."

Operator Furgis laughed in response. "Sounds like it will attack and eradicate, Doctor. I need to know what he was doing."

"It will go even further; the scarab will completely wipe out any encryption and follow any links left behind, without any danger of even a minor wipe." Dr. Gerlitz stood from his desk chair. "How's my shuttle?"

"No problems found, but, Doctor, when you're done with

the pocket pad, I would appreciate your scarab checking the protocols of *Research One* ."

"When we're done with the pocket pad, I'll show Engineer Trently how to link it in, Ken." Both men nodded before the vid coms shut down.

Dr. Gerlitz entered the lab slowly. Engineer Trently could see the data pad he was carrying had been already activated. Dr. Gerlitz approached the vid com table, ignoring everyone in the room, and glanced from the pocket pad and the sidebar data displayed on the vid com table from the pocket pad and his own data pad containing the scarab. After a quick chime informing Dr. Gerlitz of the link between the two devices, he turned to Engineer Trently with excitement. "Engineer, I told Operator Furgis I would instruct you in my new scarab." Trently stepped forward, accepting the data pad from Dr. Gerlitz with his eyebrows raised. "The scarab is designed to neutralize all encryption and bypass any walls." Dr. Gerlitz smiled as Engineer Trently realized what the doctor had created and how powerful it really was. Everyone in the room moved closer to the vid com table and watched the sidebar display flow with data as the pocket pad started to transfer to the vid com table.

Supervisor Stykes looked at Trently impatiently. "What are you getting here? Is there anything we can use?"

Trently held his hand up as he continued working the touch screen of the data pad with the scarab that rested on the vid com. Dr. Gerlitz's assistant shouted with excitement as he watched the data flow. "Wait!" Trently removed his hand from the data pad and stared at Dr. Gerlitz's assistant as he stepped in front of him and worked the controls of the data pad. The data started flowing backward for a brief moment before stopping, and Trently and Dr. Gerlitz moved close to the assistant.

Supervisor Stykes could not contain his ignorance. "Are you going to tell us what we're looking at, Trently, or do we need to guess?"

"Sorry, sir, it appears the intruder or intruders were looking for information on the Mortelis cannon and/or shields." He stared at the slowly scrolling data on the vid com table.

Officer Armela interrupted. "Did they get anything, Shaun?"

Trently held up his open hand for a moment before looking at Supervisor Stykes. "It appears they tried, but our security protocols remained intact."

Stykes smiled. "Good."

"However, something was installed—and it's extremely vague what it was."

The vid com on the control console inside *Research One* chimed. Operator Furgis exited the navigation seat and sat in front of the engineer console to answer the transmission. Dr. Gerlitz spoke quickly. "Ken, we penetrated the pocket pad. They didn't get anything of value, but something was installed."

"Well, what was installed?" Furgis noticed Chief Tylor leaning over his shoulder, also waiting anxiously.

"Sorry, we're not sure what was installed. I suggest a full diagnostics if not a complete clean of all protocols on *Research One* ."

"Agreed, Doctor," said the chief. "When you're done with Engineer Trently, send him down. In the meantime I'll get started."

"Leaf, I want you in operations; initiate a long-range trop

sweep and send Officer Armela to med lab. We need to know what the med tube can tell us about the intruder," added Operator Furgis.

Before the vid com could shut down, Marshal Scoop said, "Sir, I'll stay with Dr. Gerlitz, but if you need any help…"

"Thanks, Charles. However, your priority is with Dr. Gerlitz," Furgis answered, and the vid com shut down.

Sam Furgis set his Dou Zhe refreshment back on the vid table and reached up, activating his ear com piece. "Operator Furgis."

"Sam, everyone all right?"

Sam looked around the vid table at his companions. "Pops, what's going on?"

"We've got everything under control. It seems an intruder wanted to exchange some data with *Research One* ."

"What data were they trying to get?" Sam knew the importance of Dr. Gerlitz's work.

Operator Furgis watched the chief diagnose the protocols of *Research One* . "Some of the doctor's work," he replied. The three women at the table sat quietly concentrating on the faint sound they could hear from Sam's ear com.

"Sam, if Dr. Avers is still with you, can you ask her to meet Officer Armela in med lab?"

"She went to med lab awhile ago, and I sent Marco to check on the front desk ops while Chayton strolls through the casino. We're done here. Acela's going back to the pit, and Kelly and I will be in my office, Pops."

"All right, Sam, I don't think we'll be much longer. I'll join you in your office when we're done." The ear com chimed off.

Sam leaned across the vid table and looked at Acela

curiously. "Acela, do you know that gentleman at the bar?"

Acela turned and saw the man looking at her before quickly turning back to face the bar. "I saw him in the casino earlier, but I never spoke with him."

Kelly snickered. "Sam, Acela turns a lot of heads." She looked at Acela. "Sorry, Acela, I didn't mean any disrespect."

This caused Acela to smile, but Sam spoke quickly before she could reply. "Yeah, but look at the way this guy is dressed. He has a dress jacket over a thick vest with casual slacks." Acela and Kelly turned to look once again; Huiling was already watching the gentleman with interest.

Acela turned back with a snicker. "I get a lot of guests dressed that way; besides, I like Kelly's explanation," and she winked at the slightly embarrassed young woman.

Director Furgis did not like it. "If you notice, those are military shoes he's wearing."

"How can you tell?" asked Huiling. "I can barely see his shoes from here."

Kelly tapped her right temple. "Remember his eye, ma'am."

"Oh yes, I'm sorry, Sam," said Huiling, and he smiled with a raised eyebrow.

Acela turned to face her companions. "Here he comes!"

Sam spoke softly. "Everyone, relax. He's probably a new high roller Chayton brought in."

The man approached Acela from behind and startled her as he rested his hand on her shoulder. Looking into Sam's eyes and smiling, he said, "Do nothing to bring attention to yourself or I'll set off the Mortelis strips in my vest and split this station in two." The man looked around the table, smiling. "Howdy, everyone." He leaned back into Acela and whispered, "You will act like there's a problem in the pit. Now get up."

Acela Vega as she stood and looked at Director Furgis. "Sorry, sir, but you'll have to excuse me. I'm needed in the Solar Pit right away." Sam stood quickly with a concerned look as the gentleman followed Acela very closely out of the crowded restaurant.

Huiling Li looked over at Sam. "That was very awkward."

Sam jumped from his seat. "Did you see the ring on his finger?"

Kelly looked confused. "No, what about it?"

"They're the ring of elites Pops was talking about." He started rushing toward the restaurant's entrance. "Come on!"

Kelly and Huiling followed quickly. Sam reached up to activate his ear com piece: "Security emergency." In the middle of the retail area, he stopped and looked in both directions until he spotted the man holding Acela's arm and quickly walking toward the cargo sphere the restaurants and shopkeepers used for deliveries.

Kelly and Huiling approached Sam slowly, and he grabbed his girlfriend by the arm before shouting toward Acela, "Stop!" Sam and Kelly run toward Acela and her abductor, who turned, throwing Acela Vega to the side where she fell in a prone position. Kelly spotted the air pistol emerging from the abductor's jacket as he turned, and she grabbed Sam by the arm and shoulder and pushed him sideways as they ran. Sam stumbled and fell face down. He watched as the air pistol rose and aimed toward his girlfriend.

Kelly struggled to stop as she saw a small amount of gas leave the abductor's air pistol and then heard a slight sound of impact followed by darkness. She could hear screaming through the darkness before everything went silent. Two enforcers approached as Sam was rising to his feet. He did not notice the shots firing from their Tobine repeater pistols. These weapons did not fire gas-propelled semi-plastic projectiles; they used actual gun powdered metal bullets that caused not only severe damage but also a loud sound that created panic from the guests.

Sam slid next to Kelly, picking her up and pulling her into his chest with his hands under her head. He looked up with tears in his eyes as Pastor Li approached and kneeled next to him. She wiped the blood from Kelly's forehead only to watch more emerge from the hole. Pastor Li noticed she was kneeling in a puddle of red, and her eyes flowed with tears as she realized the abductor took Kelly Brown's life. The projectiles from the two enforcers flew by the abductor and impacted the wall as he pulled Acela to her feet and struggled to walk backward into the cargo sphere's docking chambers. He was yelling orders at Acela. "Get in or I'll break your neck!" Acela ignored the threats and continued to struggle. She knew once she was off the station the possibility of her survival was low. The inner docking sphere doors closed quickly with a hiss as the outer doors opened, and Acela could see several other men approaching through the hatch. They grabbed her and pulled her into the docked transport ship, allowing the hatch to close and depressurize. Neptune One enforcers worked in vain to establish a new seal, but the caution lights flashed and the continual warning chime sounded.

Tears flowed from Sam's eyes, but his face displayed anger like none before. He activated his ear com quickly to contact his father.

Operator Furgis was already aware of an impending emergency. Neptune One's main vid com had alerted all senior staff, but he remained calm. "Sam, what's happening up there?"

Sam wiped his mouth quickly before responding. "They took Acela, Pops. She's in the transport dock with the cargo sphere."

"We're on it, Sam, get the staff together," and the ear com went silent. Operator Furgis rushed to the pilot's seat in the cockpit of *Research One* and spoke quickly to Chief Tylor without looking at him. His concentration was on the startup procedures for the small craft. "Chief, they took Acela through the cargo sphere."

Chief Tylor was already working the touch screen controls. He used his command protocols to override the hangar bay door controls, and the vid com on *Research One* activated with a slight chime followed by a female technician's voice. "Chief, all traffic is cleared; the bay is yours."

The chief continued to work his station's controls. "Ten-four, hangar control." He pulled the seat's harness over himself and secured the safety device.

Operator Furgis was in the process of securing his harness as the docking tube released from the small craft, and he initiated half thrusters toward the massive doors. The hangar bay doors opened slowly due in part to their size. "Hold on, Chief, we can't wait," said Furgis, and Chief Tylor took a deep breath as he grabbed the edge of the navigation's console. Operator Furgis increased to full thrusters, creating more pressure; the men could feel the seat's adjustments counteracting the pressure on their bodies. As *Research One* raced toward the opening hangar bay doors, the chief cringed as he realized the width of the shuttle craft was still larger than the opening. Operator Furgis shouted, "Hold on, Chief," and Chief Tylor continued to hold the console tightly.

Research One grew closer to the hangar doors, and Operator Furgis worked the controls on the shuttlecraft; just before contact with the massive doors, *Research One* turned sideways and slipped through the opening. Chief Tylor exhaled, followed by "Excellent piloting, sir."

"Chief, get some maintenance and rescue droids out here." *Research One* banked right sharply and increased its ascent toward the cargo sphere. Chief Tylor watched the vid com on the navigation's console relay data from the troposcope. "Sir, weapons activated and we have a contact—relaying coordinates."

Furgis was grateful his chief engineer was military experienced. "Thanks, Chief. It will take awhile; they're in full thrusters and have a jump on us." He could see the chief smiling.

Research One 's vid com chimed and projected the 3-D image of Supervisor Stykes. "Leaf, clear all traffic," said Furgis. "I don't want any collateral."

"There's another intermittent contact out there, boss. We can't tell who it is." Operator Furgis checked the data on his console and looked over at the chief, who spoke calmly. "Leaf, I picked up your intermittent for a moment, but it's gone again."

Supervisor Stykes asked, "Boss, permission to activate the station's defenses and clear all traffic."

Operator Furgis grinned. "Granted, Leaf," and he left the vid com transmission on an open and secure transmission.

Huiling Li held Sam's arm as the med techs approached

with a med tube. "You need to help Acela, Sam. I'll take Kelly to med lab," and she hugged him very hard. Sam wiped the tears from his eyes, trying not to look back as he walked toward the lift. The crowd in the retail area moved aside as the young man walked past. Sam activated his ear com piece and waited for the chime and voice recognition before instructing his device, "Supervisor Stykes," and he waited for the lift to arrive. Supervisor Stykes answered quickly. "Sam, what's up?" He could hear the despair of Sam's voice.

It felt like forever before the lift arrived. "Leaf, I need to help my father; have Trently meet me in the hangar bay."

"Yes sir, and your father has authorized the station's defenses activated, Sam." Supervisor Stykes received no response.

Chief Tylor called out, "Quarter AU, sir, I can see her thrusters."

Operator Furgis worked his pilot's touch screen control panel quickly as he watched the data from the vid com. "Chief, we're closing—can you get Dr. Gerlitz's MC online?"

The chief nodded with a grin in response. "It's powered up and ready, sir."

Operator Furgis focused on the transport ship as *Research One* slowly closed the distance. He looked over at his chief engineer. "We'll try this only once; hail them." Chief Tylor attempted communications with the transport ship, but Operator Furgis's patience was at an end. "Okay, Chief, they want to do this the hard way." He worked the controls, causing *Research One* to dive slightly and straighten out at an angle that put the rear of the transport ship in firing range for the experimental energy weapon.

The small shuttlecraft vibrated slightly as Chief Tylor

readied the Mortelis cannon. *Research One* chased the transport ship well beyond the range of Neptune One, and the blue atmosphere of Neptune disappeared from view as both ships ran from her presence into open space. Operator Furgis yelled, "Fire!" and the chief gently touched the transparent controls on his console, instructing the experimental energy weapon to send a bluish cloud of pulsating energy toward the rear of the transport ship. *Research One* rocked slightly, forcing the two occupants back in their seats briefly, and they felt a wave of heat in the cockpit through the armor plating. They both squinted as they watched the ball of energy fly through space at an incredible speed.

Operator Furgis grew greatly concerned as he watched the energy ball strike the rear of the transport ship; sparks flew from a spot slightly in front of her engines as the energy ball erupted into a flash of light that caused the window of *Research One* to darken in full protective tint. Furgis and Tylor grabbed their foreheads and rubbed their eyes. Operator Furgis's fears calmed as he finally saw that the transport ship was still intact. His motive was not to destroy the ship and kill everyone on board, including Acela, but to disable the ship for boarding. "Chief, ready for boarding," he said as he worked the controls and moved *Research One* closer.

The chief looked over at Operator Furgis after a moment of gliding his hands over the transparent touch screen in front of him. "Emergency docking tube ready."

Operator Furgis grinned, knowing he would soon board the ship that violated his station and took his friend.

Research One echoed with a grinding sound after the hull of the craft hit the side of the transport ship, and small magnetic retractor cables attached to the transport ship's hull and pulled the shuttle tightly to its side. The docking tube collar extended, creating a secure chamber between the two docking hatches of the mated ships. Operator Furgis and the chief grabbed Tobine repeater pistols as the indicating lights lit up, informing the anxious duo of the secure connection. Operator Furgis nodded at the chief and when he received a ready nod in return, he activated *Research One* 's hatch control panel. The door hissed open, revealing the closed hatch on the transport ship. The chief approached with caution as Operator Furgis followed closely behind.

They stood to the side of the door as Furgis activated the hatch's control panel, and the door slid open with a hiss, revealing the corridor inside the transport ship. The chief slowly poked his head through the open hatch and saw movement, followed by the sound of a metal projectile hitting the bulkhead next to the open hatch. Operator Furgis grabbed a flash charge from his belt and held it up in view for the chief; the chief nodded, and Furgis tossed the charge into the corridor as the two men from *Research One* looked down and covered their eyes.

The extremely bright flash vanished quickly, but it allowed Operator Furgis and Chief Tylor to enter the transport's corridor with pistols drawn and ready. The chief saw movement and instantly kneeled while firing a round; Operator Furgis used the opportunity to rush to the end of the corridor with his weapon drawn and hugging his back against the wall as he approached an individual lying face down and moaning. He peeked around the corridor and moved with caution into the empty corridor; the chief followed slowly behind with his weapon ready for action. Halfway down the empty corridor, they heard a woman screaming, causing Operator Furgis to lose his precautionary concern and run to the end of the corridor. He quickly poked his head around the corner while remaining in a squatting position, and the chief grabbed Operator Furgis by the belt, pulling him back as shots rang out from the end of the corridor where the screaming was heard.

Furgis looked at the chief and held up three fingers and mouthed a few words. The Chief nodded in agreement as he stepped behind Furgis, who whispered a countdown. "Three, two, one." Both men jumped into the corridor with their Tobine repeater pistols aimed at their foes. Operator Furgis landed on his side and fired two shots while Chief Tylor hit the opposite corridor wall with his shoulder and resting in a lean. His weapon also discharged two projectiles at the four individuals facing them with their weapons drawn. Operator Furgis watched three of them fall to the corridor's floor, leaving a very angry and attractive Spanish woman shouting obscenities at her fallen captors.

Operator Furgis quickly returned to his feet. "Acela, shut up and get over here!"

The chief grew concerned as the warning lights in the corridor continued to flash with an audible alarm. "Sir, we need to go." Operator Furgis was not accustomed to seeing Chief Tylor nervous.

Acela Vega quickly kicked one of her fallen captors in the head before running toward her boss. Her hands were still in mag cuffs, but the chief was prepared with a data pad as she approached and stumbled into his arms.

Operator Furgis was concerned. "Hurry up, Chief, we got

company coming." They could hear the sound of running men growing closer. Chief Tylor quickly freed Acela and she ran toward the airlock as her mag cuffs fell to the floor. The men quickly followed her, trying to catch up as she ran faster, creating a stretch of distance between her and her rescuers.

Acela reached the airlock and quickly entered the chamber, stopping in a spin. She grabbed the edge of the open hatch and peeked back through to see Furgis and Tylor approaching her. She started waving "hurry up," but she was horrified to see a group of men come running around the corner behind her. Chief Tylor stumbled and fell, and Operator Furgis stopped quickly and turned. The older man looked up at him and said, "Keep going," and Operator Furgis turned to the airlock, jumping toward the control panel. During his flight across the corridor, he yelled at Acela, "Get out of here," and he struck the wall and panel. Acela ran into *Research One* with tears in her eyes as both hatches closed behind her. *Research One* 's main vid com acknowledged her instantly and started venting the airlock seal as she strapped herself into the pilot's seat.

Operator Furgis and Chief Tylor rolled onto their backs with their Tobine repeater pistols drawn and aimed down the corridor at the approaching men. Furgis shot first, causing one assailant to fall, while the chief dropped another before a flash charge landed between them, causing a blinding flash of light and then complete darkness.

Acela did not wait for the docking tube collar to retract. She instantly engaged full thrusters, ripping the docking tube collar from the hull of the transport ship. *Research One* rocked and vibrated as alarms sounded throughout the small vessel, which Acela ignored. The only things in her thoughts were safety and her boss. "Vid com, launch locator," and she felt another smaller jolt as a magnetic locator flew from *Research One* and landed on the hull of the damaged transport.

Acela struggled to work the controls of *Research One* using all three of the needed stations that were routed through the vid com to the pilot's console. She glanced continually between the vid com's read-out of navigation, engineering, and piloting controls as she set a course toward Neptune One. Acela knew she was at a great distance from her home, but she could still see the features of Neptune One silhouetted against the giant planet's blue light that emanated behind the station. It was a beacon of hope. *Research One* increased speed with thrusters on full, and Acela was vigilant as she watched the troposcope read-out for any contacts that may appear on her vid com. She activated the vid com communications—"Neptune One"—and heard static.

Director Furgis stood behind the technician as she worked the transparent control panel; the mood in the hangar bay control room was dismal. Supervisor Stykes turned quickly from the main vid com he was studying data on and spoke loudly to Sam. "Incoming from *Research One* ."

Sam moved near Supervisor Stykes and looked at him with concern. "The shuttle must be damaged." He pulled his pocket pad out of its holster. "I'll try cleaning it up." A faint chime could be heard from Sam's pocket pad as it linked with the main vid com. After several moments the base of the vid com flickered with the 3-D projection of Acela Vega. "Neptune One, Neptune One."

Sam responded instantly. "We got you, Acela." The image continued to flicker. "Acela, where's my father?"

After another moment of bad transmission, Sam cleared the signal enough to understand. "Furgis and the chief are on the transport ship," she replied as the transmission grew more stable.

"We'll get them, Acela. Engineer Trently and Officer Armela are heading your way in *Research Two* ; they should be there soon." Sam looked at Supervisor Stykes walking toward the technician at the control console. The young female technician looked up at the approaching enforcer and pointed at her console. Stykes's expression changed from one of curiosity to concern as an image of a warship appeared on her display panel.

Stykes quickly moved back over to the main vid com with Sam. The concern in his voice was apparent as he said, "We have a contact heading for *Research One* ."

Sam's expression turned to anger. "Who is it?" and he waited for an answer along with Acela on the other side of the vid com.

"The *Staton*."

"Acela, increase speed. You've got an Easterner destroyer approaching."

Sam was interrupted by the technician calling out data from her display. "*Research Two* clearing hangar doors, and sir..."

Supervisor Stykes quickly walked to her station. "What is it?" She pointed at the touch screen display.

Stykes turned quickly to Director Furgis. "The *Staton's* broadcasting a command code to *Research One* ."

Sam huffed with rage as he reached for his ear com and ordered, "Operations" after hearing the chime. Acela's 3-D projection yelled, "Systems are shutting down," and the vid com went back to its previous projection of data from the Neptune sector. Sam heard "Operations standing by" in his ear com piece but did not wait; he spoke quickly and with authority. "Bring our MCs on line and target that Eastern destroyer bearing on our shuttle." He turned to Supervisor Stykes. "Get that ship on my vid now."

The vid com flickered with the image of Commander Edwards appearing from his bridge aboard the SS *Staton*.

The young brown-haired and brown-eyed man spoke with a friendly voice. He looked older than Sam but was still young in his early thirties. "Commander Jonathan Edwards. What can I do for you, sir?" His smile was almost insulting.

Sam's tone was stern. "Back off of my shuttle."

Commander Edwards responded with a chuckle. "We're just trying to help, solar law states."

"Commander Edwards, I don't care about solar law. If you think your little destroyer can survive my energy cannons, then you feel free to continue your rescue operations," and the vid com terminated the transmission from the SS *Staton*. Director Furgis turned and looked at Supervisor Stykes, who chuckled. "What's with you?"

"I'm just glad you're on our side," and Sam joined Supervisor Stykes in a laugh.

Sam and Stykes leaned over the young technician working the hangar bay control console. "Is the *Staton* moving away?" Sam asked.

"Yes sir, they're moving to intercept the transport ship."

Sam Furgis shook his head in amazement. "This guy just won't give up, will he? Get Trently on the vid com."

The young woman did not look up. "Yes sir," and the vid com flickered.

Both Director Furgis and Supervisor Stykes moved to the vid com as Engineer Trently's 3-D projection materialized on the display in front of them. Trently was grinning. "Sir, I believe you convinced the destroyer to leave."

Sam did not respond with a grin or laughter; he was concerned for his father and Acela. "Trently, how's *Research Two* look?"

"Intact, sir. I think the *Staton* shut the systems down, probably what was left behind."

"All right, Shaun, tow Acela back in and we'll deal with Edwards."

"And, sir, I picked up another ship out here—not sure what happened to it though," Trently added before the vid com shut down.

Sam turned to face Stykes, who could see the worry on the tired young man. "Sir, you look like you need a break. I can stay here if you want to go to med lab." Stykes could see the tears forming in Sam's eyes and he gently grabbed his shoulder. "Sam, I'm sorry about Kelly. Huiling's in med lab."

"Leaf, my father is out there." He walked over to the technician sitting at her console, slightly irritated. "What's the status on *Research Two* ?"

"Almost here, sir." She looked over at Supervisor Stykes.

Director Furgis walked over to the observation window and looked out through the massive open doors that allowed the distant stars to faintly shine into the hangar bay of Neptune One. He studied the surroundings for a moment before issuing orders without turning from his gaze through the observation window "Leaf, I want some stealth droids launched immediately, and as soon as Trently gets *Research One* back in, he's to go back out and search for the transport ship."

Supervisor Stykes nodded. He watched the young man turn from the observation window and walk toward the hangar bay control room door. "Sir, I'll let med lab know you're coming."

Director Furgis growled loudly as he walked through the door to leave. "I don't have time for that." The doors hissed open and then closed as Director Furgis left the control room.

Supervisor Stykes watched the maintenance droids attach to *Research One* as the damaged shuttle was slowly pulled into the hangar bay by her sister ship. He reached up to activate his ear com piece, "*Research Two*," and Engineer Trently came on almost immediately. "Yes sir?"

"Let the droids park Acela. I need you out there looking for the transport ship. We have stealth droids already on their way and rescue droids standing by." Stykes watched *Research Two* turn in the hangar bay.

"Yes sir, we're on our way," Trently responded.

Stykes watched *Research Two* slowly and gracefully move through the large doors and disappear.

Chapter Fourteen

The SS *Stanton* slowly approached the transport ship and witnessed another ship docked alongside. The *Stanton* came to a complete stop and watched the two ships. Commander Edwards activated the main vid com on the bridge of the SS *Stanton* and issued his instructions: "SS *Essex.*" After several moments of silence the 3-D image of Commander Kruger was projected in front of Commander Edwards' command chair.

Kruger answered with his squawky Eastern empire accent; even Commander Edwards visualized old spy comedies when he spoke with his comrade. "Commander Edwards, report."

"Acela is back on the station, sir."

"How did that happen? The operation was sound." Commander Kruger leaned back in his command chair.

Edwards replied, "No need to worry. I was informed Operator Furgis and one of his senior staff is aboard the transport."

Kruger leaned forward with a smile. "Excellent, get them on the *Essex* immediately; we can hold a trial for Furgis interfering." He rubbed his hands together.

Commander Edwards nodded. "Will do as soon as your patrol ship leaves."

"What patrol ship?"

Now Commander Edwards was confused. He leaned back with an open hand gesture. "The patrol ship that's docked with the transport."

Commander Kruger erupted into a rage. "I didn't send any ship. Stop them now!"

Commander Edwards jumped up and commanded, "Battle stations." He watched the vid com switch to the view of the transport ship docked alongside the patrol ship and shouted orders that echoed through the bridge of the SS *Staton*. "Ready forward missile launchers." His crew worked their individual touch screen consoles.

Operator Furgis was pushed through the airlock hatch, grabbing the side of the open hatchway as he staggered, trying to shake off his dizziness from some type of drug his captors gave them. Chief Tylor was in worse condition behind Operator Furgis; he fell several times, and Furgis turned to help as he heard the heavy exhaling and grunting from his chief engineer. The transport ship personnel would not allow Operator Furgis to assist his friend as they continued to herd them through the airlock until the sound of the hatch was heard closing behind them. Furgis heard one of the men speak very loudly with a Middle Eastern accent. "Take them to their assigned quarters and post a guard." Quickly they were grabbed by the arm and led down the corridor.

Research Two was in full thruster, traveling quickly toward the locator Acela managed to tag the transport ship with. Officer Armela watched his navigation console as the troposcope projected the data from the locator. He looked over at Engineer Trently sitting in the pilot's seat of *Research Two* and said calmly, "We should have a visual soon."

Instantly Engineer Trently grew excited. "There it is!" The silhouette of the transport ship was off in the distance.

Officer Armela raised his voice slightly after noticing movement out of the corner of his right eye. "Incoming." They both watched streaks of gas trail several missiles fast approaching the transport ship. Officer Armela followed the streaks of dissipating gas back to an Eastern destroyer and called it out quickly. "Warship, starboard." Engineer Trently worked *Research Two*'s controls, causing the small shuttle to veer to port.

The crew of *Research Two* watched the bright flash radiate through space, causing the automatic tint of the cockpit window to darken. Officer Armela spoke into his open vid com. "Supervisor Stykes, a warship just hit the transport with a missile barrage."

"Hold your position; we'll handle this."

Trently brought the small shuttle to a complete stop. Within moments both individuals inside *Research Two* were shocked from witnessing a large bluish ball with a white cloud flowing around it travel past their position at an extremely high speed and strike the warship off their starboard side.

Operator Furgis was taken to a small room with a single bunk inside and thrown in; his good friend Chief Tylor followed when the impact of the missile hitting the transport ship rocked the patrol ship. One guard was thrown into the open hatch of the small room and landed face down on the corridor floor as the other guard stumbled and fell to a crawling position in front of Operator Furgis. The guard who was lying face down did not move, and the area under his head was red. Furgis used his military training to take advantage of the other guard. He moved quickly into a position behind the crawl-ing guard and struck before the guard could get his bearings. Operator Furgis's open hand came down hard on the guard's neck, forcing him to grunt loudly as he lay flat alongside his fallen comrade.

Chief Tylor sat on the floor inside the small room, lean-ing against the bulkhead as he shook his head, attempting to clear the drowsiness off. He tried to stand as he watched his boss set them both free. Operator Furgis quickly grabbed the chief. "Easy, Chief, here take this, but focus before aiming," and Furgis handed Chief Tylor one of the guards' Tobine re-peater pistols. Tylor accepted the weapon as he stood straight. "Don't worry, I won't shoot you."

Operator Furgis chuckled. "I hope not, Chief. I think we're moving." Both became still as they stood in the middle of the small room.

Chief Tylor nodded in acknowledgment. "By the vibra-tion I would say full thrusters with a lot of damage." Operator Furgis agreed as he stood with his back against the bulkhead near the open hatch. "Yeah, and we're going somewhere fast." The chief hugged the other side of the hatch.

Operator Furgis stepped out into the corridor with cau-tion; the alarm lights were flashing as he turned and waved at Chief Tylor. The chief followed closely behind as they slowly walked down the corridor. The thickness of the smoke was growing. A heavy jolt rocked the ship, sending the chief to his knees as Furgis's back hit the bulkhead. He looked at the chief through the dense smoke and yelled out over the alarms sounding off, "Another battle!" He reached a hand out to the chief and pulled him to his feet while looking at him with a questionable expression.

The chief shook his head in response. "I don't think so. It felt more like secondary explosions from inside," and he exhaled, trying to catch his breath.

Operator Furgis cautiously looked around. "We need to get off this ship." He continued to slowly walk down the smoke-filled corridor with Chief Tylor following and watching behind them as they came to another intersection. Chief Tylor noticed the writing on the wall of the bulkhead, most of which was English, but a small percent was Chinese, and he pointed to the wall. Furgis nodded and spoke quietly; the chief could barely hear him over the alarms but knew he wanted to go in the direction of Engineering.

They came to a stop and knelt next to an injured young man lying on the corridor's floor. Operator Furgis gently dragged the man to the side and leaned him against the bulkhead. "What's your name, son?" The young man stared at him. Operator Furgis tapped the young man's cheek. "Son, what's your name?" and leaned into the man as he spoke softly. "Engineer mate Johnson, sir."

"What happened?" asked Furgis while the chief stood by, looking down both directions for threats.

"Overload, one engine damaged, one off line, life support failing." The young man's head fell. Operator Furgis stood and looked at his chief engineer with urgency. "We've got bigger problems than these guys. We need to get this ship under control." He moved quickly down the corridor toward the engine room. Chief Tylor tried to keep up and turned occasionally to watch their rear.

Furgis stepped over bodies as he walked through the hatch

to the engine room; he watched the chief run to a control panel and hit his fist on the side of the display panel in frustration. Operator Furgis approached, trying to hold his breath and speak at the same time. "Chief, we need to find a working panel and vent the ship." The chief moved quickly to another panel that was lit up. He worked the controls and studied the data read-out before initiating any command inputs. Operator Furgis noticed the noise level dropping in the engine room as the chief turned to speak over his shoulder. "I've shut down the damaged engine and stopped the power supply to the destroyed engine; the emergency venting systems are starting to filter the ship."

Furgis could see the smoke starting to thin slightly. "Chief, can you get the vid coms working?"

The chief squinted at the control panel with a focused determination, then looked at Operator Furgis through burning eyes. "The vid com's on, sir."

Operator Furgis grabbed his shoulder. "Good work, Dan!" He called out at the console, "Bridge," and watched the vid com lasers flicker with static. Operator Furgis did not wait long before a 3-D image of another young man appeared. He was wearing a torn, makeshift uniform pirates liked to wear, and there were burns over the young man's face. Operator Furgis spoke loud and with authority. "This is Commander Furgis in engineering; sitrep now," and he watched the surprise grow on the young man's face as he responded. "Commander, the captain and Easterner are dead, and the bridge consoles exploded, killing most of the bridge crew." The young man looked around the bridge with confusion.

Operator Furgis was quick to act. "Son, what's your name

and who's left up there?"

The young man struggled to remain focused. "Third mate Daniels, sir. Ensign Rogers is piloting the ship."

Operator Furgis interrupted. "Daniels, inform the rest of the crew that I'm on my way up to the bridge, and my chief engineer is remaining in engineering."

The stunned crew member nodded. "Yes sir, I'll let them know, sir," and the vid com shut down.

Chief Tylor looked worried. "Sir, is that a wise idea? These kids might shoot you by accident or for the fun of it."

Operator Furgis sighed. "Yeah, you're probably right, Chief, but we need to get this ship together. When I get to the bridge I'll send you some help to get systems functioning again."

The chief nodded and returned to his working console before leaving the engineering section.

The men inside *Research Two* continued to switch their stare between the transport ship struck by missiles and the warship that was struck by Dr. Gerlitz's new energy weapon. *Research Two* slowly approached the destroyed transport ship as Engineer Trently spoke into the open vid com. "Supervisor Stykes."

"What did you find, Shaun? Any sign of Furgis?"

Trently looked at his good friend Officer Armela before replying. "Sir, the transport ship is in pieces; that missile must have struck the middle of the infrastructure with high-yield explosives." Everyone grew silent.

After a moment Officer Armela broke the silence. "Sir, we had a contact on the trop near the transport, but it disappeared quickly."

Supervisor Stykes thought for a moment before answering. "All right, Shaun, head over to the *Staton* and see what you can find."

The smoke-filled corridors grew clearer as the pirate ship's filter system worked hard to create a breathable atmosphere. The burning sensation in Operator Furgis's eyes eased up, and he could see the deserted corridors more clearly as he followed the writing on the bulkhead to the bridge. The door hissed open, allowing him to enter the command center of the damaged ship. He stood in the entry hatch of the bridge as a young man approached. "Sir, I'm Ensign Rogers." He held his hand out as he looked at Operator Furgis with curiosity, and Furgis accepted it.

"What happened, Ensign?" He looked around at the crew slumped over their consoles.

Ensign Rogers spoke with sorrow. "Not sure. We felt a large jolt, throwing everyone to the floor, and then a bluish gas came out of the vents."

"Bluish gas?!" Furgis stared at the surprised ensign.

Third mate Daniels interrupted. "It did not stay blue for long; it quickly disappeared, leaving white smoke behind."

Operator Furgis wasted no time. He instantly activated the nearest vid com, and after a brief moment, the 3-D image of Chief Tylor appeared. "Chief, I suspect Dr. Gerlitz's work here."

The chief nodded. "You're right, sir, I found it in the vid com data base already; they were trying to reproduce his work when the ship got pounded by the attack."

"Purge the system of all Dr. Gerlitz's work, Chief, and check around for an ear com piece," and the vid com shut down.

Ensign Rogers reached down and pulled the ear com piece off his captain. He stood up straight and handed the communications device to Operator Furgis. "Here, sir." The new commander looked at Ensign Rogers with raised eyebrows before accepting the communications device. Daniels worked the navigation's console but turned quickly. "Sir, the trop is damaged, but I think we have a contact out there."

Operator Furgis was irritated. "What do you mean *think*? We need to know."

Ensign Rogers could see his shipmate growing more nervous. He moved closer to the new captain of the ship as he watched him enter the command chair. "Sir, we cannot afford to run into any ship, including your Western empire ships."

Operator Furgis looked around the damaged bridge before submitting to the obvious. "You're right, Ensign. Set a course out of the Neptune Sector until we can get this tin can fixed." He paused for a moment, looking at the crew who lay on the floor of his new bridge. He looked back at Ensign Rogers quickly and saw the tall young man straightening his torn and dirty tunic; he could see the worry on his face as he stared at his comrades. "Ensign," he said loudly, and he watched the young man snap out of his distant thoughts, "get a crew together and police up these bodies, put them in the cargo hold for now, and find out if any of your med techs survived." Operator Furgis turned his attention to the vid com now flickering in front of his command station. He studied the 3-D projected navigational chart closely as he leaned forward in his command chair with one elbow on his leg.

Ensign Rogers turned before leaving the bridge. "Kai Che."

Operator Furgis looked slightly puzzled. "Excuse me, Ensign?"

Ensign Rogers repeated his statement with a slight hint of pride. "SS *Kai Che* is the name of this tin can, sir," and he turned to exit the bridge.

Operator Furgis touched the 3-D projection in front of him. "Daniels," he said, and the young man sitting at the navigation's console turned quickly. "Yes sir?"

Furgis's first thought was how inexperienced these young men were. His crew on Neptune One would answer immediately, but they would not turn and look at their superior, leaving their console unattended. "Daniels, pay attention to your console. I'm sending you a new course to plot." Daniels turned quickly as he watched the new data appear on his console's touch screen display.

Operator Furgis spoke into the active vid com to connect with Chief Tylor. He chuckled at the sight of his friend. Tylor's face was dirty and bruised, but his expression told the story of a man enjoying his work. "Chief, you're having too much fun down there."

Chief Tylor was calm as usual. "Yes sir, one of these young ones you sent down offered me an eye patch," and he watched the 3-D image of Operator Furgis laugh.

Furgis regained his composure quickly and continued. "How are the repairs, Chief? Got some good news?"

A crew member approached and handed Chief Tylor a data pad, and after a quick look the chief responded, "Very good news, sir," and a different crew member approached.

Chief Tylor listened carefully before looking back at

Operator Furgis. "We have the troposcope back on line as well as all three engines."

Furgis looked stunned. "I thought the engines required a severe overhaul?"

"Most of the damage was with the control consoles and protocols; a quick reboot and some rerouting and they came back on line." The chief looked away to direct several crew members on repair work, then turned his attention back to Operator Furgis. "Are we on course back to Neptune One, sir?"

"That depends on the status of our stealth, Chief. We've got unknown ships between us and Neptune One."

Chief Tylor shook his head. "The stealth system is in rougher condition. I'm making life support a priority followed by navigations."

"Very well, Chief, I set a course for Uranus; the last I heard it was quiet in that sector," and the vid com shut down. Operator Furgis stepped down from his command chair's platform and sat at the closest console; he worked the flickering touch screen until it steadied with the word "weapons." As he checked the read-out and status of the ship's weapons, he heard the bridge door hiss open, but he did not remove his attention from the data display as Ensign Rogers approached from behind him. "Report, Ensign."

Ensign Rogers stepped forward into Operator Furgis's view and stood rigidly. "Sir, the repair crews are assigned, and the rest of the crew is policing the ship."

Furgis quickly glanced up at the ensign. His first thought was of his son; Ensign Rogers looked to be around the same age. Operator Furgis stood, allowing another young man to sit at the weapons console. Ensign Rogers was very curious.

"Where are we headed, sir?"

Operator Furgis entered the command chair, spoke quickly, and waited as the vid com flickered. The ensign stepped to the side and stood closer to his new captain. "I set course for this sector where we can find a place to shut down and repair the stealth." Furgis leaned back, rubbing his chin. He looked at the young man staring at the 3-D chart in front of the command platform. "What's the problem, Lieutenant?"

"Ensign, sir."

Operator Furgis chuckled at the look of confusion on Ensign Rogers. "Son, I need a first officer," and he paused to allow Ensign Rogers to realize he was getting a promotion. "However, lieutenant, if you're not up to the challenge, I'm sure Daniels would appreciate the task."

Rogers nodded and said with a slight stutter, "No sir, I'm up to it, sir."

Operator Furgis smiled. He remembered his youthful days with his good friend Justin Drake in the Western Empire's solar fleet. Captain Drake not only introduced him to his wife, he also gave him his first promotion. "Well, First Officer, I could use some input." Furgis was staring at the 3-D projection of the combined sectors from Neptune and Uranus.

Lt. Rogers grew excited as he studied the projection. "Sir, we can stop off at Uranus Four; they're very sympathetic to us pira…" and he stopped in mid-sentence to stare at Operator Furgis.

His new captain chuckled, and Operator Furgis could see the uneasiness on his new first officer and decided to put his thoughts at ease. "Lt. Rogers, inform our men that when this ship is fully functional again, they will be in Western Empire's solar fleet—and part of Neptune One's family." Operator Furgis winked with a smile as he watched the crew on the bridge turn and stare.

Lt. Rogers shouted at his crew on the bridge. "Focus, com get me a secure transmission to Uranus Four and link it to the command vid com, ASAP."

Operator Furgis tried to contain his amusement. "Where's that med tech, Lieutenant?" His first officer tapped his ear com piece but Operator Furgis stopped him. "Send him to engineering and tell him that the chief needs to be checked out whether he likes it or not."

Lt. Rogers nodded. "Yes sir," and activated his ear com piece.

"Lieutenant Rogers," Furgis added.

"Yes sir?"

Operator Furgis looked around at the crew busy with the operations and repairs of the bridge. "Lieutenant, I want the ring off that traitor your captain trusted." Rogers stared at him with a blank expression, and Furgis realized he probably had no clue why they had an Eastern Empire officer on board. "Lieutenant, the Eastern officer was supposed to turn us over to the Easterner's warship but decided to take a different course when he saw some credits coming." He grew more serious as he leaned back in his command chair. "Now if you don't mind."

"Yes sir, you'll have the ring immediately."

Operator Furgis nodded with a slight smile. His attention was now focused on the chief as he spoke into the active vid com. "Chief, Lieutenant Rogers is contacting some friends from Uranus Four; I guess they're willing to help us pirates out."

The chief snickered. "Very good, sir, we could use the facilities."

The SS *Staton* was severely damaged as the ship leaned toward its port side where the energy ball from the Mortelis cannon struck. Engineer Trently could see the burn marks on the armor plating and sparks shooting out into empty space. *Research Two* slowly glided alongside the SS *Staton*. Officer Armela looked out the cockpit window in awe of the damage created by the energy weapon as he spoke softly to Engineer Trently. "Are you sure you want to talk with these guys?"

Trently sighed. "You heard your boss," and he activated the vid com. Both crew members of *Research Two* watched the 3-D projection from the main vid com flicker until the image of the damaged destroyer's captain appeared. He was very angry. "This is an act of war."

Engineer Trently took a deep breath and remained calm. "Sir, we have rescue ships and maintenance droids standing by if you require any," but the vid com abruptly shut down. Engineer Trently spoke quickly, "Neptune One," and the vid com flickered again as the video communications device switched destinations of transmission. Supervisor Stykes' image appeared. "Engineer Trently, sitrep"

"Sir, that guy is ticked; he screamed something about war."

Stykes laughed. "No need to worry, Engineer. Under solar law we offered assistance; anything else Director Furgis will handle."

"Sir, request permission to return."

Supervisor Stykes could see the concern on Engineer Trently's expression. "Granted." He released the back of the technician's chair and walked over to the main vid com in the hangar bay control room, where he contacted Director Furgis. He could hear the annoyance in Sam's voice.

"Yeah, Leaf?"

"Director, Engineer Trently and Officer Armela are returning."

"How's the *Staton* and why are they returning?" Sam was agitated.

"I'm sorry, sir, there's no sign of survivors from the transport, and the *Staton* is severely damaged. I'm sure your father and the chief are on the *Staton*."

"Sorry, Leaf, tell the guys I appreciate their help."

"They'll appreciate that, sir," said Stykes. "How is Acela?"

Director Furgis thought for a moment. He allowed a deep breath to escape before responding. "She seems all right. I spoke to her on the vid com awhile ago. When Dr. Avers is done she'll meet me in my office."

Stykes was happy to see Director Furgis focusing on the station. "Sir, Engineer Trently and Officer Armela are approaching."

"Very well, Leaf, I'll be in my office; keep me informed."

Supervisor Stykes acknowledged quickly, "Yes sir," before the vid com shut down.

The doors to Sam's office slid open and he entered quickly and walk across his office to his desk. He fell hard into his chair and rested his elbows on his desk, his head in his hands and his eyes closed in thought. He remembered his favorite psalm that Pastor Huiling taught him. "Be still and know I am God." He looked up, wiping his eyes, and sat quietly for several moments. Then he activated the main vid com and demanded "privacy mode." Sam lowered his head to look at the floor beneath him. He closed his eyes tightly, squeezing a tear out, and after watching the drop hit the floor, he began to speak softly. "Father God, I know you're the One true living God and all my love is for you, Father. I praise you for my hardships, the trials and tribulations that are in my life." Director Furgis stopped to sniffle and take a deep breath. He exhaled deeply and slowly before continuing. "I know that you have plans for me and that those plans are not to harm me but to prosper me to serve your good works, and I thank you. Father." Another quick sniffle. "I ask you, Father, if my pops is still alive, to keep him safe and if not please take care of him. I love you, Father."

Sam stood quickly and walked around to the front of his desk to activate the main vid com; his hand gently slid over the vid pic base at the edge of the desk, the display of recordings of Kelly Brown shut off. Another tear was forming as he wiped his face and activated the main video communications device and issued his commands. "Mars City Central." After several moments a 3-D image of a tall, skinny white man with dark hair and in his middle thirties appeared.

"Sam, how have you been? Bet you miss us back here on Old Red."

Sam sighed and shook his head. "Mr. Fields."

Derek Fields could see the pain in Sam's expression. "Call me Derek, Sam. Now tell me what's wrong; how can I help?"

"We have some issues here on the station I wanted to talk to Mom about."

Derek Fields saw the urgency on Sam's face. "Your mother is in a meeting, but I'll let her know immediately that you're waiting for her."

Sam nodded. "Thanks, Derek," and the vid com shut down. He was quick to issue his next command to the vid com:

"Ambassador Davis, how are you?" Sam never grew to like the short, fat Irish man, but he tolerated him at his father's request.

"Sam Furgis, how are—" Before Sam could reply the ambassador continued. "I see your father has put Dr. Gerlitz's cannon to work." Sam looked down with a grin and shook his head. Ambassador Davis became more sincere as he noticed Sam's impatience. "Sam, I don't have any news about Drake, but I'm sure they'll get this investigation done soon."

Sam lifted his head and sat up straight, his tone authoritative. "Sir, I appreciate your help with Taby, but that's not what I wanted to talk to you about. Ambassador, my father didn't return from the fight you're referring to, and in the attempt at kidnapping Acela Vega, Kelly Brown was killed."

Ambassador Davis was somber. "Son, I did not realize the gravity of the situation. My deepest condolences."

"Thank you, Ambassador, but my father may be on the disabled destroyer."

"I'll see what I can find out."

Sam Furgis was not given the opportunity to give thanks as the vid com shut down. He slouched in his chair and softly issued his commands: "jazz, early." The gentle female voice responded, "Specify," and Sam sighed heavily. "I don't know, the same as Pops would listen to," and again the vid com responded, "Specify," and waited silently for input. "Jazz from Operator Furgis's selection, any random order," Sam said and he threw his head back as his father's favorite music started to echo through his office. After several moments of relaxation with his eyes closed, he started to feel a little more at ease as he remembered to quiet his mind. The serenity was broken by a faint chime heard through the music.

Sam opened his eyes slowly and watched the name flow across the laser projection of the vid com; he sat up and adjusted his suit. "Pause jazz." He took a deep breath. "Accept Regent Furgis," and the 3-D image of his mother flickered into his office.

"Sam, what's wrong? Derek said it was urgent."

Her son fought back tears as he answered with a slight quiver in his voice. "Mom, the Easterners tried grabbing Acela, and when we tried stopping them, Kelly was killed, and Pops…"

Raynor Furgis held her hand up with confusion. "Okay, Sam, slow down and tell me what happened."

"The Easterners used an operative to try and take Acela off the station; Kelly was killed by the operative as we tried to stop them." He paused as he heard his mother say, "Oh good Lord," and he continued. "Pops and the chief went after them."

"Go on, Sam, what happened with your father? Put him on—I wanna talk with him," and she stopped in horror as she saw a tear emerge from her son's eye.

Sam looked down and shook his head. "I think he was on the transport when the Eastern destroyer blew it up."

"Absolutely not, your father is better than that, Sam. Get some search parties out there now."

"We tried, Mom. There's not much left of the transport ship, and the Easterners will not talk right now."

"Then get a boarding party over there immediately!"

"The *Staton* already threatened the research shuttle; they won't attack the station because of the damage they received from the MC, but they will not allow any smaller vessels to approach."

His mother leaned back in her chair. "Sam, you need back-up. I can't get there for a while; the Easterners are causing trouble here. Link up with the *Hammer* and let Justin know what's happening—tell him the Easterners grabbed your father and you need his help."

Sam nodded as the vid com returned to his father's jazz music. He leaned back in his desk chair to relax for a moment and gather his thoughts before contacting the SS *Hammerhead*. Sam reached across his desk and reactivated the vid pic base; the pictures from his vid recorder stored in the unit would switch at random. Sam instructed the vid pic display to freeze, and the short motion picture of Kelly Brown looped through its clip. Sam stared at the clip displayed on his desk, and the feeling of loss swelled inside. His moment of grief was interrupted by the chime on the vid com followed by "Request entry," and Sam awoke from his despair.

He sat up straight in his desk chair and adjusted his tunic as he inquired, "Who?" and waited for the response: "Acela Vega." Sam stood as he granted entry.

Acela Vega entered his office, and Sam walked around his desk and hugged the tired-looking woman. "I'm glad you're all right, Acela."

Acela looked up at Sam. "Anything to drink? Dr. Avers would only give me H2."

Sam laughed as he walked to the dispenser and turned to her with a questionable look. "Dou Zhe or do you want something with a kick?" Acela smiled as Sam turned and placed the order.

Sam handed Acela her drink before sitting in his chair. Acela waited for Sam to sit down before tasting the drink. "Very nice mix, Sam," and she watched a comforting nod from her junior boss. Both set their drinks on his desk before Acela said, "Sam, I'm really sorry about Kelly. I know if I spotted the guy quicker…"

"It's not your fault, Acela," Sam interrupted. "I just wish Pops was here."

"Did you search for the other ship?"

"The *Staton* won't let us board."

"No, the other ship."

"What other ship, Acela?" Sam was growing frustrated.

Acela leaned forward. "Sam, I heard them talking about meeting with another ship; your father could be on it."

"There could be another ship out there, but Trently and Armela checked and found only the damaged destroyer." Sam Furgis sighed with grief.

Acela stared at Sam long enough to finish her drink before asking, "Have you talked with Justin yet?"

"I was about to but wanted to talk with you first."

Acela attempted to stand. "I'm sorry, Sam, I'll let you call Justin."

Sam stood quickly. "No, stay, Acela," and he sat in the chair next to Acela, both turning to face the main vid com.

Chapter Fifteen

Commander Mela Finch sat in the command chair on the bridge of the SS *Hammerhead* as she waited patiently and nervously for Captain Drake to link with information regarding Tabitha and her hearing. The communications officer called out over her ear com piece, "Incoming link from Neptune One, sir." Commander Finch responded quickly. "Link it on the command vid com." A 3-D projection of Sam Furgis and Acela Vega appeared. Commander Finch was excited. "Sam, Acela, how are you guys?" But she realized from their expressions that something was wrong.

Sam was direct. "It's good to see you, Mela. Is Captain Drake available?"

"No, Sam, Captain Drake is with Tabitha and Karl waiting for the hearing to start." The 3-D images became silent with only the noise of the bridge from the SS *Hammerhead* in the background. Acela interrupted the silence; her voice was not as somber as her junior boss's, but Mela could hear the lack of enthusiasm. "How's Tabitha doing?"

Commander Finch smiled. "You know Taby. She's more upset over the accident than she is about the hearing." Mela paused briefly. "Something is wrong, Sam."

Sam acquired a far-off look, the look of a man with a lot

on his mind. "Mela, we have a situation I thought Justin should know about immediately." Mela sat back in her chair watching Sam grow slightly anxious.

Acela rested her hand on Sam's arm. "Mela, someone tried kidnapping me and Kelly was shot." They both watched the surprised expression appear on Commander Finch's face as she leaned forward on the edge of her command chair.

"Is Kelly all right?" Mela's voice held great concern.

"No, Mela, Kelly did not survive." Sam paused to catch his breath and held up an open hand to stop Acela from continuing. He looked toward the corner of his office where he watched the random 3-D vid pics of his mother and father displayed. Sam chuckled with a weak smile as he noticed the old vid cam sitting on display next to the vid pic base. He turned back to the 3-D image of Mela. "It gets worse, Mela. I was required to fire on the *Staton* after they destroyed a transport ship making a getaway with Acela."

Mela quickly interrupted. "Where's Ken? Is he conducting rescue?"

"He's lost," Acela said and Mela grew silent with shock.

Sam continued. "He was either on that transport or he's aboard the *Staton*."

"The chief was with him, Mela," Acela added, and before Commander Finch could reply, Sam said, "Let Captain Drake know that Von Gerlitz's energy shields are ready. I have Engineer Trently and Gerlitz installing them on my research shuttles."

Mela nodded. "All right, Sam, I'll let him know and ask him to talk with you immediately."

"Mela, what's your schedule?" Acela asked.

Mela looked at her data pad, working the touch screen and watching the linked data appear on a smaller vid com in the bridge. She set her pad down. "Depending on how long the hearing is, we have several stops in our patrol route, including Taby's championship match." Mela paused for a moment. "Captain Drake will let you know." She nodded with a smile before the vid com shut down.

Captain Drake stood outside the hearing chamber's doors with his arm around his daughter, waiting for the commissioner's summons. Karl Hobbs was concerned but calm. He could see the worry on Tabitha's face, but he was convinced there was no fault from his armor warrior friend. "Taby, they should be asking for us soon. No need to worry."

She was ready to reply with a slight smile, but she heard her father's ear piece chime. Captain Justin Drake reached up and activated it, and his expression turned from concern to curiosity when he heard the name "Commander Finch."

"Captain, Sam Furgis was looking to link up with you."

"Mela, tell Sam we'll link up later; we're hoping this hearing will start soon."

"There's been an issue on Neptune One. I informed Sam you'll link up as soon as you can."

Captain Drake nodded. "Thanks, Mela."

Karl looked at Captain Drake curiously. "What's up? Everything all right?"

The captain scoffed. "Ken's got some issue on Neptune One and Sam is asking for us."

"They'll have to get in line," Karl replied. When he saw the concerned look on Tabitha's face he added, "What I mean is, the easy issue first," and he smiled and winked at Tabitha.

J. W. DELORIE

The three remained silent for a while as they looked down the hall leading to the council chambers and watched other individuals passing by in the main lobby. Karl thought of how crowded the main lobby was, knowing most of the crowd was from the solar news. He was also aware of the seriousness of the enforcers at the entrance; if the security droid sensed you were too close and the DNA scan did not match any authorization, then certain action would be taken. Karl smiled as the image of his favorite news broadcaster came to mind.

His thoughts were interrupted as the door hissed open, followed by a loud chime, and an enforcer with a holstered air pistol pulled the military-preferred Tobine repeater rifle from his shoulder as he moved to the side of the large entry door, standing at attention with his rifle ready for action. Karl thought about the stare of those nonmoving eyes and how very eerie they were. Suddenly the commissioner's assistant emerged from the open door and stopped abruptly in front of the enforcer; she was quickly followed by a droid hovering slightly above and to her side. Tabitha scoffed slightly; she always respected her elders, but she was not ready to listen to this older, gray-haired woman with a snappy voice that made the hairs on the back of her neck stiff. Her father used his arm he was holding her with to turn them directly toward the commissioner's assistant. Karl was already standing in front of her. "Hello, ma'am."

The commissioner's assistant looked at him briefly before focusing her attention on Tabitha. "Tabitha Drake, the commissioner has summoned you." She stepped to the side, allowing Tabitha to walk past. Captain Drake looked surprised as he was stopped from following his daughter by an extended hand

from the commissioner's assistant. "I don't think so, ma'am. That's my daughter and I'm going in." The enforcer stepped forward with his weapon still against his chest.

Karl chuckled falsely as he stepped forward, watching the two uniformed men stare each other down. "No need for chest-beating," and the commissioner's squawky voice echoed through the corridor. "Very well, let him through."

Captain Drake gestured to Karl to enter and followed close behind; the entry door hissed closed with no sign of the assistant, and Karl laughed. "That's good." Captain Drake shook his head and smacked Karl on the shoulder, moving him forward through another door into the council chambers. The captain compared these chambers to some of his good friend's old video displays.

A rough, loud voice was heard from the tall, aging man sitting slightly higher than his associates. "Tabitha Drake, this hearing has found you negligent on a third-degree charge."

Tabitha's father and friend stepped up onto the podium and stood next to her. A hover droid instantly lowered behind them, and both Captain Drake and Karl turned as they heard the mechanical noises produced from the aging droid.

The commissioner continued. "Captain Drake, I figured you would join us."

"Sir, with all due respect, this is my daughter." Captain Drake knew the importance of respect, but it was irritating watching three grown men wearing old-style robes with an Earth insignia on the left side talk about his daughter and her fate. The commissioner took turns leaning to each side to listen to his junior commissioners; he straightened up in his seat and continued to look down at the three individuals standing in his hearing chambers.

"You may stay, Captain, but if you interrupt, my droid will escort you out immediately." Captain Drake nodded with a frown. The commissioner turned his attention to Tabitha and ignored Karl completely. "Tabitha Drake, we have reviewed the fight droid's recordings of the Mech fight." The commissioner spoke quickly. "Vid com link, Simpson Desert Mech fight," and the chime of the vid com bench was heard as the droid linked the recording.

The commissioner and his junior commissioners watched the downloaded recording from the administrative droid. Tabitha Drake could not see the 3-D projection the commissioners watched, but she could see slight movement from the transparency top that created flashbacks of the Mech fight that took Ben Swells' life. After a long moment, the commissioner spoke. "Armor Warrior Drake, this hearing, after reviewing all the facts, finds you guilty of negligence, minor degree."

Captain Drake looked at his daughter with shock as he saw her brown eyes widen in surprise. He looked up at the commissioner, his hands at his side in a fist and the right one rising suddenly with a finger in a pointing gesture. "Outrageous! Unacceptable!" He quieted quickly as Karl grabbed his shoulder. The commissioners right hand went straight up in the air and came down hard, causing sparks to fly as the balvel struck its base; the noise echoed through the hearing chambers and a security droid sped by, stopping just behind Captain Drake. He could hear the intermittent chime from the droid as it hovered close by.

"I already told you no interference," the commissioner warned.

"My apologies, sir," the captain replied.

The commissioner leaned back in his chair. "As I was stating, the charges have been reduced to negligence, minor degree. If you feel this is inappropriate, you may request council; however, I will warn you now, if you choose to seek council, you will be charged with two hundred and eighty-three counts of negligent fatalities and of course the accompanying injuries."

Karl was quick to gently grab Tabitha by her arm as he spoke softly. "Don't push it, Taby."

The young lady in her formal armor warrior uniform stood stiffly. "Sir, I agree." She cringed as she heard the balvel strike its base with an echoing sound.

The commissioner stood, instantly followed by his junior commissioners. "The ruling of this commission is final." Captain Drake moved back slightly as the administration droid quickly moved around him, stopping in front of the transparent vid com podium. Tabitha watched the twenty-four-inch droid hover with a bounce as she smiled, shaking her head at Karl. They both had the same thought about the practice droids Mech fighters used: The administration droid was outdated, very slow, and extremely clumsy. Fight droids were smaller and quicker. The administration droid chimed and a yellow light emerged and illuminated Tabitha Drake as she stood at the transparent vid com podium.

Her father could see the irritation on her face as she removed her pocket pad from its holster and activated the small device. Karl turned to step off the podium, and his eyes widened in surprise as the administration droid chimed louder and the light turned red, illuminating all three individuals. Captain Drake gestured to Karl to return to his position. "I don't think it wants anyone leaving until its business is done."

Karl noticed the security droids patrolling the perimeter of the hearing chambers and relaxed. "Okay, have it their way," and Captain Drake laughed.

Tabitha didn't have to wait long to receive the linked data to her pocket pad as she pulled the device closer after the administration droid terminated its link. She stared at it with confusion; her father held his hand out and studied the data with a curious look until Karl's patience ran thin. "Well, what gives?"

Captain Drake chuckled. "It seems Taby is required to complete some community service for the Tribune."

Karl looked at them both with confusion. "What's humorous about that? Some of those tasks are dangerous."

Captain Drake followed his daughter off their individual spots and joined Karl closer to the exit of the large hearing chambers. "It states Taby is to report to the Tribune or her party, and her party being the Western Empire, she falls under this subsection of the ruling that states her community service will be at the Western Empire's discretion." Her father smiled at both of them. Before Tabitha or Karl could understand what Captain Drake was stating, they watched him input his identification code into her pocket pad and speak loudly. "Tabitha Drake, assignment, Western Empire space fleet, SS *Hammerhead.*" He handed the pocket pad back to his daughter. "You can start by cleaning your quarters," and her father gave her a wide smile.

Karl's smile was just as big as he watched his good friend lunge forward into her father's arms. "I love you, Daddy." Captain Drake kissed his daughter on the forehead before releasing her. He reached up and activated his ear com piece to contact the SS *Hammerhead*.

"Sir, I was getting concerned," said Mela Finch. "Everything all right?"

"Everything's fine, Commander. How's my ship?"

"Very good, sir. Will everyone be joining us?"

Captain Drake watched the smile grow on Karl Hobbs. He gently grabbed his daughter by the shoulder and pulled her in for more hugs. "Yes ma'am, we're all on our way," and he heard a slight sigh of relief through his ear com piece. "Mela, we have no need to stop at our quarters; we're headed directly to *Hammer One*. Have our support ship ready to leave as soon as we dock."

Mela Finch could not restrain her happiness at the return of all three. "It will be good to have you back, sir," and the link between the captain and his ship was shut down.

Commander Finch activated the command vid com and waited for the chime and acknowledgment to follow. "Attention all vessels, prepare for immediate departure," and the vid com switched at her command as she addressed the crew of the SS *Hammerhead*. "All stations prepare for departure; hangar bay prepare to receive *Hammer One*."

Commander Finch leaned back in her command chair. "Helmsman, set course for Mars and ready for departure." The lights on the bridge of the SS *Hammerhead* dimmed as the vid com projected Earth sector and all the vessels including the colonies on the moon and stations around both astro bodies.

The 3-D projection of the sector changed to the image of the shuttle bay door opening. Commander Finch was amazed by how quickly Captain Drake arrived at his ship. She knew firsthand that he was uncomfortable with the politics from Earth. The operations officer of the bridge chimed in a link to Commander Finch as he sat at his station. "*Hammer One* docking, ma'am."

Commander Finch answered, "Prepare for departure," and she switched the vid com back to the 3-D projection of Earth sector with an outline of the course set for the SS *Hammerhead*.

Captain Drake watched the large conning tower of his ship rise into the view of the cockpit window as *Hammer One* started to lower into the large opening; he also noticed the maintenance and security droids moving around in the docking bay as his shuttle slowly turned to face its assigned berth. Gas was escaping the combat shuttle before dissipating in the vacuum of the hangar bay. As the shuttle gently landed on its extended landing skids, Captain Drake offered a casual salute with a nod to his ensign inside the hangar bay control room. He knew formal salutes were only used in ceremonies but always liked to praise his crew. The external light faded as the large hangar doors closed and the slight impact of the docking tube contacting the hull of the combat shuttle was felt by the crew of *Hammer One*.

As soon as the confirmation chime for the docking procedure was heard, Mela Finch spoke over the vid com for the SS *Hammerhead* and its small support fleet. "Let's go, gentlemen." She watched the smaller ships on the 3-D projection fall into standard formation, the SS *Hammerhead* along with her five escorts completing a wide turn to line up with their intended destination. Within a brief moment, Commander Finch could feel a slight pull and watched the bluish rings and patches with white cloudy streaks appear on the projection. She looked down at her helmsman as he worked his navigation's console with precision. "Helm, report."

The helmsman maintained his focus on his console as he answered through his ear com piece, "All ships in formation and on course, Commander."

Mela grinned as she looked around the large bridge of the SS *Hammerhead*. The entry doors on the second level of the bridge slid open, allowing Captain Drake, his daughter and Karl to enter. Captain Drake stepped up to the command level and watched Commander Finch quickly exit the command chair and stand rigidly close by. "Good to have you back, sir."

Captain Drake smiled. "It's good to be home, Mela."

Karl stepped forward. "Mela, it's good to see you," and Mela chuckled. "Good to see you, Karl." She winked at Tabitha.

Captain Drake interrupted the greetings. "Sitrep, Commander," and leaned forward to study the 3-D projection as he moved the view to the sidebar.

Commander Finch answered her captain's inquiry. "Sir, all ships in formation with a course for Big Red."

Captain Drake leaned back in his chair and grinned with pride as he watched his bridge crew. Tabitha stepped closer to her father and put her hand on his shoulder. "I'm going down to the bay and check my fighter, Dad."

"All right, Taby. We've lost some time on Earth, but you still have enough time to get ready for Masoko."

Tabitha turned toward the upper-level command bridge stairs. Karl Hobbs followed. "We need to stop at your quarters and start cleaning." Tabitha allowed him to walk alongside of her as she smacked the tall, muscular black man in the chest.

Commander Mela Finch waited for them to leave the

command level before speaking. "Sir, you need to call Sam," and Captain Drake looked up with a nod as Commander Finch stepped down to the navigations level.

Captain Drake leaned back in his chair and contacted Director Furgis on Neptune One. His wait was slightly longer than usual. He and the Western Empire were aware of the Eastern Empire's interference with the solar satellites the vid coms used. The lasers flickered for several moments before a slightly distorted 3-D image of Sam Furgis appeared. Captain Drake responded immediately to his greeting as he watched the young man display a certain amount of worry through his tired expression. "Sorry, Sam, Earth would not speed things up."

"We have some issues, Justin."

Captain Drake paused with his open hand up. He looked down at the second level of the bridge and watched Commander Finch nod before returning his attention back to Sam. "Sorry, Sam, needed to know we were on a secure link. Now what is going on?"

"Pops is gone," Sam said calmly. "The Easterners tried taking Acela, and when Pops and the chief stopped them, they disappeared."

Captain Drake remained calm as well. "Any idea where?"

Sam took a deep breath. "The *Staton* destroyed the transport and I damaged the *Staton,* so they won't tell me anything except making threats of war."

"Yeah, the Easterners are getting brazen with their war dances lately." Captain Drake watched the 3-D image of Sam Furgis flicker with static.

Sam yelled at his vid com, "Enhance," and the projection

slightly cleared.

"Sam, calm down, there's a possibility that we have a stealth ship close by trying to jam." Captain Drake nodded once again at Commander Finch. She activated her ear com piece, instructing the communications officer to enhance and trace any unwanted signals interfering with her captain's link.

Sam continued. "Justin, I think they're on the *Staton*."

"Don't worry, Sam, if they're on the *Staton* they won't be harmed. Do not bow down to the Easterners; stand your ground. How's Acela?"

"Acela's fine, but Kelly's dead."

Captain Drake moved forward in his command chair with surprise and anger in his voice. "How?"

Sam Furgis held back the tears in his eyes as he answered. "The abductor fired a round at me, and Kelly got in the way."

Captain Drake could see that Sam was having a hard time dealing with this issue and decided to remain calm.

Commander Finch stepped next to Captain Drake. "Hi, Sam."

"Hi, Mela, thanks for letting Justin know I was looking for him."

Mela Finch's eyebrows raised and she smiled. "Not at all."

Captain Drake interrupted. "Sam, I take it you spoke with your mother?" Sam nodded. "All right, here's what we're going to do. We cannot divert from Mars, so I want you to have droids searching for your father and patrolling your sector." Captain Drake shook his head slightly. "Sam, I'm not supposed to reveal this, so do not repeat this to anyone."

Sam replied with wide eyes, "Yes sir," as Captain Drake spoke with more authority.

"The Western Empire has a fleet heading your way, so do not give in to the *Staton*. You have them outgunned, Sam. We'll be there soon."

Sam relaxed even more. "Thanks, Justin." The vid com shut down.

Captain Drake leaned back in his chair and looked at Commander Finch. "The situation with the Easterners is getting worse."

Finch snickered. "Nothing the *Hammer* can't handle," and she stepped back down to the navigations level. Captain Drake frowned before reactivating the vid com into link mode so he could connect with Raynor Furgis on Mars.

She replied quickly. "Justin, been waiting for you."

Captain Drake watched the full-figured attractive black woman who once served under his command lean back in her desk chair. "Yeah, Ray, been busy with the Earth Commissioner, but I did talk with Sam."

"Just, it seems Ken got himself into a mess again." She shook her head with a grin.

"Ray, I think he's on the *Staton* along with Chief Tylor."

Raynor started laughing. "Not trying to be funny, but if he is, he'll be running that ship in no time at all!"

Captain Drake chuckled. "Ray, I thought you were going to Deimos to deal with the Easterners?"

Raynor frowned. "Just, they turned me away, said I do not have the Solar Counsel's permission." Captain Drake laughed. She looked at her former commander with surprise. "What's so funny, Just?"

"Ray, I would have guessed you'd reform the Mars Independent Army by now."

"Sorry, Just, the link is weak. You said something about the MIA?" and she waited as the link grew slightly stronger.

Captain Drake briefly waited until the link cleared. "I said you can always reactivate the MIA."

"I would love to, but I think anything more than my police force will give the Easterners an excuse."

"There's a lot of that going around. When are you going back to Deimos?" He leaned forward in his command chair.

Raynor picked up her pocket pad from the desktop and activated the personal assistance device; she scrolled the transparent touch screen briefly before replying, "Looks like Derek will have to handle the Mech fight championship." She paused. "Just, I told Sam there's nothing I can do about Ken right now—can you help?"

"Ray, I would love to, but I follow orders as well. Look, if Ken is on the *Staton,* then only Ken will get him off without giving anyone an excuse to start a major incident. But Ken has some friends heading his way."

Raynor gave a fake smile. "All right, Just, I'll let you know what's up with Deimos," and they both nodded as the link severed.

Uranus was similar to Neptune in color and size, allowing Ken Furgis to feel at home as the SS *Kai Che* navigated around several of the large planet's astro bodies toward the ship's destination. He watched the 3-D image of the small station known as Uranus Four hover above the massive rings of Uranus; the station was only half the size of Neptune One, and with the large rings dominating the image of Uranus Four, Ken grew concerned over the quality of assistance his new ship may receive. He sat in his command chair watching the crew of the SS *Kai Che* work their individual consoles on the single-level bridge. He activated his ear com piece and waited until hearing the chime and voice acknowledgment, "Lt. Rogers," and his newly appointed first officer turned quickly and approached the command chair.

"Lieutenant, can you link with your contacts and set up a quick repair schedule? I don't want to be caught with an anchor out."

Lt. Lewis Rogers looked confused. He was soft-spoken and replied in almost a whisper. "Anchor, sir."

Operator Furgis laughed. "Sorry, son, I don't want any company while we're moored with the station."

Lt. Rogers grew stiff and straightened his stand. "Yes sir." Operator Furgis smiled as he watched his first officer walk to the communications console and lean over the crew member operating the touch screen console. Operator Furgis activated the vid com and issued his commands after the usual chime and greeting.

Chief Tylor stood in front of the environmental control console working the purge system and immediately accepted the link from Operator Furgis.

"Sir, I believe all environmental systems are purged and two out of three generators are at full capacity."

"Thanks, Chief. We're approaching Uranus Four now, and Lieutenant Rogers is setting up a maintenance crew from the station."

Chief Tylor was quick to respond. "Still working on the com and long-range troposcope, sir. Will you be going on station to contact Neptune One?"

Operator Furgis sighed with a slight frown. "No, Chief, as far as I'm concerned, we're in hostile territory and I don't want to risk the Easterners knowing our location."

The chief looked puzzled. "The Easterners work with pirate ships on occasion when it's in their interest."

"They'll consider this a Westerner ship if they know we're on board."

The chief smiled with a nod. "Very well, sir."

Operator Furgis continued. "How's the stealth drive?"

"Sir, I have a list as long as my arm of damaged components."

"Chief, give a list of tradable material to Lieutenant Rogers and see what he can do for you. If we're in a pirate ship, we probably should act like it."

Lt. Rogers stood behind the navigation console watching the helmsman work his touch screen control; he would switch his stare from the console and the vid com projection of the data received from the troposcope showing the station grow larger as they approached slowly. Operator Furgis grinned as he watched his nervous first officer concentrate on both the vid com and navigation station; he knew the helmsman was getting jittery over the hovering senior officer. "Lieutenant Rogers." Furgis's voice echoed throughout the small bridge, and he contained his urge to laugh as he witnessed his first officer quiver at the sound of his voice. Lt. Rogers turned and approached Operator Furgis. "Yes, Captain?"

Operator Furgis gestured to his first officer to stand next to the command chair and face the vid com projection. Lt. Rogers nodded, "Yes sir," and clasped his hands behind his back. Operator Furgis continued to watch his ship approach the station on the vid com projection. "Lewis, are these men on our bridge capable?"

Lt. Rogers was surprised at the question and hesitated before answering, "Yes sir."

"Then let them do their job. I've got another assignment for you." Operator Furgis leaned back in his command chair watching the vid com's 3-D projection. He allowed Lt. Rogers to stand still and wait for a while before explaining his new orders. Operator Furgis wanted to take this opportunity to teach his new first officer patience and discipline.

Lt. Rogers wanted to sigh in relief but refrained as Operator Furgis said, "I informed the chief of your assistance in acquiring parts for our stealth drive. Do you think this station will be able to assist in this?"

"Yes sir, and, sir, I can have our weapons store replenished as well." Lt. Rogers grinned.

"Well done, Lewis!" Operator Furgis was impressed with Lt. Rogers's enthusiasm.

The young voice of the helmsman interrupted through the vid com. "Vid coms linked, sir, docking maneuvers at Uranus Four's discretion," and both Operator Furgis and Lt. Rogers watched the 3-D projection of the SS *Kai Che* docking with Uranus Four.

Uranus Four's vid com linked with the SS *Kai Che* navigation vid com, allowing the small outpost station to control the docking procedure as several docking tubes extended toward the side of the ship. Lt. Rogers stood stiffly next to Operator Furgis, who was sitting in the command chair, and he glanced on occasion toward his new commander. They watched the gas from the maneuvering thruster dissipate quickly in the vacuum of space. Operator Furgis grinned as he felt the small ship vibrate slightly at the impact of the docking tubes, and his helmsman turned his head slightly in response. "Docking maneuvers complete, sir."

Operator Furgis was impressed with the small ship, but his thoughts remained on teaching his new crew to acknowledge without looking away from their stations. "Thank you, helm, keep focused on your console," and he stood. "Vid com, engineering," he instructed.

Chief Tylor answered with his heavy English accent. "Yes sir."

Operator Furgis answered with a grin. "Chief, we've docked."

"I know—you can feel everything on this tin can."

Operator Furgis laughed. "All right, Chief, Lieutenant Rogers will be down. Link what you need into his data pad."

"You don't want me to go with him?"

Operator Furgis grew serious as he looked at Lt. Rogers and then back to the 3-D projection of Chief Tylor. "No, Chief, I think it's best if we stay on the *Kai Che* and out of sight from the station." Operator Furgis nodded at his first officer and could see the pride and loyalty on the young man's face.

Chief Tylor was always respectful of Operator Furgis as he continually reminded himself of the first day they met on Neptune One. Tylor had been left to maintain a rundown, damaged, and abandoned station from his Eastern Empire and was sure this new man taking control to turn a military station into an entertainment establishment during these hard times in the systems would ask him to leave.

The chief answered with respect. "Yes sir, and we have the long-range troposcope functioning."

Operator Furgis chuckled with a shake of his head as the vid com shut down.

Chapter Sixteen

Captain Drake sat in his command chair on the bridge of the SS *Hammerhead* with his attention diverted from the navigation's vid com projection. He watched Karl Hobbs and his first officer Commander Mela Finch flirting on the second level of the large command center. Captain Drake grew curious as he watched Karl start laughing. Commander Finch continued to talk with a smile and her hands moving as she expressed her thoughts. Captain Drake grinned and gave in to his impulse to interrupt with a loud voice. "Karl, what's so funny down there?" Commander Mela Finch exchanged her wide smile for a slight grin as she realized her commanding officer was watching.

Karl looked up at Captain Drake with a smile. "Mela was just telling me some war stories, Captain." He looked over at Mela with a passionate smile.

"Well, Mela, you want to share some of these funny war stories?"

His first officer grew rigid, "Sir," but before Captain Drake could continue teasing, the main command level vid com lit up in yellow accompanied by a claxon alarm. Commander Finch quickly stepped around Karl and stood behind the helmsman's station. She was in full military mode; her voice remained sensual but there was a deep tone of authority in every word. "Action station, condition yellow throughout the ship." She watched the bridge crew of the SS *Hammerhead* quickly man their duty stations.

Captain Drake sat up straight in his command chair. "Report." He studied the main vid com 3-D projection and sidebar displaying the troposcope data link.

Commander Finch turned toward the command level. "Ship in distress, Captain." She climbed the short stairs to the command level, leaving Karl leaning over the helmsman.

Captain Drake spoke quickly to the main command vid com. "Fleet." He started his command issues before the chime was complete. "Space normal speed, half thrusters," and he watched the 3-D projection of the vid com displaying his fleet in formation with his command ship. More data appeared on the sidebar from the command level vid com, and Captain Drake studied this data intently as he leaned forward with an elbow on his knee and his hand rubbing his chin.

Commander Finch switched her focus between the vid com's 3-D projection and the crew manning the individual station. She was loud as she bypassed her ear com piece and the vid com. "Weapons, report."

The weapons officer activated his ear com piece with haste. "Weapons ready, sir."

Captain Drake interrupted as he looked from the 3-D projection to his first officer. "The SS *Sojourner*."

Commander Finch watched the data on the sidebar before responding, "A Christian ministry ship, almost as large as the *Hammer*, sir."

Captain Drake focused on the 3-D projection as it grew in

detail. He was silent as he watched the damage appear on the ship. Sparks and smoke dissipated into the vacuum of space as quickly as it appeared, and he could see the smooth hull buckled and torn as debris floated nearby displaying individual signs of damage. The *Sojourner* was a large and impressive ship; the smooth hull gave the ship a sleek look, and the two conning towers resembled the newest ships from the Andromeda cruise line fleet. However, there were only three engines, and all of them were shut down as the ship listed to port. He called out, "Battle stations, one-third thrusters," and stood as he watched his crew jump into action. Captain Drake snapped at Commander Finch, "Long-range trop now."

Commander Finch replied quickly, "Yes sir," and stepped down to the navigation station.

As the new data from the troposcope linked in with the vid com's 3-D display, the captain used his data pad to outline his desired course. Commander Finch rejoined him on the command level as he started issuing orders.

Commander Finch was unafraid to interject, "Sir you have the *Mustang* moving in on the starboard side; should the *Hammer* stay back for support?"

Captain Drake studied his plan for a moment, respecting the insight of his first officer. "No, I want the *Hammer* closer to the *Sojourner*. We don't know if there are any survivors or if this is a trap."

Commander Finch studied the 3-D projection again. She was ready to offer more input but was interrupted by the vid com chime and the voice of the weapons officer. Her young voice was slightly shaky, but the captain could hear pride and assurance. "Sir, the weapons signatures were disguised as pirate weapons, but they appear to be Easterners."

"Appears? I don't want *appears*, I want definite!" Finch said.

Captain Drake looked up from his command chair. "I think we both know who attacked this ship, Mela" and she nodded with agreement. Drake activated the command vid com and said, "Fleet wide, secure." The vid com acknowledged the link to all his fleet ships. He took a deep breath. "*Mustang* approach from starboard, keeping a long-range missile's distance as the *Hammer* proceeds directly in. The SS *Timbers* and *Hatchet* will proceed on the port side with a tighter range for patrol ship maneuvering. Hopefully this is a simple rescue mission, but with the Easterners' growing aggression, I want all ships on battle ready. God speed."

Karl stepped closer to Commander Finch. "I believe Pastor Li said 'God speed' was quoted from Titus three verse thirteen."

Captain Drake smiled. "We'll confirm that later. Let's do it," and he watched his fleet start to move.

The command level vid com projected the entire area in 3-D, showing the bright light and dissipating gases from the SS *Mustang* as the Western Empire's destroyer started a wide arc approach. The two patrol ships gained a slight amount of distance from the SS *Hammerhead* but remained close with a direct course on the left side of the larger heavy cruiser they supported. Captain Drake watched the disabled SS *Sojourner* grow closer as the *Hammer* moved in; he heard Commander Finch calling out her orders: "Stay on that troposcope—we don't need surprises!"

Karl leaned into Captain Drake. "There's a rescue hatch. Should we use shuttles?"

Captain Drake shook his head without removing his concentration from the vid com's projection. "No, Karl, shuttles will be too vulnerable. Slow one-third thrusters," and he watched his crew with pride. "Helm, bring us along her port side for standard docking procedure." Captain Drake paused before turning his attention to his first officer. Commander Finch stood nearby with her hands behind her back, watching the vid com as Captain Drake spoke softer. "Mela, anything from her yet?" He turned back to the vid com as his first officer responded, "No sir." Captain Drake worked the data pad docked in its base on the arm of his command chair as his eyes switched between the data pad and vid com.

Both Captain Drake and Commander Finch watched the main vid com on the command level with great anticipation. Karl stepped closer to Commander Finch. "Why not send the escort ships in first?"

She took a deep breath and spoke softly as she continued to watch the vid com projection. "The *Hammer* can handle a direct attack, if this is a trap like the captain believes." Commander Finch called out, "One and a half GMs to target; reduce speed to one hundred and twenty-five KMs." To Karl she said, "The *Hammer* will have time to get out, provided we're not tied down to the docking tubes, if the patrol ship was docked and hit."

Captain Drake watched the vid com's 3-D projection of his fleet, and he was satisfied at the position of his three support ships. "Dock with her, Mela." Commander Finch stepped down to the second level and stood behind the helmsman. Captain Drake watched the SS *Hammerhead* slowly maneuver alongside the damaged vessel; he could see the gases escape from the SS *Hammerhead's* thrusters and dissipate quickly.

Commander Finch spoke to the bridge crew. "I want long-range trop updates continuously." She turned to face Captain Drake in his command chair, who asked, "Sitrep." "In the tube, sir," she responded.

Captain Drake stood. "Mela, any readings from the vid com link?"

"Cannot link, sir, the *Sojourner's* main vid com is down."

The captain studied the projection of his small fleet and ordered, "Take Gunny with you. We don't know what anyone's left behind." Commander Finch stepped down toward the bridge entrance on the mid-level and activated her ear com as she left the bridge. Captain Drake sat back in his command chair. "Are those recon droids still linked?" He heard a faint "Yes sir" echoed through the bridge as the sidebar of the vid com projection displayed several transmissions from the recon droids.

"I didn't know we had recon droids," said Karl.

"It's standard procedure when battle stations is called," the captain replied.

The sound of the communications device was faintly heard over the other consoles operating throughout the bridge. Captain Drake answered immediately. "Mela, report."

"With Gunny standing by, sir."

Captain Drake took a small breath as he looked at Karl. "Do it," and the vid com went into record mode.

Commander Finch looked at the very large white man standing next to her at the docking tube hatch. GySgt. Lesko was six foot two inches and filled his marine uniform with very large muscles. "Grif, your men ready?"

Gunny Sergeant Lesko turned to his small group of elite space marines. "Sgt. Provovich," and instantly a female voice shouted out, "Gunny!" GySgt. Lesko stared at her with his permanent angry frown. Sgt. Provovich was not intimidated; the short brunette had earned her respect already and could control the rowdy group of fighters. Gunny Lesko spoke loud and with authority. "Ready weapons," and Sgt. Provovich turned to her marines with a shout, "Weapons ready!" as she readied her assigned Tobine repeater rifle.

The marines prepared their own Tobines as the corridor of the SS *Hammerhead* echoed "Hoorah" and the mechanical clicking sound was dominating throughout the corridor. Sgt. Provovich pulled her pocket pad out of its holster and linked with both hatch controls of the docking tube; the hiss of the hatch opening from the SS *Hammerhead* was heard. Three marine privates followed by their corporal quickly entered the brightly lit docking tube and ran in formation to the hatch of the damaged ship. Commander Finch followed Gunny Lesko and Sgt. Provovich. She unstrapped her pistol and pulled the weapon from her holster. "The hull's intake, Gunny, let's go," and Gunny Lesko nodded at Sgt. Provovich.

The short brunette marine sergeant's uniform did not allow for any feminine features to show, and her short hair under her combat helmet gave a false manly image. She pushed two privates aside and stepped closer to the hatch control; holding her pocket pad in line for a strong link, she nodded at her marines. The SS *Sojourner's* hatch slid open, allowing smoke to enter and briefly obscure their view. Sgt. Provovich shouted over the mechanical noises, "Go, go, go!" and the three privates followed by the corporal quickly entered the damaged vessel. The sergeants and commander followed closely.

Commander Finch's combat helmet immediately adjusted the visor, allowing her to see through the darkness and smoke. She did not like what she was witnessing. Commander Finch was a veteran of space combat and watched ships sustain heavy damage and the loss of life that followed the damage; however, she knew this was a civilian ship. She stopped with caution as a marine squatted with a bent elbow and his fist in the air. Her ear com piece was already linked with the marine's communications devices. The voice of the private on point was heard loudly: "Movement, Gunny," and before GySgt. Grif Lesko could respond, Sgt. Provovich said, "Corporal, take the private and check it out."

With weapons at combat ready, the corporal moved slowly, hugging his back against the hull as they made their way down the corridor where the movement was seen. The rest of the marines stood close to the hull, waiting and ready for whatever situation presented itself. Commander Finch kept her back against the corridor wall opposite Gunny Lesko, her pistol held tightly in her hand. She heard Sgt. Provovich's voice on the ear com. "They have crew with them." And she watched the corporal approach followed by a group of crew members. Commander Finch stepped forward as the leader of the SS *Sojourner's* group stepped out front. He was tall with dirty blond hair and he coughed while he spoke. "Will Scott, ma'am."

Commander Finch accepted the hand he held out. She looked around quickly. "Is this it, Will?"

After a slight cough the missionary answered quickly, "Yes, ma'am, the rest of the ship was vented."

"Gunny, time to go," and Finch activated her ear com.

Captain Drake was watching the main vid com display the surrounding area when he heard the chime followed by the recognition voice of the vid com. "Mela, sitrep."

Commander Finch spoke quickly and slightly out of breath as they escorted the missionaries through the docking tube. "We have six survivors, Captain." She did not receive a reply; all she could hear were the claxons from the bridge.

Captain Drake stood as the claxons sounded and his weapons officer called out loudly, "Incoming!" He watched as six missiles appeared on the troposcope linked to his vid com and called out, "Anti-missile batteries." The vid com displayed the closest patrol ship initiating defensive action. Anti-missile projectiles shot from the small patrol ship, SS *Timbers*, creating a wall of projectiles. Captain Drake yelled loudly over the vid com as he watched the other patrol ship, SS *Hatchet*, initiate intercept maneuvers. "Mela, get the docking tube off that ship. We've got incoming!" Karl was tightly grasping the back of Captain Drake's chair.

A barrage of anti-missile projectiles quickly shot from the SS *Hammerhead* and joined the barrage from the SS *Timbers*. The wall of projectiles was strong but not perfect. Five missiles exploded as they entered the barrage of anti-missile projectiles, but two missiles penetrated the defensive attempt. One missile found its target on the stern of the SS *Sojourner*, and the explosion of the missile ripped through the back of the ship with great force, causing fire and smoke that dissipated quickly into space. The sparks and debris shot out from the back of the ship as the stern pulled away, leaving the SS *Sojourner* split in two. As the alarms on the bridge sounded with the strain of the

Sojourner pulling at the failing docking tube, the captain yelled into the vid com, "Mela, get that tube stowed," but he heard nothing.

He watched another explosion on his command's vid com as a missile impacted the bow of the SS *Timbers*. The small patrol ship was engulfed in fire that quickly dissipated. Captain Drake took a deep breath and exhaled as he watched the SS *Timbers* emerge from the impact area; suddenly the small ship listed to port and stopped moving.

Karl Hobbs was confused and angry. "What the he—"

Captain Drake turned and interrupted quickly. "They're using stunners," and he watched another missile appear on his troposcope. The SS *Hatchet* was in range and released another barrage of anti-missile projectiles. Captain Drake called out to his helmsmen, "Where's the *Mustang*?" and a large fireball erupted from the SS *Timbers*.

Another volley of missiles emerged on a direct course for the SS *Hammerhead*. Captain Drake shouted into the vid com as he watched the remaining section of the SS *Sojourner* pull free from the docking tube. The missionaries waited inside the airlock of the *Hammerhead* as Commander Finch followed Gunny Lesko through the hatch. A loud metallic ripping sound caught her attention as she turned to look at the docking tube connection with the SS *Sojourner*. The marine corporal was the last in the docking tube and also paused to watch the metal hull of the tube start to buckle under the stress. The atmosphere inside the docking tube erupted into a deafening sound as the seal with the SS *Sojourner* failed.

The marine corporal aggressively pushed Commander Finch through the docking tube's hatch before the docking hatch controls sensed the breach and slammed the hatch closed. Mela Finch turned quickly to look the corporal in the eye through the hatch window; suddenly the corporal's face froze and he was swept backward at an incredible speed when the docking tube lost its hold on the *Sojourner*. Gunny Lesko was soft-spoken but forceful. "Mela, you're needed on the bridge. I'll see that these guys get to med lab." Gunny Lesko could see the shock on Commander Finch's expression. She activated her ear com piece. "Captain, we're free," and she waited for a response as she exited the airlock.

Captain Drake was loud. "Get up here." He watched the projection as a large barrage of anti-missiles emerged from above the SS *Hammerhead* to join the ordinance from the SS *Hatchet*. The SS *Mustang* traveled directly over the *Hammerhead*, releasing its weaponry. A volley of seeker missiles launched from the destroyer's bow and flew straight into the vastness of space where the assault on her sister ships originated from. She wanted revenge. Captain Drake spoke loudly into his command vid com. "Fleet wide, stay clear of those seekers. *Mustang*, if they travel back, destruct immediately." He turned his attention on his helmsmen. "What are those droids doing? I want that ship's location now," and he watched his bridge crew work with precision.

The 3-D image projected from the command level's vid com chimed before sounding the claxons, and Captain Drake focused on the area displayed from one of the recon droid's link. He used his data pad from the command chair's arm to enhance the area as he and Karl watched a movement of distortion appear. Before either could confirm, an explosion erupted in the exact spot.

Karl laughed. "I like seekers."

Captain Drake looked up at him with a grin before addressing his fleet through the vid com. "*Mustang,* check that out. *Hatchet*, check the *Timbers* for survivors. I think there may be more than one, so keep vigilant."

Commander Finch entered the bridge and approached the command chair quickly. "Sir, the survivors are in med lab."

Captain Drake continued to watch the main command level's vid com. "Sorry I couldn't give you heads-up on those missiles."

"Not your fault, sir, but I regret to inform you that Gunny lost his corporal."

Captain Drake looked at Mela. The anger he felt was hidden by the sympathy in his eyes. "I'll talk with Gunny."

Commander Finch nodded before she asked, "Sir, did we get them all?"

Captain Drake gestured at the projection. "I believe so, but we're sweeping the area before we continue to Big Red."

Commander Finch surveyed the bridge before joining Captain Drake and Karl Hobbs in their study of the vid com projection. "Are you all right, Mela?" Karl asked quietly.

Commander Finch smiled as she grabbed his lower arm. "I'm all right, Karl, thanks." She cleared her throat. "Captain, the survivors said they were attacked by pirates."

"If pirates had stunner missiles, they would use them for boarding and raiding, not destroying."

Commander Finch nodded with a grin. "Agreed, sir."

The vid com chimed, interrupting the conversation. Captain Drake authorized the data transmission from the SS *Mustang* to appear on his main command vid com.

Karl said, "You're right, Captain," and Commander Finch agreed as she stepped closer to the data in the sidebar of the projection. "That was an Easterner, sir."

Captain Drake leaned back with a grin. He could sense the conflicts growing in the inner system. The main vid com chimed, catching their attention, and the voice recognition was heard clearly: "Com."

Mela replied quickly, "What is it, com?"

The communications officer was professional. "I have something from Earth on the solar news, sir."

Commander Finch replied, "Link it up," and the captain switched the 3-D projection of the SS *Hammerhead's* course to the sidebar.

The solar news broadcaster appeared on the main vid com; his 3-D image stood outside in daylight with a tall building in the background. The building resembled saucers stacked on top of each other and rose extremely high. On the top of the building was a larger section that was diamond-shaped with an excessive number of antennae. Fire swept from the sides of the building originating from the midsection and ran up all sides, engulfing the entire top section. The news broadcaster described the scene. "It did not take long for the evacuation tubes to empty the building; however, there are reports of casualties in the Tribune's council chambers. No reports or identities of the victims are released at this time."

Karl broke the silence as they watched the report. "Why would they attack the Terran Tribune? What good would that do?"

Commander Finch answered the armor warrior's query. "A lot of good if you want chaos and confusion throughout the system."

Captain Drake stood from his command chair and looked around the bridge, stating his orders loudly. "Commander, I'll be in the briefing room; you have the bridge."

Commander Finch grew slightly stiffer. "Yes sir." She sat in his chair as he left the bridge.

"Where's he going?" asked Karl. "We're on course for Big Red."

Commander Finch chuckled. "Maybe. The captain's contacting Western Command. When he comes back to the bridge, we'll know if we continue to Big Red or not." She leaned back in the command chair.

Raynor Furgis spoke softly to the 3-D projection of her son. "Sam, I know your father's alive. What you need to do is concentrate on the operations of the station until he gets back. Don't forget you have a good staff there. Use them."

Sam's voice was sad. "I know, Mom. I just worry for Pops. What if he doesn't come back?"

Duncan Jennings was quick to interrupt. "I've known your father for a long time, Sam. Trust me, he'll be back."

Raynor continued. "he's probably commandeered an Eastern vessel and is building a fleet."

Sam forced a laugh. "That would be Pops." He tried shaking the feeling off. "All right, Mom, I'll try. If you hear anything, I want to know. Love ya, Mom."

"Love you too," and the vid com shut down. Sam reactivated it and waited for the chime and recognition to finish. The vid com quickly flickered and produced the 3-D image of Huiling Li standing next to one of the airlocks on the hangar bay.

"Sam, we're ready." She could see the tears forming in his eyes. "Thanks, Huiling, I'll be right there."

Sam stood from his chair as the vid com shut down. He walked slowly to his desk and picked up the vid recording base, switched the device on, and watched the looped 3-D image. Tears ran down his cheeks as the vid recording of Kelly Brown spoke to him. He stood watching the playback for a long time before setting the vid base back on his desk. He left the device on as he turned and exited his office.

Huiling Li worked the airlock's controls, inputting commands that left the double hatch doors to the inner airlock chamber open. Dr. Avers and Dr. Cole stood inside alongside Kelly Brown's casket at military attention in their dress med uniforms. Chayton and Marco De Luca approached slowly, both wearing impressive and expensive suits. Huiling handed each a vid stick as they entered the large cargo airlock. Ambassador Davis followed Marshal Scoop, and the marshal stepped aside, allowing the ambassador to approach Pastor Li first. She nodded, "Blessings," as she handed each their vid sticks.

Dr. Gerlitz and Seth Adams waited their turn to enter while Supervisor Stykes stood behind looking around on occasion. He looked nervous as he realized the danger this cargo airlock offered Sam Furgis's senior staff. He reluctantly followed his friends inside after receiving the vid stick and blessing from Pastor Li. Huiling watched Sam walk toward the entrance with Acela Vega holding his arm. They stopped in front of Huiling Li as she handed him a small rectangular box. Sam held back his tears as he opened the chrome-plated box with Kelly Brown's name appearing across the lid when touched. He stood for a moment and stared at the personalized vid stick hovering in the middle of the box.

Sam looked at Acela with a sad smile before stepping through the entrance hatch. Pastor Huiling Li gently grabbed his arm with both hands and offered another compassionate smile. Acela spoke very softly, almost a whisper, as she stepped through the entrance. "Thank you." Huiling nodded as she followed them inside the inner airlock. Acela stepped closer to Sam on the left side of the hovering casket; she held Sam's arm with both hands as she looked at Kelly through the transparent top. She looked up at Sam and saw a tear escaping the struggling young man. His thoughts continued to switch between his father and Kelly.

"Dr. Avers and Dr. Cole did a great job, Sam," she said softly. "She looks beautiful."

Sam choked up. "Yeah, you can barely see the hole." Acela saw the anger grow in his face.

Pastor Huiling Li slowly dragged her hand across Sam's shoulders as she walked behind him. "She's at rest with the Father now." She took her position at the front of the hovering casket, cleared her throat loudly, and bowed her head. The friends who gathered around Kelly Brown followed Pastor Li in the same gesture. After a moment of silence, Pastor Li spoke loudly. "Shaun De, you are our Father and we praise you, Lord. You are our strength and refuge. We ask that you hear us as we say our farewells to our sister, your daughter." Pastor Li paused as she slowly looked around at the individuals surrounding Kelly. "The vid recordings on these vid sticks are from Kelly's personal pocket pad." She nodded at everyone as they held up their vid sticks. Pastor Li smiled at Dr. Avers. "It's time to say good-bye."

Dr. Avers stepped close to the hovering casket. She could see Kelly through the transparent top, and she realized how beautiful Kelly really was. Her blonde hair flowed gently over her shoulders and rested on top of her pink blouse with her hands on top of each other in a restful position.

Dr. Avers held up the eight-inch vid stick and activated the recording device; a quick distortion appeared above the vid stick briefly before a 3-D image of Kelly in the same blouse appeared. The image was one foot tall and hovered in a gracefully looped motion. Dr. Avers said, "Hi Kelly," and the image came alive. "Hello, Brook. It's been a real pleasure knowing you, Doctor. If I could do things all over again, I would want to be a doctor and learn from you. My love is with you," The image of Kelly returned to its graceful prerecording display with a red light surrounding the image indicating the presence of a personal message.

Dr. Avers stepped back as Dr. Cole moved forward and greeted the image of Kelly. Her message to Dr. Cole was quick but polite. "Dr. Cole, I did not know you very well and did not have the time to talk with you much, but my heart tells me you're a very good man and a friend of Brook's. I will miss the chance to know you better; my love is always with you."

Seth Adams stepped forward and activated his vid stick. "Seth, on the outside you're a pirate." The 3-D image of Kelly started chuckling. "But on the inside is a very kind and giving man. I wanted to thank you for introducing me to ancient rock at Grav Zero. Sam and I had some really special times there. Thank you, Seth, my love is always with you." Seth shut the device down and stepped back with his head bowed.

Chayton stepped forward holding his slim vid stick up and extended above Kelly's casket. Chayton smiled at the 3-D image. "Chayton, I will miss you. You're a really special guy. You have taught me so much on how to be a responsible adult, and you did it while being a good friend. My love will always be with you."

As Chayton stepped back, Marco De Luca grabbed his shoulder and nodded as they exchanged eye contact. He continued to the casket except he held his vid stick closer to himself. Kelly started with a laugh. "Marco, I will miss your humor; you always made me laugh," and the 3-D image of Kelly paused to laugh. "Don't let Sam fool you—he enjoys your humor just as much as I have, something I will really miss. My love is with you, Marco," and he stepped back as the vid stick turned red.

Leaf Stykes approached the foot of the casket and stood slightly to the left as he activated his vid stick. The 3-D image of Kelly appeared in its initial position before Stykes allowed the image to come alive with his greeting. Kelly smiled at him for a moment before speaking. "My protector, thank you so much for your kindness, sir. I know what you did for Sam and how good of a…" She stopped to look off into the distance before continuing. "…boxer, I think it is called. I will miss you, Leaf; my love is always with you." Supervisor Stykes held back a tear as he smiled and stepped back.

Ambassador Davis stepped forward quickly, and no one responded as they watched the comfort he displayed. He quickly held up his vid stick and greeted the 3-D image of Kelly before it was finished materializing above the slim device. "Ambassador, I thank you for your good-byes and I really hope you're not too uncomfortable. I never got a chance to congratulate you on your promotion to ambassador." She bowed her head slightly. "Congratulations, Ambassador. Please help Sam and his father in any way you can. Thank you. My love is with you."

Next to step forward was Marshal Scoop. Kelly's image nodded with a smile. "Sir, I realize you're a very good enforcer and like things done by the law, but I would like to ask you a personal favor." As she paused, Marshal Scoop could feel the stares from everyone. "Acela Vega is one of the smartest and wisest women I have ever known, and she is so compassionate and loving. Instead of trying to arrest her, please help her; she is a very good person. My love and gratitude are with you." Marshal Scoop smiled and nodded at Acela Vega as he stepped backward.

Dr. Niclas Gerlitz stepped forward and casually held up his vid stick as he looked around at the individuals staring at him. Pastor Li nodded with a gesture to activate his vid stick. The 3-D image appeared in the initiation loop of the recording device, and Dr. Gerlitz spoke in a low voice. "Hello, young lady." She chuckled as the 3-D image looked directly at him; her head followed his eyes as he moved the vid stick around nervously. "Dr. Gerlitz, please allow yourself to have some fun on occasion; if you need help with this, then ask Seth. He can show you how. May my love be with you." Dr. Gerlitz stepped back with a feeling of relief as he realized there was no red light surrounding her image.

Acela released Sam's arm as she stepped forward; tears appeared in her eyes as she tried to wipe her eyes and hold her vid stick at the same time. Marco De Luca and Supervisor Stykes each pulled out a pocket cloth and offered it to her.

She subconsciously accepted Marco's cloth, knowing his would be finer. As she wiped her eyes, she held her vid stick up; her hands were shaky as the 3-D image of Kelly appeared. Acela Vega activated the vid recording with a shaky voice. "Hi Kelly." The 3-D image came alive. "Hello, Acela, please do not cry. I do not want you to feel sad. I know why they call you Lady Diamonds. Your heart shines and you bring a spark to everyone."

Sam smiled as he looked at Acela's black dress shoes and followed her lower legs up to see her black skirt and Meraty dress jacket. The beautiful black jacket was low cut, covering a very small lighter black dress shirt. His smile grew slightly as he watched the sparkle from the large diamond necklace that hid Acela's cleavage. He knew Kelly always admired Acela's jewelry. Acela sniffled as Kelly's projection continued. "Acela, I thank you for being such a good friend and inspiration to me. May my love always be with you." Her projection was illuminated in red. Acela stepped back and held Sam by the arm as she smiled at him.

She released his arm as Sam stepped forward. He stared at Kelly for a moment before activating the vid stick. "Hey, baby, I miss you so much." Kelly's arm extended forward in a gentle touching gesture. "Sam, my dear love, I will miss you so much. Please do not grieve for me." His senior staff could see the strength and control leave him as he started to cry. Acela stepped forward and held his shaking hand. "Sam, do not grieve for me. Pastor Li would be the first to tell you I am with the Father now, and I will be here for you." The red illumination appeared as Acela stepped back with Sam.

Pastor Li stepped forward, bowing her head as she held

her pocket pad; her hand gently flowed across the transparent screen releasing a very faint chime. She looked up and around at Kelly Brown's friends before sharing in her gentle, soothing voice, "The Lord is my shepherd, I shall not be in want. He makes me lie down in green pastures, he leads me beside quiet waters, he restores my soul. He guides me in paths of righteousness for his name's sake. Even though I walk through the valley of the shadow of death, I will fear no evil, for you are with me; your rod and your staff, they comfort me." Pastor Li looked around at the bowed heads; she heard Sam and Acela crying as she activated the transparent hatch that separated the inner and outer chambers of the cargo airlock.

She stepped aside as the hovering casket gently and slowly moved into the outer airlock chamber, with the voice of Arina Petrov singing "Amazing Grace" in the background. Two halves of the transparent hatch emerged from inside the bulkhead walls and came together with a hissing sound. Sam and his senior staff gathered behind Pastor Li. Sam rested his hands on the hatch as the light inside the outer air chamber turned red.

Officer Armela sat in the pilot seat of *Research Two* wiping his eyes as he listened through the vid com to "Amazing Grace." The vid com chimed with the voice recognition over Kelly's favorite song. "*Research One*." Officer Armela let out a heavy sigh to regain his composure. He answered with a somber voice. "Hey, Shaun," and Engineer Trently replied with the same tone. "Get ready, Juan." They watched the crack of light from the cargo hatch grow wider as the doors started to part.

Small thrusters on Kelly Brown's casket, along with the vacuum of open space, accelerated the hovering casket into a slow speed that allowed the casket emerge into space. Sam felt helpless and alone as he watched the casket depart Neptune One and travel into the faint bluish light from Neptune. As the casket traveled past the research shuttles, they activated the Mortelis cannons at very low power, creating two small bluish balls of energy that crossed paths in front of the casket. As the Mortelis energy blasts erupted into a display of blue fireworks, the casket's small thruster ignited, propelling her deeper into the void of space.

Chapter Seventeen

Commander Finch sat in the captain's chair on the bridge of the SS *Hammerhead* watching the vid com 3-D display of the area her ship traveled through. Her head turned quickly and sharply as she heard the doors to the captain's chambers hiss open. Captain Drake approached quickly. She stood abruptly from his chair and said, "Bridge is yours, Captain."

The captain of the SS *Hammerhead* sat in his command chair, "Sitrep," and pulled his data pad from the docking port on the arm of his chair.

Commander Finch replied, "On course to Big Red, sir. Should I change course?"

"No, Mela, command said they want the match to go through."

Karl Hobbs climbed the short steps from the mid-level of the bridge and approached the captain. "That's good for Taby; she said she's ready for the final fight."

After realizing the captain was waiting patiently to hear all opinions, Commander Finch said, "It's good for the Mech fighter fans, but not for the system," and she paused to look at Captain Drake, grinning. "Karl, we all know the Easterners are up to no good; we should be preparing for war."

Captain Drake's voice was loud and determined. "That's

not for us to decide, Commander. We'll leave those mistakes to the diplomats." He leaned forward as the vid com chimed with the acknowledgment of arrival at Mars sector. Captain Drake enhanced the vid com's 3-D projection with his data pad. While studying the image of Mars sector, he said, "Navigations, sitrep."

Commander Finch and Karl grew quiet as they watched the intense traffic of ships around Mars.

The navigations officer spoke into his station's vid com with all stations throughout the bridge on an open link. "Standard orbits are crowded, sir."

Commander Finch responded, "Nav, park us above the upper pole," and she stepped closer to Captain Drake's command chair.

The captain leaned back and looked at Karl. "Tell Taby she can drop at any time; her Mech fighter is to go through inspections at the hangar, and you and I will take *Hammer One* and meet her after I see Ray." He turned to Commander Finch. "Have *Hammer One* standing by with Taby's equipment." Commander Finch smiled with a nod.

Captain Drake focused his attention on the main command vid com. "Raynor Furgis, Mars City Central." The 3-D image of Derek Fields appeared. The tall, slim white man wearing a deep red suit appeared; his voice was rough but held a slight amount of excitement. "Justin, how are you?"

Captain Drake smiled. "Derek, you're still on Big Red. I thought you'd be running Mother Earth by now."

"No need for Earth. We've got the politics we need here."

"Yeah, I can tell. I barely found a place to squeeze in."

"Here she is now. She can explain that." Derek stepped out

of the projection range of the vid com.

After a moment Raynor Furgis stepped into the projected view and appeared in front of Captain Drake on the bridge of the SS *Hammerhead*. The captain could see how tired she looked, but her voice did not reveal the fatigue as she smiled with excitement. "Just, it's about time you got here."

Captain Drake laughed. "You could have saved us a parking space." Commander Finch approached and stood next to his command chair, and Captain Drake's excitement wore off as he saw Raynor's expression.

"Hey, Mela." She did not give Commander Finch time to respond. "I wish I could have, Just. In fact I wanted to link up but there's been a lot of broken links around here lately. Come on down and we'll talk before I head to Deimos, and tell Taby to get a move on before she forfeits." The vid com returned to its operational display.

Commander Finch looked at Captain Drake with puzzlement. "That does not sound good, sir."

Captain Drake nodded as he spoke over his shoulder. "Broken link is code for enemy jamming." Commander Finch pulled her pocket pad out of her holster and zoomed the 3-D image from the vid com toward Deimos. Captain Drake stood abruptly and exhaled. "Okay, Mela, the *Hammer's* yours. Park in the upper quadrant at battle ready and launch a stealth toward Deimos." He paused as he approached the stairs leading to the mid-level. "Tell Hobbs to be at *Hammer One* when I get there. All links on secure status."

Commander Finch responded, "Yes sir," and occupied the command chair as Captain Drake left the bridge.

The SS *Hammerhead* and her two sister ships in Captain

Drake's fleet added to the traffic around the red planet; most of these ships were from the Eastern Empire's fleet. One of the two rear shuttle bay hatches started sliding apart, revealing the stars and the glow of the red planet to the occupants of *Hammer One*. Captain Drake looked out the cockpit window, caught in the beauty of the giant red planet. As *Hammer One* turned, he could see white clouds covering the red surface with a touch of blue in the atmosphere from all the terraforming domes scattered over the surface.

Captain Drake activated his ear com piece. Karl Hobbs was slow to respond. His attention was on the engineering station's console. "Yeah, Captain?" He continued to work the transparent touch screen controls.

"How's Taby?" The captain continued to watch the white clouds engulf *Hammer One* before emerging into slight atmospheric traffic. He gestured at the large city in the distance and watched the pilot nod. He could hear Karl's voice clearly through his ear com piece.

"Captain, Taby's in the Mech fighter hangar. Mars Central granted a delay, but she needs to prep and get her Mech fighter to the Mariner Desert quickly."

Captain Drake grinned. The main vid com chimed and displayed the words "incoming transmission." Captain Drake assumed it was his first officer and accepted without confirmation. The vid com 3-D projection flickered briefly before Raynor Furgis appeared. "Just, are you almost here? I've got a meeting with the devil on Deimos I need to attend."

Captain Drake laughed. "I told you to leave that boy alone. We're approaching the hangar now." He paused. "Oh, and thanks for the delay, Ray."

Raynor chuckled. "Don't thank me, thank Derek. I'll be in my office." The vid com shut down as *Hammer One* slowed and entered the landing line with the other shuttles arriving.

Raynor sat at her desk when Captain Drake entered her office with open arms. She accepted the hug immediately and looked Captain Drake in his eyes. "Any word on Ken yet?" She answered her own question from the look in her former captain's eyes.

Captain Drake sighed. "Not yet, Ray, but don't worry. He and the chief will escape the Easterners. Speaking of Easterners, who's this devil you need to see?"

Raynor turned both chairs in front of her desk around and said, "Bad choice of words, but they act like they are. The Easterners, as you know, put a base on Deimos without the Solar Counsel's approval." She turned and picked up a data pad from her desktop and handed it to the captain. He scrolled through the transparent touch screen. "Is this data from stealth droids?" He handed the data pad back.

Raynor Furgis tossed it on top of the other pads on her desk and turned to Captain Drake with a concerned look. "Just, they're trying to hide a fleet." She activated her main vid com.

The 3-D image of Deimos appeared with numerous Eastern Empire warships orbiting the large satellite. Raynor pulled her pocket pad out of its holster and worked the controls. The 3-D image zoomed in on the Eastern Empire's base built on the surface of Deimos. Captain Drake leaned forward and looked intently at the base and surrounding structures as the view rotated. "There they are!" Raynor paused the movement of the 3-D image, and Captain Drake pointed at several locations. "You can see them here and here."

Raynor shook her head in anger. "I knew it. They've got missile batteries and anti-missile batteries."

Captain Drake held his hand out. "Let's see what else is around here." He worked the controls of the pocket pad, causing the 3-D image to unzoom and scan the area around Deimos. He stopped the movement of the display and said, "Check it out."

Raynor sat on the edge of her chair for a moment before responding, "Is that what I think it is?"

Captain Drake whistled. He worked the controls of the pocket pad to zoom on the location, displaying images that were unfocused and hard to recognize. Raynor took the device from Captain Drake as she stepped closer to the vid com projection and worked the controls until Captain Drake spoke abruptly. "Stop." They both stared at the 3-D image. Raynor looked at Captain Drake with deep concern. "I knew they were up to no good, but this is unacceptable."

He shook his head with disapproval. "The SS *Courageous*, wonderful." He leaned back in his chair with a sigh.

Raynor shut down the vid com. "From what Chief Tylor said, the *Courageous* is the most powerful carrier ship in either fleet." She stood and walked to her desk chair.

Captain Drake quickly followed and grabbed her arm. "Ray, there's no need to go up there."

Raynor gave him her usual frown and activated her ear com piece. "Derek, get my shuttle ready. You're taking care of the Mech fight while I'm visiting our new neighbors."

Captain Drake knew how stubborn Raynor could be. "All right, Ray, I don't blame you. But I want you to wear this link so I can track you if needed, and I'm telling Mela to put the *Hammer* on standby alert." Raynor nodded and accepted the locator link.

Karl Hobbs sat at the engineering console inside *Hammer One*. Tabitha Drake could be heard clearly over the vid com. "All set, Karl, ready for drop ship."

Karl grinned as he answered, "You're a go for entry, Taby, and you be careful on this one. The Sword is brutal." He heard the hiss of the shuttle's doors and saw Captain Drake enter. He could tell the captain held more concerns than his daughter's Mech fight. "Captain, everything all right?"

Captain Drake approached the console, his voice displaying the concern he felt. "Just helping Ray deal with some unwanted guests."

"The Easterners and their little space fleet again," Karl said.

Without turning, the captain said, "Not as little as you think, Karl." Captain Drake looked into the cockpit of *Hammer One*. "Let's go" echoed through the rear cabin. The pilot's hands glided across the touch screen console as he input his command, and *Hammer One* lifted off its retractable landing skids as the gases from the thrusters swirled across the landing deck. *Hammer One* turned slowly as the forward momentum was felt by its crew, and the light from the atmosphere of Mars brightened the interior of the combat shuttle. Captain Drake spoke loudly. "Let Taby know we're on our way to the Mariner Desert," and Karl nodded before activating his ear com piece.

Hammer One traveled at a low altitude with increasing speed. The features of Mars passed by the cockpit window quickly as the bluish-red atmosphere's light reflected off the panels inside the cockpit of the combat shuttle. Captain Drake could feel the thrusters decelerating and he checked his vid com display as he adjusted the shuttle's troposcope. "Lieutenant, status."

The pilot continued to concentrate on his control console as the vessel slowed. "We're at the Mariner Desert, sir, taking assigned fight position." The crew of *Hammer One* became quiet as Mars' planetary anthem was heard through the vid com.

Karl laughed and turned to look at Captain Drake. "Glad we're not late."

Captain Drake chuckled as he swiveled in his engineering station's chair. "Fine with me. I never liked the Red anthem." He grew more serious. "How's Taby?"

Karl swiveled his chair to face his operations station and paused to check the console's vid com display. "They're both closing on the drop zone, sir."

Captain Drake's vid com chimed and flashed his first officer's name across the 3-D projection of the Mariner Desert. The captain leaned back and said, "What is it, Commander?"

The vid com link was briefly full of static before Commander Finch's 3-D projection cleared enough to hear. "Sir, there's a lot of jamming up here; switching to battle link." Captain Drake adjusted the vid com on his console. Suddenly the image of Commander Mela Finch appeared with lifelike detail.

"Sir, Earth's been attacked, and numerous Mortelis warheads have been detonated. All command contact in that sector is gone."

Drake could hear the claxons and alarms in the background of the bridge. He switched into military mode immediately. "Put the fleet on battle stations, and set a course for Io. This match is over." He swiveled his chair toward Karl. "Karl, wake up. Lieutenant, put us in the drop zone. Karl, get a link with Taby ASAP."

Karl turned his chair forward to face his console. His hands worked fast as he called out his report. "Captain, cannot link; she's already dropping."

Captain Drake left his engineering station and climbed into the copilot's seat. "Ready all weapons, Karl. Lieutenant, bring us behind her drop site." The pilot did not respond as he operated the controls in reply to Captain Drake's orders.

The vid com link from the Mech fight council was faintly heard over the noise of the shuttle and internal communications. Captain Drake recognized Derek Fields ordering all civilian hover stands and ships to clear the area. Captain Drake watched the two Mech fighters appear from the bluish-red atmosphere; their Mechs were descending fast with thrusters firing from the back of the Mechs and under their feet. The pilot of *Hammer One* worked fast and continually to keep the combat shuttle from the impact area, and the crew inside strapped their harnesses quickly as the ship moved violently. Captain Drake watched the Sword drop first in a half-kneeling position. She stood quickly as her opponent, Darkstar, arrived, causing a larger cloud of dirt from her full kneeling position.

The Sword launched long-range missiles toward Darkstar, and the captain worked his console's controls quickly, instructing *Hammer One* to join the fight. A barrage of anti-missile projectiles emerged from *Hammer One* and intercepted the Sword's arsenal. Explosions erupted all around Darkstar as she lifted off the ground with full thrusters. The vid com chimed with an intrusive link to Captain Drake's battle link. "Dad, what are you doing?"

He did not have to wait long before he heard the match's termination order in the background. "Taby, the match is over; get out of there." Before he could explain, a missile attack on the surface began, and one of these missiles impacted the Sword directly, causing a large fireball to erupt and shoot straight into the air.

Captain Drake called out quickly over the vid com link, "Taby, eject, we'll get you," and he turned to look at Karl unstrapping his chair's harness. Karl struggled to get to the external entry hatch of *Hammer One* as the combat shuttle was rocked back and forth from the violent explosions of the missile barrage. The rear cabin filled with dust and smoke as the hatch opened to the red planet's atmosphere. Karl had already secured his harness to the hull of the combat shuttle, and as he leaned out, he felt the ship turn to port while rocking in the turbulence. Darkstar was already descending when she activated her ejection thrusters, causing the harness of her Mech to release all connections to her armor warrior suit. She watched helplessly as her Mech fighter fell away, leaving her suspended in midair. She knew the emergency thrusters on her suit would not last long.

Hammer One was gracefully dodging the debris from the missile attack as the combat shuttle abruptly stopped close to Taby while she hovered in the chaotic surroundings. Karl lifted a retractor gun up from his harness and pointed the rescue device toward Taby; he waited for the proper moment when the shuttle calmed enough in its turbulence to aim and shoot. Tabitha reached for the retractor cable as it shot from the open entry hatch in her direction, and the muscles in her arm strained against the turbulent surroundings as she attached the retractor cable to her armor suit. Her back arched and her chest was pulled forward from the thrusters, and the pulling force on the retractor cable was the only assurance of rescue Tabitha Drake had from *Hammer One*.

Captain Drake unbuckled his harness and tried exiting his copilot seat to assist Karl in the rear cabin. The more he worried about his daughter, the harder he struggled. But the violent maneuvering from *Hammer One* was too great to overcome. Captain Drake activated the vid com's internal communication and yelled as he turned in his chair to look back into the cabin. "Karl, is she in?" The silence was painful.

Karl secured the retractor gun in the built-in attaching bay at the entry hatch and worked the controls; he could catch glimpses of Tabitha through the thick clouds of dust as *Hammer One* was beaten by the aggressive atmosphere. Suddenly the ship leaned on its starboard side, and Karl could see directly down and on top of Tabitha. He immediately increased the retraction speed to full, knowing the stress in this position was acceptable for the cable's rating. Tabitha reached for the hatch as the combat shuttle straightened out, with her nose acquiring a ninety-degree pitch up. Karl reached out of the hatch and grabbed Taby's arm with as much strength as the G-force would allow. He yelled through the vid com internal communications, "Go, I've got her!"

Captain Drake looked at over at his pilot. "Go."

Hammer One went to full thrusters, shooting straight up at an incredible speed. It emerged from the atmosphere of the giant red planet above the northern pole and the orbital parking space of the SS *Hammerhead*. Captain Drake was concerned for his daughter but focused on the intense battle the combat shuttle was encountering. The pilot flew evasively as Captain Drake's attention went directly for his ship. He watched a barrage of anti-missile projectiles strike numerous missiles on a direct course for his ship. The battle link to his first officer was already open. "Mela, we're coming in hot; hangar bay one. Roll the *Hammer* to port and give us some cover."

His first officer shouted out orders, causing the large Western Empire heavy cruiser to roll left. Captain Drake looked back over his shoulder quickly to try and catch a glimpse of his daughter before continuing. "Mela, set a course for Io, and get the fleet moving. We're outgunned here." The combat shuttle jumped and bounced around explosions, and both the pilot and Captain Drake grew completely still as they watched a missile fly by the cockpit window. They both turned their heads to see the target the missile was aiming for as a flash of light quickly dissipated, giving Captain Drake something to grin about. He knew the SS *Mustang* was not an easy target.

Hammer One entered the open hangar bay door of the SS *Hammerhead* at full thrusters; the crew could hear the retractor cables from the bay strike the hull of their combat shuttle before the sudden force of stopping pinned them briefly in their harnesses. The retractor cables quickly and gently pulled the shuttle into its berth. The lights turned yellow and the hangar doors started quickly closing.

Commander Mela Finch sat on the edge of the command chair as she worked the touch screen console of the data pad docked with the arm of the command chair. The main vid com already displayed the sector of space where the Western fleet was engaged in battle. She plotted a new course and issued the commands to the fleet through the battle link on the vid com.

The main vid com on the bridge of the SS *Hammerhead* displayed the fleet movement along with combat engagement of all warships. Commander Finch watched a green flash on the vid com and issued commands through her data pad to enhance the sector where the unknown friendly identification was transmitting from. The entry doors to the bridge hissed open, and Captain Drake quickly entered. He did not slow his pace until he was next to his command chair. Commander Finch immediately stood. "Bridge is yours, sir."

Captain Drake sat in his chair and picked up his data pad. "Sitrep, Commander." He watched the data change on the vid com 3-D projection.

"Sir, the fleet consisting of two cruisers, three destroyers, and a patrol ship is on course for Io. I was ready to change course for the unknown friendly here, sir" and Finch gestured to the green unknown on the 3-D projection.

Captain Drake grinned as he watched his fleet launch countermeasures and retaliatory strikes at the Eastern Empire ships. "Negative, Commander. Have the *Hatchet* check it out; a patrol ship accelerates quicker and is more maneuverable." Commander Finch nodded and gestured at the communications officer.

Captain Drake leaned back in his chair, watching the 3-D projection from the vid com. His focus was interrupted by his first officer. "Sir, how's Taby?"

Captain Drake looked up with a sigh. "She's in med lab with Karl. She's bruised and shaken up, but she'll be fine." He could see the look of relief on Commander Finch's expression. The conversation was interrupted by the communications officer chiming in on the vid com. "Sir, the ship is a shuttle from

Mars Central; she's taking a pounding, sir."

Before Captain Drake could reply, he watched the 3-D projection of the SS *Mustang* assist the SS *Hatchet* in recovering the shuttle. Missiles and projectiles crossed paths in open space as the *Mustang* intercepted the ordinance from several Eastern Empire ships targeting the *Hatchet*. Captain Drake stood quickly from his command chair as he watched the 3-D projection of a missile striking the *Hatchet* under the command coning tower of the small patrol ship. "*Hatchet*, reply!"

The vid com flickered with static before focusing on a young man wearing a slightly torn uniform. "Captain, Mendez here."

Captain Drake calmed a bit. "Sitrep." Commander Finch stepped closer. They watched the young man look around the smoke-filled bridge. Sparks occasionally would shoot from a console. He turned to face the vid com, and Captain Drake could hear the fear in his voice. "The captain's dead and the first officer is unconscious, sir." The vid com shut down.

Captain Drake looked at Commander Finch, but the vid com reestablished the battle link. "Sorry, Captain, we got some damage over here."

Captain Drake looked back at Commander Finch. "Have the *Mustang* run on her starboard in support." He turned back toward the vid com. "Listen, son, at this time that's your ship. I want you to proceed on the port side of the *Mustang* for cover; the fleet is slowing, so make it quick. Then I want a damage report and to speak to that shuttle commander." The acting captain of the SS *Hatchet* nodded, "Yes sir," before the vid com on the SS *Hammerhead* switched back to the 3-D projection of the sector.

Commander Finch approached the command chair. "The *Stang* is covering, sir. She says there's no trop contact on the VC."

"I don't care what the vid com says. I don't like that they had us outgunned four to one and they stopped." Captain Drake looked at Mela with a cautious expression. "Why?" Commander Finch frowned. The vid com chimed, followed by the vid com's voice. "SS *Hatchet*." Captain Drake leaned forward and accepted the battle link.

The vid com's projection focused, leaving a 3-D image of a full-figured black woman on Captain Drake's bridge. He smiled with excitement. "I knew it, Ray, you're the only one I know that would attack the Eastern Empire with a shuttle."

Commander Mela and Raynor Furgis laughed. "I see I had as much luck as you," said Raynor. "I'll be right over, Just."

"No need. Commander, the *Hatchet* is yours, so I suggest you make repairs before we get to Io."

Commander Finch was smiling and nodding. Commander Furgis also nodded in response. "No sir, we intercepted a link to Io. They're getting hit pretty hard, but the report said they're holding their own."

Captain Drake looked intently at the sidebar of the vid com. Commander Furgis waited patiently. She had served under Captain Drake when he was a commander and held high respect and trust in his judgment.

"All right, Commander, we're setting course for the Saturn sector and then on to Neptune; hopefully we'll find your other half. Fall in between the *Hammer* and the *Stang*." The vid com shut down. Captain Drake stood and gestured at the 3-D projection. "Mela, I want the destroyer *Yama* up front, the light cruiser *Liberty* on our port, with support from the destroyer *Enapay* and the *Hatchet* tucked in between us and the *Mustang*."

Commander Finch nodded and stepped down to the second level of the SS *Hammerhead's* bridge.

Operator Furgis leaned back in the command chair of the SS *Kai Che*. His first officer, Lt. Rogers, stood close and they watched the 3-D projection of Uranus Four slowly growing smaller as the patrol ship gained distance. Operator Furgis looked over at Lt. Rogers and nodded with a grin. "You did good, son."

Lt. Rogers returned the grin. "Thank you, sir."

Operator Furgis could see the trouble in his young first officer's expression. "What is it, Lieutenant?"

Lt. Rogers sighed and shook his head. "Just thinking about Earth. You think they really irradiated her with Mortelis, sir?"

Operator Furgis activated his ear com and waited for the chime and voice recognition before issuing his commands. "Chief Tylor." Almost instantly he heard the heavy English accent. "Yes sir." Operator Furgis grinned. He felt reassured with the chief in engineering. "Chief, we're headed back to Neptune One, but we're taking the long way around. Is the solar drive ready?"

"Whenever you're ready, sir."

Operator Furgis looked at his first officer as the ear com shut down. "Set a course, Lieutenant. The solar net is down, giving us no info on Earth, so concentrate on our course instead." The first officer nodded as he walked over to the navigation station.

The 3-D projection continued to update the course of the SS *Kai Che* from the troposcope data. The sidebar flowed with details as the troposcope communicated with the vid com. Operator Furgis leaned forward as the vid com started broadcasting claxon warnings and highlighting a large area of space the ship was approaching. "Space norm speed, half thrusters, engage stealth mode and launch recon droids."

Lt. Rogers relayed his commands, then stepped closer to the command chair. "What is it, sir, Easterners?"

Operator Furgis remained quiet until the troposcope displayed the required data. "No, it's the *Hammer*, and she's being attacked by stealths." He yelled, "Battle stations," and ordered the vid com to enhance a section on the far side of a Western Empire's destroyer. "There, Lieutenant, the quick flash is our target!"

Lt. Rogers was impressed but also concerned. "We need to be quick—the destroyer's trying to intercept for the patrol ship, but it's getting hit hard." Both could see the SS *Hatchet* receiving numerous impacts through the defensive wall the SS *Mustang* provided. Operator Furgis watched a large explosion with debris shooting out from the side of the *Hatchet*, and he interrupted his first officer. "Launch seekers." Noticing the surprised look on Rogers' face, he added, "It's a gamble, son, but we need to do something about that stealth." They watched their stealth missile travel in an arc pattern toward the last position of the stealth attacker. After watching the missile adjust its course, Furgis and Rogers shouted, "Yeah," as a bright flash was displayed on the 3-D projection. Their shout was heard throughout the bridge, causing a chain reaction of cheering from the bridge of the SS *Kai Che*.

Operator Furgis looked around with pride before speaking with his first officer. "If you wanna kill a stealth, use a stealth."

Lt. Rogers gestured at the vid com, and Operator Furgis leaned back in his command chair as he watched the display of action.

The *Mustang* proceeded toward the explosion from the *Kai Che*'s missile strike; the Western destroyer was not merciful. A barrage of missiles shot from the starboard side and struck the exposed patrol ship. Operator Furgis watched the small vessel light up on every strike until the ship was floating in numerous pieces. As he watched the fires shoot into space and extinguish themselves along with the sparks and debris, he leaned forward and spoke loudly to the vid com. "SS *Hammerhead*," and then he waited for the image to focus.

Operator Furgis laughed as soon as the vid com's image was clear. "Just, was that fly bothering you?"

Mela Finch stepped closer to Captain Drake's command chair as Furgis's surprised former captain answered, "I should have known it would be you sneaking around out there. Ken, what's your sitrep?"

"Just, I got a new ship, but I'm running on a skeleton crew, taking the scenic route back to the station."

Captain Drake grinned and held his hand up as he spoke softly and indistinctly to his first officer. Commander Finch turned and walked out of the vid com's link. Captain Drake faced Operator Furgis again as he leaned back in his command chair. "Ken, I got a crew for you."

"All right, Just, what do you have in mind?"

"You're gonna like this, Ken." He paused for a chuckle and a slight shake of his head. "The *Hatchet* is too badly damaged and is now a liability. I'm sending her crew your way to help out. I think Commander Furgis would make a good first officer."

Operator Furgis's eyes grew wide. "What is she doing over there?"

"She was on her way to Deimos when the cowards pulled their surprise attack; she had enough sense to head away from Mars, and we picked her up on the way out. Your new first officer will be there shortly." The vid com shut down as he looked at Lt. Rogers. "We're lucky he didn't make her captain. Prepare for guests, Lieutenant."

Operator Furgis watched the hangar bay doors slide closed on the 3-D projection of his ship along with the rest of the fleet moving information on a course for Neptune One. Soon after the hiss of the doors' opening caught his attention, he stood from his command chair as his new first officer entered the bridge. "Permission to come aboard!" she said and stood at attention.

Operator Furgis quickly approached and pulled her in for a hard hug. "Permission granted. Ray, I'm sorry I didn't get here in time to save your ship."

Commander Furgis put her hand on his chest and took a breath. "There's nothing you could have done; they surprised us with stunners, and the first hit shut all electronics down."

Operator Furgis put his hand on his wife's cheek before pulling her into another hug. He stepped aside, allowing Lt. Rogers to approach. He quickly snapped to attention, and Ray laughed. "The first time I ever saw a pirate at attention."

Lt. Rogers spoke with a deep and proud voice. "Lt. Rogers of the Western Empire's warship SS *Kai Che,* ma'am."

Raynor looked at her husband with raised eyes and a smile. Operator Furgis chuckled before explaining. "At ease,

Lieutenant. Ray, the lieutenant and the rest of the ship have been acquired by the Western fleet."

Raynor looked around the small bridge. "In other words, you recruited them." She smiled and shook her head.

Operator Furgis nodded at Lt. Rogers, "Stations," and stepped closer to his wife. "You know the Easterners are going to hunt the pirate ships down."

"Most likely the Mars confederacy as well."

"I don't care about the Mars mob. They can stay with the Easterners. But the pirates have a pretty good stealth fleet we could use."

Raynor agreed and she looked at the crew's pirate uniform and laughed as she realized they were all slightly different.

Operator Furgis activated the main vid com and asked for Chief Tylor.

"Ray."

Raynor chuckled with excitement. "Now I know how Ken got this tin can moving."

Operator Furgis looked sharply at his wife but was interrupted by the vid com's battle link. He quickly dismissed the chief. "Yeah, Just, what's up?"

"Ken, link with the stealth droids behind us."

Operator Furgis picked up his data pad from the arm of his command chair. Raynor moved closer and behind her husband's chair as the 3-D image of Captain Drake moved to the side allowing the image from the stealth droids to quickly appear. "I can make out three heavy cruisers, a dozen or more destroyers with a lot of support ships—oh, and that larger vessel they're trying to keep in the back must be the *Courageous*." Operator Furgis sighed heavily.

Captain Drake asked, "Did you link with Neptune One?"

Furgis's wife looked at him with surprise. "Not yet, Just."

"Now's the time," said Captain Drake. "Tell them to get ready," and the vid com returned to the full 3-D projection of the pursuing Eastern Empire's fleet.

Raynor knew that when she was on the SS *Kai Che* or any other Western Empire warship that she was considered his first officer before his wife. "So you haven't spoken with Sam yet?" she asked softly.

Operator Furgis could still hear the slight anger in her voice as he turned to respond. "We've been under no link protocol, and until we arrive at Neptune One, Captain Justin is in command and thinking of the fleet, Ray."

Sam Furgis leaned back in his chair as his senior staff continued to offer reports concerning the affairs of the whole system and of Neptune One. He struggled to keep his thoughts from wandering. Acela Vega and Chayton jointly were reporting on the status of the station's civilian personnel and guests when they were interrupted by the vid com chime. Sam was curious when the words "SS *Kai Che*" were displayed, followed by the vid com's voice. His entire senior staff turned to face the vid com as Sam sat up straight in his chair.

Chapter Eighteen

Director Furgis almost fell out of his chair when the 3-D image from his vid com focused in on his mother and father in front of him. He stood quickly, along with his senior staff, and using his arms and hands to quiet his staff, he shouted and laughed with joy at the same time. "Pops, what!"

"Calm down, Sam, we've got a problem," his father interrupted, and Sam sat back in his chair with a smile and tearful eyes. "Sam, is the senior staff there?"

"Yeah, Pops, everyone but Ambassador Davis—he's on a secure link in his office."

Operator Furgis spoke quickly. "We're on our way to the station to meet up with another Western fleet. I need you to get that station ready with the MCs, and tell Gerlitz it's imperative that these weapons are on line."

"Pops, what happened on Earth and what's up with Mars? The solar net is down."

"Sam, we'll discuss that later. We're on approach, so don't fire any MCs, and tell Engineer Trently the chief wants the hangar bay doors open. We're retrofitting our fleet with MCs, starting with the *Kai Che*."

Sam nodded and sighed. "All right, Pops," and his office vid com shut down.

Karl Hobbs sat on Tabitha Drake's docked med tube and watched her laugh and smile at her father on the main med lab vid com. Her time with her father was interrupted as she heard the battle link chime in the background.

Captain Drake answered the vid com quickly. "Sitrep, Ken."

"Just, Sam's getting the station ready. The *Kai Che* will go in first for MC upgrades." Operator Furgis smiled.

Captain Drake chuckled. "I see you still have a little pull on that floating corn pipe."

"Of course. The chief said it will be quicker to upgrade the *Kai Che* and end up with an equivalent of another cruiser."

"All right, Ken, we're approaching Neptune sector now and there's no sign of the other Westerners. We'll see you there."

Operator Furgis leaned back in his chair watching the projection of the Neptune sector. His arm hung over the side of his chair as he held Ray's hand and they both anticipated seeing their son.

Two research shuttles emerged from the large hangar bay doors on the massive station. Operator Furgis could not help feeling great pride as he watched the SS *Kai Che* approach along with Captain Drake's Western fleet. He leaned back in his chair with a smile after hearing the vid com's battle link chime. "*Research One*, you're a welcome sight."

The image of Engineer Trently was quick to reply. "Operator Furgis, welcome home, sir. Is the chief with you?" Trently was smiling wide.

"Who do you think got this ship running?"

Trently grinned. "That explains everything. Tell the chief the engineering crew are ready in the hangar bay, sir."

Operator Furgis grew more intense. "Shaun, I need you

and *Research Two* to set up a defensive patrol around Neptune One and assist Captain Drake. We've got company coming."

"Yes sir, I let Juan know. He's in *Research Two,* sir," replied Trently, and the main vid com on the SS *Kai Che* returned to the 3-D image of Neptune One as the small patrol vessel slowly entered the hangar bay.

Operator Furgis stepped down from his command chair and turned to his wife. "Ray, I need you to stay with the *Kai Che*. I'll be with Sam in operations."

Raynor nodded. "All right. From what the chief said, it won't take long to upgrade to MCs."

Operator Furgis winked. "The ship's yours, Captain," and he turned to leave the bridge. As the doors hissed open, he could hear his wife shouting orders, and his smile grew wider. He knew a commander of a ship was called captain when on the bridge and enjoyed watching the pride his wife was feeling.

Captain Drake sat straight in his command chair as he watched his fleet create a battle formation around Neptune One. He spoke sharply. "Commander."

Commander Mela Finch turned and approached the command level. She stood next to his chair with her hands behind her back. "Yes sir."

Captain Drake held great respect for his crew, and as he watched his first officer he was reminded of the reason. "Mela, I want the destroyer *Yama* in for MCs next. Have the light cruiser *Liberty* take up the slack."

Commander Finch offered a quick nod and "Yes sir" before she stepped back down to the mid-level. Captain Drake leaned forward in his chair as he watched the movement of his fleet on the vid com display. He spoke softly, "*Research One.*" and waited patiently.

Engineer Trently quickly appeared on Captain Drake's vid com display. "Yes sir."

"Shaun, I need you and Officer Armela to provide a wide reconnaissance around the Neptune sector." He continued to study the sidebar projection of the sector

Engineer Trently replied, "Yes sir, we'll link up with the reconnaissance droids, sir, and provide as much of an early warning as possible."

Captain Drake nodded as the vid com sidebar of the sector enlarged to full view. The surrounding lights turned red, along with claxons sounding a warning as the battle link projected an intruder. The captain stood quickly and issued his order. "Take that stealth droid out of my sky."

Before he finished his order, a volley of projectiles from the SS *Mustang* had already struck the enemy droid, causing a quick flash before disappearing. The battle link chimed, "Neptune One." Captain Drake sat back in his command chair. "Ken, they're closer than we think." He could see the concern on Operator Furgis's face, but he could also see the joy and quickly imagined how his good friend felt when he saw his son.

Sam Furgis stood next to his father in the 3-D projection on Captain Drake's bridge. His voice was full of joy and confidence. "No need to worry, we'll deal with them." His father looked at him with a smile before turning to Captain Drake. "The station's defenses are ready, and the civilians who did not transport to the mining colonies are tucked away safely, Just."

Captain Drake grinned. "All right, Ken, hopefully they'll give us more time for more upgrades."

Operator Furgis smiled. "The *Kai Che* is almost ready. She's leaving the bay now while the crew finishes."

The SS *Kai Che* slowly emerged from Neptune One's hangar bay. The SS *Yama* waited patiently on the other side of the maintenance bay and slowly started to move forward as the *Kai Che* exited.

Operator Furgis turned to Supervisor Stykes as the main vid com in Neptune One's operations shut down. "Leaf, make sure the main MCs are on line and ready to go."

Leaf Stykes held up his data pad in one hand with a grin. "We're all set, boss."

Operator Furgis turned back to the vid com. His son stood close as he instructed the communications device, "*Kai Che.*" He watched the 3-D image of his wife appear on the vid com. She adjusted her new Western Empire military uniform as she answered. "Ken, we're almost ready. The chief stayed in the maintenance bay to assist with the destroyers; he said they require a slightly different touch."

Operator Furgis laughed. "That sounds like the chief, Ray. Take your position and get ready quickly."

Sam Furgis watched the eye contact between his parents before the vid com returned to its battle link display, and his father noticed his smile.

The SS *Kai Che* gained speed as Captain Furgis issued orders to her first officer, Lt. Rogers, who stood close to her command chair. He relayed these orders quickly to the appropriate stations on the bridge and felt pride in his crewmates who were once a pirate crew. Suddenly the bridge of the *Kai Che* lit up with red illumination, and the sound of the claxon alarms echoed through the small bridge.

Captain Drake looked at the missile barrage quickly

approaching the fleet on the main vid com. She grasped the arms of the command chair. "Counter, anti-missiles now." She watched the missile barrage meet the barrage of anti-missile projectiles from the Western Empire's fleet. "Lt. Rogers, set a course directly for those contacts. Our bow is a smaller target, and have the forward MC ready." Lt. Rogers repeated her orders as she watched the troposcope link the identification of the approaching warships. Another barrage of missiles launched from the small destroyer, *Staton*, with the heavy cruiser, SS *Essex*, following closely. Suddenly small bluish balls of energy emerged close to the *Staton*, striking the destroyer on each side.

Captain Furgis watched the two research shuttles fly by each other quickly as they escaped the impact area. As the sides of the SS *Staton* erupted in explosions, causing sparks and debris to shoot off into open space, she called out her orders loudly. "Fire!" A larger ball of bluish energy struck the bow of the SS *Staton*. Captain Furgis was heard once again as she watched her enemy ship's slow speed. "Ninety degrees starboard, ready port cannons." Her small patrol ship gracefully turned, and a large energy sphere of bluish color with white circulating clouds sped by. Captain Furgis stood in awe as the energy sphere from Neptune One struck the conning tower of the SS *Staton*, resulting in an immediate blinding light that was quickly reduced by the vid com's 3-D projection.

Captain Drake stood from his command chair on the SS *Hammerhead*, his mouth open and his eyebrows squinted in awe. The entire bridge crew watched the image of the SS *Staton* slowly appear through the dissipating residual energy; large sparks shot out from where the conning tower was, and the hull under the extremely damaged area started to open in a large gap as the small Eastern Empire destroyer slowly broke in two like a snapping stick. The captain shouted, "Stations," as the SS *Essex* slowly flew through the debris field. He sighed with relief as he watched the enemy warship sharply bank to her starboard side in a retreating maneuver.

Operator Furgis sat at his command chair in Neptune One's operations center; the main vid com was chiming with civilian traffic. He switched the vid com to the battle link only and allowed his senior staff to calm the civilian populace. He grinned as four individuals appeared simultaneously on the main vid com: Captain Drake, Captain Furgis, Engineer Trently, and Officer Armela. Captain Drake spoke first. "Ken, as soon as the *Yama* is done refitting, I would like the *Mustang* next."

Operator Furgis nodded with a grin as his wife interrupted. "I wanna know what you put in that last one. Those poor souls had no chance." He could see her 3-D smile clearly.

Officer Armela joined the conversation. "Sir, my trop link with the stealth droid shows the Eastern fleet holding position outside the sector."

"I confirm that, sir," said Engineer Trently. "The *Essex* is moving away at flank speed."

Operator Furgis could see the grins growing on his crew. He remained in military mode. "Captain Drake, sit rep. Any damage or casualties?"

"No sir."

Furgis turned his attention to Officer Armela and Engineer Trently. "Unless you have any damage, I need you patrolling the sector's perimeter."

The vid com chimed: "Ambassador Davis on emergency interlink."

Operator Furgis spoke quickly, "Stay sharp out there," and switched the vid com to the diplomatic link Ambassador Davis used. Furgis could not restrain a slight snicker as he watched the short, fat, balding Irish man wearing his old worn-out rainbow tweed cap appear. He was amazed at how little Ambassador Davis had changed over the years he had known him. "Ambassador, we're a little busy at the moment."

Ambassador Davis held up his hand. "It's all right, Ken, I just spoke with the Eastern Empire's ambassador. Commander Kruger is standing by. He's been asked to meet with you in my office."

Operator Furgis was growing angry. "Stand by, Ambassador." He paused the vid com and turned to Supervisor Stykes, but Sam was first to speak. "What do you think, Pops?"

Operator Furgis paused long enough to realize he should take the advice he gave his son. He smiled and grew calmer. "My first reaction is to say 'Go to H-double hockey sticks.' However, if there's a possibility of ending this madness, then we should try." He looked at Supervisor Stykes as he nodded in agreement. He reached out and rubbed the back of his son's head. He was grateful his son was there; Sam reminded him of the importance of principles over personalities.

Operator Furgis turned back to the main vid com. "Resume." Ambassador Davis reappeared quickly, and Furgis chuckled as he realized Davis offered the perfect look of a diplomat.

Ambassador Davis set his data pad back on his desk and spoke calmly. "Ken, I think we should do this."

"All right, Ambassador, here's the play. One ship with

Kruger on board will dock with the docking spheres. He will be met at the glide tube station and escorted to my office." Ambassador Davis nodded. Before the vid com shut down, Operator Furgis quickly added, "Any deviation or anything suspicious will result in immediate retaliation." The vid com sidebar went back into full view.

Operator Furgis quickly turned to Supervisor Stykes. "Meet Kruger in the glide tube station. Sam and I will meet you and our guest in my office. Oh, and Leaf, tell Acela to keep this station looking like a casino resort."

Supervisor Stykes nodded before leaving. "Yeah, boss." The doors hissed closed.

Operator Furgis spoke to the vid com, "*Hammer* and *Kai Che*," and watched the split screen of the vid com display Captain Drake and Captain Furgis. "Just, Ray, we've got company coming. One ship with Kruger on board will dock with the station for negotiations. Just, have the research shuttle patrol the perimeter of Neptune One while they're docked." Both captains nodded as the vid com returned to its tactical projection.

Operator Furgis and his son watched the vid com display patiently for what Ken thought was an eternity. Suddenly the vid com displayed a 3-D ship entering the defensive zone of the large station; it identified the ship as the SS *Essex*. Operator Furgis chuckled as he turned to his son. "Let the games begin." He knew Sam needed more diplomatic experience and thought this would allow for a good lesson. "Let's get to my office." Sam followed his father out of the operations command section, listening to him issue orders to the crew manning the various consoles before they exited.

Supervisor Stykes stood in front of his squad of armed enforcers anticipating the glide car's arrival in glide tube station A. The station's vid com audio announcement echoed through the station Supervisor Stykes had evacuated earlier. "Glide car A arriving." He watched the cylindrical car pull into the station and hiss to a stop. He activated his ear com piece and said, "Marshal Scoop."

Marshal Scoop answered as Commander Kruger exited the glide tube car followed by another Eastern Empire military officer. Supervisor Stykes motioned to his enforcer to surround the two Easterner personnel as he spoke to the marshal. "Charlie, keep an eye on Gerlitz and his lab; we have Easterners aboard."

Stykes stepped closer to Commander Kruger. "Sir, you are supposed to be alone."

Kruger scoffed with his eyebrows squinted in a disrespectful expression. "He's my first officer, sir."

Stykes did not like Commander Kruger's tone. He motioned to his enforcers with a nod at Commander Kruger's first officer, and immediately they displayed their Tobine repeater rifles at chest level. "Well, your first officer can wait in the holding chambers until you leave." Two enforcers escorted the Eastern Empire's first officer to the holding chambers. "Commander, Operator Furgis is waiting in his office, if you would follow me." Supervisor Stykes did not wait for an answer; he walked off quickly, followed by Commander Kruger and his Neptune One enforcer escort.

The door hissed open to Operator Furgis's office, allowing Supervisor Stykes, Commander Kruger, and his two escorts to enter. Operator Furgis stood with his son and Ambassador

Davis. Commander Kruger was quick to approach Sam Furgis with his right hand extended in a greeting gesture. Sam smiled; the thought of shaking Kruger's hand with his stronger bio arm was appealing. He grabbed the commander's hand quickly and squeezed hard.

Commander Kruger looked Sam in the eyes, his voice full of sarcasm. "You have the latest model, and I see a spark in your right eye." Sam frowned and let go of his hand immediately.

In the past when Operator Furgis spoke with Commander Kruger, he wanted to laugh at his comical accent, thinking he would fit into one of those old twentieth century spy comedies. But now he was more annoyed. "Are we here to play games, Commander?"

Kruger chuckled. "Of course not. Ambassador Davis, it's good to meet you in person." Ambassador Davis stepped forward and shook his hand.

Operator Furgis sat back in his chair and picked up his data pad. "Shall we?" He gestured toward the chair in front of his desk as the vid com flickered to life with a 3-D projection of the Neptune sector. "Before we start, I want to know if you have authority here."

Again Commander Kruger chuckled. "Absolutely, Ken, my word in any matter is good."

"Then why the surprise attack?" Sam asked angrily.

Ambassador Davis stood, gesturing toward Commander Kruger and Operator Furgis. "All right, all right, gentlemen, this is going nowhere." He turned to Commander Kruger. "What is the Eastern Empire proposing?"

Kruger smiled and pointed at the vid com. Operator Furgis took the cue from his adversary and handed him the data pad from his desk. The vid com zoomed out to project the 3-D image of the entire solar system.

Commander Kruger said, "The Eastern Empire will stop at Io."

Operator Furgis scoffed. "You're mad."

"Let him finish," the ambassador admonished and nodded at Commander Kruger.

Kruger sat back in his chair facing the vid com and operated the linked data pad. "Everything else will remain with the smaller Western Empire."

"No sir," said Ken, "your fleet may be larger, but ours is more powerful. If your young emperor wants to stop this madness, then you'll back off behind the main belt."

His office was silent for several moments before Commander Kruger stood quickly, startling Supervisor Stykes and the two enforcers. He looked at Operator Furgis for a moment before laughing. "You can't blame me for trying. All right, Ken, the powers to be have already convinced the emperor that he has gone far enough for now." Kruger sat back in his chair and turned to face Operator Furgis.

Ambassador Davis set a data pad in front of the commander and said, "Insert your identification, and the Neptune Accords will be in effect." Commander Kruger picked up the data pad and entered his personal identification; the data pad quickly scanned his eyes before sounding a chime of confirmation.

Operator Furgis reached across his desk and pulled the data pad toward him. He picked up the personal assist device and entered his identification followed by the scan and confirmation. Ambassador Davis leaned over Operator Furgis's desk to grab the data pad. Commander Kruger stood slowly as he watched the enforcers with a smile. "Good work, Ambassador," and shook his hand. He turned to Director Furgis and held out his hand.

"I hope you keep your word," Sam said. Before Kruger could reply, Operator Furgis turned to Supervisor Stykes and said, "Have our guest's first officer escorted to glide tube station A."

Supervisor Stykes nodded as he stood sideways with an open-handed arm toward the office door. Operator Furgis could hear Commander Kruger talking as he exited his office. "Leaf, I was hoping to stop at the Sports Depot to place a wager…"

Operator Furgis sat back in his chair, and a few minutes later his senior staff entered his office. Both Marco and Chayton pulled out chairs for Acela. Operator Furgis said, "Thank you for joining us, Seth," and pointed at a chair in the corner of his office. Operator Furgis worked the data pad in front of him, allowing time for the vid com to switch projections before talking to his anxious staff.

They turned to face the vid com as the terms of the Neptune Accords slowly scrolled down the sidebar. Operator Furgis said, "I know everyone in this room, and I know each of you will find this hard to accept. The system has been through a military coup d'état." Everyone started talking at the same time.

Director Furgis stood quickly and said, "Quiet down. Look, it is what it is. The system is now divided between the inner system and the outer system."

Operator Furgis grinned with pride for his son. "The systems are pretty much equal. Earth is most likely irradiated with Mortelis, and the inner system is in major defiance."

Sam spoke softly. "I guess our task would be securing the outer system."

Operator Furgis smiled at his son. "Sam is correct. Seth, I need you to establish your contacts on the black market; tell them we're still operating as an entertainment establishment and there's lots of profit coming this way."

Seth Adams nodded. "I'll try, sir," and he left the office.

Acela Vega said, "Ken, we have a lot of civilian ships heading our way. I'm not sure what kind of condition they're in."

"We'll be fine, Acela. Let's do our best to help everyone and keep this station functioning as it was intended." Operator Furgis smiled with confidence as his senior staff stood to leave. "Hold on, Sam," Ken said quietly. Sam turned around and slowly approached the front of his father's desk. His father walked over to his observation window, and his son stood next to him with his hand on his shoulder. They both stared out the window for a moment, and Operator Furgis started chuckling. "I remember a moment years ago when we stood here worried about your mother arriving."

"I remember, Pops, and I'm glad she came. She's a blessing from the Lord." Sam could see the SS *Kai Che* off in the distance.

His father pointed at the same ship. "She's also a fine captain, and I want you to join her as first officer of the SS *Kelly Brown*." Operator Furgis smiled, knowing his son needed a moment to understand his orders.

Sam laughed at first, then became inquisitive. "The *Kelly Brown*?"

Operator Furgis turned to his son and held his hand out. "I ran it by your mother, and she approves. The SS *Kai Che* is now the SS *Kelly Brown*, and your first assignment as first officer will be recon around Io." Sam Furgis pulled his father in for a large hug. Operator Furgis grew serious. "It is important the Easterners leave Io alone, Sam. They will push, trying to provoke a fight."

Sam interrupted. "Of course, if they capture the *Kelly Brown* they will have Mortelis weaponry."

Operator Furgis nodded, realizing his son was aware of the situation. "You best get going, Sam. I'll let Huiling and Juan know."

Sam walked toward the office door with slight disappointment. He turned and said, "Tell them I said congratulations on their wedding, Pops," and he left for his new assignment.

The battle link on Operator Furgis's vid com chimed, and he turned from the observation window. He sat at his desk and accepted the transmission from Captain Drake and Raynor. The vid com moved the 3-D projection of the Neptune sector to the sidebar as the two captains appeared. Captain Drake said, "Ken, the SS *Essex* is passing us now; she'll be out of range shortly."

Operator Furgis snickered. "I know what you're thinking, but let her go."

"I know it's not honorable, but it would have gone a long way at solving our problems."

Operator Furgis laughed with a nod, then grew slightly more serious. "Both you guys were linked during our meeting?" The captains nodded. "Very well, then you know the deal."

Captain Drake interrupted. "Ken, the chief said the *Liberty* is next for refit; after her I'll be bringing the *Hammer* in."

Operator Furgis grinned as he heard the name of his

favorite ship. His thoughts wandered briefly before replying, "Sounds good, Just."

His wife was concerned. "What's wrong, Ken? You look a little distant."

"I was just thinking of the good old days when we were on the *Republic*." Both captains joined him in a quick laugh.

"Sam's shuttle is here, Ken. We're almost ready to take the long way to Io."

"Very well, Ray. Go it easy out there and keep an eye out for that Western fleet that was supposed to be here along with any more civilian ships. God speed."

Captain Furgis replied, "God first," before the 3-D image of Captain Drake expanded to the full view of the vid com.

Drake said, "Ken, I've got some missionaries on board who want to know if it's safe to travel over there."

"Why am I not surprised? Of course they can travel over here. Use *Hammer One* and we can refit her after you drop them off."

Captain Drake raised his eyebrow. "*Hammer One* is already done; the chief instructed my chief engineer."

Operator Furgis watched the image of his good friend look out of the view of the vid com while holding his hand up in a waiting gesture. After a moment Captain Drake returned his attention to Operator Furgis. "It seems one of my missionaries wants to stay." He started laughing.

"You could do worse, Just. In fact it may be good for morale. Look at what Huiling has done for Neptune One!"

"You're absolutely right, Ken. For some reason I just thought it was funny."

Operator Furgis shook his head. "Remember, we've grown

past those vexations."

Captain Drake could not restrain his humor. "Yeah, we persecute for other reasons now."

The vid com battle chime interrupted their conversation.

"Just, I've got Ray linking in," said Ken and he watched his good friend nod. "Meet me at the solar house in a few. I'm buying," and the vid com switched.

The 3-D image of Captain Raynor Furgis replaced Captain Drake, and Operator Furgis smiled when he saw his wife, with his son in a first officer's uniform standing behind her. "The fighting Furgises," he said with a laugh, but calmed as he realized neither his wife nor his son was amused.

Ray spoke softly. "Ken, I just got word from Mars." He could see his wife's eyes tearing up. "Derek Fields was executed. They shot him in the public courtyards of City Central."

"Son of a…"

Raynor Furgis interrupted quickly. "There's more… Before he was taken into custody, he sent a personal messenger. Derek's message said the emperor's son did not kill his father; in fact he only had a daughter."

Operator Furgis nodded patiently. "And so we're dealing with an empress, not a young emperor." He grinned and leaned back in his chair.

Sam interrupted. "No, Pops. You've met the emperor already."

Operator Furgis leaned forward, confused. "What are you guys talking about? Stop with the riddles and tell me what's up," he said impatiently.

"You just made a treaty with him," his wife said. "Derek's message said Commander Kruger was a distant relative and assassinated the whole family." Sam Furgis watched his father's expression change instantly. Operator Furgis quickly stood and shouted, "Kruger?! You're telling me Kruger is..." He tried to shake the stunned feeling off. "Is the *Essex* still on the troposcope? Where is it?"

Sam Furgis snickered. "He's gone, Pops."

Operator Furgis leaned back and relaxed; the shock was wearing off. "Does Just know?" He did not wait for an answer. The look from both his wife and son answered his question. He laughed loudly while staring off through the large observation window. "I bet he's laughing as much as I am." He turned back to face the vid com's 3-D projection of his wife and son. "If you get a chance to take him out, do it," and the vid com chimed. "It's the chief, Ray. Like I said, if you get a shot..."

Raynor nodded. Operator Furgis accepted the link from the chief's office quickly.

Chief Tylor sat straight in his desk chair, holding a data pad. "Sir, we just retrieved a droid from the King David."

"What happened, Chief?" After a moment of watching the chief study his data pad, Operator Furgis grew impatient. "Well, what happened?"

The chief set his data pad down. "It appears to be just a flight vid they launched before entering WH-12."

"Appears? You can't tell?" Operator Furgis leaned back in his chair in frustration.

"No sir, the droid requires a command authorization before completing its download." The chief leaned forward in concern. "Sir, I don't want to overstep here, but is everything all right?"

Operator Furgis looked out his window at the bright blue

of Neptune. He turned back to the vid com and sighed. "Chief, did you get the Neptune Accord download?" The chief nodded. "Then you're aware that Kruger signed the peace accord." Again the chief nodded. Operator Furgis laughed. "Well, Chief, the intel is that Kruger is the new Eastern Empire's emperor, and he was sitting in my office negotiating."

The chief shook his head. "That figures. Sir, the Krugers have always been devious, and it does not surprise me, so don't let it get to you. You'll get another chance." They both laughed. "Kruger will honor the accord for a while until he thinks he has the upper hand and it's in his best interest."

Operator Furgis nodded. "Yes, I know. I've got the *Kelly Brown* heading toward Io, and Justin said you're almost done with the refitting."

"Yes sir."

"All right, Chief, meet me at Dr. Gerlitz's lab and we'll get that droid downloaded." The vid com switched to a vid recording of light jazz from Mars City Central.

Epilogue

Operator Furgis stood at his observation window with his hands behind his back; he watched several of Captain Drake's warships in the distance silhouetted by the giant blue planet. His thoughts were interrupted by the chime over his favorite music from the vid com. "Request entry." Operator Furgis closed his eyes and took a quick, relaxing breath before turning his head toward the vid com. "Who's at my hatch?" The vid com projected the name "Huiling Li" followed by its voice recognition. Operator Furgis sighed. He wanted privacy but welcomed Huiling's company. "Granted."

Pastor Huiling Li approached slowly with a smile; she hugged Kennith tightly and received a small hug and smile in return. Operator Furgis's voice was full of compassion. "It's always good to see you, Huiling."

"Thank you, Ken. Both Juan and I wanted to thank you for performing our wedding ceremony." Operator Furgis smiled as he realized their wedding was on the next full cycle. Huiling held Operator Furgis's arm with both hands and continued to look up at him. "The chief told me what happened with Commander Kruger… Ken, you did the right thing by letting him go. Remember, God first."

Operator Furgis smiled. He looked back out the observation window. "Huiling, your sister is on the *King David*, correct?"

Huiling stepped closer to the window. "Yes, she is."

Operator Furgis looked down into Huiling's eyes. "Let's go down to the science lab and unlock that droid." Operator Furgis put one arm around her as they exited his office. Neither of them heard the hatch door hiss closed.

CPSIA information can be obtained at www.ICGtesting.com
Printed in the USA
BVOW07s2311280813

329809BV00001B/23/P